Always Another Villain

TARA LYNN THOMPSON

Copyright © 2020 Tara Lynn Thompson
All rights reserved.
ISBN: 9798590231737

DEDICATION

To all the kindred spirits. You know who you are.

The Another Series

Not Another Superhero
Just Another Sidekick
Always Another Villain

1

Always follow the doctor's orders, unless the doctor orders you into the trunk of a car. Then get a second opinion. Ask around. Read medical journals. Spend hours on WebMD. Don't let the doctor lock you inside the trunk of a 1980's Cutlass Supreme and drive off with you inside.

Ninety-seven percent of the medical profession agree this is stupid.

I blinked at the suffocating blackness and banged my fist against the lid.

"Locking women in trunks is against your Hippocratic Oath!"

I yelled so the driver, dressed in arrogant authority and a white lab coat, could hear me above the road noise. After that last sentence, I decided shorter statements tasted less exhaust fumey.

"Jerk!"

I considered my surroundings. All I remembered from my brief glimpse of the trunk before being closed inside was a spare tire resting at my head. Spares are important. That way, if you get a flat tire while driving to a secluded area to bury a body, you won't have to call AAA's 24-hour roadside assistance.

"You're limited to how many assistance calls you can make in a year." I kicked the inside of the trunk. "Some restrictions do apply!"

This was getting me nowhere. Even if he did respond, I wasn't sure I'd hear him. What I needed was out of here. Better still, what I needed was to have never ended up here in the first place.

Impatience is what got me into this mess. Impatience always gets me into messes. One day, I will address this character flaw. But later. When I have time for stuff like that.

"What happens if I need to go to the bathroom?!"

I did, by the way.

This series of events started while I was guzzling too much of whatever orange liquid comes out of the soda fountain in the hospital cafeteria. That's where the doc found me and the moment the evening took a disagreeable turn.

Before that, however, it had been an average Tuesday evening with Jackson Christy. Despite our supernatural abilities, we were no different than most couples. I was reading him magazine relationship quizzes, and he was lying there in a coma.

"Here's a good one," I told him earlier, folding the magazine in half. "Listen to this. 'Find out if your boyfriend is an emotional stud or a clueless dud.'"

Three days ago, I got shot in the gut by Senator Chad McBride's widow, whose first name I still can't remember. But I wasn't the one now missing a spleen. Jackson had - somehow - healed me of the wound, and, in doing so, took the injury on himself.

Emergency responders found us in the empty office building where we'd been held captive earlier. They did their best for Jackson by stopping the bleeding and rushing him directly into surgery. He had survived the night but, now three days later, still remained unresponsive.

Although I begged, pleaded, threatened, and bargained with him to open his eyes, he refused. Annoying him with relationship quizzes was my only move. If he wanted me to stop, he needed to wake up and say so.

I had propped my feet on his bed, snuggled into the plastic chair inside the ICU, and clicked the pen. "This will be fun for everyone, but more so for me."

After nineteen questions, he wasn't faring well.

"This is the last one, Jackson, and you are in desperate need of a studly answer. Here we go. 'When you're having a bad day, does your boyfriend: a) listen attentively while not offering advice, b) try to fix your problem while making you feel bad because you're upset, or c) ignore you.'" I fiddled with the pen while thinking it over. "A is the answer we want, but is that you?" I looked at Jackson's serene expression. "Do you think you've earned an A?"

What he didn't do was respond. What he did do was lie there. With his eyes closed. And his chest rising with the beat of the heart monitor.

I clicked the pen. "C it is."

Doctors weren't offering optimism. Now in his third coma day, the medical staff had gotten quieter and quieter. What they could tell me was that the gunshot to his abdomen was healing extraordinarily fast. What they couldn't tell me was why he remained unconscious. The latest theory was that the excessive blood loss had caused brain damage. They'd be able to pinpoint why he wasn't waking if he ever woke up.

There was a Joseph Heller novel in there somewhere.

In the meantime, while we all waited for Jackson to wake up, I'd been sleeping on a cot in his ICU room. The nursing staff allowed me to stay as long as I promised to stop singing Celine Dion's "Where does my heart beat now?" every time they checked Jackson's vitals.

Living here wasn't so bad. Even in the chaos, life creates a rhythm. In the last three days, I'd discovered the best waiting rooms to find women's magazines, where to get frozen yogurt inside the hospital after the cafeteria closed, and the quietest corners of the building where you could pray and cry during the difficult hours.

For the loved ones of critical patients, this place existed on the border between the life that was and the life when our waiting ended. Either for good or bad, nothing outside these doors would ever be the same again. We all knew this. It was reality, one we acknowledged with brief nods as we passed in the hallways.

We were the haunted ones in this building. Half here. Half alive. Halfway to acceptance, halfway in denial.

One bright spot for me had been the nurses. In my fear for Jackson, my appetite had been nonexistent. Bullying me like true friends, they'd forced bites down my throat from their own plates. Nurse Corinne had been the most successful because she ate mostly Greek. I finished off three teaspoons of fasolada soup yesterday and two bites of a lamb gyro at lunch.

Tonight, however, Nurse Neal was on duty. He was a highly energetic 32-year-old with an athletic build, unreserved swagger, and brown hair so boring it didn't deserve a description. He loved three things that I knew about: comic books, soccer, and scarring the inside of his mouth.

"How much pain will this cause me, Neal?" I asked him earlier, while holding a paper plate of one-fourth of his dinner. It burned my eyes simply by existing.

"You're going to love Vindaloo, Sam. It'll be your new favorite Indian dish," he smelled his cardboard takeout box.

I poked around at the mustard-colored meat blobs. "I had an old favorite Indian dish?"

His eyes glazed over in hunger. "Doesn't that smell make your mouth water?"

I wiped my cheeks. "It's making my eyes water. Does that count?"

"Just try it. You'll thank me later."

Neal walked away, digging into his own container. Moments later, I heard his "hot damn!" exclamation from the nurse's station.

This was going to hurt.

After two bites, guzzling an entire glass of water wasn't cutting it. I needed liquid flavorful and sugary enough to mask the pain. I headed to the cafeteria in search of better weaponry.

Considering my current situation, it's too bad curry breath can't burn through trunk locks.

∼

While I gulped down fluid from the soda fountain and mopped the perspiration on my forehead, a doctor walked up wearing blue-scrubs, a white coat, and that dismissive manner required by the state to obtain a medical license.

He approached with a cup in hand and the kind of apathy to other's needs that meant he'd drink all the orange soda.

When he stopped in front of me, I put a protective hand in front of the soda spout. "I ate Indian food, Doc. I'm going to need all of this. Have you tried diet sodas? They taste almost real."

The doctor raised one disinterested eyebrow, which matched the pinching of his disinterested mouth. "I don't drink diet."

I scanned the selection on the soda fountain. "How do you feel about raspberry tea?"

"That little old ladies adore it."

"Cola?"

"Liquid battery acid."

"Lemon-lime?"

"Consumed by no grown man ever."

"Root beer?"

"Remove the root, and we can talk."

I scanned the dwindling fountain options. "You should drink water. As a doctor, you are a representative of the healthcare profession and need to set an example."

The disinterested eyebrow lowered, replaced by the raising of a disapproving one. Then again, that could be his typical face. The soured lines around his mouth alluded to a tongue as biting as the teeth outside it. This was not the kind of person ever denied orange soda.

"Do you mind stepping aside?"

I did mind, but I conceded anyway.

The doctor moved to the carafe at the end of the fountain. A tight elbow pinned a thin stack of files to his side while he held his cup under the dispenser. Black smoking liquid poured out.

The doctor took a methodical, demonstrative sip from his cup, while watching me indifferently over the rim.

"Right." I nodded in understanding. "Coffee. Didn't see that there. Coffee is a good choice. Straight up. No frills. You look like a no-sugar, no-cream, black coffee drinker."

He lowered the cup an inch. "And what does that look like?"

I had no idea. It was only something to say until he moved on. But, now that he asked, it looked like him. A no-nonsense kind of guy with a straight, no nonsense kind of nose. Grey eyes that rarely blinked. Laugh lines that cut his face without mirth. He stared down at me as if he always watched civilization from somewhere on high. Not because he was aloof, but because he was positioning himself so civilization could never get the jump on him. That wasn't the look of a doctor. It was the look of a soldier. But he had it anyway.

His atypically thick hair, which he wore cropped close, had turned completely white. It topped a face that had gone a few bloody rounds with life, evident by the softening at his jawline. Otherwise, he held his distinguished age well. If I had to guess, time was too intimidated by him to get too close.

I bit at the end of my straw, weighing what answer would move him along the fastest. "Like a man who's got things to do."

He "hmm"ed at that, dismissing the conversation, and turning to his files. "Speaking of," he pulled out one file from the stack in his hands and flipped it open. "You're Samantha Addison, the fiancé of Jackson Christy, correct?"

Fiancé. Girlfriend. Woman responsible for his coma. The definitions are so similar.

"That's me." I wasn't his fiancé, and the girlfriend part wasn't official, but the title gave me more access to him, not to mention the fact I've watched *While You Were Sleeping* one too many times.

The doctor paged through the contents inside his file, which he balanced unceremoniously on the rim of his coffee cup. "You were pointed out to me earlier. I've been asked to consult on Mr. Christy's condition, and I may have news for you."

"News?" My burning tongue stuck to the roof of my mouth. "What news?"

He casually checked his watch. "I don't have time to chat now. I've got to be somewhere else. I'll come find you tomorrow, and we can talk then."

Tomorrow? I couldn't wait until tomorrow. "Tomorrow is too far away. How about now?"

"I don't have time now."

"Where do you need to be? I'll walk with you."

He closed the file, casually slipping the whole bunch back under his arm. "In my vehicle leaving. Let's talk tomorrow when I have more time."

He had to be kidding. "Tomorrow is twenty-four hours longer than I have patience to wait. I'll walk you to your vehicle, and we can chat on the way."

The doctor realized I wouldn't be taking 'no' for an answer. "That's fine. If you can keep up." He headed for the elevator.

I looked lovingly at the fountain, while shaking the ice inside my empty soda cup. "If I could just…" When I turned back around, the doctor was out of sight. There would be no more orange soda.

Oh, Neal. You've got to start eating more alkaline foods, buddy.

In the lobby, I spotted the doc stepping into the elevators. I double timed it across the lobby, through a group of visitors, around a loud cell phone talker, and slipped through the doors before they closed.

Inside, the doctor sipped his staunch coffee, the smell wafting around us like smoke, and scanned his files.

"I'm here!" I caught my breath and leaned against the wall, motioning for him to start talking. He wasn't looking so the motion accomplished nothing. "Go ahead. What's the news?"

The doctor sipped and scanned. "Hmmm?" Then it was back to the file and his coffee again.

Before I spoke another word, the elevator dinged. The doors swooshed open, sucking in the bitter chill and stale air of the second-floor garage.

The doctor, pacified with his reading material and beverage, walked out.

"Excuse me. The news?" I followed the coffee smell around a parked Chevy Suburban.

The doctor sauntered at a reasonable pace, unlike the one he'd used to jettison himself into and out of the elevator. Now, he walked as unhurriedly as he sipped, while clicking his heels rhythmically against the soiled cement.

"I have a few questions for you, also, Miss Addison." He smacked his lips, swallowing any residual caffeine. "For example, the surgeon notes in Mr. Christy's chart that a bullet was not recovered during surgery." He moved past the Suburban to the next aisle and around a Toyota Land Cruiser. "That's concerning."

I pranced along working to get in front of him. Each time I tried, he outmaneuvered me by taking a zigzagging pattern through parked vehicles. I couldn't tell if he was purposefully moving erratically to keep me out of his way or he was just a moving erratically kind of guy.

As for the bullet, the doctor wouldn't have recovered one, of course, because the bullet went into – and possibly through – me, not him. I had no scars left by the injury, so I had no idea if the bullet passed through me or was still inside rattling around somewhere in there.

My stomach took that moment to growl, as if it found the idea of a nine-millimeter appetizing.

"There was an exit wound," I explained.

The doctor cut between two brown Volvos looking too depressed to be driven.

"Not an exit wound. An exit tear. As if the skin had separated or been pulled apart, not severed by a bullet."

I nodded, seeking a way past this line of questioning.

According to the police report on Jackson's injury, he was shot during a carjacking. He and I had been struck by a black SUV three nights ago. Two thugs, who looked identical minus their hair color, rammed into Jackson, shoved us off the road, then dragged us outside of the vehicle. During the skirmish, Jackson was shot, his vehicle taken, and the two of us stranded in a snowstorm.

Now stuck in worsening weather with Jackson badly bleeding, I spotted a nearby uninhabited office building. Luckily, a door was left unlocked. Inside, I started a fire to keep Jackson from going into shock.

That's where authorities found us after being notified by an anonymous caller who saw the smoke coming from the building.

As for the broken window in the conference room, I told them we'd found the place like that. And that's where the flow of information from me stopped.

None of that actually happened, of course. The only true part of the story was that the two thugs did look-alike minus their hair color. Everything else was a lie. But a believable one, which was the important point.

The truth was Jackson and I had been held prisoner in that office building after the other sidekicks escaped through the broken window. Then, Senator McBride's widow had shot me in the gut, and Jackson had miraculously transferred the injury onto himself.

You can't tell police stuff like that. If you do, they feel obligated to prove you wrong.

"It's strange," the doctor concluded.

I shrugged, treating his inquiry with disinterest. "I guess, but this is information I already know. You said you had news."

"I do." The doctor walked to the back of a powder blue 1980's Cutlass and inserted a key into the trunk.

"And?"

The lid creaked as he lifted it.

Inside was nothing. Just an empty trunk with a spindly looking spare tire. There was no change of clothes, no golf clubs, no box of pamphlets or bag of instruments. Not a single extra coat or extra blanket. Not even a heavier pair of boots. Nothing you might find in a trunk.

I can't say why, maybe my instincts were waking up, but the serenity of the space unsettled me.

"Are you needing something out of your trunk?" I took a second look to make certain I hadn't missed anything. He was holding a thin stack of files, nothing normally placed inside a trunk, and nothing was in the trunk to be removed. Yet here we stood with it open.

That's when I got suspicious.

This entire scene was off. The details, upon closer consideration, didn't fit. For example, why a Cutlass? There's nothing wrong with the vehicle, but doctors usually drive Mercedes and Lexuses, BMWs and Porsches. Why was he parked in the farthest spot from the elevators? Doesn't the staff have better parking spots available?

My eyes settled on the doctor. His blue scrubs. His white coat. The medical staff wore one or the other. Blue scrubs without the coat or the coat without the scrubs. Where was his ID badge? Or his name inscribed on the coat?

My eyes dropped to his feet. They weren't in tennis shoes or supportive wear. Not the kind you'd expect from a medical worker on his feet all day. He wore boots. Western style. The brown leather toe looked worn, dark in spots from oil and lighter in spots from wear. These were boots accustomed to outdoor weather exposure. These were not the shoes of a man moving from patient to patient in a sanitized environment.

My eyes raised to meet the doctor's gaze. I'd scrutinized the man earlier. Now, I ran my mind down his slightly scruffy cheeks and worn but rough build. My earlier assessment stood. He was all I'd thought before – a dismissive, arrogant, hardened, black coffee drinker. But there was a patience I hadn't picked up on. The patience of a lion sunning in the grass, who spotted an unsuspecting lamb. The doctor, noting my shifting expressions, took a lingering sip of his coffee. He watched me as if I was the one about to make a move, not the other way around.

I took in a deep, satisfying breath in preparation for moving like lightning when the moment required it. A smile tipped the corners of my mouth. Not only did I know I could handle this guy, I knew I'd look good doing it. A confident woman is a beautiful woman.

"You don't know this yet," I hooked a strand of hair behind my ear, "but you're in over your head."

The doctor, finished with his coffee, crushed the cup and shoved it into his white coat pocket. He looked disappointed. "No," his mouth sagged with boredom, "it doesn't look like it."

That's when a person approaching from behind took me and my ego by surprise. A shove in the small of my back, perfectly upsetting my balance, sent me sprawling forward into the trunk. Before I could process the mortification of gloating while being played, the lid locked.

Vindaloo will never be my favorite Indian dish.

2

Before congratulating yourself on being too clever to be outsmarted, factor in the ego's tendency to overestimate itself. That way, if you find yourself locked in a trunk, you'll feel less humiliated.

I rubbed the itchiness from the trunk's carpet lining out of my arms, pulled down the sleeves of my sweater, and considered how much trouble my cockiness had gotten me into now. Cold leached into the trunk space without being hampered. We'd driven half an hour and still no stopping.

As the doctor, or his partner, drove us out of the city, I kept a semi-cognizant idea of where we were headed. Kyle Alice, a music columnist at Oklahoma Now and old friend from my beat reporter days, frequently reminds me I'm directionally challenged. He recommends I memorize the patchwork, potholes, and repair seams in the streets. They're so distinctive, he claims, I'd never be lost again.

"Why don't I just use street signs," I asked him once, after arriving late to dinner one night back in September. I was meeting Kyle and the newspaper boys for our quarterly barbecue binge and catch-up session. By the time I got there, all the complimentary bread had been devoured.

"Okay," Kyle had bitten into a buttered roll, "but that doesn't seem to be working for you."

Navigating via road work could be the way to go. Kyle is blind, but he's never lost.

As the vehicle bumped along through the city streets, I focused on the feel of the ride. Underneath, the tires spun over rhythmic tar seams. Ka-clunk. Ka-clunk. Ka-clunk. A deep groove in the road bounced my hip bone. Ka-clunk. Ka-clunk. Ka-clunk. With a slight leaning, we curved to the left. Then, right. All the while, we ka-clunked forward at a speed faster than a school zone and slower than the Autobahn.

If I had to guess, we were near the Twelve Oaks Country Club and Golf Course off Granger Street. The road curved like an old coke bottle and was notorious for poor patchwork that, if driven at thirty-five miles per house, sounded like "Tainted Love" by Soft Cell.

At a cross street, we turned right. We drove north toward a section of town with less pretension but smoother roads. Within a mile, the tired played nothing but wind noise. We merged onto a seamless highway. The speed flattened out the street Braille. All I detected was the driver hitting a shredded chunk of tire. We now headed north on 75, or west on 412, or southeast on 351.

Sorry Kyle. I make a terrible blind person.

With my bladder getting more uncomfortable, I banged on the lid again. I opened my mouth to yell something biting and witty, but I have uncreative moments, too.

"You…you…you…"

I had nothing.

"Never mind! I'm not going to tell you what I was going to say. You can wonder about it forever!"

The vehicle leaned to the right on an off ramp. A few beats later, it stopped and accelerated again. Wherever we were going, we were close.

Underneath, the road turned from paved badly to gravel. Pieces of rock, like enemy fire from a bb gun, pinged against the undercarriage. The vibration buzzed against my shoulder and hip. My hand, palm down in front of me, helped balance the bumps.

What could I do? I could still use my speed, but after the humiliation of being locked in here, I felt less cocky.

We were moving slow enough now that I could jump out without killing myself, if I could pop the trunk. Earlier, I'd felt along the walls for the possibility of an emergency trunk release lever. Beginning in 2002, all vehicles were required to have one. This vehicle, however, was from the 80s, a decade unburdened by safety issues.

Even though the release levers glowed in the dark, I felt around in case I'd gone blind in the last hour from degenerative eye disease. I found nothing but a hard plastic trunk lining and two wires. I yanked them out of their proper place because I was in a destructive mood.

The vehicle slowed. We turned twice, each time slowing to a cautious forward roll. Any minute, we would stop completely. Then, the real nightmare began.

I had no weapon. Not even a high-heel shoe to beat him back. I wore sheepskin-lined, gray knit boots because, after my hypothermia from nearly drowning last Friday, my feet were constantly cold.

I needed a strategy other than jumping out superfast. Not that I wouldn't, but if this fake doctor knew about my quick attribute, he would have made allowances. Like getting a second person to sneak up behind me. Those kinds of allowances. The uncomplicated, successful ones.

If only I could ask Jackson. He would know what to do.

As the vehicle stopped, I closed my eyes and imagined Jackson's face. Whatever was coming, I wanted him to be my final thought. I pictured him standing in my backyard with his black-hood guy garb. The hood was down so I could see his face. The moonlight washed one cheek with a soft, bone white. He stared at me with that curious, crinkled brow expression, the one he gives me 85 percent of the time.

It was the night of our first kiss. Had that only been five days ago?

He came over late to make sure I was safe, and I had accosted him with my Triple Defender Pepper Spray Gun. Instead of being annoyed I'd avoided him for three weeks after the Durant Ball, he opened up and shared his feelings. He told me about the night, seven years earlier, when Senator Chad McBride had died and Jackson saved me from falling off the Oklahoma Now building. He shared his memories from that night hoping I'd stop seeing black-hood guy as a separate person.

"When you think about this black-hood character you've created, I would really love it if you see me, too."

After being so vulnerable and open with me, I couldn't help myself. I walked up to his confused face and kissed him. If he was going to share his feelings with me, I'd do the same with him. But nonverbally. Words are overrated.

Jackson hadn't expected that, but he never suffers surprise long. He gave me a few seconds to enjoy the upper hand, then he took it away. When his arms pulled me in tighter, I decided, in this area, I'd defer to his lead.

His mouth – warm and sincere and wanting – pressed against mind. I wouldn't have been able to dial down my feelings for him at that moment if I'd wanted to, and I didn't. I sank deeper into him until my bones no longer held. The man could flip a switch inside me that went all female all at once. Talk about living dangerously.

When the kiss ended, his smile made my ankles wobble. I could have kissed him again for that smile. Come to think of it, a couple minutes later I did.

That was one excellent moment. When you're possibly facing death at the hands of a faux doctor, that's the kind of moment you want to relive. Not the moment less than 24 hours later when I started doubting him. Or the entire night after that I spent running away from him. Or the time after that when he fell into a coma.

What I wanted to remember was the moments we spent together when my heart overruled my head. We had so few of those moments I could review most of them before the doctor put the car in park.

"Oh, Jackson. I need you so desperately. What am I supposed to do now?"

Blame it on breathing exhaust fumes for an hour or my earlier consumption of high fructose corn syrup, but I heard Jackson answer, "Fight, Sam. Now you fight."

∼

"Jackson?" His voice had been muffled, as if talking through a scarf, but still distinctive enough to understand. "Jackson? Is that you?"

Outside, the driver's side door opened and closed. Feet crunched gravel as they punctuated the ground with heavy footfalls. The doctor, or whoever shoved me in here, was coming.

I wasn't ignoring the approaching danger, but, at that moment, I was a little distracted, too.

"Jackson?" I whispered. "Jackson? Are you in here?"

I listened with any sixth sense I possessed. Where did his voice come from?

I'd had a similar experience earlier today. While begging Jackson to come back, I'd thought I heard him say we needed to talk. As quickly as his voice came, it left. Or, if I'd been imagining it, then my imagination stopped imagining.

Jackson's voice came again, this time quieter. More intently. A muffled whisper in my ear. "Pay attention, Samantha."

"I am," I whispered. "But where are you?"

I felt around the darkness. The trunk, though decently sized, didn't have space for two without both knowing. Even the 80s, an era of cars big enough to transport the era of hair, limited storage space. Jackson was not in here.

"Focus." His voice came again.

Definitely my imagination.

"Jackson?" I whispered. "I think I'm going crazy, babe."

Jackson laughed softly. "Going?"

The footfalls stopped outside the trunk. Knuckles rapped against the lid. "You still alive in there?"

I recognized the raspy southern drawl. It was the fake doctor. Hopefully, his fake costume came equipped with a fake stethoscope so I'd have something to strangle him with for real.

I crossed my arms over my chest. "No. I died."

"You didn't find a way out yet?"

"I did, actually. This is a recording."

The car shimmied, as if taking on the weight of a boot on the bumper. "You do want out, don't you?"

He sounded directly above my feet, so I estimated the approximate placement of his head. I pulled my knees into my chest so I could kick with more enthusiasm when the lid opened.

He knocked again. "Well?"

"You ask me now that I finally got comfortable?"

The boot left the bumper. "Suit yourself."

Footfalls ground out until lessening, lessening, and disappearing. Where was he going?

"Are you going to let me out or not?"

No answer.

"Hello?"

No answer.

"What happened to dragging me through the woods and making me dig my own grave?" Wasn't that how these things usually ended?

No answer.

The breeze whistled in toil and trepidation. A coyote whined in bewilderment. The car pinged with exasperation. It was a perplexing situation for everyone concerned.

I strained to pick up minor sounds outside, like a twig snapping, gravel grinding, or coffee sipping. I heard more wind. Not a sound or shimmy suggested anyone was around.

Did the doc leave with me locked in here? That's it? Lock me in a trunk, abandon the car, and leave without dumping my body? I'll never understand kidnappers.

Cold leaked in from outside giving me the shivers. Also, I still needed to use the facilities. Time to get out of here.

"Jackson?" I whispered. "You still there?"

"Yes, Sam, I'm still here."

I sighed. "Of course, you are. You're a figment of my imagination. You aren't going anywhere until I want you to go."

"I'm not a figment of your imagination, Sam."

"Apparently, it's important to me for me to believe that. Now, help me think." I tapped my finger against my forehead. "I need a way out of here."

"You've already searched for an emergency release lever?"

"Yes."

"What about the trunk release cable? Can you find that?"

"I felt around for it, but this trunk has a hard plastic lining covering that area. And I can't get through the lining without tools."

I strummed my fingers on the floorboard while running through ideas.

"What about the backseat?" Imaginary Jackson had an idea. "The bolts keeping the back of the seat in place could be loosened, if you can find something to use as a tool. Then you could crawl out that way."

I considered it. "Not a bad idea. But how did I know about that? I don't remember learning how a backseat is bolted."

"I'm not imaginary, Sam."

"Of course, you're not, sweetheart." I felt around the space once again. "Now help me find some tools."

~

During my glimpse of the trunk, I noted the cleanliness and emptiness. Considering it now, it seemed the doctor had, with painstaking detail, removed any chance I'd find a discarded penny or loose pen to use as a makeshift tool. The trunk was immaculate, but he'd forgotten to remove one item so expected in a trunk you look right over it.

"The spare tire," Imaginary Jackson said. "Lift it up and look underneath. That's where the jack is usually stored."

I couldn't lift it up. No room. I could, however, scoot it out of the wheel well.

"What," I grunted, while tugging the wheel, "can I do," I braced my good leg against the wall for more leverage, "with a jack?"

"Use it."

"Use it how?"

"Use it to pop the trunk open," Jackson clarified.

Jack open the lid? "Would that work?"

"It's worth a try."

I blindly felt around the tire well until I cut my finger on the jack. "Found it! Maybe this could work. How did I come up with that idea?"

"You didn't."

"Don't get me wrong," I wrangled the clunky object and sat it in front of me, "I'm not saying I'm a genius."

"Mm hmm."

"But there are times," I ran my fingers along the jack for a knob or button or lever or on-switch, "when I'm delightfully innovative."

"Insert the handle into the socket and position it as close to the latch as possible."

Handle. Socket. Right. I knew that, apparently. "Of course. Makes sense. I knew I'd think of something."

I dug back into the wheel well, found a heavy bar inside a vinyl bag, and found a round-sized hole on the jack that accepted the round-sized handle.

Before raising the lever, I snuggled into the opposite corner and placed the jack in front of the door lock to give me room.

On the first pump, I misjudged the height of the trunk and hit my funny bone, which isn't a bone but a nerve and isn't funny but agonizing. The next pump smashed my fingers. The third pump scraped my knuckle.

"I'm loving my plan less."

"Keep going, Sam. And it was my plan, not yours."

By the fifth pump, the lid creaked in displeasure. The louder it moaned, the faster I pumped. The faster I pumped, the heavier I breathed. The heavier I breathed, the more the space shriveled. Even in the dark, the space shrunk and spun, turned and tightened.

I wanted out of this trunk. The darkness. The cramped area. The lack of freedom. The closer I came to escaping, the closer I came to hyperventilating.

News to me, I have claustrophobia. It's always good to find these things out about yourself.

"Calmly, Sam. Calmly. You're doing fine," Jackson's voice came again.

"I want," I sucked in a shaky breath, "out."

"I know. You're almost there. Just slow your breathing."

I forced myself to stop, breathe, and regain control. "Jackson?"

"Yeah?"

"I miss you." I took another calming breath. "I miss you so much it hurts."

There was a pause before he answered. "I miss you, too, Samantha. Every moment." He cleared the huskiness from his voice. "But, right now, you've got to focus. Come on, baby. Get yourself out of there. Slow but steady."

I nodded to no one and started pumping again. The hard plastic lining inside the trunk was giving warning signs of shattering under the jack pressure. The lid, however, still hadn't popped open.

I inhaled deeply and gave one long exhale. Then I sped up the pumping again.

"Almost, Sam." Imaginary Jackson cheered me on. "Almost."

A metal brace in the lid cried out as it dented. Another pump and the lid popped. It rushed upward as the latch disconnected and bounced as far away from the jack as the hinges allowed. The lid popped open so hard it reverberated back and nearly took out my skull. I raised my arm in protection, while sucking in the sharpened air. Cold surged over me in a swelling of an icy breeze, as if God had dumped a bucket of Gatorade on my head after a big win.

I scrambled out of the trunk. When my feet hit the ground, my knees dipped but held.

While stomping around to increase blood flow, I scanned the area. There were no lights, but, compared to the utter darkness in the trunk, I saw everything clearly. A line of hibernating trees groaned and swayed in the moonlight along the abandoned road, which wound forward into shadows of nothingness. In the distance, a faint rush from far away highway traffic slithered into the rustle and crack and snap of the wooded nightlife.

What I didn't see was a fake doctor or his shovey sidekick. I was alone. Abandoned in a car trunk and left nowhere and for no reason.

"Jackson?" I spoke above a whisper in case I wasn't alone. "Jackson? You still with me?"

I waited, but there was only silence. He'd been a figment of my imagination, after all. A way to comfort myself while being frightened. But, who said I was done being comforted?

"Jackson? Please answer me."

Nothing.

"This is why you got a 'c' on that relationship quiz."

3

In Chinese folklore, dragons breathe fire, are poisonous, and guard gold. In Oklahoma, dragons drive semi-trailers, transport citrus fruits, and snack on cheese crackers.

"I'm not saying I'm a dragon right now, but I was one in a past life." The man hunched toward the steering wheel of his rig, as if willing all 18 tires to propel him faster along the open road.

His name was Mart Katirci, and he was my ride. He was also the guy with a nine millimeter resting on his thigh and the reason my parents told me to never hitchhike.

"I get what you're saying Mart." I didn't, but there's no reasoning with a mythological serpent. "But I don't need you to avenge me. I only need a ride."

We started this discussion ten minutes after I climbed in the cab of his semi. He had spotted me walking along the darkened highway shoulder. He pulled over and offered me a ride. With no phone, no idea where I was, and no arch support, I climbed in.

He seemed harmless enough. In his early 40s, Mart was on the pudgy side. He was also covered in black, curly hair. It sprouted from his arms, sprung from his face, and bounced from his head. In the blue light of the dashboard, he had the silhouette of a snowman – a round circle resting on top of a larger round circle. He also had light gray, almost silver, eyes and an open, guileless expression.

Of all the weirdos I might run into along the highway at night, I thought he'd be less weird. I may have been wrong about that.

At first, we chatted about his truck load of red navel oranges and golden grapefruit, why everyone should consume one citrus fruit a day, and how Vitamin C was the key to immortality. As a truck driver for

Daffodil Groves, a citrus farm in Brevard County, Florida, he delivered his sweet bounty all over the United States and was a true believer in the product. On this current delivery, he'd already logged 1200 miles and had another thousand to go. To pass the time, and for companionship, he frequently picked up hitchhikers along his route.

And now we're back to me.

"Why were you out here alone?" He'd been transferring the contents of a Cheez-It box to his mouth without forfeiting too many crumbs. After three to four handfuls, he'd brush his belly free of residue and resume the workflow. It was efficient. Even hypnotic. He offered me a box of my own, but I told him they would only add to my thirst. So, he offered me a soda, but I told him that would only add to my bladder.

"Well, Mart, it's a funny story." I didn't tell the funny part because it didn't exist. "I kind of, in the loosest sense of the words, ended up in the trunk of a Cutlass that drove me out here."

That's all I got out before the snacking rhythm stopped, and Mart's head turned in my direction. His eyes brightened as if freshly polished. They looked so much like silver dollars I wondered if their minted date was stamped at the bottom.

Without knowing him or his expressions, I went with the always reliable and often guileless, "What?"

His single, black eyebrow raised. "Was it done as a practical joke?"

I hadn't considered that. "I don't think so, but maybe?"

"Whose car was it?"

"I don't know."

"How did you get locked inside?"

"Someone shoved me in and slammed the lid."

"Did you see who did it?"

"Technically, no."

"How did you get out?"

"With brilliance. And a tire jack."

His head took on a series of mini-nods and, from what I could determine through the beard, his mouth twisted on one end and then the other. Mart was weighing this news.

"This person's going to be mad you escaped," he pointed out.

I considered that, then dismissed it. "I don't think he cared one way or the other."

Mart looked disquieted. Would he insist on involving the police? I couldn't let that happen. The police already watched me as if I was in labor and due to birth another crime spree any minute.

"Mart, it's fine. I mean, I'm fine. These things happen, right?"

He shrugged. "Not really."

"Look, I'd rather not make a thing out of it or get the police involved. OK?"

His head gave one last, accepting nod. "OK. We won't involve the police."

I exhaled. "Thank you."

Mart tucked the flaps of his Cheez-It box closed and set it next to his chair. "We won't need them. I developed skills, ancient skills, of thwarting adversaries during my previous life as a dragon." He dug under his seat and pulled out a nine-millimeter. "We'll take care of this foe ourselves."

~

To win any argument, toss in details of your past life as a lizard. There are simply no good counter arguments to that.

I would call Mart crazy, but you never call actual crazy people crazy.

"This idea seems…" I chose my word carefully, "unwise."

Mart wasn't deterred. "I still have the soul of a dragon, Samantha." He raised his long eyebrow as if to say, 'impressive, no?' "I can take care of this for you."

I slumped in my seat. Unbeknownst to the medical community, high doses of daily Vitamin C may have hidden side effects.

Mart scanned the road ahead for an approaching off-ramp where we could turn around and go back to the scene of the crime. No matter what I did tonight, strangers kept driving me to abandoned country roads.

"I appreciate the gesture, Mart. But there's nothing back there but an abandoned vehicle. Whoever locked me in the trunk is long gone."

Up ahead, a roadside traffic sign noted the approaching exit for LaVille Road, another unpopulated path to nowhere. Mart took the exit, turned left under the overpass, and adroitly steered us back onto the highway to cross miles we'd already traversed, while oranges and grapefruit followed obediently behind.

I was never going to get to a bathroom.

"Mart, it took a great deal of effort to escape that place. If you're looking for a damsel to rescue, the city is ripe with them."

Mart shifted through the ten gears until we were flying past the nondescript wooded terrain along the highway exactly as we'd flown past it going the opposite direction.

"We have to strike while our enemy is expecting retreat." He grabbed his Big Gulp from the cup holder and sucked down liquid of the dark variety. Vigilantism is known to cause dry mouth. "What's the exit, Samantha?"

I considered not telling him, but what would that accomplish?

"It's up ahead. Another three'ish miles or so."

"Jessen Road?"

"Sure."

I didn't know the name. When I'd left, I hadn't paid attention to road signs. Why would I? I hadn't had any intention of returning.

What Mart didn't know, and couldn't know, was that I'd already taken a quick inventory of the area and found no one. My legs had made quick work of the gravel road, while the gravel road made quick work of my shoes.

Seeing my knit boots coming to a tragic end, I slowed down to a mortal pace and headed toward the glow in the sky. That's where Mart found me walking the highway shoulder wishing for Timberlands.

Now, we exited onto the off ramp back toward my Bermuda Triangle.

"Left or right," he asked at the one stop sign.

"Left."

There were no homes out here. Or visible commerce. The road had to have been established for some reason, but I couldn't say what. Back roads are considered the veins of this state. Some peeking here. Others bulging there. Whatever their size or purpose, they crisscross all of Green Country and can take you anywhere you want to go – if you survive them. What a backroad journey won't do is hand you your destination on a clearly designated, smoothly paved platter. You'll have to earn it. That means you may lose a tire or two, as well as your shocks. The chances your paint job will survive is sixty-forty. And just when you think you've finally got these dusty beauties beaten, your vehicle will break down, and you'll die alone in the wilderness.

The sunsets, however, are gorgeous.

Mart slowed as the asphalt turned to gravel. "How much further?"

"Further."

He shifted uncomfortably in his seat. "I can't take my load down roads like this. I could get stuck."

"Yep."

He slowed to a stop. "Going any further would be a bad idea."

"Bummer." I wondered how long it would take him to turn this baby around and get us back on the highway.

Mart idled behind the wheel. "Looks like we'll have to walk from here."

Ten minutes later, Mart and I stood in the middle of the gravel road checking out the nothingness. I'd hoped his dragon soul could fly us here, but we'd had to walk.

"Where's the Cutlass?" Mart swung his flashlight from one end of the road to the other, back and forth, as if we'd only be able to see a four-door sedan if he got the lighting angle just right.

I stated the obvious. "It isn't here."

"Where could it have gone?" The flashlight beam disappeared as Mart pointed it down the empty road one way and then the other.

"I don't know."

"You think west? Maybe east?"

"Maybe."

"Back to the highway?"

"Maybe."

"Down some sideroad?"

"Mart," I waited until the flashlight hit me in the face, "I don't know, OK? I don't know."

The light dropped to his shoes. "It's weird, is all. You said no one was around when you got out of the trunk, right?"

"Right."

"So they came back later and drove off?"

I scanned the line of sloth-like trees lazing around at the edge of the road. A sea of moonlight gray weeds lapped at their trunks. No signs or sounds of a vehicle disturbed the natural habitat's lethargic lifestyle.

"It's as good a guess as any."

"And you're positive this is where the car was parked?"

I confirmed it for him.

"You're sure?"

I pointed to a tree with a mass of knots around its gut. "See that tree?"

Mart squinted in the dark before remembering he had a flashlight. "That one? What's special about that one? They all look the same to me."

"It has five knots shaped like a handprint."

"I don't see it."

I scooted two steps to the left. "Stand right here." I pointed exactly where I'd been standing.

Mart shifted over, while dancing his flashlight into a dizzying storm of light and shadows. "A handprint?"

He was a few inches shorter than me so maybe it was the angle. "Raise up on your tiptoes."

Still nothing. "And stop moving your flashlight around. Turn it off for a minute. You'll see it better in the moonlight."

Mart clicked the flashlight off and waited for his eyes to adjust. "Oh! I see it. A handprint." He held up his pudgy fingers to compare. "The knots are the fingers with the big one the thumb." He suspiciously squinted back at me. "You saw this earlier?"

I kicked at a piece of gravel. "I have ancient skills, too."

We took another five minutes of walking around, kicking gravel, and spotlighting one homogenous tree after another with his flashlight before Mart gave up his quest. Before we headed back, I told him I wanted a minute alone to process my emotions. That was bull, but he bought it. Once he was out of earshot, I tried one last time to conjure Jackson back into my head.

"Jackson," I asked as politely as possible, "could you come back here for a minute?" I waited in the silence and slapped my thighs in exasperation. "Is one minute really so much to ask?"

~

On the drive back, Mart put away his gun and went back to being a Vitamin C enthusiast.

To distract me from my bladder pressure, I asked Mart how he knew he'd been a dragon. During a particularly long and lonely haul last year, he'd discovered a local AM talk show in Nevada discussing past lives. That's when the flashbacks started.

"I was a luck dragon." He'd switched from Cheez-Its to trail mix. "I had white fur and pink scales. And large teeth with floppy ears. I also had a friend, a young boy named Atreyu. I flew him everywhere - over mountains, across oceans, through a storm once. I don't remember why we were flying through a storm. It was cool, though. I loved flying."

"I see." I didn't have the heart to tell him his past life was the movie, *The Neverending Story*. "Then it looks like you were destined to always be in motion."

Mart, in command of the open road, brightened at the idea. "I guess that's right."

Being a true luck dragon, Mart took me directly to the hospital entrance and dropped me off without another glitch. Before we said our goodbyes, he handed me a grapefruit and told me not to neglect my Vitamin C. Then he told me to "never give up and good luck will find you."

He must have watched *The Neverending Story* a lot as a kid.

I gave him a kiss on his fuzzy cheek and told him to keep picking up hitchhikers, but keep the gun handy, too.

As soon as he pulled out of sight, I hustled to the lobby bathroom before I gave myself a bladder infection. Even after a night of being kidnapped, locked in a trunk, abandoned on a gravel road, and driven by a dragonkin, there's something humanizing about the freedom of using the facilities when needed.

After washing my hands, I dampened a paper towel and cleaned off the layer of dust riding shotgun on my face. I ran my fingers through my tangled, brunette curls as a makeshift hairbrush. My reflection told me I needed sleep. And lipstick. I wet my lips, rubbed at my cheeks, and brought life back to my weary skin. At least now I looked alive. Tired, but alive.

With the prep work done, I grabbed my grapefruit off the counter and headed upstairs to spend time with Jackson before crashing on my cot.

Even though the hospital never truly sleeps, the patients try. In the early morning hours, this place sank into slumber mode with lights dimmed in the empty waiting rooms, voices only heard in pockets near nursing stations, and hallways empty minus the squeak of medical personnel shoes or the insomniacs haunting the halls.

I took the elevator up to ICU alone. The quiet soothed the lingering unrest from being kidnapped by a fake doctor. I didn't know who he was or why he'd locked me in a trunk and left, but that was a question I could obsess about tomorrow after I talk it over with Jackson. He couldn't respond, but I could hold his hand, feel his warmth, rest my head on his shoulder. And that connection would keep the boogeyman away until sunrise.

As the elevator doors dinged open, the solemn quiet of the hospital shifted to ominous. Down the hall, two female nurses I'd met only once, along with Nurse Neal, were talking in hushed tones. Officer Chuck Reilly, followed by a female cop I didn't recognize, exited the ICU entrance doors. All five turned in my direction and stayed turned as I walked up. Whatever this was, it was bad. It was very bad.

"What's going on?" I asked Reilly, who I hadn't seen since the Durant Ball a month ago when he and Officer Bart Simpson dragged Jerome DeLuca, a psychotic videographer, killer, and mugger, through the lobby in handcuffs.

Seeing him here now felt familiar, but not in the comforting sense of the word. It felt familiar like a sore tonsil reminds you of the beginning stages of the flu.

Reilly, towering over everyone else, shifted his utility belt on his broad hips. He always had a treasure trove of snacks in his patrol car. I wondered if he had anything that would pair well with a grapefruit.

Instead of speaking, Reilly looked at Neal as if handing it over to him. Neal, in response, toyed with a rubber band.

"Neal?" I tilted my head in his direction. "What's happening here?"

Instead of answering, he pulled at the rubber band until it snapped. The guy who could fearlessly chow down on ghost peppers wasn't making eye contact.

"Does someone want to tell me what is going on? Or, you can get out of my way so I can get to bed."

Reilly cleared his throat. "Okay, Sam. Here's the deal." He glanced at his female partner, a slim brunette with a stubborn jaw and a get-down-to-business nose, for help. "We've been trying to reach you because something has happened."

I nodded impatiently, motioning for him to finish. "On with it, Reilly."

His big hand rested on my shoulder. "The thing is Sam, I'm sorry, but Jackson's gone."

4

Misunderstandings with the English language have been screwing up communication for eons.

For example, you can lie about something or lie down on something. Object to an object. Refuse refuse. And wind up in the wind.

How you use a word, spell a word, and pronounce a word can define a word. For this reason, and for all the wars, skirmishes, brawls, and battles started over bad translations, I asked for Reilly to clarify his statement before I went into meltdown.

"Reilly, what do you mean, 'gone'?"

"Well…now…um…Sam, it's like this, see. The thing is…you know…well…"

I didn't possess patience for hemming and hawing. Pushing my way through the group, I punched the button to the ICU entrance and rushed into Jackson's room. The lights were all on making the space look like a staged reproduction of an ICU room instead of a real ICU room. When contrasted with the earlier pitch blackness of the evening, the room I'd been living in for three days now felt like the scene of an alien autopsy.

I scanned the room. Nothing much had changed. My cot rested against the wall and my suitcase, toiletry bag, and purse sat shoved underneath. The only change was Jackson's bed. It was gone. Along with Jackson.

I dropped my grapefruit on the bedside table, which still held my uneaten plate of Vindaloo. Behind me, footsteps entered and stopped. I diagnosed one of them as Reilly from the melody of his utility belt.

"Where is he?" My voice came from a place that didn't want, but desperately needed, the answer.

"I can't say, yet." Reilly stood on one side of the doorway, while Neal took the opposite side.

I picked up the grapefruit and frantically tossed it from one hand to another like a baseball. "Why not?"

"Because we're still piecing things together."

"What things?"

"Things that'll tell us why he's gone."

This couldn't be true. Jackson wasn't dead. He couldn't be. I'd feel it, would I? Wouldn't I know the moment my heart broke? Do people feel things like that in real time? Wouldn't I sense the emptiness in a world that no longer held him in it?

I didn't feel any of that. I felt nothing.

"Reilly, I need to see him."

He pursed his lips sympathetically. "I understand, Sam. We'll do our best to make that happen."

"Why can't it happen now?"

Reilly nodded. "So true, so true."

What did that mean? What was I missing here? Now that I think of it, why was Reilly here at all? Police officers don't attend the death of hospital patients unless foul play was expected. Or something else was happening...

"Reilly, Jackson is..." I couldn't bring myself to say the word 'dead.' "...gone. Isn't that what you're saying?"

"Yes. He's gone."

"As in...not here anymore."

Reilly nodded.

"As in...we lost him."

He looked chagrined. "We did."

"As in...left the building."

"Yes. He's definitely left the building."

He kept answering me as if embarrassed, not mournful.

"As in...slipped away."

Reilly nodded.

"As in"–I leaned in to study Reilly's expression–"departed."

"Sam?" He wasn't going to play along forever. "Why do you keep asking me this?"

I grasped one of Reilly's bulky arms. "Tell me once and for all,

Reilly, please, are you saying Jackson is…" I swallowed, "that Jackson is dead?"

Now, it was Reilly's turn to study my expression. "Dead? Why would you think that?"

Why would I think that? Was he kidding? My grip on his arm tightened until he flinched. "So, you're saying he is not dead?"

Reilly's forehead creased in concentration. "I mean, I don't think so. You can't be positive about a person's status unless they're within sight, of course. So, I can't say for sure…"

"Reilly!"

"Yeah Sam. Not dead. As far as I know, anyway. But he is missing."

I dropped my forehead on his bulky chest, inhaling the scent of pine trees and mustard. "Missing. He's missing." Releasing Reilly, I plopped down on my cot with my grapefruit, the juice now oozing from the beating I'd been giving it. "Missing. Not dead. Missing. Gone."

"Yes. Gone. Departed. Not here anymore. However you want to say it. We've searched every floor. He's definitely left the building."

I looked up from my slumped position. "Those are all phrases that could also mean…" I caught Reilly's bewildered expression, "Never mind."

He moved on and caught me up on the details. "His disappearance is why we were called in." Reilly motioned toward Neal, still standing in the doorway. "I was here getting some additional info from Neal. He was the last nurse to see him."

"Neal." I crooked my finger at him and pointed to the far wall. "You. Come in here. Stand there." Then I caught Reilly's eyes and pointed to the far wall again. "You stand there, too."

They exchanged looks but complied, both taking up a section of the wall.

"Get yourselves comfortable." I closed the sliding glass door in the face of the confused female officer. "We're going to have a conversation where you two tell me how I can leave my boyfriend in a coma three hours ago and return to find the hospital has lost him, and the police can't locate him. Then, when I'm satisfied I know everything, we're going to bloody well bring him back."

I studied the back of the officers' heads from the backseat of the patrol car. We headed west on 412 with Reilly in the passenger seat and the female officer, introduced to me as Tandy Meyers, doing an excellent impression of Mario Andretti.

We weren't running hot, but Officer Tandy wasn't the type to mosey. On the highway, speed limits were for chumps and civilians.

We clicked westward after Neal explained how Jackson could be in a coma when I went to the cafeteria at 9 pm and gone when I returned around midnight.

"I came in and saw you were out," Neal told me earlier, while toying with a replacement rubber band. He needed an object to fiddle with more than me, so I handed him the grapefruit. "I chatted with Jackson while replacing his IV bag. He's a soccer fan like me, right?"

He wasn't even a little bit of a soccer fan. "Sure."

"I thought so. I've always gotten a real soccer vibe from him. So that's what we talked about." Neal tossed the grapefruit from hand to hand unconsciously, not noticing the drops of juice splattering with each palm slap. "When I turned to leave, I noticed his hand twitch once. Then again. I asked him if he could hear me and, if so, to open his eyes. And he did."

I jumped to my feet. "He opened his eyes?"

Neal nodded. "For a moment. So, I called the doctor in. Jackson responded to several directions, like squeezing the doctor's hand, opening his eyes again, attempting to speak when asked a 'yes' or 'no' question."

I wiped a tear running down my cheek. "He opened his eyes."

"He was in, what we call, a minimally conscious state, Sam. So that's good. That's progress."

I plopped back down on my cot. "He opened his eyes. They're blue. Beautiful, aren't they?"

Neal shrugged uncomfortably. "Okay, sure."

For three days, all I could do was wait for any sign he would return. I never wanted to see someone open their eyes so much in my life.

I motioned for Neal to go on.

"The doctor ordered a new MRI to check for any change that was leading to this progress and, hopefully, get more insight as to why he'd fallen into a coma in the first place. I had Marshall take him down to the lab."

"Who's Marshall?"

"An orderly."

I waved my hand for Neal to continue.

"And that's when Jackson went missing."

"When exactly, Neal? I need details."

"When Marshall wheeled him into the patient holding area just outside the lab. He left to notify the technician. When he came back to wheel Jackson into the lab, he was no longer in his bed."

"And?" I prompted.

"And…" Neal dropped the grapefruit, which landed with a plop. "We don't know what happened to him."

Medical personnel searched the hospital. But, in a minimally conscious state, there was no possibility Jackson had fully awakened, jumped out of bed, and walked off. Even if he had, miraculously, become fully conscious, he wouldn't have had the strength to go anywhere, yet.

That's when the police were called.

"We did another thorough check of the hospital, but there was no sign of him," Reilly said earlier. "And no one saw anything strange or suspicious. With you missing, too, and with the two of you always in some kind of trouble together—"

I interrupted. "We aren't always in trouble together." Sometimes we're in trouble apart.

"Well," Reilly begrudgingly added an addendum, "OK, not always but a lot. So, I assumed, somehow, he was with you."

Neal studied me as if realizing I was cooler than I looked.

"Where could he have gone?" I eyed the blank face of Reilly, then the blank face of Neal, then Reilly again. "What are your theories?"

Neal suggested it had to be a kidnapping.

Reilly wasn't convinced. "But how do you smuggle a six-foot-two coma patient out of a hospital without anyone noticing?"

"Minimally conscious patient," Neal corrected. "And maybe it was a Weekend at Bernie's kind of thing."

I nixed the idea. "No one walks a 'drunk' guy out of a hospital. They walk him in. Someone would have noticed."

Officer Tandy, quiet enough to only be the shadow of a person and not a person herself, spoke up. I didn't know when or how she'd gotten into the room. "Maybe he was transferred to a different wing of the hospital." She leaned against the corner where the light never fully reached. "And we've overlooked him somehow in our search."

Her theory was more plausible than Neal's, but what about the bed?

"The bed was there. But empty, right?" I directed the question to Neal.

He nodded, vetoing Tandy's idea. Not only was there no paperwork to suggest it, Neal explained, but Marshall would have seen other medical personnel taking Jackson. There's no way to hide coming in and out of the patient holding area.

"The nursing staff in this hospital knows everything that happens on their assigned floors. That's our job. And we're good at it. You know this first-hand Samantha."

He was referring to the fact the nurses had caught me sneaking wine into Jackson's room. Twice. "Right, right. Any other ideas?"

"Wait." Neal stepped away from the wall with his hands raised in a stop gesture. "Empty bed. No body. Vanished in a moment." Neal's eyes, larger now than at any time while eating his dinner, turned to me.

I shrank back. That look said it all. Neal had fit the pieces together – the implausible story of what happened the night Jackson was shot, the oddities of his injury, the wonders of his rapid healing, now his unexplained disappearance. He knew Jackson, somehow, was less fragile than the rest of us. He knew it all.

"Guys," Neal paused, looking at everyone around the room. "Could it be…I mean…this might sound crazy, but…"

How should I act when he suggests Jackson had superhuman abilities? Should I act confused? Shocked? Annoyed?

"was he…maybe…"

Dismissive? Disbelieving? Should I faint? Roll my eyes? How does an innocent person act in a situation like this? And how do guilty people fake that?

"I'm only throwing it out there…but…"

As soon as he mentioned the possibility of Jackson having super abilities, would all the missing pieces click for Reilly, too? Would he know Jackson was behind all the close saves in my life back in October? How I survived my mugging? How the SUV tailgater was smashed into a tree? How the drive-by shooter ended up with a butter knife wedged into his forearm? How we were able to disarm Jerome DeLuca on the roof of the Durant Hotel the night of the ball?

"...could he...I'm only suggesting..."

Once Neal made this implausible suggestion, and before I could fake innocence, would Reilly finally make sense of it all?

"...could he...I'm just going to say it...could he...have been raptured?"

False alarm. Neal knows nothing.

"Whoa." Reilly waved the idea off. "That did not happen."

"I don't know," Neil countered. "Seems strange though, doesn't it? There's no trace of the guy. Just the sheets where he was laying."

"Listen to me. It did not happen," Reilly tossed the idea without effort. "I spoke to my Nanna an hour ago. If there had been a rapture, she would have been in it."

That's one way to gauge the end of days.

"You want to know what I think happened?" Reilly looked each of us in the eye for dramatic effect. "I think he woke up and walked out."

"Not possible," Neal countered. "His body wouldn't have the strength."

"You don't know this guy when he's awake," Reilly stood straighter, the look of a pastor before delivering a powerful sermon. "This guy held onto a grown man while he was dangling over the roof of the Durant Hotel."

Neal opened his mouth to ask a question, but Reilly kept going.

"With a bucket of—"

"Two buckets," I corrected.

"Two buckets of spackling paste—"

I held up my finger to interrupt again. "Grout adhesive."

"Right. Grout adhesive," Reilly continued, "tied to the guys ankles. Those things weigh about 50 pounds—"

"Sixty-one-point-five," I amended.

"Sixty-one-point-five," he repeated to Neal, "a piece."

Neal looked impressed. So did Officer Tandy, if shadows have facial expressions.

"He saved the guy's life." Reilly respected Jackson, obviously. Smart guy. "And then took out a guy with a gun."

"Uh," I raised my hand, "I was there, too."

"Oh, yeah," Reilly halfheartedly acknowledged, "Sam was there, too. I'm telling you Neal, this guy is a serious badass."

I couldn't argue with him there.

Neal took it all in. "And he's a soccer fan, too. Very cool dude."

Reilly leaned back against the wall as if finished with the altar call. "That's all I'm saying. If anyone could walk out of this hospital after being shot and in a coma for three days, it'd be Jackson Christy."

∼

Reilly had a point. He also had a piece of information that sent me out the door.

When Reilly had called Jerry, Jackson's grandmother and emergency contact, about Jackson missing, she responded with, "Isn't that curious." Then hung up.

She knew something. She always knew something.

I reached the elevator before remembering Jackson's SUV was parked on the second-floor parking garage. In the section over from where I'd been kidnapped earlier. To find Jackson, I was willing to confront my fears but not willing to be delayed inside another trunk.

"Where are you going, Sam?" Reilly shuffled up to me at the elevator with Officer Tandy standing behind him and to the side like a good little shadow.

I eyed them long enough that Tandy stepped back into the light.

"What's that look about?" Reilly could be so suspicious of me sometimes.

"Don't be paranoid, Reilly. I'm not looking at you with any particular look." I was, actually. "I don't want anything from you." Except, I did. "But let's talk about your suspicions anyway."

When the elevator doors opened, I stepped in. "Walk and talk, m'kay?" I held open the door and motioned the officers inside.

Reilly wasn't convinced, but he came anyway. And Tandy, attached to Reilly for all of time, had no choice. The elevator jostled under their weight as I released the doors.

To ward off any lurking kidnappers, I needed the officers to walk me to my vehicle. Reilly knew better than to believe me when I said I didn't want anything. Will people never learn?

"And off we go."

On the elevator ride down, Tandy said nothing, which I expected. Reilly merely repeated his, "Where are you going, Sam?" question before the ding signaled our arrival. As the doors slid open, I hung back and let the officers step outside first.

"You guys see any doctor hanging around out here?"

Reilly and Tandy shared a look.

"Or a pale blue Cutlass?"

Reilly scanned the garage. "No. No doctors. Not Cutlass. Why Sam?"

"No reason, Reills." I pointed to the far west side of the garage. "That way." I followed Tandy, who followed Reilly. We looked like the Beatles crossing Abbey Road.

"Sam, are you going to tell me where you're going? I have to file a missing person's report so is there something I should know?"

I decided to answer honestly. Many times, honesty really is the best policy. And, yes, that surprised me, too.

"I'm heading to Jackson's house to see his grandmother."

Reilly stopped at the western wall, waiting for me to catch up. "Good idea. She'll appreciate you coming over to offer some comfort tonight."

That wasn't my plan. "Right. Comfort."

Reilly motioned toward the three vehicles parked along the wall, none SUVs. "Which one is his? I remember him driving a dark, full-sized SUV."

I checked the area. "I must be turned around. It has to be parked along the opposite wall."

Out of politeness, I assumed, Reilly and Tandy stayed with me. When we reached the far wall, his SUV wasn't there either.

"Not here either?" Tandy scanned the row of vehicles.

"No. I must be mixed up, but I can fix this." I reached into my purse and rummaged around. "I'll hit the alarm button on the key fob."

Reilly had been using his height to scan the whole of the garage. He held his head up and back, prompting his slack mouth to naturally hang open. "We're looking for the SUV, right? The same one he drove that day we went around questioning all your magazine clients back in October?"

"Mmm hmm." I wasn't finding the fob.

"I thought that was the vehicle that got car jacked when Jackson was shot."

"Well, yes," I babbled my way around the false story, "the SUV was stolen…"

After initially giving the police the carjacking story, I'd called Theo Erickson, Jackson's adrenaline junkie buddy and my favorite Asgardian, to drive the SUV off the road into a ditch. Leave it. Then call the authorities with an anonymous tip about an abandoned vehicle.

The police recovered the "stolen" car and returned it to me that afternoon. I didn't even need a rental for a day.

"…but, it was recovered," I finished.

I shoved my face in my purse to hide that look liars get when they lie. Reilly never knew when I was hiding something. Tandy, however, had an otherworldly way about her and otherworldly people pick up on stuff.

I fished through the zippered compartments, side pockets, and shadowy unknown realm lying at the bottom of all women's purses, but found no keys.

Meanwhile, Reilly and Tandy stood in that patient, impatient manner cops have perfected over centuries of evolution.

"They aren't here." I held my purse to my ear and shook it. "No jingle. No keys. I don't know what's happened to my vehicle."

"Jackson's vehicle," Reilly corrected.

"Yes, Jackson's vehicle." Sheesh. The bromance. "He wouldn't mind me driving it, Reilly. Mine was lost in the flood. My insurance doesn't provide for a rental, and I haven't had time to shop for another. Also, why am I explaining this to you?"

He shrugged. "I don't know. But I don't think it's here."

"It has to be here."

"Not if he took it."

Is that what happened? Or had the Widow McBride planned his abduction and staged it to look like he left on his own?

I would get no answers standing here.

"Reilly," I slung my purse strap over my shoulder, "I need a favor."

He rolled his eyes and motioned for me to head to the elevator. "One ride, Sam. One. Don't tell Detective Casey. And don't ask again."

5

No one ever forgets having their home broken into. If you did the breaking, they don't let you forget, either.

"Why don't you ever call first before coming over?"

Jerry Christy waited in the limp twilight for me to explain my purpose for being on Jackson's front step at this hour. Her hands rested in the pockets of a terry cloth bathrobe the color of bananas one day past green and three hours before brown. Silky red pajamas pants, peeking out below, billowed against her petite legs.

With her starched hair disoriented from sleep and her eyes slanted with suspicion, she looked like an angry, droopy-eyed garden gnome.

"We need to talk." I darted my eyes to point out the idling patrol car in the driveway behind me. "Are you going to let me in?"

Jerry pushed the door open further and dissolved into the blackness inside. "At least you rang the doorbell this time."

I gave Reilly and Tandy the signal they were free to go. As their patrol car lights bounced over me while reversing out of the driveway, I stepped into the cavernous space within.

Walking into Jackson's entrance hall always felt like passing through the pearly gates into an illustrious afterlife. Inside, you knew you'd find climate-controlled temperatures, comfortable seating, a safe haven, and a generous warrior.

The only time I wasn't on the receiving end with Jackson were the times I refused to accept what he offered. Or the times I tried to take it without asking, like the night I'd broken in and Jerry caught me.

She's never liked me, and I can't figure out why.

Tonight, I was back at Jackson's home looking for him, but he wasn't here. I could feel the emptiness between the walls.

I felt my way along the veiny grooves in the plaster to Jackson's study where a lamp begrudgingly emitted low-watt illumination. Cheerless shadows curtained off all four corners of the room. Jerry sat in the low-lying darkness with a Ray Bradbury book open in her lap, but, unless it was printed in braille, she wouldn't be reading it in here.

I lowered myself into the opposite chair. We were back where we first met.

"I made you some tea," Jerry nodded toward a vintage teacup sitting delicately on the coffee table. "Drink up. You look dehydrated."

I lifted the curved lip to my mouth. The tea was still hot.

"Chamomile and vanilla?"

"With manuka honey."

"You saw me coming?"

"I always see you coming, Samantha."

Jerry had known I would break into Jackson's house that night back in October, too. So she'd planned and waited. At the time, I assumed it had been my bad luck and her good. Now, I knew better. My déjà vu flashes, what I called the brief glimpses into the future that seemed to always rotate around my death, are a superpower we now shared.

Knowing the ability originated with her meant her mystery had faded a skosh. I could read that woman like, well, tea leaves.

She lifted her own teacup to her wrinkled mouth and sipped contentedly. Our relationship dynamic had changed since then. During my first visit, I was looking for evidence Jackson wasn't to be trusted. Now, I was here because I loved him. It made her like me better, I think. Or, at least, tolerate me.

Taking the last sip, I relaxed into the mollifying nature of chamomile. "I know he's not here, Jerry. So, where is he?"

She set down her tea, eased the book closed, and clasped her hands over it. "I don't know where he is, Samantha."

Jackson often gave Jerry information, followed by telling her not to share it with me. Keeping things from me was Jerry's favorite hobby.

"You don't know? Or you haven't been given clearance to tell me?"

Because her eyebrows were white, I could see her raise them in the gloom.

"Clearance from whom?"

"Jackson, of course."

"Jackson does not tell me what I can or cannot say, young lady."

"Strongly suggests then?"

Jerry snorted. "We're both less devious than you give us credit for."

"I doubt it." I held up my hands to stop her from derailing my questioning. It took more effort than it should. The weight of my arms dragged them back down instantly. Exhaustion was setting in. "What's happened to him, Jerry?"

She tapped one banana-colored slipper against the thick cut-pile rug. "I don't know."

"You don't?"

Jerry continued tapping her foot while feeling no obligation to answer me a second time.

"Do you think he's in trouble?"

She tapped one finger on her book in the same contemplative rhythm. "He usually isn't."

I snorted. "What are you talking about? He's always in trouble."

"No," she answered dryly, "you are always in trouble. He's always getting you out of it."

"Oh, right. That."

We sat in the dark silence, while the grandfather clock in the hallway ticked off the moments left in life. With each tock, my eyelids drooped further. I shook myself awake and focused back on Jerry.

"The hospital says Jackson opened his eyes before he disappeared. Do you think it's possible he's awake, Jerry? Could he finally be back?"

Jerry spoke to the window and, just beyond, the moonlight dusting the creaking tree limbs with powdered sugar. "Anything is possible."

Drained of energy, I relaxed into the chair as it grumbled from its wiry bowels. "I can't believe I hitched a ride all the way out here," I paused for a eye-squeezing yawn, "for a 'possible.'"

Jerry, dragging her attention back to the room, opened her book and pretended to read again. "You could have called."

∼

Jerry insisted I stay the night. Mostly, because she didn't want to drive me home or let me borrow her car. There wasn't much of the night left anyway. It ticked and spun and dwindled at its regular, undaunted pace. Undeterred by fake doctors, dragon truckers, or vanishing boyfriends, the witching hour cackled at the devilry it had caused. Then it slipped through the fog and boarded a gondola where an Italian in a blue striped shirt and flat straw hat rowed the witching hour into the next day.

Fatigue had me at two glasses in. One more hour awake and I'd be over the legal limit. But I had things to do, superheroes to save, and boyfriends to find.

Jerry, on the other hand, doggedly sat in the darkened gloom. The sooner I could get her to go to bed, the sooner I could steal her car and search for Jackson.

I knelt down beside her chair, stumbling with my dissipating coordination, and put my hand over her bony one.

"You're worried, aren't you." Me, too. Which is why I needed her to GO TO BED.

Jerry patted my hand with her free one. "No."

"Then what?"

"I'm just…" she finally met my eyes, "waiting."

"For what?"

"For you to pass out."

Her joke caught me off guard.

"Cute, Jerry." As soon as I said it, my head swam and a temporary dizzy spell unbalanced my weight. I pressed a hand into the plush rug fibers for stability.

Jerry leaned forward in eager, nearly giddy, anticipation. "Are you getting lightheaded?"

I cast my eyes upon the horizon to seek an unmoving piece of land. Seeing as how bookshelves don't dance, I picked that. "No."

"Yes, you are." Jerry tapped me on the shoulder. "You should lay down."

Plopping down on my butt, I dug my fists into the rug to brace against the twisting room. "What's happening to me, Jerry?"

She motioned toward my empty teacup. "I added some intrigue to your tea."

My head spun and righted. "Intrigue?"

"Nothing to concern yourself with. Just some valerian root, Hops, GABA, L-theanine, and enough honey to mask it. All perfectly natural.

But, to be on the safe side, I also added five milligrams of Ambien."

Jerry pushed herself out of the chair, while moving with an ageless ease, and whistled. The bedraggled dog, who I hadn't seen hiding under my chair, stood at obedient attention.

"Get some sleep, Samantha. I'd crash on the couch, if I were you. It's unlikely you'll stay conscious long enough to climb the stairs."

I reached out to grasp her robe but missed. "But, Jerry, why?"

"Because you need sleep. With Jackson missing, you won't take it. So, I helped. You can thank me later." She tucked her book under her arm. "Also, I don't want you stealing my car."

I reached out for her, but grasped only air, which felt weighty in my hands. "You're crazier than I gave you credit for."

Jerry shrugged, turning for the door.

"Wait, Jerry." My tongue never felt so heavy. And fat. And lazy. I nudged it to move, but it sank into my mouth like a Barcalounger and started flipping channels on the tube. "Please. I need to know something."

One question, one haunting question, threaded through and over and under my brain these last three days. No one, except Jackson and maybe Jerry, could answer, but I hadn't had the guts to ask because I wasn't sure I wanted the answer.

"You should ask quickly, Samantha, before you lose consciousness."

My chest shook on the inhale. "How did he do it, Jerry? How did he take my place?" The words came out slowly, but at least they came. "I need to know."

Jerry's small frame towering over me seemed to stretch all the way to the ceiling, like the elongated shadow of an elf. As intimidating as she appeared in my addled, drugged brain, her voice sounded softer, warmer than I'd ever heard before.

"He loves you that much, Samantha. How else?"

I studied the carpet fibers, unable to meet her eyes. "I tried to heal him, Jerry. For three days, I've tried to take it back. But I failed. If I can mimic others' abilities, like his speed, like your visions, like talking to animals and all the other weird things I've done, then why didn't it work? Is it because my love isn't enough?"

Jerry rested her warm hand on my shoulder. "No. It's not about being enough. Love him with everything you are, Sam. Always love him with everything you've got. That's enough."

"But, what about my failure to"–I waved my hand around to push the words out–"mimic, to heal him."

Her bony, warm fingers squeezed. "I think, dear one, this might be an ability you will never have." Typical Jerry would use this as an opportunity to criticize, but she spoke comfortingly. Even motherly. "It simply isn't for you, sweet girl. It's Jackson's alone. Accept it gratefully. And remember it," her tone sounding less comforting and more prognosticating, "in the times when you doubt him."

I nodded, wiping away plump tears as my brain swished around inside my skull. The cocktail of herbs and narcotics walked through my mind switching off lights.

Jerry patted my shoulder once, airing out the room of emotion. "Now, enough of this. Take the couch. Goodnight."

She glided toward the stairs with her banana slippers whispering secrets against the floor. The dog clicked his nails behind her.

"Goodnight Jerry," I called after her, "you devious crackpot. Goodnight..." I didn't know the dog's name because no one ever used it, "dog."

I ambled to my feet and stumbled down the hall. I'd show her. I could make it to a bedroom. Leaning against the stair bannister, I gazed at the ascending steps, which plucked away at gravity. Jerry had climbed them already and disappeared. And she was 150 years old. I could do this.

I lifted one foot and dropped it. "Another night."

Slipping back into the darkened study, I collapsed on the broad, plush window seat. Planning her deception to the letter, Jerry had left a folded quilt on one end. Tugging off my shredded boots, I flopped onto my side, pulling the blanket to my chin. The pillows tugged me deeper into delirium.

I sighed, embracing the narcotics.

Outside, the wind puffed against the house in open, expansive breaths. The inhales tugged at the glass panes in a high pitched "ah." The exhales released the windows to chatter in place with a low mumbling "uh." I timed my breathing to the wind as consciousness staggered away.

~

Dreams rarely give me insight. Mostly, when I dream, it's about whatever I ate last. It's boring, but typical. Over the last three nights at the hospital, my typical changed. I started dreaming about Jackson, which wasn't surprising. But these dreams didn't feel like dreams. They felt like memories. Only, not my memories.

The first came after Jackson came out of surgery on Saturday night. I'd been awake for more than forty hours, spending most of those hours surviving a flood, a lightning storm, angry domesticated dogs, an out-of-control forklift, a rattlesnake, a kidnapping, a gunshot, and an actor. Sleep was going to happen with or without my permission.

With Jackson out of surgery, I'd pulled a chair next to his bed, held his hand, and dropped my forehead on his arm. I was out. Then, the first dream came.

Dad said it was too dangerous. He said not to try it, but he never said I couldn't watch Theo try. And Theo would always try.

"What do you think, man? That limb up there?"

Theo blew at his pale hair, which crowded into his eyes, while hugging onto a tree from twenty feet up.

"That's too high, Theo. Just tie it off where you are and come down."

I stood at the base, watching my best friend scurrying up the bark of an old elm for the perfect place to secure a rope swing. He wanted to climb to the top. But that was Theo. Theo always wanted to go further than he should.

"Hold on. I can make it a little higher," he shouted down, scratching at the bark with his tennis shoes. Pieces flitted down like snow, getting in my eyes and mouth. I spit them out and wiped my face with my t-shirt.

We were in the hills behind my house. Dad said I wasn't allowed to climb the tree that high, but he hadn't said Theo couldn't. Not that it would matter. Anything you tell Theo not to do, he'll do. He's been that way since we were kids. Heck, I guess we were still kids. But not for much longer. We'd both be driving in less than five years, and the idea of Theo behind the wheel scared everyone. Except me. I knew Theo would be okay. Sure, he'd wreck whatever vehicle he got. A few times, probably. But he'd still be okay. Theo was always okay.

"Come on, man. Tie it off and come down. Any higher and the rope will be too short, anyway," I shouted up at him.

Theo scooted out onto a sturdy, brittle limb, his knees grasping each inch and then pushing forward again. He shoved his hair behind his ears, but it was too short to stay and too long to manage. Theo's mom couldn't keep up with the speed of his hair growth any more than she could keep up the speed of her son. Each had been racing past her in a blur for twelve years.

"Almost got it," Theo tossed the end of the rope around the limb, created two loops, and worked it into a double running bowline knot, a skill Dad taught us both.

Finished, he tugged on it twice, making certain it was secure.

"We're good. I'm coming down, Jackson," Theo yelled. "Look out below!"

Before I could stop him, Theo, with rope in hand, swung out kicking, hooping, and hollering. "Woo hoo!" Sunlight grasped at Theo, who swung from the light to the shadow, from the tree base to the branches, from one cloud to another like the son of Zeus.

Then Zeus dished out some tough love.

Blinded by his unruly hair, Theo lost sight of a heavy limb in his blind spot. Sliding down the rope, it hit his shoulder hard, knocking the strength out of his grasp. The rope sped up, slipping through his hands. He flailed. He fought. He seemed suspended in that moment forever.

I saw what was happening, knew what was coming, but what could I do? Staring up into that bitter afternoon sunlight, I was powerless. Could I catch him? Could I break his fall?

Theo's partnership with gravity dissolved and he fell hard and fast, striking the back of his head on a limb. Unconscious and bloody, his meteoric decline landed in a heap on top of me. I'd cushioned the ground, but the damage had been done in the air. The gash in the back of his head dyed his matted blond hair in a deep, wet ruby.

He wouldn't wake up. He wouldn't take a breath. He couldn't die. Not Theo. Not my best friend. Not if I could do anything about it.

"Theo, hold on! Just hold on!" I lugged his deadweight across my shoulders. "I'll get you help!"

I ran from the deepest part of my fear. I ran like I'd never run before. I ran fast enough to make the sunlight beating down on us work to keep up. I ran until I found help to bring my best friend back to life.

I woke in the ICU with my head on Jackson's arm, now wet from tears. It wasn't from my emotion, but Jackson's. These were his memories and his fears of nearly losing a best friend.

Always Another Villain

Like comatosed Mr. Portelli, what I was seeing was in Jackson's head. Whether he meant to share them with me or my superpower allowed me to be intrusive, I didn't know. If it helped me connect with Jackson, however, I also didn't care.

An hour later, I passed out again on Jackson's shoulder.

"Pace yourself, son. The control will come…in time. If you try this on your own, before Hal says you're ready, you'll only end up getting hurt."

Dad had a voice that epitomized authority. He spoke plainly, clearly, and with a wisdom that originated from before time was time. It was always folly to take Dad's instruction lightly. It was absolute foolishness to ignore it completely.

But I did. I had to know what I could do.

After dark, I snuck out of the house, laced up my shoes, and ran. I ran to the end of the neighborhood, then to the dairy farm three miles away, then to the city limit sign five miles further, then into a tree. The next night, I tried again. This time, I hit the side of Mr. Patterson's barn.

Every morning at breakfast, Dad would note the new bruises on my face and arms. He'd repeat his advice, and I'd repeat ignoring it.

On my fifth night, the advice finally stuck. Instead of taking the roads, I zigzagged through a nearby neighborhood, raced between alleyways, felt the ease of the speed in my legs, and increased it by a notch. That's when I ran into Mrs. Dunning's yard and got a lesson in listening to Dad.

I'd awoken in a gasp. I blinked the oozing blood out of my mind's eyes.

"Oh, honey," I traced the straight scar across his neck, "a clothesline?"

~

His memories weren't always complete stories. Some were clips strung together, like the replay of his most painful highlights over the years. There were broken bones and body gashes, cuts and scrapes and bruises, twisted joints and torn muscles. Controlling his speed didn't come overnight. Or in a year. It came like all things eventually mastered ever come—through loss of sleep and skin and blood.

Putting himself into harm's way to save others meant he couldn't always control the circumstances. A few memories flashed from his military service overseas: Jackson protecting a young girl from an exploding building, Jackson shoving a civilian away from an IED, Jackson dragging an injured soldier out of enemy fire.

The two purple hearts for his service made more sense now. With his ability, he couldn't stop himself from running to wherever violence unfolded. He wasn't Superman, but he was giving it his best shot.

One memory lingered long after I woke. Afterward, I'd laid in my cot inside his ICU room and stared at the white tiled ceiling for an hour. It was the memory of him rescuing me from the Oklahoma Now roof the night Senator Chad McBride died.

What is that man doing? Is someone up there with him?

I bolted through the Oklahoma Now lobby, stirring papers and tipping coffee cups as I went. The security guard didn't blink. The janitor vacuumed. A newspaper pile flapped. The elevator dinged.

I took the stairs. Up, up, up. I moved floor to floor to floor to floor. Gravity gave no objections. Empty and echoing, the sound of my own feet reached the roof door at the same time I did. We both crashed through.

I lunged over the ledge to grab the hand slipping. It wasn't McBride. McBride was no more. His body lay half in and half out of a Buick LaCrosse windshield below.

The woman in my hands looked straight ahead but saw nothing. She didn't blink. Didn't breathe. She hung there frozen in time. Conscious, but unaware. Alive, but unresponsive.

Slowly, I pulled her over the ledge and lowered her to the ground.

"You're safe now. I've got you." I spoke in a cautious, gentle tone. "Can you hear me? Are you hurt?"

She looked straight up. Blinked once. And took a shuddering breath.

No words. No tears. Nothing.

She was hurt. I could see it in the unnatural curve in her hips, the way they were now tilted from the rest of her body. One shoulder bulged forward, too. Possibly dislocated. I checked for any life-threatening injuries, any blood loss, and found nothing. Her feet were bare, but uninjured. Other than the cuts on her hands from the ledge, her injuries looked internal.

I smoothed the dark waves from her face. She had eyes the shape of almonds but size of walnuts. Normally, they were almost too large for her face, if I had to guess. Right now, they were alien. Swollen beyond their normal size from shock. Her mouth quivered, then stilled. Her lips puckered to speak but flattened. She tested the muscles in her face with an eye twitch, a nose wrinkle, a jaw reset, and back to mouth puckers. I didn't know what she was doing, but I liked watching it. She had an unconventional beauty about her that made me curious to see what expression would come next.

"Everything's going to be okay now," I whispered, while the twitches shifted to the other eye, the other cheek, the other side of the mouth.

She puckered again and breathed out. "You can do this," she said on an exhale.

I leaned in closer. "What?"

She took another breath and again breathed the words out. "You can do this."

I laced my fingers around her hand and tried again. "Do what?"

"You can." The words came with more conviction. "Do this. You can." She shivered. "Do this. You can. Do this."

I sat back on my heels. She was giving herself a pep talk. Right now? She couldn't even register her body's pain, yet. Nor my presence. The shock still had her tracing Orion's Belt with her eyes. But she already had the determination to overcome whatever had already happened and beat whatever was now coming. She was coaching her mind back from its place of rest and retreat.

I'd never seen anyone handle trauma like that before. Not while in the heat of it.

"You're..." I smiled, thoroughly impressed, "something else, aren't you?" I kissed her hand. "Whoever you are, you're right. You can do this."

The next memory was from later that same night. He sat in his study talking to Jerry.

"You didn't cause this," Jerry said. "Why are you blaming yourself?"

Because I knew that guy was weak. Because I knew he may become unstable. Because I should have seen it coming.

Months before Sen. McBride's public destruction went national, I had approached him with a friendly piece of advice.

"Be wary of your own weaknesses, Senator. Power without humility is dangerous. Hold it lightly or it'll destroy you even as you destroy others with it."

He took the advice like I expected by shrugging it off.

I'd approached him one night after spotting him in a parking lot in the isolated, industrial sector off the Arkansas River. What he was doing there, I didn't know. I'd been in the area checking on a homeless encampment. When I'd seen him, I chalked it up to chance. Later, as his reputation and life imploded, the encounter felt more divinely designed.

McBride didn't know me. And, even if he had, I didn't let him know it was me. Dressed in my black hoodie, I kept my face out of the light. I knew the warning wouldn't mean much to him, but I hoped, even subconsciously, it would resurface when he needed it. Maybe it did. More likely it didn't.

At the time, I had no idea what was coming for him. I only knew the darkness that will always be an orb around political power. As a state senator, his actions and even votes had always leaned more toward his need for public approval. He wasn't a man with inner strength. And he was vying for a higher position of power, which he was unequipped to manage.

The warning was meant kindly. Whether he took it that way or not, I left up to him.

After I spoke to him briefly, I disappeared. I'd warned other politicians in the past, too. Few took it to heart. Many were still in power, though clumsily. Some were gone, scorned out of office through one scandal or another. Others ceased being relevant except to those who could control them.

What they did with their authority was their decision to make and their consequences to face. All I could hope was that the warning pricked their conscience from time to time.

When the end of McBride's political career hit the news, it caught me by surprise. I feared for the guy, for his ineptitude, for what destruction his greed and ego would bring, but I hadn't expected the destruction quite that fast.

"I should have kept a closer eye on the guy, Jerry," *I told her now.* "He was weak. And I knew it."

Jerry strummed her fingers together. "He was a grown man. Capable of making his own decisions and responsible for their outcome."

I leaned back in the chair and stretched my legs out. "Yes, but that outcome has now hurt an innocent person."

"The woman."

"Yes, the woman."

"Who is she?"

I shook my head. "I don't know. Yet."

"Is she going to be okay?"

I met Jerry's eyes. "She's alive, if that's what you're asking."

Jerry wasn't going to let me second-guess all night. "Jackson, honey, you're human. And so am I. I can't foresee everything, and you can't use your body as a shield for every danger to every person on the planet. We do what we can."

I knew that. I didn't even question it, but I didn't have to like it. "Tonight, it wasn't enough."

Jerry's clear eyes narrowed. "What's really bothering you? You didn't know the man was going to dance around on a ledge tonight. Or that he'd nearly drag a woman down with him. Why is this bothering you more than others?"

I turned my head to the window and studied our reflections against the glass. A single lamp burned over Jerry's head, creating a near halo effect. That was as much light as she ever turned on in this room. She came in here, usually, to gaze at the moonlight. And hide in the shadows.

"What do you want me to say?"

She shifted in her chair. "I want you to say what about tonight has gotten you so upset."

I tapped my foot on the carpet. "I don't know."

I thought about the woman. About her resolve. About her voice. About her hair. There was something about her that felt familiar, that felt similar to something similar in me. Her face wouldn't leave me. Nor her stubborn spirit. I couldn't say what it was about her, yet. Only that there was something.

I stopped tapping my foot. "Maybe I do know."

Jerry raised an eyebrow. "The woman."

I took a deep breath, "Yes, the woman."

Now, I laid in Jackson's window seat and gazed at the chair where he'd been sitting in the dream-that-isn't-a-dream-and-memory-that-isn't-my-memory. What I wouldn't give for him to be sitting there now.

Stretching with a catlike contentment, I blinked once, twice, three times, slowly, slowly, slowly and turned over. The intrigue Jerry slipped in my tea had mellowed my mind, unwound my muscles, and had me mentally floating.

If anything could float, it should be the brain.

Outside the window, I blinked a shape into focus, then out of focus, then into focus again. My unfettered mind moved over the curves of the shape, the lines of the shape, the way the shape stood there staring down at me.

"Hi, Jackson," I told the face outside the window, as I sank into the bewitching couch cushions.

He raised one hand in an awkward 'hey there' gesture, and I slipped into a dream about chickens stoking a fire.

6

Manipulating people makes them not trust you. I did not see that coming.

"I'm telling you, Jerry, he was here."

She was preoccupied punishing innocent egg yolks.

"You dreamed it, Samantha." Jerry added in a gulp of milk and kept beating.

"I did not. Jackson was here last night. In fact, he told me to tell you to fix pancakes for breakfast."

She shook, pinched, and sprinkled black pepper, basil, rosemary, and chives over the egg mixture. "I'm making omelets."

I shifted on the snack bar stool. "He was here, Jerry. I'm serious about that."

She didn't interrupt the rhythm of her whisk. "You're saying he stood outside the window…"

"The big one above the window seat."

"He stood there," she repeated impatiently, "watching you sleep and…waving?"

"Like this," I demonstrated with a half-hearted wave and a 'what's up' face.

This morning, nursing a minor Ambien and herb hangover, I'd awakened to the memory of Jackson standing outside the window and me, thanks to Jerry, too drugged to do anything about it. She, in turn, told me I was incorrect.

"Never happened."

I leaned onto the counter in a way I thought demonstrated sincerity. "Why don't you believe me?"

Jerry didn't bother to roll her eyes, but the spirit of an eye roll was there. "He wasn't here, Samantha. You dreamed it. Or you're lying. Hard to know with you."

"What reason could I possibly have for lying?"

Jerry decapitated the head of a stick of butter and flung it into the hot skillet. "If one exists, you'll find it."

Theo, dressed in his usual sidekick gear of jeans, boots, and red flannel, stomped into the room with his head tilted back as the aroma of browning butter led him by the nose. "Jerry, is that bacon?"

She marched the egg mixture into the skillet. "Not yet, but it will be."

To keep an eye on things with Jackson gone, and because he had no home, Theo had been crashing in an upstairs guest room. I got the feeling he lived here more than he didn't. Calling it "a guest room" was probably in deference to Theo's disdain for staying still. In one place too long and he'd bolt. To irritate his inner commitment-phobe, I was going to hang a Thor poster above his bed.

"Hey Raggedy." Theo snatched a bottle of orange juice from the refrigerator in one big-handed grip and walked it to the breakfast nook. He had no idea why I was here and, due to his nonexistent curiosity, wouldn't be asking.

"Morning, Theo. In case you were wondering, I stayed over last night because Jackson has disappeared from the hospital."

He sipped his juice, sucking the pulp off the scruff on his upper lip. "Oh yeah? Guess he's feeling better, then." Theo viewed Jackson's coma as his way of catching up on some much needed R and R.

"Sam's been telling me this morning that Jackson came by last night for a visit." Jerry bombed the center of the eggs with shreds of cheese and shards of tomato. She fired spoonful after spoonful of sautéed mushrooms and spinach. "Then left."

I swiveled on the stool to face Theo. "He did."

Behind me, Jerry coerced the omelet. "She dreamed it."

Theo's thick fingers wrapped around the small glass. With no additional effort, he could have substituted the glass for a whole orange and simply squeezed however much juice he wanted directly into his mouth.

"Dreams are often the manifestation of a mere whisper in the mind, Raggedy." He raised his glass as if offering a toast. "I wouldn't ignore it."

"I'm not ignoring a dream, because I didn't have one."

Theo raised his eyebrows over the glass as he continued chugging it down.

"Okay," I corrected, "I did have a dream. But it wasn't relevant, and it certainly wasn't a dream when I saw Jackson standing outside my window."

Jerry stabbed a spatula under the omelet and plopped it on a plate. "I think your blood sugar is low." She shoved the plate at me. "Eat while it's hot."

I took it cautiously. "Are there any herbs in this thing I should know about?"

She stabbed the center of the omelet with a fork. "Eat and find out."

With food and utensil in hand, I slid into the booth across from Theo, who wouldn't be getting breakfast until Jerry finished frying a whole pig. In the meantime, he satisfied himself with another glass of juice, which he slipped between the tufts of shaggy hair framing his mouth.

"Don't get upset, Raggedy." Theo draped one heavy arm across the back of the bench. "You can't expect us to believe everything you say."

I can't? "Why not?" I shoved in a bite of omelet.

"Because, when it comes to being open, sometimes you…" Theo searched for the word, while Jerry jumped in with an answer.

"Lie."

Theo openly considered it. "Not lie. Maybe a better word is–"

"Lie," Jerry repeated, while wisps of pork-fattened smoke nudged her nose.

"Well, or–"

"Lie."

I shot Jerry a dirty look.

Theo countered. "Control. That's more accurate. Control."

"Or lie."

He considered it as if she hadn't said it thrice already. "A good way to explain it, Sam, is that you tinker with the truth."

Jerry added, "Which is his way of saying 'lie.'"

While the two of them tossed around ways of insulting me, I finished my omelet. Adding rosemary was a nice touch.

"Look, both of you, I think I've got the gist. You think I either dreamed it because I was heavily medicated last night, or it's my usual manipulating self coming out."

Jerry clanked down a plate in front of Theo. She'd made him an omelet stuffed only with bacon. He inhaled the cholesterol.

"Manipulating?" Theo shoved half the omelet into his mouth and swallowed it. "Yes. That's the best description yet, Raggedy."

I waved them off. "Yes, yes. I'm horrible and all that. But I bet you couldn't name one instance where I've been less than upfront with either of you."

∼

They gave three examples and wanted to give more, but Delaney called. Talking to my boss was hell, but hell with a disconnect button.

"Oh, that's my boss calling. Gotta take this," I put the phone to my ear in the middle of Jerry's rant over breakfast, which didn't stop her from muttering a final "you turkey." I mouthed an insincere 'so sorry,' and Jerry finally got around to rolling her eyes.

Sliding out of the breakfast booth, I skipped away from the kitchen. The relief of escape lasted three seconds and ended when Delaney spoke.

"Are you coming in today?"

Delaney wasn't one for phone pleasantries. Most of the time, she starts talking before confirming I'm on the line. This has led to many tediously long voice messages of her accusing me of giving her the silent treatment. To address the issue, I've re-recorded my voicemail greeting five times, starting with, "You've reached my voicemail." When that didn't clarify it for her, I tried, "Let me start this message by saying, this isn't me," "This is a recording, I'm not actually here," and "You can't talk to me right now because I'm literally somewhere else." When none of those worked to inform her how voicemail operated, I gave up and went with, "Hey, Delaney, what do you need?" This, of course, confuses everyone else.

"Today, today, today." I softly clicked my tongue. "Thinking…"

"I've emailed you the contact information for that psychiatrist person, Virgil Fairchild. I've sold him a full page of space in the Christmas issue, and he's ready to move forward with the article. He's expecting your call. So, talk to him today. I told him you'd be writing the article and now all he does is ask me questions about you. His buy isn't big enough and you are not interesting enough to keep me answering his calls" In my mind, I could see Delaney's Botoxed facial muscles warring with her natural scowl.

"I'll get an interview scheduled."

"Also, that reporter from *Oklahoma Now* is scheduled to shadow you today."

Delaney had, without my permission, okayed a reporter from my old newspaper tagging along with me today. According to her, the paper was doing a feature on local media by highlighting a "typical day" with an editor. Because *Promotion Magazine*'s biggest competitor, *You Preferred Magazine*, was participating, and because *You Preferred Magazine*'s publisher is Delaney's ex-husband number two, I was obligated to participate.

"That's today?"

"The reporter is scheduled to meet you at the office in an hour. I also gave her your name and number, so she'll be calling. Don't embarrass me on this. Your Christmas bonus is riding on it."

Is that what she calls a gift certificate for six Laser Lipo sessions?

"I'll do my best."

"And Samantha? If your boyfriend is still in a coma by Friday, you need to break-up with him so his condition doesn't interfere with your work."

I hung up. Hell called back, but I hit ignore. My voicemail would keep her occupied for a while.

Done with the call, I hovered in Jackson's main hall considering how to get keys to any nearby vehicle without returning to the kitchen. If I went back in there, Jerry and Theo would return to their list of grievances.

"You purposefully kept me out of the escape plan when we were being held hostage," Jerry pointed this out before Delaney called. "And, you never have returned that ball gown."

I'd dismissed the accusation. "That wasn't me manipulating you, Jerry. That was me letting you sleep so I wouldn't have to hear your opinion. And, as for the gown, I'll check my closet again." She was never getting it back.

Theo, who chose to eat biscuits instead of engage, had his grievances magnanimously covered by Jerry, who accused me of being a pickpocket who always needed a ride.

"Speaking of." I'd turned to Theo. "I need another ride."

Ultimately, Theo explained their real issue with not believing me was the fact I wasn't a team player.

"You're a lone wolf, Raggedy. Or think you are. And I get that. I've lived a lot of my life that way, too. Did I ever tell you about that time I…"

"Yes," Jerry and I interrupted.

Theo wiped strawberry jam off his mouth. "Well, anyway, the point is you are not alone anymore, but you refuse to believe it. If you can't trust us, how can you expect us to trust you?"

I wanted to give a flippant answer, but I didn't have one.

After I ended my call with Delaney, I avoided returning to the breakfast table inquisition by stealing Jerry's Prius. I needed to find Jackson, whether he wanted me to or not.

I believed I'd seen him last night…mostly. I mostly believed. Jerry had a point, though. I could have dreamed it. I dream a lot of weird stuff these days, possibly more when dosed with herbs.

Jackson was out there somewhere, and not here. I needed to find out why.

Jerry and Theo, on the other hand, preferred eating a leisurely breakfast. When I asked Jerry to give me a straight answer about what or where she thought Jackson was, she said he was most likely "busy doing stuff." Then, she put another pan of biscuits in the oven.

Jerry and I parted ways with my way happening inside her car.

Here's the one thing I knew for sure: Jackson would never make me worry needlessly. He was too considerate for that. If he was willfully keeping me in the dark, he believed it was for my good.

Here's the other thing I knew for sure: I didn't care what Jackson thought was for my good.

"What do you think, Gin? Do they have a point?"

The last place Jackson had been seen was at the hospital. That was where I was headed. Maybe there was a clue that Reilly and Officer Tandy missed. Maybe Nurse Neal knew something more. Maybe I'd stick my nose in a few places it didn't belong and see what happened.

That's my usual repertoire and, in unexpected cases, it worked.

On the drive back into town, I called Gin Duncan, my redheaded, mechanical, childhood friend, who was obsessed with two things in life – his clunker van Beatrice and his clever girlfriend Angel. He knew me and Jerry and Theo and Jackson, too. We were all thrown together in this crazy superhero and sidekick world, now.

I called him because those who knew you as a child usually know you best. He could tell me if, like Jerry and Theo suggested, I manipulated situations.

"Well," a background sound of metal grinding against metal clanged across my speakerphone, "you did steal Jerry's car, right?"

I angrily jerked the Prius around the curves. "I don't know why I called you. You don't know me at all." A beep interrupted the call. "Hold on, Gin. I've got another call." I switched over. "Yeah?"

It was Delaney again. "That Virgil person is bugging me already this morning."

I counted to five, taking one long, patient breath, before responding. "I'll call him back now."

"Why haven't you called him back already?"

A beep interrupted my second long, patient breath. I switched over to the new incoming call.

"Hello?"

"Samantha Addison?" It was a sloshy male voice, one trudging through rising levels of spit to emerge out of the mouth. I'd never heard it before. "My name is Virgil Fairchild."

"Yes, Mr. Fairchild." I switched to my professional, peppy voice. "You were on my list of calls to make today."

"Good. We really need to talk."

"Right. About your ad." Another beep came through. "I'm sorry. Give me one moment. I need to wrap up a conversation I was on when you called." I switched over. "Gin?"

"Sam," it was Fred, the owner of Fred's Used Books and my hacker friend who I used all the time to do me favors at a moment's notice, "I need a favor."

"Fred? You never call me."

"I'm calling you now because, like I said, I need a favor."

Such terrible timing. "Fred, it's not that I don't want to help you, but–"

"No buts Sam. You owe me so many favors I've lost track. So, no buts."

He was right, I did, and he knew I did and knew I knew I did. "Okay, Fred. You're right. I owe you. Can you hold on a minute? I was on the other line."

His tone calmed. "Yes. I'll hold."

I switched to the next waiting call. "Gin?"

"Samantha Eloise, did you steal my car?"

Crap. "Jerry, legally speaking, it isn't technically considered stealing."

"It most definitely is technically stealing. If you get one scratch–"

Another beep.

"Sorry, Jerry. I'm getting another call. Gotta take it." I punched the "switch" button. "Hello?"

"Is this Samantha Addison?" The female, harmonic voice on the other end didn't sound familiar.

"Yes?"

"Hi. My name is Trudy Greene. I'm the reporter from *Oklahoma Now* who's shadowing you today."

I'd forgotten all about her. "Right." Another beep. "Can you hold on a minute, Miss Greene?" I switched over before she could answer.

"Yes, Miss Addison. Like I was saying–" It was Mr. Fairchild.

"I'm sorry, Mr. Fairchild. One more minute." I hit the switch again. "Gin?"

"Again, no."

"Hey, Jerry. Hold on." I punched the button again. "Gin?"

"No, I don't want any gin, Samantha." Delaney had stayed on the line. I hang up on her all the time, and she never stays on the line. "Why would you be offering me alcohol at ten in the morning?"

"That's not..." Oh forget it. "Delaney, I got this covered, okay? Mr. Fairchild is on the other line."

"Make sure he doesn't call me anymore."

"I'll try. You could also start screening your calls, which is what we all need to be doing more of." I clicked off Delaney and took the next call in the cue. "Gin?"

"Look, Sammie. I didn't mean to hurt your feelings." It was Gin. At last.

"You didn't. Not really. You were only being honest."

"It's just that you do manipulate people and, well, situations sometimes. Usually with the best intentions, though."

Leave it to Gin to try bleaching my bad spots.

"I get it," I let him off the hook. "Apparently, I have a trust problem or something. I'll seriously think about it, okay? But I don't have time to talk about it right now."

"Okay. We can talk about it later, but Angel wanted to say something before you hung up."

He put her on the line before I could stop him.

"Hey," Angel's melodic voice came over the line. She loved me because I'd been the one to push Gin to finally make a move. "I heard part of the conversation. I've got a thought."

"It's not that I don't want to hear it, Angel, but I've got work–"

"Right. I'll make it quick. I think you have an overdeveloped sense of responsibility. Like, you think everything's up to you. Or, that everyone is depending on you. So, you're trying to manage situations on your own, and it comes off like manipulation. When, really, it's that you're super horrible at asking for help."

"Could be," I tossed out lightly, "but I've got to take this other–"

"And I think there's a root fear there of what could happen if you can't take care of everything yourself. You know? Like you're afraid of needing anyone, while also thinking you don't have the right to need anyone. Make sense?"

This was turning into a much longer conversation than I'd planned. "Angel, I really appreciate your insight. Can you hold on for a minute?" I clicked over. "Mr. Fairchild?"

"It's Fred, Sam. Still holding."

"Sorry. Hold again?"

He sounded less calm. "Do it."

Done with guessing who was the next call in the cue, I switched over and went with, "Speak."

"Samantha, I log my miles on that car." Jerry was still holding. "So I'll know exactly how far you drive it. I expect it to be returned by the end of the day with a full tank of gas."

"You got it."

"Also…"

"I have to go." I hung up on her and waited for the next caller to emerge. "Hello?"

"Why are you calling me?" It was Delaney.

"I didn't call you. You were still on hold. Why were you still holding?"

"I don't know what you're talking about."

I clicked off Delaney, and the next call came back. "Yes?"

"Hey, girl. It's Angel. You seem busy, so I'll let you go. Just remember what I said about asking for help, okay? And, not beating yourself up for needing to ask. Gin and I? We're here for you."

That would have brought tears to my eyes if I'd had a moment to blink. "Thank you, Angel. That means a lot." I switched off and took the next call. "Speak."

"Excuse me?" It was Fred.

"Okay, Fred. What favor do you need?"

Fred took a breath. "I need you to pick up something at an old college buddy's house."

"College? Fred, you went to college?" Fred never told me anything about himself. The only thing I'd gathered over the years, other than his love of peanut butter and information, was that he appeared to be suffering from agoraphobia. He never left his bookstore or his apartment above the bookstore.

"You're wasting time," Fred ignored my personal question like Fred always does. "Do you have time to waste?"

Come to think of it. "No. Let me call you back in a few minutes, and I'll get the details then, okay?"

"Sam..." He wasn't mad, but he was cruising the neighborhood.

"Just a couple minutes, Fred. Let me wrap up the calls I have holding on the other line. Then I'll call back and get all the particulars on this favor you need."

He huffed. "The next time you show up on my doorstep needing something–"

"You're going to make me wait for it. I know." I hung up on Fred and waited for the next holding call to ring back. "Mr. Fairchild?"

"No, this is Trudy. From *Oklahoma Now*. Are we still on for today?"

No, I'm busy. "Sure. I'll meet you at my office."

"That sounds great, what about–"

"Sorry, Ms. Greene. I've got another call." I switched over. "Mr. Fairchild? Are you still holding?"

"Yes, Miss Addison. I'm still here. We really need to talk now."

I started to schedule a time to interview him for the ad, but I was interrupted when a vehicle tapped the Prius from behind. In the rearview mirror, a baby blue Cutlass rode my fumes.

"Mr. Fairchild, I need to put you on hold again."

7

Lightning does not strike in the same place twice. Vehicles, however, do.

Here, once again, I was skating the tight curves after leaving Jackson's home, and a car was breathing down my bumper. There was bad juju for me on this drive. If I looked at it from a ratio standpoint, approximately one out of every three times I drove this road alone someone tried to push me off it.

The vehicle bumped me again.

Yeah, yeah. I know this game already, buddy. I don't need refreshed on the rules.

Gripping the steering wheel for better control, I glanced into my rearview. That was definitely the same unmistakable baby blue Cutlass from last night. I'd recognize that trunk anywhere.

The driver, a darker-complected guy with dominant cheekbones, didn't look familiar or friendly. He squinted, either from the sunlight glaring into his left eye or due to astigmatism. Next to him, riding comfortably with another coffee cup in hand, was the fake doctor.

I waved at them in my rearview. To let me know they weren't in a friendly mood, Cheekbones bumped me again.

Both hands flew to the wheel as I wrestled with the forces of thrust and drag. The tires gripped and slipped. The car shimmied. A wobble ran through the vehicle in a shiver. Then, as quickly as it came, it left. The Prius, once again, found balance.

Jerry was never going to believe her dented bumper wasn't my fault.

The Cutlass chomped down again on my exhaust plume. If the fake doc wanted me dead – and people often do for no reason – it would have been more efficient to check that "to do" last night.

A fourth bump put a kink in my neck. If Cheekbones didn't take it easy, Doc was going to spill his coffee.

Usually in this situation, which is sad I have a "usual" in this situation, I speed up and attempt to outrun the tailgater. That method has worked exactly zero times. Back in October, when the Cutlass was a Chevy Tahoe and Cheekbones was a gambler named Furmann, I'd survived because Jackson plowed him off the road.

A few nights ago, during one of my dreams-that-aren't-dreams-but-memories-that-aren't-my-memories, I'd relived that night from Jackson's perspective. After walking me back to my vehicle, which I'd parked in the woods outside his house, Jackson was met at the front door by Jerry, who'd had a vision of me being run off the road. He'd jumped into his monster truck and roared down the road with only seconds left before the SUV made one final contact.

In case Jerry had a flash about this moment, too, I shrugged helplessly. "Jerry, just remember, this wasn't my fault."

With Jackson currently AWOL, I took the only other option I could think of: I slowed down. Speeding hadn't worked. Why not try something different? If Doc wanted to run me off the road, he could. I couldn't outrun that Cutlass, and I didn't outweigh it, either. He and Cheekbones were the cat. I was the ball of yarn. And yarn knows better than to fight back.

As the speedometer ticked lower, I waited for their next move. They, in turn, appeared to be waiting for mine. We traveled the road in close proximity but with enough space for maneuverability on both our parts. The Cutlass hung back in preparation of whatever I was about to do, and I did nothing just to screw with their heads.

We were at an impasse. A slow and steady, minimum speed limit, impasse. The speedometer ticked lower and lower until we hit 25 mph. It was the most boring car chase in human history.

On the slight straight away before the casino entrance, the Cutlass moved into the opposite lane and sped up to pass. The noise of the motor rumbled in my blind spot. The grill inched into my periphery.

Gaining more ground, the Cutlass entered the no-friend-zone of all civilized, driving nations. It's the point between pulling even and passing where the driver of the slower vehicle does not make eye contact with the challenger. I made eye contact with the challenger.

When I glanced in his direction, Doc surveyed my ten and two position with a twitchy, critical eye. His right hand, bronzed and wiry, thumped impatiently on the window seal. He shook his head as if, once again, I'd gravely disappointed him.

Done with whatever game he and Cheekbones were playing, I looked Doc in the eye and mouthed, 'What?'

Returning to leisurely sipping his coffee, Doc motioned for Cheekbones to pull ahead. In return, I eased off the accelerator even more. I hoped I could coast to a stop, and Doc would be so engrossed in his Colombian dark roast he wouldn't notice.

In case that wouldn't work, I added a twist to my plan when the casino's flashing sign came into view.

Why not. Today's as good a day as any to lower my standard of living.

~

My quick turn into the casino entrance wouldn't lose the Cutlass, but finding a place to turn around on that road and in that size of a vehicle would buy me a few minutes.

I sped along the uphill drive, which curved this way and that as if hypnotizing the driver to leave all their financial scruples behind. Large boulders, freshly planted trees, neatly trimmed landscaping and the continual incline gave you a sense of entering a world set apart from another, as if the drive itself was a drum roll before the big reveal.

Finally, cresting the hill, the neon sign announcing the Cash Mountain Casino flashed dimly in the morning light. Behind it, a modern, windowless building shut the day out and the risk in. I zipped through the expansive parking lot. It was neither crowded nor vacant for a casual Wednesday morning. People, with more money or less fulfillment than I, were spending their hump day on pure entertainment, while I was spending mine wearing the same clothes I'd slept in and fleeing strangers with an empty trunk. Someone needed to reassess their life choices.

Spotting two full-sized pickups parked a space apart, I squeezed into the slot between them as a temporary hiding space. Next to these metal behemoths, Jerry's Prius felt like an adorable toddler toy.

Now parked, I took a beat to think about my next move. It took less time than I'd budgeted, because I didn't have a next move. Trouble was still finding ways to take me by surprise.

Only a couple of days ago, Jackson had warned me a life with him would be challenging. It's one of the reasons he had so patiently allowed me to spend seven years finding my way to him, instead of him pushing himself at me. It's why he never told me he'd been the one to save my life that night with McBride on the roof of the Oklahoma Now building. It's why he'd kept his distance during the months we worked together on his Hearts For Homes section in Promotions Magazine. It's why he never told me about what I could do, instead letting me discover my super ability on my own time. It's why he wanted to train me as soon as possible but gave me the freedom to avoid it anyway. And why, while we took shelter in the Noble Park pavilion during the rainstorm on Saturday night, he asked me straight out if I wanted to be with him.

I could still see the tawny light from the fire he'd built brushing against his left cheek. That look of vulnerability, the one he could unload on me at a moment's notice, peered back from across the hearth.

"Sam? I'm asking you now to be honest with me. Do you want to be with me? If you don't, now's the time to say."

What I'd wanted to say was, "Yes! More than anything." Or even a, "Hell, yeah." But all I could get out was a single nod. I knew the seriousness of what he was asking, but I also knew I couldn't live without him.

Now, here I was facing that seriousness of a life with him but without him. Not my kind of day.

Taking a solid, mind-clearing breath, I looked around the area and assessed the situation. I'd successfully positioned myself in a parking lot with only one way in, which happened to also be the only way out. If I couldn't escape via a vehicle, then I'd escape on foot. One way or another, I was going after Jackson, and there wasn't a Cutlass alive that could stop me.

Shoving Jerry's keys in my purse and my phone in my jean pocket for easier access, I bolted toward Lady Luck. If I found her, maybe she could give a girl some advice on how to ditch clingy men.

Crossing through the casino entrance, I walked into a haze of cigarette smoke and recycled air, accompanied by the ringing, dinging, tinkling, tolling, beeping, bonging, jingle jangle of foolish enticement. Rows of slots ran lengthwise, widthwise, and crosswise in both directions while Whitney Houston's "I Want To Dance With Somebody" competed for air time.

Seeking to clear the line of sight from the door, I made a beeline straight through the middle and took a hard left. I walked down the slot row passing a woman nursing an oxygen tank and an unshaven man in plaid pajamas. So, maybe I wasn't the only one wearing what they'd slept in.

The whole place, filled with a lethargic crowd, smelled like early morning depression, what I'd describe as cigarettes, old perfume, and sweaty skin in a base of rubbing alcohol. No wonder people get addicted to these places.

In the next aisle, two middle-aged men wearing t-shirts stretched across their round bellies leaned on one machine. One man in a ball cap pushed buttons, the other watched over the man's shoulder while blowing cigarette smoke in his ear. A cowboy hat lay on top of the machine behind him. I picked it up as I walked by and kept going.

At the farthest east side of the room, two televisions entertained patrons at the bar. They consisted of a group of four ladies having morning mimosas and a single elderly gentleman with a beard down to his clavicle. I removed my neutral sweater for the black tank top underneath and tied it around my waist. I dropped the cowboy hat on my head and sidled up next to the old, bearded gent.

Positioned under a heating vent, he looked to be slowly melting, skin and all. His mouth sagged at the corners, his face sagged at the jaws, his arms sagged at the elbows. Every part of his spine sagged to the floor. He sat as if poured into a chair Jell-o mold.

"Hey there," I greeted him.

He responded by not acknowledging that neither I nor the world existed.

I took a seat.

The guy wasn't being rude. If I had to guess, he'd most likely died at least thirty-six hours ago and was now in the process of putrefaction, even though his hand rhythmically pushed buttons on a touchscreen. Despite being a corpse, his beard wasn't a bad place to hide behind.

With my back turned, my hair up in the hat, and my new friend beside me, I might pass temporary inspection when my pursuers came into view. It all depended on if Doc and Cheekbones were thorough when in pursuit or more haphazard and rushed. I was betting on the latter.

~

It didn't take long for me to spot Cheekbones. Watching the room over my shoulder and through my decaying friend's beard, I caught his husky form near the Willie Nelson slot that chimed erratically in no pattern I could detect.

As he moved down aisle after aisle, the flashing, hyperactive slots splattered his face with a neon rainbow, which the cavern under his Cheekbones absorbed without even trying. Even in this erratically lit, windowless room, I got a clear look at the man. At six feet, not over, his chest was broad and bulky. He wasn't heavy. He wasn't thin. He was that middle-sized thickness that comes from living a good life with potatoes. I'd guess him somewhere north of 40, south of 50, with skin that never will wrinkle. He didn't have a single strand of hair on his head, but he wore the nothingness well. His hairless caramel head also matched the gold of his eyes, so it all blended in nicely to create one dangerous-looking hulk of a man.

Moving with a continual scan of the faces as he passed, Cheekbones turned down one aisle and then another until only the bar remained. I leaned into my dead friend, putting a lazy arm up on the bar, and did my best slouch. Cheekbones sailed by and turned the corner.

Watching him go, I mumbled, "Maybe this is my lucky day."

My dead friend, still punching buttons into the machine, got chatty. "Ain't they all."

Are they, though? "Right on, man. Right on." I climbed off the barstool as the heating vent belched out a breath of uncharacteristically cool air. "See you around."

"Yep." Disinterested in my parting, he tapped at the screen. "Don't forget your phone."

Phone? I patted my right butt cheek pocket. Where was my phone? I scanned the spotted and swirled red murky carpet. Meanwhile, my dead friend, in a brief animate moment, reached across the bar, snatched my phone I hadn't remembered placing there, and passed it to me over his shoulder, all while keeping his right hand tapping the touch screen.

"Thanks, man," I returned it to my back pocket.

He grunted in reply, returning once again to the business of decomposing. I left him there with his organs breaking down and took off for a game of cat-and-mouse with Cheekbones.

His formidable form moved through the aisles like Pac-Man on his way to gobble up a Power Pellet. So, I hunted him like Clyde, the orange ghost with the stalkerish tendencies.

Staying in whatever aisle he'd vacate, I hunkered down below the machines and stayed ten paces behind. When he moved, I moved. When he reversed direction, I reversed direction. I watched and pursued until Cheekbones turned toward my general direction, then I fled to regroup.

What did I hope this would accomplish? Mostly, I wanted Cheekbones to rejoin Doc, wherever he was, and leave. Mostly, I knew that wouldn't happen. So, mostly, I watched and waited until there was an opening to escape out the front door.

Cheekbones entered the casino's small cafe, which was lined with glass walls so you could eat while watching the action-packed button pushing happening live on the casino floor. He stood facing the slots, crossed his arms, and surveyed the room. If I hadn't been following him, his position would have been ideal. Slightly camouflaged by the slot lights reflecting off the cafe glass, I wouldn't have noticed him until after he'd noticed me. Lucky for me, that's not how this was going down.

Keeping my cowboy hat below his line of sight, I moved down an abandoned line of slot machines two rows up from the cafe as Air Supply, belting out a soulful tune for mid-morning gambling, convinced everyone that even the nights are better. Standing in front of spinning pictures of bananas, I got a clear line of sight on Cheekbones' view and the front entrance, which was not currently in Cheekbones' view. If there was a time to make for the door, it was now.

Dropping to my knees, I speed crawled along the side of the aisles toward the front, through another cool gust from the heating vent, and into an oxygen tank.

"Hey," the woman from earlier, breathing in better air than the rest of us, obstructed my exit.

I smiled from the floor. "Hey."

"Is that yours?" She pointed behind me to a phone on the red, swirly floor.

Once again, I smacked myself in the butt. Once again, no phone.

"Guess so." I crawled over and stuffed it back into my pocket. "Don't know why it keeps falling out."

The little woman, neatly pressed in slacks and supportive shoes, pulled her oxygen tank closer. "It would probably stay in your pocket if you didn't crawl around on the floor."

I gave her an appreciative nod. "Good tip."

With that, she headed toward a slot called, "The Big Bang Theory," with her own air supply, and I headed out to prove the band Air Supply was right that days are better when someone you love is beside you.

8

Trudy Greene asked too many questions.

"I'm a reporter. That's what we do. You did know this was an interview, not just a free ride, right?" She asked, while giving me a free ride.

I don't usually ask strangers for rides. Well, okay, maybe I do. All the time, actually. When it's convenient. And free. But I wouldn't have asked her, except she kept calling me.

After escaping the casino, I'd nearly run right into Doc, who had been lazily leaning against Jerry's Prius while sipping his coffee. Distracted by his Colombian roast, he hadn't changed positions when a retirement home van pulled up to the casino entrance to unload takers of the early lunch buffet.

I'd exited the casino amidst the white-haired mob and used the van for cover. As it slowly pulled away, I jogged alongside it until I reached the corner of the casino. One hard right and I was out of sight.

On the east side of the parking lot, a frazzled, unshaven older man wearing grey sweatpants, a grey hoodie, and crazy grey eyes paced the side of the casino mumbling to himself. He kept saying stuff like, "It was the smallest jackpot," "I played the highest denomination," "Did I hit the max credits?...Yes, yes I did," "Maybe switch to video instead of reel spinning." He had a stone or a coin in his hand, which his thumb rubbed every time his heel hit the ground.

So sad. How does a person get to this point?

I moved around him as a sharp breeze hit me from behind. That reminded me to slip back into my sweater. Before I had it fully pulled over my head, the sweatpants man poked me in the side.

"Your phone," he pointed to the ground. "It fell out." Then he went back to pacing and mumbling.

My phone? Again?

There it was. On the ground. Once again, out of my pocket and making a break for it. This made no sense. My pockets were of normal size. My jeans tight enough. Items don't wiggle out on their own like that.

Wait…items don't wiggle out on their own.

"Jackson?" I hissed under my breath. "Are you here?"

I scanned the east side of the parking lot. Was Jackson pickpocketing my phone? And, then dropping it? I stood still, waiting to see if the wind would blow again. Nothing. Not on this side of the casino. The building blocked the breeze from this corner. Where had that breeze come from, if not Jackson? And, what about inside? Hadn't I felt a burst of air inside before my phone would fall out, too? Those cool bursts had to be Jackson jetting by, right?

"It's you, isn't it? You're here!" I spun around, heading back the way I came and passing the pacing man on another pacing round. When I got near the corner of the building, I headed back again, all while scanning the area for any glimpse of him. "Where are you? Why are you hiding? What is going on? What are you trying to tell me?"

The pacing man passed me on the right still talking to himself about betting limits and strategies. I went to the farthest south corner of the casino parking lot, looked around, and turned back.

"Is there someone I should call? Is that what you're trying to tell me?" I spoke to the air, in case Jackson was near enough to hear. "Why can't you tell me? Should I call you? But you don't have a phone. Those twin thugs took it on Saturday before handcuffing you to the warehouse pole."

Somehow, in the pacing, I'd synchronized with the grey sweatpants guy, and we were both walking and talking side-by-side. Just not to each other.

"I should choose a more aggressive jackpot."

"Did you get a replacement phone?"

"I should bet max coin."

"Is it the same number?"

"But, first, I should prime the pump."

"Would a text be better?"

"I should grab the slot at the end near the entrance."

I turned to the pacer and shushed him. "Can you keep it down? I'm trying to have a conversation here."

His distracted grey eyes focused on my forehead. "Have you ever tried the Reverse Martingale strategy?"

So, this is how a person gets to this point.

Time to go. "I'm leaving now. Here." I handed him the cowboy hat. "Return this to its rightful owner inside the casino, and it'll bring you good luck."

He looked at the hat with widening eyes. "Really?"

"Well, it can't hurt, right?"

I pivoted on the ball of my foot and headed for the woods. The parking lot ended abruptly at the crest of a sloping hill. With no fence or obstruction of any kind, I plunged into the wooded terrain and didn't look back.

Ten minutes into my downhill hike off Cash Mountain, my phone rang. And rang again. And again. I didn't answer because it was my office calling. By the fourth call, they'd broken me.

On the other line was Trudy Greene, the reporter scheduled to shadow me today. She had arrived at my office, but I had not. And, Delaney wasn't having it. I could hear her in the background telling Trudy to go to the hospital. "She's probably there. Her boyfriend is dying or something, and she refuses to break up with him."

I needed to step in and take control of this situation. "Why don't you meet me here, Trudy?" If she was going to go to the hospital anyway, I might as well get a ride.

"Sure. Where are you?"

That took some explaining. I wasn't completely sure, to be honest. I knew, if I kept heading downhill, I'd hit a sideroad eventually. But what sideroad? To keep this as uncomplicated as possible, I told Trudy to head toward the Cash Mountain Casino. Ten minutes later when I emerged from the woods and saw the road sign, I called her back and told her to pick me up on County Line Road 2533. Driving a little blue Ford Focus, she pulled up twenty minutes later.

"Hey there," I leaned into her open driver's side window. I stood next to a mailbox at the end of a long, dirt driveway in the middle of a lonely, dirt road. "Let's get this typical day started."

"You were out here on a story?"

Trudy had been asking questions from the moment I climbed into her cramped two-door hatchback. She wasn't as young as I'd expected. Shadow assignments usually end up on the desk of lower-level writers because anyone with seniority will opt out of following a person around all day. But she looked about my age, except with a sentimental roundedness to her chin that gave a kind impression. Although not beautiful, she had a dreaminess to her appearance that made her look slightly out of focus. When she glanced in my direction, she tilted her head a degree higher than needed, as if her nostrils wanted a good look at me, too.

Beyond all that, the most amazing thing about her was a full, luscious head of dynamic reddish-blonde hair with auburn streaks that stopped at the shoulders of her creamy sweater. She reminded me of an inquisitive strawberry cupcake.

"Research, specifically. Nothing too exciting." I told her. "Just, you know, normal managing editor kind of stuff."

She was driving us to the hospital for me to continue doing more normal managing editor stuff, which wasn't normal at all or connected to my job in any way.

On my earlier walk downhill, I'd had a heart-to-heart with Jackson in case he was listening. Namely, it consisted of statements like, "If you can hear me, please show yourself," "Hiding from me isn't good for our relationship," "This makes no sense," "I miss your face," and, my personal favorite, "What the hell is going on?"

What I got in reply was the sound of leaves breaking under my feet and a few "whoa"s from me when I twisted an ankle on a tree stump.

After the waning, unchecked silence, I started to doubt my own theory. Breezes can be only breezes. Phones falling out of pockets can be only phones falling out of pockets. Not everything was a secret message to be deciphered. In the back of my mind, I knew I could be making it all up. The sight of Jackson at my window last night, the sense of his presence today, it could all be imagined out of my desire to see him again. To know he was awake. To believe he was safe. To be moments away from hearing his voice and looking into his eyes. To lose myself inside the safety of his arms.

Or, I could not be imagining it, and he could be close. So close. Just outside my grasp. And, if that was true, all I had to do was figure out what was keeping him away. Maybe this was the final mystery keeping us apart. Solve this, and he comes back and never leaves.

"Is that it, Jackson?" I'd asked the silence earlier. "If I can find out why you have to stay out of sight, will you come back, then?"

A rock answered my question by tripping me.

"I would assume you'd have a vehicle." Trudy asked me now. "Don't you have a vehicle? Where's your vehicle?" She had a higher-pitched voice than me. More girlie, yet maternal. Add to that a heavy southern accent, and she had a disarming charm to her questions that, although still annoying, made me want to answer.

"I borrowed one from a friend, and it was time to return it." By return, I meant text Jerry its location and let her come pick it up. Something I'd be doing when the urge struck.

"Well, you need to get a vehicle of your own, now don't you." It wasn't a question, it was instruction. Although it was annoying to get advice from a stranger, her lilting voice and gooey face made it cute.

"Yes, I suppose so. Mine was totaled during that flash flood over the weekend. I've been too busy to get it replaced."

"But you could get it replaced."

Well, sure, it wasn't an impossibility. "Yes."

"Of course, you can." She grabbed a piece of individually wrapped gum from her console, unwrapped it, and judiciously popped it into her round mouth. "You can make time. Then, you won't need to bum free rides off others and borrow your friends' cars. You'll have more freedom that way."

She had a point. I mean, she was a know-it-all. She was obnoxious. But she had a point. I could get a new vehicle. The insurance company was only waiting on me to pick my replacement. Then, I'd have my own wheels.

"You're right, Trudy," I had to acknowledge. "I should get that done soon."

"Today?"

"Sounds like a plan." I answered before I thought about it. Today? How in the world would I have time to go buy a car today? I had a boyfriend to find. "Err…or soon."

Trudy nodded approval, ignoring how I'd walked my agreement backward, and moved on to the next thing about me obviously bugging her.

Now escorting us both to the hospital per my instructions, she eyed my ragged appearance. I could read the disapproval in those ghostly green eyes of hers. From the mud on my boots to the dirt on my pant legs, from my disheveled sweater dotted with leaf bits to my hair carrying a twig or two, I looked a mess.

"So, about your typical morning activities." She popped her gum. "Do they usually include a shower?"

Instead of the hospital, we ended up at my house so I could "address the chaos of my appearance," Trudy explained. Delaney gave her my address earlier to track me down. So, home we went, with or without my permission.

I could have stopped her. This didn't have to happen now. I didn't look all that bad. I mean, yes, I was still dressed in my clothes from yesterday. Yes, the clothes I'd been locked inside a trunk in. Yes, the clothes I'd hitchhiked down the highway in. Yes, the clothes I'd trekked down a deserted dirt road in. The clothes I'd slept in. Then crawled around on a casino floor in. Then hiked down a hill through the woods in.

Okay, she had a point.

At my house, I let us in and told her to make herself at home. She did by busying herself in my kitchen, while not asking permission to do whatever she was doing. Meanwhile, I took a long, hot shower and re-emerged feeling human.

For today, I dressed strategically. When hunting your boyfriend, you've got to put effort into your appearance. I chose a dark pair of stretchy jeans, high brown leather boots, white button-up long-sleeve shirt, long green cardigan, maroon knit scarf, and pocket-sized pepper spray, which is one of those accessories that simply goes with everything.

The jeans would provide flexibility for any ass-kicking moves I'd need to execute. The boots would protect my legs from vermin should

I need to hike through the woods again. The shirt and cardigan were simply a smarter choice than a heavy sweater because it was warming up outside. Also, green was a good color on me and, not to be overlooked, when I found Jackson I wanted to look good.

My hair I blow-dried, letting the curls do what they fight me to always do – run free. With a touch of color on my cheeks and lips, I looked more alive than I'd felt in days. Sitting all day at a bedside waiting for the person you love to live or die speeds up the aging process. A shower, a change of clothes, and hope turns back time. Even my eyes, shifting from brown to hazel due to the green cardigan, had a light in them now. That's what possibilities do. And, today, it was possible I'd see Jackson alive and well and awake.

While Trudy created a hot, buttery aroma in the kitchen, I casually walked through my house looking for any messages from Jackson. If he was awake, free, and flitting in and out of my day, it was possible he'd left me a note or message or clue to what was going on. Without rousing any suspicion, I employed my sharpest sleuthing skills and searched my house.

"What are you looking for?" Trudy set two plates of sandwiches on the kitchen table.

"What? Me?" I climbed out from under the table, while testing the stability of the table leg. "I'm not looking for anything."

"You obviously are. What is it?"

I slapped the leg, satisfied. "Everything looks good here. Just checking on the general," I waved my hand around, "sturdiness of things."

"Okay, sure." She sat down, pointing to the other plate in front of me. "I made paninis."

I sat down and eyed the sandwich, lifting a corner to view the insides. She had stacked cheese, tomato, olives, red peppers, hummus, and a thin strip of sliced chicken between two slices of bread, grilled it in olive oil, then sliced it diagonally down the middle. I took a bite, relishing in the crunch sound as my teeth sank into the bread.

"Whis is inwebible," I told her around a mouthful. "Whewah wid ew et uh wummus?"

Trudy chewed analytically, calmly weighing out the flavors with her tongue. "I understood 'hummus.' The rest was gibberish." She sipped her iced tea.

I waved it off, more interested in eating than speaking. "Not in'ortent."

Finished with lunch, we headed to the hospital. With the sun high past noon, we pulled into the Hensley Medical Complex comprised of a hospital, a children's wing, a rehabilitation center, a heart institute, an urgent care center, a cancer treatment center, a wellness center, and a building of offices for bone and joint specialists, neurosurgeons, and a health club. With my brother and sister-in-law working in this complex, I knew a few secrets about the place only known to insiders. For example, everyone thinks the parking behind the rehabilitation center is for employees only. And the employees want people to continue thinking that.

I directed Trudy to the rehab center across the street from the hospital and to the supersecret parking behind the building. No way was I going back into that hospital parking garage.

Jumping out of her hatchback, I scanned the area for any lurking blue Cutlasses. We were in the clear.

"We'll cross the street and walk over." I looped my purse strap across my chest. "The fresh air will do us good."

Trudy fanned her face as a truck passed by spitting out exhaust. "Real fresh."

Reaching the sidewalk, we stood at the intersection, while I hit the crosswalk button.

A hot shower, fresh clothes, and a delicious sandwich does wonders for a person's outlook. Even though I had no idea what I would find inside, or if I'd find anything, I felt uncharacteristically optimistic. Soon, I'd locate Jackson. He'd be healthy and strong. Life, with us finally together, would then only get better and better.

Not that I believed in 'happily ever after.' No way life works like that. I'd experienced too much of life at my age to fall for any such naivety. There was too much pain and disappointment, heaviness and hardship in life. But, even in tempestuous journeys, there are moments of lightness, of laughter, of sunlight full on your face.

That's how I felt, now. I tipped my face up to the sun, closed my eyes, and listened to the crosswalk voice repeatedly telling me to "wait" in that male robot voice.

Wait: a word I knew well.

"It must have been a hard couple of days here for you." Trudy watched the traffic passing, while her hair grabbed at the sunlight. "How have you managed it?"

I squinted into the blazing light. "I read a lot of magazines."

Trudy wasn't satisfied. "And?"

"And..." I held the word out, deciding how much to say, "I prayed. I cried a lot. I pleaded and threatened him. I cried some more. And went back to praying."

She nodded, processing a heavy thought of her own. "Yes, I can see you did."

While we waited for the sign to change, a white catering truck, probably headed to the wellness center cafeteria, pulled up to the light in front of us and stopped about the same time my phone started ringing. Rummaging through my purse, I grabbed the phone and answered, "Hello?"

"Yes, Miss Addison," the slurpy voice greeted me, "this is Virgil Fairchild again."

I started to apologize for not calling him back sooner when my eyes landed on the passenger in the white catering truck. It was Doc. Sitting there drinking coffee. Giving a half-hearted wave when our eyes met.

"Oh, man," I grumbled. "Not you again."

Mr. Fairchild responded with an "excuse me?" and Doc responded by sipping his coffee.

Before I could figure out how to run like the wind while carrying Trudy, the side door of the van opened, and Cheekbones jumped out. I dropped my phone and reached into my pocket for the pepper spray. As soon as I yanked it out, Cheekbones slapped it out of my hand and jabbed two fingers into my forehead.

I'm fast. Superfast, actually. But, unless I get a running start, hand-to-hand combat isn't my strength. And, not to discount his own ability, Cheekbones was shockingly fast himself. Not a heightened speed, but swift enough and obviously skilled enough to throw off my equilibrium with two strategic moves.

Although the jab to the forehead wasn't painful, it jerked my head back and exposed my throat. Cheekbones locked his hand around it, while tossing a hood over my head. It all happened so quickly, so forcefully, I hadn't formulated a good counter move when he tugged me into the van.

Unable to see Trudy or know if she was being manhandled by a second thug with strong facial bone structure, I yelled through the hood, "Don't freak out, Trudy! This is all part of a typical day!"

9

People don't need to always be in the know. Not knowing can have its charms, too. Like, not knowing all the ingredients in a hotdog before eating it. Not knowing your college ex-boyfriend's wife is hotter than you. Not knowing how a city's wastewater treatment plant works. Not knowing you owe additional income taxes before vacationing in Vegas. Not knowing where a van is going when you're locked inside of it.

"I don't know, Trudy. Okay? I don't know."

Trudy had been rapid-firing questions at me from the moment we found ourselves co-captives in my latest kidnapping adventure. If I thought she was curious before, I didn't fully appreciate the word. Her questions, however, felt more like a therapy session than a woman trapped inside a speeding catering van headed to destinations unknown.

"What are you thinking about right now?" "Where do you think they are taking us?" "Have you thought about what is going to happen next?" "What do you think is the best move in this kind of situation?" "Have you formulated any ideas on how we can escape?" "Considering the odds, do you believe escape is possible?" "When in uncontrollable situations like this, how do you mentally combat your fear?" "What do you think you did wrong to get yourself into this situation?" "Was there a way you could have prevented this from happening?"

Trudy was proving to be one of those annoying journalists who question everything until discovering the truth, which is so passe in that profession. I didn't answer her questions because they were annoying.

"What are you doing now?"

Lying on the floor.

"Why are you lying on the floor?"

I have my reasons.

"Do you have a good reason for doing nothing but lying there?"

Of course.

"Why are your eyes closed? Do you think it's a good time to nap?"

Honestly, yes. I was still full from lunch, and a nap sounded awesome.

"I'm not napping, Trudy. I have this friend who's blind, and he says…" I looked up at her curious, cupcake face. "Never mind. Just trust me, okay? I'm trying to figure out if they're taking us to the same place they took me last night."

"If this happened to you last night, too, how did you let it happen again? Did you not take the time to formulate a heightened safety protocol?"

What was she talking about?

I exhaled loudly and abruptly and went back to ignoring her. She wasn't my favorite person right now. When Cheekbones tossed us into the van, I assumed we were both tied up with hoods on our heads. Not so, a fact I learned after tugging my hood off by using my knees as claws. When I could finally see again, I found Trudy sitting pretty on a bench built into the van wall. She wore no hood and no zip ties.

Did that seem odd? I thought it seemed odd.

She could have helped me get free but sat there smacking a fresh piece of gum instead.

"Thanks for the help," I'd muttered.

She had looked at me with her bulbous green eyes. "Oh? Did you need help? You didn't ask, so I just assumed."

This is why I didn't tell her that bench, coated in an aluminum lining, was going to bruise her tailbone when the van hit potholes. She never said she didn't want a bruised tailbone, so I'm just going to assume.

Now, ten minutes into this situation, I'd finally formulated a plan. A hint of a plan, anyway. And it started with me laying down.

I wiggled my hands down my spine until my arms slipped over my hip bones. Then, pulling my arms forward, I stretched the ligaments in my shoulders until my zip tied wrists moved forward down my legs and, eventually, over my feet. Now, at least, my arms weren't tied behind my back but cuffed in front. Finished, I stayed on the ground, feeling my way down the city streets.

"Where did they take you last night? Do you remember?"

Was she kidding? "Do I remember? Of course, I remember."

"Where was it?"

"A deserted road off Highway 75."

"What exit?"

Um…

"You don't remember what exit?"

Well…

"You must have situational awareness in circumstances like this. Escaping could all depend on the details." She paused, as if catching herself being a know-it-all. "I mean…so I've read."

"Thanks, Trudy. Super helpful. I'll remember that for the next kidnapping."

She glanced off, appearing to rethink her obnoxiousness. When she spoke again, her voice was less instructional and more curious. "So, what happened exactly? How did you escape?"

I rolled off my side and sat up, resting my bum on the floor because I don't like bruised tailbones. "They tossed me in a trunk. I used the jack to pop it open. Then, I hitchhiked back to civilization."

"That must have been scary. What do you think these guys want?"

"No idea."

"Are we heading back to the same spot?"

"I don't think so. We haven't gotten on a highway, yet, but anything's possible."

"So," she glanced toward the cab of the van, which was walled off, "what do you think happens next?"

I shrugged. "If we're lucky, we run into a dragon."

∼

Half an hour later, the van stopped. I glanced at Trudy and, puzzled, she glanced back.

"What do ya-ya think will ha-happen now?" Her green eyes barely had green in them. Mostly, they were white and grey and bulging wider and wider with each drop in the temperature.

Our van wasn't just any van. It was a refrigerated van. A refrigerated van whose cooler kicked on twenty minutes ago. Ten minutes later, we'd both entered the uncontrollable shiver stage.

Not only did the cold air zap us of strength and clarity to fight back, but the blowing air muted the sounds from outside, too. We couldn't hear anything over the rushing of our blood fleeing our freezing extremities.

Trudy, tired of the battering her tailbone had been taking, sat with me on the aluminum-lined floor. Our backsides were numb. To spare the rest of my body the same fate, I'd curled my knees into my chest, hooked my tied arms over them, and squeezed myself with each shiver, shake, and shudder. Trudy opted for a cross-legged posture on the floor and a crossing of her arms over her chest. With both of us dressed in jeans and light sweaters, we wouldn't last long in here.

I released a trembling exhale, watching my breath head to the heavens, and sniffed more cold back in. "Hard to say. They either leave us. Move us again. Or drag us out of here and make us dig our own grave."

She shot a wide-eyed look my way. "Da-dig our own gra-graves? Wa-where wwwould you ga-get an idea like that?" She rubbed her arms, while I tunneled into my own body heat.

"Nevvver ask me about...where I get ideas, Tru-da-dy. Once you know, you can ne-never un-na-know."

She shrugged or convulsed. Hard to tell. "You're ma-making ja-jokes?"

I rubbed my ear against my knee to generate heat. Then switched to my other ear and my other knee. "Tra-trying."

"Oh ka-kay. Ma-maybe that's na-not such a ba-ba-bad thing. It's ya-your coping mech...a...nism, re-right?"

I gave up warming my ears and went to work on my nose. "Shhhhure."

Trudy curled further into her cream sweater. "Where. Do you tha-think. We are? Ca-could you? Ta-tell? From the ra-road noise?" She needed out of here or, at the least, for the refrigerated air to kick off. Neither one of us could take this for long.

The only thing I knew for sure was that they hadn't returned to the deserted road from last night. Today's drive had been less curvy, less seamy, and less lengthy. Thank you Kyle Alice, you beautiful blind bastard.

Knowing where we weren't, however, didn't tell us where we were. Other than knowing our drive didn't include any highways or brick roads, I had little else to offer.

"Not…shh…shh…ure," I stammered out.

Trudy moved her mouth, but it took a half beat later before any sound came out. "Do you think they la-la-left again?"

As the minutes ticked by, the air kept blowing and neither Cheekbones nor Doc opened the door. The likelihood had increased that they were repeating last night's pattern. "Seems sa-so." My whole body shook and calmed. The strap on my purse across my chest turned stiff from the cold.

Trudy glanced around the van, as if only now taking in her environment. "And there's no-no-no way. Of get-get-getting out. Of here?"

I shook my head no.

"You're shhhhhure?"

I did the same glancing around. "None I can sa-see."

She motioned her head toward the back and side doors, while keeping her hands rubbing her arms, her legs, or themselves. The cold was getting to her. Even her hair streaks didn't glint with the same reddish fire.

"You tra-tried the doors?"

I shot her a 'really?' look.

"Okay. Stu. Pid. Ques. Tion." Trudy sat in silence for ten peaceful seconds. "They ra-really left."

I tried to shake my head 'yes' but my spine was frozen.

"I ca-can't ba-lieve they. Just. Left." She sounded surprised. "With the free. Zer on."

I tried to shrug my shoulders, but my shoulders were frozen.

Trudy released a gravelly growl, a sound you'd expect from an irate woman disgusted with hypothermia. She turned her rebellious green eyes toward me. "So, do you want to kna-know how to ga-ga-get. Out of those zip ties or. Na-not?"

Of all the questions this woman had asked me in the three hours I'd known her, this question caused my right eyebrow to raise in a 'come again?' expression. Then my eyebrow froze like that.

Trudy motioned in stiff, choppy movements towards my hands, as if I needed reminded I was bound.

"I ca-can help." Slow and a little achy, she got on her knees. "Someone taught…t me. A trick. Once. To ba-break out of. Those things."

So, that's why she wasn't bound. I thought Cheekbones just didn't like me.

She worked her mouth to limber up the taut, bloodless facial muscles. She looked less cold, but madder. I liked her mad. Mad generated heat. Get her mad enough and maybe I could warm my hands on her cheeks.

Whatever she was saying now, if I was understanding her halting speech correctly, intrigued me.

"Okay." I was willing to try anything. "What tra…ick?"

Trudy showed, instead of told. Standing tall on her knees, she mimed having her hands bound. She raised her arms over her head, shaking from the cold as she did, and yanked her hands down quickly to hit herself near the hip bone. She separated her arms to demonstrate being free and looked at me with a 'got it?' expression.

I nodded and moved into position. It took me longer because I didn't have warm fury welling up inside. I've been kidnapped and held captive too many times to get irate over it anymore.

Now, on my knees, I raised my arms above my head and, taking in a deep breath, jerked my arms down against my hip bones. It hurt. It hurt badly. And it didn't work.

Trudy, coursing with hot rage against zip ties, examined the ties. She yanked them tighter around my now bruised and cut wrists, positioned the locking mechanism at the top and center of my two hands, and scooted back to give me space.

I nodded hesitantly but tried anyway. Raising my arms, pausing to get a good breath between the trembling, I closed my eyes and yanked down hard.

Still nothing.

She nudged her head at me, as if encouraging me to try again.

"I da-don't know, Trudy. It's not wa-wa-working. And, it ha-ha-urts."

Trudy shot her green eyes directly into my hazel ones. It was a look of knowing, of seeing, of slapping. Right across the face, actually. That stinging look left an imprint.

"You can do this, Samantha. Do you hear me?" Her voice struggled against the cold, but she spoke smoothly.

I paused.

"Do you?" She repeated.

I nodded an affirmative. I one hundred percent believed her. I know, it shocked me, too.

"Good. Now, do this. Do it now."

Taking a shaky breath from the cold, I raised my arms, feeling a sense of total confidence, empowerment, possibility, and hope. I could do this. I knew I could.

Yanking my arms down with force, suddenly my hands were simply free. Released from captivity. No pain. I didn't even feel the restraints break.

"It worked!" I rubbed the redness from my wrists while Trudy gave a short 'yay!' We attempted a spontaneous high-five and missed.

As if all the wrongs in life were righting themselves, the air kicked off. Stooping under the low ceiling, we excitedly bent and straightened our knees. In the cramped space, it was the closest we'd get to jumping up and down.

I caught a noise from outside.

"Trudy, hold on." I dropped back down to my knees and leaned my ear against the side door. Outside, I heard two cars pass by slowly, three car door slams, and, what I think, was mumbling voices. "I hear people!"

She leaned over me to listen. "People?"

"People!"

We both went back to bending and straightening our knees.

Trudy stopped first. "I want out of here before that air kicks back on."

"Agreed."

Trudy looked at me expectantly. "So now what?"

"Now," our celebrations gave me an idea, "we make a ruckus and hope someone calls the cops." She looked at me not understanding. "Jump, Trudy!" I explained. "And yell. And beat on the doors. You take the side door. I'll take the back. We need to draw attention."

I didn't have to tell her twice. Both of us went to work. We bent knees. We straightened knees. We pushed our weight into the floor and jerked our weight up, creating a bounce in the shocks. We yelled for "help!" We beat the doors and the walls until our hands ached. When her voice got tired, I yelled louder. When my voice broke, she yelled. Ten minutes later, we heard commotion at the back door.

"Someone's at the back door," I told her.

"We're saved!" Trudy and I both embraced in a stooped hug.

At the back, a sound like a metal bar wiggled around in the door guts until, finally, we heard the lock release. One door opened. Sunlight splayed across the bitter walls, bringing heat and life back into the van.

In the brilliance, a broad male form stepped forward.

I caught my breath. "Jackson?"

10

The only difference between driving a vehicle you've stolen and driving a vehicle you haven't stolen is that one comes standard with a prison sentence.

"Are you sure you can drive this?" Trudy rode shotgun, glancing in her rearview mirror to give me the go-ahead on changing lanes.

"Sure, I'm sure," my hands flexed on the wheel. "It's only a class one van. Nothing too fancy, minus the refrigerator in the back. And this beaded necklace," I fiddled with a pink, white, and red necklace hanging from the rearview mirror, "that smells like," I leaned forward to get a better whiff, "chocolate-covered cherries." I turned the radio on. "Let's check out the speaker system."

Trudy leaned over from her bucket seat and flipped it off. "Let's concentrate on driving."

For a calm, cool, collected chick when being kidnapped, frozen to death, or lying to cops, she wasn't handling me in the driver's seat with as much aplomb.

"What's got you so nervous?" I motioned for her to check if I was clear to change lanes again.

"I'm not nervous." She motioned for me to get in the next lane. "I'm…in shock."

I doubted that. Trudy had yet to be phased by anything, including captivity.

"Because you've never been kidnapped before?" I waited for an answer, but she was too busy watching her rearview mirror. "It's okay if you haven't. Lots of people haven't. Nothing to be ashamed about. But, the more it happens, the better you'll get at it."

She continued ignoring me, so I tried again.

"Because we stole the van? And, really, is it stealing when it's been abandoned with a key inside? And it was used to kidnap you? The law may have some gray areas there."

Still nothing.

"Is it because we lied to a cop? You shouldn't worry about that, either. I lie to that guy all the time. He doesn't expect me to tell him the truth anymore."

Officer Bart Simpson said as much after he opened the door and got Trudy and I out of the van. He was disappointed to see me again, and I was disappointed he wasn't Jackson.

When Simpson jimmied the door open and got a glimpse of my frozen face, all he said was, "Of course, it's you," and then stepped out of the way for us to climb out. Simpson was determined to loathe me for all of time.

Trudy glanced my way. "I wouldn't take comfort in being thought of as a liar." Ouch. "From his reaction to seeing you, I take it he's not your biggest fan."

I swallowed the lump of shame in my throat and moved on. "Hard to imagine, right? I'm so cute."

Trudy neither agreed nor disagreed. "How do you know him?"

I checked my speedometer and increased it by five. Vans get better traction at higher speeds. "He, along with another officer named Reilly, were my protection detail last month. It's a long story, and it's also off the record, by the way."

Trudy held up her hands in a 'that's fine' gesture.

"In fact," I continued, "so far, this entire day is off the record."

Per typical Trudy, she wasn't phased. "I read about you taking out some guy with a gun during the Durant Ball. Did the protection detail have something to do with that?"

I chewed on my lower lip. "Something."

Trudy settled comfortably in her seat, visibly relaxing for the first time. With the heater on full blast, our blood warmed nicely.

"Is it also the reason you didn't tell Officer Simpson about the men who grabbed us outside the hospital and locked us in the back?"

I chewed on my upper lip. "Possibly."

Although authorities believed Jerome DeLuca, my original mugger, had been the person behind all those assassination attempts on my life back in October, they'd never been able to prove it.

They couldn't link him to the online hit posted on Craiqslist with a *q*. They also couldn't get a confession out of Jerome because he was actually innocent of that. Nothing else, though. He was guilty of everything but that. Everything like trying to kill me at least three times. Or nearly killing Trevor Maessen, my date to the Durant Ball and an old flame. Or the assaults and murder videoed on his phone. Not being guilty of posting an online hit job was the least of his legal worries.

Who authorities knew nothing about was the Widow McBride. She posted the hit. She had me and the sidekicks kidnapped. She shot me in the stomach. And she was possibly guilty of kidnapping me again.

Although, the last one I doubted. That power hungry femme fatale wanted me dead. Doc and Cheekbones seemed more interested in messing with my head than knocking it off. If the Widow McBride had been behind the last two kidnappings in the last twelve hours, I was sure there'd have been some grave digging by now.

As for what was really going on, I couldn't share that with the authorities, either. I needed them to see me as a boring, law-abiding citizen with nothing in my life that needed investigating.

So far, they had accepted my story explaining Jackson's injury. Not because they believed me. Of course, they didn't. But because they couldn't prove otherwise.

If any other odd mishaps involving me were to happen, however, like being kidnapped and locked in a trunk or a refrigerated van, their barely their forbearance would end. My life would be turned upside down and all the contents shaken out. To protect Jackson's supersecret identity, along with myself and the other sidekicks, I had to live the straight and narrow. Or, at least, appear that way.

For this reason, I had told Officer Simpson the van was Trudy's, and we had accidentally gotten ourselves locked inside.

"Why did you drive a refrigerated van to a furniture store?" He had asked, while scribbling notes in his metal ticket book and standing in the Second Love Furniture Warehouse parking lot off 121st E. Avenue. Authorities had been called after a shopper heard us yelling from inside the van.

"Well, you see, that's an easy explanation," I had said, before realizing I had no easy explanation.

Trudy, leaning against the van with her face blissfully soaking up the heat, offered a cover story. "I need a new dining table. The only other vehicle I own is a hatchback, and the table wouldn't fit in there. I didn't know the child safety locks were engaged. The refrigeration getting switched happened by mistake."

Why did Trudy play along? I had no idea, but I had a few growing suspicions.

Simpson had scrutinized her, scrutinized me, then written something down and told us to be more careful. Then, he sat in his patrol car, filled out paperwork, and, possibly, waited to see if we'd lock ourselves in the back again.

To sell our story, Trudy and I climbed in and debated our next move.

"Search the cab," she told me. "Maybe there's a spare key somewhere."

I chuckled. "That's cute, Trudy. Who leaves a spare key in their unlocked vehicle?"

Kidnappers, that's who.

Trudy found one in the glove compartment, right before locating her purse and my phone shoved under the passenger seat. With me already in the driver's seat, I took the key, started the van, and we both waved at Officer Simpson as we drove off.

Doc obviously wanted us to take the van, or he wouldn't have left a spare key. He may be crazy, critical, and addicted to caffeine, but he wasn't careless. I saw the pristine state of his trunk. He wanted us in this van. So, we needed out. Right after I burned through his gas tank running an errand for a friend. And, in the process, did a little digging into Trudy. Something about her, like not freaking out and blabbing to police when you've been kidnapped, wasn't adding up.

Was I paranoid? You know it.

"So, this Fred person, he's a good friend?"

Trudy found individually wrapped pieces of gum in the glove compartment and chewed contentedly.

"One of my closest." While stopped at a stoplight, I hurriedly typed out a text to my friend Kyle Alice. I needed a favor, and he was the perfect go-with-the-flow kind of guy this favor needed.

"What's his last name?"

I finished the text and hit send. "Who?"

"Fred."

"I don't know."

"About how old is he?"

"Hard to say."

"Is he married?"

"I doubt it."

"Has he ever been married?"

"I've never asked."

"Is he from around here?"

Kyle texted back, asking for more details. I hurriedly typed out my instructions and then accelerated through the green light. "Could be."

"But you're close?" Trudy sounded skeptical.

I crossed my fingers. "Like this."

Earlier, Fred had given me the details of his favor. Not wanting to upset my free online support, I'd called him back this morning while waiting on County Line Road 2533 for Trudy to pick me up.

It was a simple favor, thankfully, and wouldn't deter me long from my Jackson hunt. All I needed to do was swing by the house of his old school chum, pick up a yellow manila envelope, and drop it off at Fred's Book Store.

That was it. Miniscule. In the universe of favors, it was Mercury. It was also something he wanted done three hours earlier. That's why I wasn't surprised when my phone rang on my way to perform said favor.

"I've called five times, Samantha. Five. Why have you been ignoring my calls?"

I drove along Harvard, climbing the hills in a refrigerated van loaded down with nothing but myself and a bossy redhead. We were flying.

"I wasn't ignoring you, Fred. I was kidnapped and locked in a refrigerated van."

He grumbled. "It's always something with you."

Fred's concern over me being in danger was, as always, absent. He considered threats to my life as a way to liven it up.

"I was driving there when you called, Fred. I am literally headed there now." I increased my speed.

He wasn't buying it, even though it was the truth for once.

"Is that the commonly accepted definition of 'now' or your definition of 'now,' which may or may not actually mean 'now'?"

Next to me, Trudy's eyes were twitching as trees and lawns and gated neighborhoods passed by in a blur. "Do we really need to drive this fast?"

I resituated the phone between my shoulder and ear to free both hands. "Hear that, Fred? Trudy is nervous. That means I'm making excellent time."

"Who's Trudy? Never mind. I don't care." He hung up.

I dropped my phone in a cup holder. "Fred isn't what you'd call a patient man."

Trudy had no interest in understanding Fred. "Do you think you could slow down a little?" Her nails sunk into the seat. "So we don't wreck?"

I took a curve without slowing down. "You bet." I increased the speed by five miles-per-hour. "Right after this next curve. Speed helps with traction."

Trudy braced one hand against the glove compartment and gripped the door with the other. "No, no that's incorrect."

The next curve brought out a squeal from the tires. "It's true. I read it somewhere."

"You did not!"

The residential entrance was up ahead. "Oh, look. Our turn."

I braked for a quick left into a residential area, while Trudy sucked in a ragged breath after being slammed against the passenger door and nearly swallowing her gum. We squealed through the entrance, and I slowed to a reasonable, yet aggressive, pace.

Fred's old college chum lived in an upper middle-class neighborhood if the year was 1968. Located in an elegant, yet older, area of town, the collection of retro-style brick homes kept company with bulky trees that buckled the sidewalks to the great delight of weeds.

We rolled into the neighborhood in our pristine white van and curved along Temple Street until it wound uphill and to the right. Fred's friend, a guy named Eugene Percy, lived in a ranch-style burgundy brick home with a short, stubby concrete porch decorated with three potted plants.

I parked in front of the house, shut off the engine, and read an incoming text from Kyle. He was a 'go.'

"What are you smiling about?" Trudy squinted at me.

Ignoring her, I shoved my phone into my back pocket. "Here we go!"

We climbed out, crossed the lawn, and mounted the two porch steps. I rang the doorbell, and we waited.

"Do you know this Mr. Percy?" Trudy cupped her hands against the front window to peek inside.

"No, he's some old school friend of Fred's." I rang the doorbell again.

"An old school friend of the very close friend you know nothing about?"

I rang the doorbell again. "Fred likes peanut butter."

Trudy turned away from the window. "What does that mean?"

"It means I know something about him." I knocked twice, waited, and gave up. Fred said Eugene Percy might not be home.

"So, we're here to pick up an envelope? What's inside?" Trudy stepped away from the window as dried leaves scratched their nails across the porch.

The temperatures had warmed for November, but the breeze still bit down when it blew. Cold rain, thankfully no sleet, was moving across the plains of the state now. It would be on us within the next hour or so. You could sense it in the chilled moistness of the air.

I squatted in front of the third potted plant and tipped it to one side. Water seeped out of the bottom and drained off into the grass. I picked up the hidden house key where Fred said Eugene Percy said it would be.

"Should you be using his hidden house key?"

I wiped off the dampness from the key before inserting it into the lock. "I have no idea."

"You have no idea what's inside the envelope? Or you have no idea if we should be using the hidden house key?" Even Trudy couldn't keep up with all her questions.

"Not so hidden if I could find it, now was it."

"So that's a 'no' then?" Trudy stood behind me as I jiggled the key, which didn't get enough regular usage. "Let me make sure I've got this straight. We're picking up an envelope, but we don't know what's inside, from a guy we never met, but are entering his house anyway, to give to your dear friend who you know nothing about except he likes peanut butter."

When the lock finally gave, I smiled back at her. "All part of a typical day."

The door hinges protested being awakened. Inside, the house felt dead, devoid of life for weeks not hours. I stood in the center of the living room surveying the open expanse. Trudy stood next to me, doing the same thing.

The whole place had a charming cottage feel, although the air smelled stagnant. Eugene Percy needed to open some windows every once in a while.

The living area opened to the dining room, which opened to the kitchen. Wood floors covered the breadth of the space, from the front door to the back wall and down the narrow hallway. A thread-bare Egyptian rug took up the centerpiece of the living room, surrounded by colorless furniture and dark-wood tables. Various eclectic art pieces collected dust around the room. I recognized an African tribal Mossi doll, a Norwegian rosemaling pewter bowl, a Canadian Coat of Arms collectible plate, and, on the wall, what looked like a heavy wooden cutout of Idaho. Stuffed in chairs and on the couch were antique tapestry pillows.

I walked through the dining room, the kitchen, then came back and stood next to Trudy, who was rubbing the worry out of her arms. "Are you sure it's okay for us to be in here?"

"Sure, I'm sure." She didn't know me well enough not to believe me.

~

Fred said the envelope would be in Eugene Percy's office inside his desk in the bottom, right-hand drawer. I checked. No envelope. So, I checked the left side bottom, right side top, left side top and both sides middle.

No envelope.

My phone buzzed with a text from Fred. "Bottom. On the right."

Didn't we already cover this?

The 19th Century French Mahogany desk was another antique collectible in a house weighed down by history. Antiques often had hidden compartments. In case Fred meant "secret" bottom, right-hand drawer, I ran my hands along the smooth finish, touched the golden overlays, and came up empty.

No envelope.

I checked the bottom, right-hand drawer again. Under a stack of files and a dark leather book, I found a white envelope.

Fred texted again. "Yellow manila."

Right. Yellow.

My feet sank into yet another Egyptian rug as I stepped lively around the office, skimming my fingers along the built-in bookshelves. No hidden compartments. No envelope.

Fred again. "Check the Biedermeier."

I looked around the room, mumbling to myself, "What's a Biedermeier? How am I supposed to know what a Biedermeier is?"

Fred again. "It's a coffee table."

A pale, natural grain, wood coffee table squatted in the center of the room. Was that a Biedermeier?

"Center of the room," Fred texted.

I got down on my knees by the table. "You must be a Biedermeier," I told the table. "And I need to check you." I felt along the sides and bottom for any hidden compartments, like prepping a cow for milking. "Sorry about the cold hands."

Fred texted. "Stop goofing around."

Looking around the room, I fired off a reply. "How did you know I was goofing around?"

"Lucky guess."

I skimmed the upper corners of the room, finding a security camera above the door and another in the opposite corner above the bookshelf.

I hastily sent another text. "Don't tell me you hacked Eugene Percy's security feed."

"Ok, I won't tell you."

I moved into the direct path of the camera above the door and glared. "Fred."

He sent a reply. "Don't make a big thing of it."

Un-freaking-believable. "So, you can see me. Can you hear me, too?"

He texted back, "Yes."

Just great. "Fred, before I'm questioned by authorities, could you tell me whether or not Eugene Percy gave you permission for me to be in his house?"

Fred texted his response. "You should hurry."

I shook my finger at the camera. "I'm trying to live a boring, law-abiding life here!"

My phone buzzed in my hands. "You really should hurry."

I crossed my arms defiantly. "What's in this envelope, Fred?"

"Hurry isn't a suggestion."

I pointed my finger at the camera, then ran it across my neck: a universal sign that didn't need interpretation.

He texted, "What part of hurry do you not understand?"

I glared.

He texted again. "Security feed on loop. Alarm off. Eugene out of country but plane lands soon."

I didn't need so many friends. I really didn't.

Hurriedly, per Fred's instructions, I checked the Biedermeier drawers, found a yellow manila envelope, and shoved it into the back waistband of my pants.

"Trudy! We have to leave. Like now." I scurried around the room, wiping down anything I'd touched. "Did you hear me?" She was somewhere in the house, presumably the front living area. "Yell if you can hear me!"

From the living room, I heard a yell.

"That works! Be there in a minute." My boots pounded on the wood floor as I walked down the hall and emerged back into the living room.

Trudy stood next to a French faux wood floor lamp with her hands up, her body motionless, and her eyes focused on a man holding a knife.

"Trudy," I eyed the knife, "what have you gotten us into now?"

11

You don't need to be skilled with a blade to be a threat with one. Put a rusty, antique knife into the hands of any ne'er-do-well, and you've got yourself a serious situation.

Judging by the amount of white I could see in her eyeballs, that was the thought going through Trudy's mind about now.

The man, who was not homeowner and antiques enthusiast Eugene Percy, stood between the kitchen and dining room with the knife floating around in his hand like a balloon. Under his breath, he hummed, "Touch of Grey," which was easy to guess due to his Grateful Dead shirt that said, "The sky was yellow and the sun was blue."

Yellow-lens glasses hid his eye movements, while his black shaggy hair, stylishly gelled to make the most of the shag, stuck up in wayward places. Not unlike little blades. The grey at his temples looked cold, unyielding, but stylish, too. A sign he had and would continue to age well. He tapped black converse shoes against the wood floor to sound out the rhythm to his humming, while he rubbed the blade of the knife as if summoning a genie.

"I'm short on time," I told them both, "so we need to wrap this up."

Trudy, who had backed up against the arm of the couch, held her hands out like an airplane. Body language experts might say that indicated a desire to "take off."

"Psst," I called to her. "Remind me later to tell you how much trouble we're in."

Wide-eyed, she blinked back at me.

"Ladies, have you ever seen such a thing of beauty?" The man finally spoke, while still caressing the blade. "A Moran knife. That man was a bladesmithing genius. A lyricist with steel. Can you see this stamp?" He held the blade out sideways, while pointing to a small black engraving near the handle. "It says W.F. Moran. He started using that stamp in 1973, so this twelve-inch beast is valuable."

Fascinating.

"I mean, wow. I found it hanging on the wall in there in the kitchen," he pointed the knife listlessly behind him. "What a find! I wouldn't really call myself a hunting knife enthusiast, but the craftsmanship is impressive. Personally, I'm more partial to a chef's knife."

I glanced over at Trudy to gauge how she was doing. Her legs pressed against the arm of the couch hard enough to scoot it back one inch, then two.

So, she was fine.

"I mean, the chef knife has so many uses," he spoke in a soothing tone, caught up in his childlike excitement of cutting things. "You can use it to cut anything into any size you desire."

Interesting phraseology.

"For example," he went on, "when I'm making French fries, I usually go with the batonnet cut. That gives the fries a slight crunch at the edges, while staying soft inside. Now, that's a great fry. Heavy on the salt. But you've got to get the oil good and hot. Come to think of it, French fries sound good right now."

He flipped the knife, blade over handle, once and palmed the maple grip again. Squeezing the handle, he jutted the knife into the air twice, testing the weight and his own quick reflexes.

"I'm getting hungry," he smiled. "Who here wants fries?"

Trudy gulped. I yawned.

"Here's the thing." I jumped in before we learned his thoughts on the best julienne vegetables. "We need to leave. A hiccup in my day has occurred and, sadly, our time here needs to be cut short."

In my hand, my phone vibrated with a text. Fred again. "Get rid of this yahoo."

I found the nearest surveillance camera in the corner of the living room and rolled my eyes at it.

Meanwhile, the man shifted his weight from one Converse to another. He wasn't a towering man, nor small either. His medium-frame looked wiry, but there was muscle tone under his clothes and dimples under his facial scruff. That last point isn't important but cute enough to deserve a mention.

"I see." He ran his thumb repeatedly down the pointed edge of the knife, making a soft scraping as the blade moved across his fingerprint. "So, what you're saying is, whatever I came to do, I need to hurry."

Trudy gasped. I burped.

"Excuse me," I pounded once on my chest. "Heavy lunch."

Resigned to bringing the festivities to a close, he smacked the blade against his palm three times. "Too bad we have to end this so soon. It was getting fun, but I understand. Time to get on with it."

Before anyone else could move, Trudy, having reached the end of her calm, jerked back. Forgetting about the couch behind her, she lost her footing and went down like a champ swinging arms and kicking legs. The panic didn't solve anything, but it did knock the wooden Idaho off the wall. As soon as her back hit the couch, Idaho hit her stomach and rested there like a sack of potatoes.

The fall had Trudy stunned into silence. I walked over and stood above her.

"Geez, Trudy. What's gotten into you?" I pointed my thumb over my shoulder to the man preoccupied with tossing the blade over and over in the air. "That's just my friend Kyle stopping by for a visit."

∼

Trudy took more time than we had available to get her rage under control. After situating Idaho back in the northwest, she stomped around Eugene Percy's kitchen seeking edible things to slice. She needed to unwind.

Cutting fruits and vegetables for her is like popping popcorn is for me. Not all girls drink wine in a bubble bath.

Kyle and I combed through the kitchen for edible, sliceable produce. We found a bag of carrots, five apples, a chunk of sharp cheddar, and a jar of pickles. She started slicing apples.

Right away, she noticed Kyle's blindness. It only took him telling her three times, right after she asked him to "look for a pineapple" in the refrigerator, "tell me what you see" in the pantry, and "inspect the cheese for mold."

By his third reminder of "I'm blind," Kyle went with, "Sure, why not."

Once her chopping got under way, the anger flowed. "I can't believe..." she diced half an apple into tiny squares, "I just can't believe," she mushed the tiny squares into pulpy juice, "you let me believe he was here to..." She stopped, waving the knife from me to Kyle and back again.

We stood there snacking on apple slices.

"What, Trudy? What did you believe?" I crunched, snagging another slice while her blade was motionless.

She opened her mouth, fumed, and went back to dicing.

I handed the slice to Kyle, who took it and munched contentedly.

"I was scared," Trudy spoke softly. "I was truly scared, Samantha. You knew that and said nothing." She turned her knife back to pointing at us both. "You guys did that on purpose to freak me out. Who treats people like that?"

Trudy. That's who.

I'd suspected her and stopped suspecting her and suspected her again as someone working with the kidnappers about half a dozen times over the last hour. Once we climbed into the van, she'd unknowingly confirmed my suspicions. She was definitely not on my side.

That's when, while on the drive over here, I'd texted Kyle to help me give her a taste of her own medicine. He was as chill as they come and always up for anything if I promised him food. I'd asked him to help me scare her a little. The knife bit was him improvising.

Not bad, Kyle. Not bad at all, my dude.

From the pinched look on Trudy's face, she didn't like being manipulated any more than I did.

I rested my arm across Kyle's shoulders. "Let me catch you up on what's going on, Kyle." I spoke to him but kept my eyes connected with her. "Trudy is upset because she thought we were in danger. I, of course, knew we weren't in danger, but I didn't tell her. And she thinks that's a rotten thing to do to a person. What do you think?"

Not hearing her knife hammering on the chopping block, he

reached for another slice. Trudy pushed the cutting board closer within his reach.

"Sounds rotten." He tossed an apple slice into the air and caught it with his mouth. "Did we find any peanut butter to go with these?"

Trudy rolled her eyes. "Samantha, do all your friends obsess over peanut butter?"

I thought about it. "Quite a few."

She turned away to rummage through the refrigerator for peanut butter. It also allowed her to hide her face, which looked more guilty than cupcakes should ever look.

"Let's have the truth now, Trudy. We're not leaving until you explain what's going on, and that might upset Eugene Percy when he returns home."

My phone buzzed with a text. It was Fred. "Peanut butter on the third shelf. Eugene in baggage claim. Hurry doesn't look like this."

I turned to the camera in the kitchen and slowly, very slowly, chewed on an apple slice.

Trudy found the peanut butter, grabbed a spoon, and dropped it into the jar. Then handed it to Kyle, who took his bounty to the dining room table.

"Look, Samantha"—a deflated Trudy had less red in her hair—"I know you won't believe me now, but I am your friend."

I raised an eyebrow and grabbed another apple slice. "I'm thinking about having fewer of those."

Trudy, defeatedly, put her knife to bed. "When did you figure it out?"

It took me awhile, but she didn't need to know that. "Almost immediately."

"How?"

From the dining room, Kyle called out, "Um, Sam?"

"Yeah, be there in a minute." I fished two water bottles out of Eugene Percy's refrigerator. "Really? It's like you guys weren't even trying. You weren't zip-tied. Nor did you have a hood shoved over your head. When I was grabbed, you didn't scream or run away. You seemed more nervous at the refrigeration being left on than you did of being kidnapped."

She crossed her arms, leaned against the kitchen cabinet, and listened. "Those knuckleheads switched it on by accident." She thought about it. "I think."

I continued presenting my evidence. "You knew the van had a spare key and where to find it. And, if that wasn't enough, there was the gum."

Her cupcake forehead wrinkled. "Gun?"

"Gum." I chewed on nothing as an illustration. "It's individually wrapped in a private label. Girly print. Pink and green colors. I couldn't make out the name, but it's distinctive enough. And in the glove compartment of both your hatchback and the van. That's no coincidence."

"The gum." Trudy shook her head, disbelieving. "I completely forgot about that."

"Feel free to jump in with some flimsy explanation at any time. Your buddies have now locked me inside a vehicle twice in less than twenty-four hours. Are these the kind of people you want your mother knowing you associate with?"

Trudy gave me an impatient-but-trying-to-be-patient face. "You don't understand what's going on here, Samantha."

I pointed my water bottle at her. "Exactly. I don't. But I'm about to because you're going to tell me everything." I swigged down a few gulps of chilled water and took the second bottle into the dining room.

Kyle, sitting with an ankle crossed over a knee and his free foot swinging away contentedly, took the water, twisted the cap, and tossed back half of it.

"Peanut butter really dries the mouth. I like to keep hydrated, keep the lips moist." Kyle smacked his lips to illustrate. "But that wasn't why I called you. We've got company."

"What do you mean?"

"The same SUV has circled the block three times and has now stopped in front of this house." As soon as Kyle said it, two car doors slammed. "I think your hiccup is here."

∼

Outside, two men stalked up the cracked sidewalk toward Eugene Percy's house. Neither were the traveling homeowner, according to Fred's text that simply said, "Not Eugene."

Trudy and I huddled in the dark dining room and spied on our visitors through slits in the miniblinds. Kyle sat behind us gnawing on a banana.

"Who are they?" I whispered to Trudy.

She shrugged, whispering back, "I don't know. Not more friends of yours? Stopping by for a visit?"

I shook my head. "Not more of your buddies? Swinging by to lock me in a trunk?"

Kyle spoke around an oversized bite, "They drove a Cadillac Escalade. It doesn't have what you'd call a trunk. It's cargo space. Nothing you can be locked inside of."

"Thank you for that educational factoid, Kyle."

Trudy whispered to me, "How does he know that if he's blind?"

Kyle held up his hand and pointed back down at himself. "Blind. Not deaf, dear."

I leaned into Trudy and whispered, "His hearing is excellent."

Kyle swallowed the last of his banana. "What did you say Sam?"

I looked at Trudy and mouthed the word, 'Never mind.'

"Trudy, to answer your question, the cadence of an idling Cadillac Escalade is distinctive." Kyle leaned back in his chair. "It's like a John Paul Jones riff, low and rapid, nearly opposite of a Nissan Armada, which is lighter and higher, but fluid, and sounds more like Enya. And both are different than other large-sized vehicles. Take, for example, a GMC Yukon..."

Kyle continued his musical review of the latest luxury SUVs, while Trudy and I watched the men surveying the house. One guy, bald with a jagged neck tattoo, repeatedly flexed his shoulder muscles as if warming up to break bones. The other guy, who looked like a grown-up Opie Taylor from The Andy Griffith Show, wore khaki trousers, a yellow polo, and repetitively wiped his mouth of extra saliva with a white handkerchief.

"...and that's why you never play Led Zeppelin in a Land Rover," Kyle finished his musical engine presentation.

Remembering I'd unlocked the back door so Kyle could gain access after Ubering here, I tiptoed toward the kitchen to lock it back.

As I passed by, Kyle held out his banana peel. "If you're going that way anyway."

I grabbed it and hushed him. "Could you keep your voice down?"

"Of course, I can." He didn't even try, more interested in

rummaging through the fruit bowl on the dining room table in search of a kumquat.

When I returned, Trudy shook her head at me. "I think we're in trouble here, Samantha. These guys are up to something. I think they're coming in, whether we let them or not."

Kyle, making as much noise as a chair scooting back on a vinyl floor can make, meandered to the window and pushed one muscular, unconcerned shoulder against the textured wall. "You girls don't really think these guys are here to hurt you, do you? Sam? Do you?"

"You're coming late to the party, Kyle. There's a history here you know nothing about."

Bored, he scratched at his facial scruff. "Look, ladies, there's no reason to be anxious. You're getting all worked up over nothing. These guys could have been hired by the homeowner to assess his property, for all we know. Or they're landscapers. Or roofers. Or Mormons. Whatever. Relax. Is there any Nutella around here?"

I gave him a dirty look before remembering that didn't affect him. "So that you understand what kind of situation we might be in, and by 'we' that includes you, here's the short version: strange men like to hurt me now. Or, kidnap me and not hurt me. I never know which way it'll go."

Trudy backed me up. "It's true. They do."

"And, if they're coming for me, to kidnap or not kidnap," I pointed out, "they won't leave you here snacking."

Kyle gave a placating nod and a patient exhale, as if willing to go along for the time being. "Okay, then. Let's have it. What are they doing? What do they look like? Tell me what you see. Maybe I'll agree." He tongued a chunk of fruit in his back molars. "Maybe I won't."

I watched the bald one hanging back in the yard, while khaki pants talked momentarily on the phone. You could hear his garbled voice, but I couldn't make out any words.

"One looks like Mr. Clean from the alternative, evil universe. Brawny. Bald. Over pumped. Jagged tattoo up his neck. Wearing a gray business suit which, I think, is hiding a gun. Walking around like an idiot, an idiot about to do something idiotic."

Kyle considered it. "Okay. And the next guy?"

"An older Opie."

"So, Ron Howard."

Trudy weighed in. "But younger."

Kyle leaned forward, moving closer to the sound of her voice. "Richie Cunningham?"

"That's too young. Past his acting days."

"*Willow*?"

Trudy thought about it. "Closer to *Apollo 13*."

I shushed them both. "Now is not the time to debate how Ron Howard has aged."

"Besides," Trudy spoke to Kyle, "what difference does his appearance make to you?"

Kyle casually crossed his arms over his chest, either as a power move or to show off his gym membership. "You're a tactful soul, Trudy. I picked up on that right away."

I shushed them both again. They could get acquainted later.

"Zip it. Both of you. Opie's on the phone. Kyle, can you make out anything he's saying?"

He leaned his ear closer to the window and listened for a moment. Trudy and I, without discussing it, both held our breath to be as silent as possible. About the time we needed to exhale, Kyle straightened. "Okay, I agree. Run for it."

12

Running for your life gets a bad rap, as if only doomed people do it. But there's nothing shameful in scurrying away so you can live to scurry away another day.

Our only other option was sitting around a house we'd unwittingly burglarized and waiting for death to come knocking. But death usually just kicks in the door.

Fred agreed with Kyle by texting, "What he said."

Trudy and I grabbed Kyle by the arms and ran out the back door, through Eugene Percy's backyard, out his gated fence, through his neighbor's yard, and into the next residential block. On the way, we shouted out instructions to Kyle like, "limb," "hole," 'bush," "swing set," "fence!"

This neighborhood had not been structured well for running with a blind guy. The sidewalks were uneven and cracked. Landscaping was a to-each-his-own style. Vehicles parked without rhyme, without reason. Broad trees interrupted clear access to and through yards. Kids laid out traps in no recognizable pattern. Kyle tripped through a hydrangea bush and kept going.

Our clearest option ran down the center of the street. Kyle needed room to navigate. He could run fast, but not always straight.

We kept to the asphalt, hoping to gain distance if not concealment. That worked until a bullet whizzed past Trudy's head and lodged into an elm.

Each of us found the nearest object to hide behind. I chose an idling UPS truck. Trudy chose a tree. Kyle ran into a yard, tripped over a wall of decorative railroad ties, and chose that.

"I'll hang here!" he yelled.

I peeked around the UPS truck to catch a glimpse of Mr. Clean. He'd only fired one round, possibly a warning shot, but I didn't know how many warnings Mr. Clean gave before he mopped the floor with you.

Hauling his bulky upper body around looked exhausting. That might have been why he didn't give chase and, instead, took a call on his cell. That or Opie was on the phone, telling him to wait while he retrieved the Escalade. It was the less fatiguing option. With us on foot, they could easily mow us down with 420 horsepower and room enough for eight.

I didn't know who these guys were, but, if I've learned anything about being hunted, it's that the "who" isn't all that interesting of a reveal.

While I hid behind the truck, the UPS delivery guy, clad in the customary brown uniform and brown legs, jogged back from dropping off his delivery, jumped into the driver's seat, and took off. He either hadn't heard the gunshot or did hear it but guaranteed overnight delivery is guaranteed overnight delivery.

When he parked in Mr. Clean's line of sight for another drop off, Trudy and I grabbed Kyle and made a hard right at the next cross street.

Mr. Clean hadn't seen where we went, but it wouldn't take long to hunt us down. We needed to get lost fast.

"What did you hear, Kyle? What did Opie say on the phone?" Trudy, ever the curious one, asked in a shaky voice as her feet pounded along the pavement.

"All I heard was the last part of a question, 'do with the witnesses.' Landscapers don't use the word 'witnesses.' So, ladies, you want to fill me in? What is going on here?" Kyle ran between us, close enough so we could be his eyes when necessary.

"No idea. Pothole," I pulled him closer to me and released him when his path was clear again.

"Oh, you know. Just us girls. Getting all worked up over nothing," Trudy sputtered out sarcastically between breaths. "Left at the next block."

As we ran, a few neighbors glanced up momentarily, but, otherwise, weren't too interested. Three grown adults in street clothes running down the middle of the road was, apparently, a common occurrence in this neighborhood.

No one seemed particularly concerned about hearing a shot fired, either. If anyone heard it, they most likely dismissed it as a car backfiring. Then went on with their duties of raking leaves, unloading groceries, and pulling their kids' bikes into the garage before the storm hit.

That gave me an idea.

"Follow me, people. I've got a plan."

Once we crested the hill, I led us right at the next cross street and slowed to an easy jog. Trudy and Kyle kept pace.

"What are you looking for Sam?" Kyle could, quite possibly, hear my eyeballs moving around in my head.

"A garage."

Trudy shot me a questioning look.

"An open garage," I clarified. "One unmanned."

It was early, yet. Adults were arriving home from work, which meant pulling into their garages. Afterward, many, I noticed, were leaving them open.

With the storm blowing in, this was typical Oklahoma behavior. There's not a smell on earth as fresh, as alive, as the air ten minutes before a severe storm hits in the Heartland. The cooling air is less dense. The oxygen sweeter. Each sudden burst of wind feels like hope pushing all the broken-heartedness out.

You couldn't help but gulp it in. You wanted that air everywhere – in your lungs, in your house. This was the moment windows were flung open, and garages aired out. Car windows rolled down and doors left ajar. Until all was shut back up again when the rain air bombed everything.

Once the lightning moves into the horizon, residents often stand in their yards, pop open lawn chairs, or congregate on porches. You watch. You point. You gauge whether or not you should take cover while the weatherman on the television pleads with everyone to take him seriously and take cover.

If the storm is severe, some will only stay minutes before retreating inside. Others stay to the last final breath. When the thunder vibrates their chest, the lightning snaps overhead, the wind blows them down, or the rain comes in fat plops or a slanted sheet, they race for the safety of their garages.

This was prime time in Tornado Alley to find an impromptu hiding place.

What we needed was a garage with one vehicle, preferably a Lexus or Audi sedan. No kid's bikes or toys around. Tools neatly hung or shelved. All storage containers organized and, possibly, stackable. All connected to a single-story house with a manicured lawn, lush flower garden, and wind chimes.

I found it three doors down on the next block, perfectly situated on the north side of the street.

"A Mercedes-Benz," I told Trudy and Kyle, who were too winded to speak. "That should do it."

~

We slowed to a walk so they could catch their breath, and I led them toward the open garage. When Trudy saw my direction, she grabbed my arm. "What are you doing?"

I motioned to the garage. "I'm hiding."

"In someone's garage?"

"Do you have any better idea?"

She thought about it for so long I moved on.

"Kyle, what about you? Any objections?"

Kyle sniffed twice at the air in two quick inhales that tugged at his thin nostrils. "At some point, you will explain to me why men are chasing you," it wasn't a suggestion, "but, other than that, I'm good. This house smells like lavender, potting soil, and cookies."

We crossed the threshold of the darkened garage. Inside, a meteorologist urged viewers to "get inside." He knew about the addictive pre-storm air, too.

"TV on. Channel 6," Kyle filled in for me. "Should we knock?"

"No," I whispered. "We're only going to hang out here long enough to form our next plan of action. We won't touch anything. We won't disturb anything. She won't even know we were here."

"The touching part." Kyle put his hand out into open space. "Does that apply to me?"

Trudy looked around the space. "She? Do you know her?"

I shook my head no. "A hypothesis only." I pointed to two metal shelves taking up one-third of the garage. "Over there. Behind the storage boxes. Hurry. This plan only works if we're not spotted milling around by the door."

Trudy and I found a spot behind the boxes where we put our backs to the wall and our eyes on the road. Although the sun hadn't completely set, yet, the storm drastically reduced visibility and deepened the corner shadows. From our position, you couldn't see our heads peeking over the containers from the road unless you had infrared goggles or turned the garage light on.

Kyle, sitting across from us with his back to the shelf, found an open cardboard box of hand tools and ran his fingers along each one.

"Trowel. Shears. Garden knife. Hand rake. Scissors." He set the box back on the shelf at eye level. "Enthusiastic gardener. So, now what are we doing?"

"Thinking." I eyed a passing SUV, which didn't match our pursuers. "And hiding."

"Your hypothesis," Trudy never let anything go. "Why do you think the homeowner's a she? And why did you pick this garage?"

I pointed to the vehicle. "Mercedes-Benz sedan. High end vehicle. Very clean. Not a vehicle you purchase with toddlers or teens at home. I'm guessing retired and widowed. Garage is neat, but largely unused. No mower. A retired man would have a mower. No man around? A woman will hire it done. Stackable, neatly organized storage containers meant she has no need to access most of this stuff. It's kept for sentimental reasons. Men would be less sentimental and want the space. One story house means the owner is likely less mobile than in previous years and requires less space. So, possibly elderly. This means she's unlikely to go outside during a storm, but she still wants to air out her garage. Well-kept flower garden means she's home often and with time on her hands. Another age indicator. The wind chimes at the door are a friendly voice to keep her company, which means she most likely lives alone. Therefore, there's no one else here to walk outside and find us hiding." I met Trudy's eyes, which appeared impressed for the first time. "Again, hypothesis only. So, let's keep our voices down in case I'm wrong and we've invaded the space of a 28-year-old pro wrestler."

With the wind wailing at a higher pitch, we settled in, glad to be out of the elements. Thanks to Jackson, I could run without getting as physically exhausted as my companions. Trudy and Kyle needed rest, and all of us needed a plan.

Habitually, we checked our phones for reception. Trudy had one bar. Kyle had none. My phone battery died thanks to all of Fred's texting. We needed help, but from whom?

Jackson was the only person I fully trusted to get me out of this mess. Where was he?

Trudy, unburdened by indecision, strolled through her contact list to make a call. I reached over and snatched her phone.

"I'm using that," she grabbed at it and missed.

"Not right now, you aren't." I lowered my voice. "I don't know who you are, what you want, or why your pals have, twice"–I held up one finger then two just to be dramatic–"locked me in a vehicle. So, you've lost your phone privileges."

Kyle propped his arm on a raised knee. "What have you gotten yourself into, Sass?"

Trudy's phone went into the pocket of my green cardigan sweater. "I'm not sure."

Taillights on the street drew my attention. They bounced as the vehicle moved, then stilled as they stopped. A black SUV, one that looked vaguely familiar, stopped outside our hiding place.

Kyle whispered. "Chevy Suburban. Not the Lincoln."

So, not our pursuers.

Inside the Suburban, the interior light came on, while the male driver checked his phone for messages, and the passenger snacked on Cheetos. Both men looked nearly identical, all except the color of their hair.

~

I sucked in a breath and ducked down, pulling Trudy and Kyle's head down with me.

"What's going on? Who are they?" Trudy whispered, looking as panicked as I felt.

"The twin thugs," I could barely get the words out. "They kidnapped me and some friends over the weekend."

Kyle forgot to keep his voice down. "Another kidnapping?"

"Yes," I hissed. "I told you it happens a lot."

Trudy chimed in, "She did tell you."

The last time I'd seen the twin thugs, they left Jackson and I locked in the warehouse with Jude something, the thespian fixer with the impossible last name. That'd been right before the Widow McBride showed up and shot me in the stomach.

Now, they idled in the road near the end of the driveway. The brunet was texting, the blond was eating. Both glanced around periodically. Neither showed our garage any particular attention. They didn't know I was in here, but they knew I was in this neighborhood. There's no way their presence now was a coincidence.

"These guys are muscle for hire. I had a run-in with them this weekend while…"

Kyle hushed me. "Sass, your life is madness. I respect that, but, also, be quiet. I'm listening."

That's fair.

"What do you hear?"

Kyle bobbed his head hesitantly, while humming. Under his breath, he mumbled, "'Cause I can't fight this feeling anymore…' They're listening to REO Speedwagon. That's a soulful choice for thugs. You sure they're as bad as you think?"

I thought about the déjà vu flash I'd seen last Saturday of the blond shooting Gin in the chest while we were escaping the conference room.

"No, they're worse," I confirmed for Kyle.

Trudy, whose hair showed signs of increasing moisture in the air, leaned her head in.

"What should we do now?" She whispered.

I wasn't sure. As for coming up with a plan, I'd found us a safe place to hide until a plan was formed. That's as far into a plan as I'd gotten. When we entered the garage, we'd reached the end of my ideas.

I pushed back at my thickening hair and then at Trudy's. There wasn't enough room scrunched up in a ball like this for all this naturally curly hair. Sick of beating it back, I lifted my head for a breath of fresh air and that's when I saw it. Outside the garage. Between me and the thugs. A black blur.

I sat up and blinked. What did I just see?

"What did you just see?" Trudy asked from a pool of red frizz.

That woman needed to get out of my head. "Nothing. I think." Or was it something? Was it what had my heart hammering in my chest?

Was it what I'd been so desperate to see during the last and longest three days of my life? Was it the one person in this world I couldn't live without?

Was it Jackson Christy, dressed in his black hoodie, racing by? If it was and if he wasn't allowing me to see him right now, and if, while not allowing me to see him, he was still keeping an eye on me, how did I get him to stop running away?

Or was it only the last light of day reflecting off a sheet of rain?

"I have an idea." I didn't. "I can get us out of here." I couldn't. "We're all going to be fine." Eh. Probably not. "I need you to stay here, stay hidden, and not leave this garage until I come back to get you."

"You aren't going anywhere without me." Trudy wasn't having it. I wondered if her assignment was to keep me in sight at all times.

Kyle, on the other hand, still rifling through anything within reach, found a life jacket to use as a pillow. "Wake me when you get back."

Trudy nudged his thigh with her foot. "You're going to let her go out there by herself?"

Kyle, leaning against the metal shelving, resituated to get comfortable. "You obviously don't know Samantha well. There's no 'letting.' Whatever the girl gets determined to do, she does. I can't stop her, but I can conserve my energy." He snuggled his head into the life jacket. "You should, too."

I nodded in agreement. "You really should, Trudy. He knows me better."

Getting on my feet but staying in a crouched position, I maneuvered around Trudy, who grabbed my arm before I reached the Benz.

"Wait." She spoke in a harsh whisper. "Are you planning to use your..." here she paused so I did, too.

"My what?"

She held up a finger in a 'wait one minute' gesture. Then, leaning toward Kyle, she waved her hand rapidly in front of his face.

"I'm not asleep, Trudy," Kyle murmured. "But I am still blind."

"How did you—"

"Your hands still smell like apples. And I am capable of feeling air being battered right in front of my face." He waved a hand dismissively. "Whatever you want to ask Sam privately, try sign language. I'm not fluent."

Trudy turned a bewildered face in my direction.

"What, Trudy? Just ask." She needed to hurry. Squatting cut circulation to my feet.

"Are you going to…" She used two fingers on her right hand to walk across her left hand.

I squinted at her cupcakiness. "Walk?"

She shook her head 'no' and tried the gesture again, only this time her fingers "walked" faster. I finally got it. She was asking about my super speed. So that answered that question. Her, Doc, and Cheekbones knew about my abilities. Or at least that one.

I nodded to show her I understood.

"Here's what I'm going to do," I turned away and walked out of the garage.

~

Dramatic exits are more dramatic when you don't go back for a raincoat.

Outside, the rain was in that dumping phase where clouds grab buckets of water and turn them upside down. The icy air pushed the wet into your north and out your south.

I stepped outside the garage and stepped right back in. Next to the door between the house and garage was a series of four pegs, one holding a windbreaker, one an apron, one an umbrella, and one a raincoat. I went with the raincoat. It would allow more maneuverability than an umbrella. It also fell down past my knee boots, while the two-sizes too big hood and four-inches too long sleeves covered me entirely.

Maybe my hypothesis about the home's resident was closer with the 28-year-old pro wrestler than the elderly woman.

Bundled into dark blue water repellent material, I headed in a less dramatic exit for the storm. In the corner, Trudy frowned and Kyle snored.

With the oversized hood swallowing my head, I stepped under the waterfall again and into the shadows. The sun hadn't completely set, yet, but it might as well have. The thick storm clouds sealed off the light.

In the hazy visibility, while camouflaged by the midnight blue raincoat, I easily moved through our host's front yard without the thugs noticing. Once in the shadow of the yard, I changed direction and approached the SUV from behind.

If Jackson was out here, he'd chosen to avoid me. Would I trust him and respect that choice?

Come on. It's like you don't know me at all.

I needed to force Jackson, against his will and better judgement, to do what I wanted, a true sign of a healthy relationship. That meant getting myself into serious trouble, so he'd show up to save me. Two thugs wouldn't do it. I'd need four.

This is why I continued pushing against the wind and rain to sneak up on the twin thugs' idling suburban. Although water futilely sloshed against my knee-high boots, the sound was little more than a whisper among the screams of a thundering downpour. Step by slushy, sneaky step, I trudged through the runoff racing to join its fallen brothers in nearby ponds, creeks, and gutters.

Almost there. Almost…

Once I reached them, I'd subtly get their attention, prompt them to give chase, then join up with Opie and Mr. Clean. With four thugs against one me, Jackson would be compelled to intervene.

If Jackson wasn't standing outside my window this morning, or pickpocketing my phone at the casino, or racing through the thunderstorm to keep an eye on me, then I was putting myself into a sticky situation I might not be able to get out of.

The things I do to control the ones I love.

Reaching the back of the suburban, I scanned the area for a black blur. Nothing. But just because I couldn't see him didn't mean he wasn't there. Jackson played this invisible spying game with me before.

Here goes nothing.

I walked along the side of the suburban, intent on knocking on the glass and giving a friendly wave, when the twin thugs chose that moment to shove the car into drive, gun the accelerator, and squeal tires racing away. A fury of water crashed against my overachieving raincoat, rocking me backward several steps, as the suburban's back tires bullied their way through the runoff. It wasn't until the suburban's red devil-eyed brake lights glowed through the weepy haze that I picked my jaw off the road.

What part of my plan did they not understand?

13

The backseat of a 1980s Cutlass has more legroom than the trunk. I think the design engineers intended it that way.

"This is madness." Kyle, sitting behind the driver, engaged in a heated debate with Trudy, whose hips and hair filled the space between us.

"You need to be more open minded, Kyle." Trudy wasn't backing down.

"More open minded to madness?" Kyle wasn't backing down either.

The three of us bounced along in the backseat. Up front, Cheekbones suspiciously eyed every passing mile from behind the wheel. Doc relaxed in the passenger seat acting disappointed the world lacked the backbone to defy him every once in a while.

They'd found me in Eugene Percy's neighborhood still trying to get all the thugs together in one spot and finding them uncooperative. The twins had taken off, leaving the neighborhood for more snacks or mayhem. Meanwhile, Opie and Mr. Clean had resurfaced near the housing edition's private playground and jetted off to an adjoining neighborhood in pursuit of something not me. I hadn't moved fast enough to get their attention. While standing there deciding which thug couple to follow first, Doc and Cheekbones pulled up next to me with Kyle and Trudy in the back.

Doc rolled down the window and motioned for me to get in.

"How did you find..." I never got the "me" out. In the backseat, Trudy held up her phone and jiggled it between her fingers.

I reached into the raincoat and checked my cardigan pocket. She had lifted her phone when she stopped me from leaving the garage.

My cool, dramatic exit was getting more pathetic by the moment.

Seeing my embarrassment when I realized she'd outplayed me, Trudy grinned. Cupcakes are far too self-congratulatory.

"Get in, Addison." Doc ordered in his customary bored tone. "I'm getting wet."

With that, he rolled his window back up and, defeatedly, I climbed into the back.

Running away wouldn't work. Doc had proven he'd find me whenever he wanted. I also couldn't leave Kyle behind, considering I'd been the one to drag him into this mess. Also, worth noting, I wanted to know who these people were and what they wanted.

I climbed in behind Doc, pulled Fred's manila envelope out of my waistband so I could sit comfortably, and had been listening to Kyle and Trudy argue ever since.

"I thought blind guys would be better listeners," Trudy shot back.

"Just because I can hear your earrings brushing against your hair doesn't mean I should come around to your way of thinking."

Trudy fingered the gold hoops in her ears. "You can hear my earrings?"

There was no end to Trudy being impressed by Kyle's heightened senses, all except his taste buds. That's what the argument was over. Not where we were being taken. Not why. Not what Trudy and her pals wanted. Kyle was disgusted by Trudy's opinion that corn belonged in lasagna.

"Are you impressed enough to stop this foolishness with the corn?"

Trudy laughed. "Absolutely not."

Kyle didn't laugh. Kyle never laughed. If you were able to honestly amuse him, he rewarded you with a slight upturn of the mouth and a "huh."

With Trudy, however, he got as close to a smile as Kyle got. They were flirting.

I wasn't up for witnessing a blossoming romance, so I went back to ignoring them.

In front of me, Doc watched the landscape out the passenger window. His head didn't move much, nor did his eyes. He looked disinterested. But a few brief eye twitches and a momentary squinting made me wonder if I should reconsider the assessment.

As Trudy and Kyle moved on to debating lime juice or lime oil on pan seared fish, I zoned in on Doc and the back of his thick, white-haired head. I couldn't say this because I knew the man, I didn't. And, I couldn't say this because he gave me any reason to believe it, he didn't. But I got the impression his attention was heightened. That he wasn't bored at all. That his laidback attitude was a cloaking technique. That those unflinching eyes were catching every movement out the window in anticipation of something coming. That Cheekbones, also, wasn't merely driving defensively but transporting us through a war zone. That we were all in some serious trouble.

Then again, maybe not. What did I know? Doc and Cheekbones could be mentally replaying their favorite sports team's highlights.

What I did know was that Jackson hadn't swooped in to save the day. That meant Doc, Cheekbones, and Trudy weren't dangerous enough to warrant his intervention. Or it meant I'd imagined his sporadic appearances and was now in deep doo-doo.

I had no training to rightfully diagnose this or any other dangerous situations or people. Nor did I have knowledge on how to avoid either. So far, when faced with safety challenges, I made the most of my common sense and penchant for harebrained ideas. But logic and stupidity could only get you so far. Without Jackson, I needed the know-how to get out of these jams on my own.

That's where I was now. In a jam with three people who hadn't hurt me but had conspired against me for the last twenty hours. And me and my friend stuck in a vehicle with them taking us west out of town.

What was I feeling at this moment? Anxious about where this ride was taking us.

What was Kyle feeling at this moment? Indignation over Trudy's recipe for oatmeal cookies.

"You don't add chopped pecans? What kind of heathen are you?"

I tuned him and Trudy's conversation out for the third and final time. It was distracting. And making me hungry.

Jackson had predicted one day I'd get in trouble without him. He told Theo his concerns recently, according to one of my dreams-that-aren't-dreams-but-memories-that-aren't-my-memories.

The night settled in. Stars poked white holes in the black blanket overhead. One red twinkle identified a satellite from the rest of the sprinkled mass. Over the back-porch banister, naked branches stripped of green swayed and creaked companionably in nature's moaning winter chorus. The air felt warm, comforting, hypnotic as heat emanated from the nearby chiminea.

I could feel it all, see it in detail, breathe in the spices of a November night because Sam had awakened my senses tonight, and they weren't sleepy yet. The hour-old memory of her softness in my arms and her sweetness on my lips replayed and replayed in my mind.

Man. I had it bad.

"Hey, brother, you plan on coming back or are you out for the night? Hello? Jackson Christy. You still in there?"

"Huh?" *I turned to Theo, while taking a swig of a chilled beer.*

When I'd gotten back home tonight from Sam's, Theo had been lounging on my back patio and drinking my beer. The only reasonable thing to do was join him.

"You were telling me about Sam eating a mouthful of sour cream?" *Theo raised his eyebrows, waiting for me to return to our conversation.* "Earlier tonight? When you went to her house? To talk to her about how she's been avoiding you since the Durant Ball? Then you spaced out. Any of this registering, brother? Or would you like me to let you return to whatever thoughts you were entertaining with that grin on your face?"

I cleared my throat and got my head back in the game. "Right. From earlier. She thought it was yogurt," *I continued my story.* "Shoving food in her mouth gave her an excuse not to answer my question."

Theo gulped down an ounce. "Creative. That's one way of avoiding you."

I smothered a smile. "Yes. One way."

"By that smile you're fighting, looks like you ended the avoidance."

I took another swig of beer and worked on my poker face. "We talked about it."

Theo, mimicking my movement, rolled the cold liquid around in his mouth weighing this out. "Talking's good. You cover all the bases?"

Using my thumb, I rubbed at the paper wrapper on my beer bottle until the edge started curling. "You mean the deadline? The training? Hal?"

Theo nodded with each question.

"Not." *I thought about that kiss again.* "Exactly."

"What about her vulnerabilities? You go over any of those?"

I shook my head no. "Not yet."

"Sounds like you did a lot of talking."

"I..." How did I say this? "Told her."

Theo's arm, the one clutching the beer, dropped onto the armrest and lazily hung there while he weighed out my words. He knew how long I'd been keeping a careful watch over her. He also knew that I'd fallen for her somewhere along the way. Not making that information known had been for her safety. Getting involved with me would complicate anyone's life. Getting involved romantically would make her an instant target for anyone wanting to control, punish, or manipulate me.

That's why I'd kept our relationship professional, why I kept a safe distance, why I'd warred with ever telling her at all. Theo had been the one to nudge me to reconsider. After her mugging, I'd feared it happened because of me. Because I'd gotten too close. Let my guard down. Shown someone watching how I felt. That's why I'd decided to end our working relationship the next day, a move that had backfired. All I'd done was awaken her curiosity.

"Let her know, brother," Theo told me after her mugging. "It should be her choice whether or not to risk being with you. Stop denying her the option."

I'd finally agreed to tell her...when I thought she was ready. That hour had finally arrived. So, tonight, I shared a little of how I saw her and how I wanted her to see me, not just this black-hood guy persona.

I didn't tell her everything. Like, how my heart races at the mention of her name. How, when she is in a room, nothing else could get my attention. How I saw her. Really saw her. Even the vulnerable parts she hides. How I wished I could be with her all the time. How I feared my desire to be with her would put her in danger, and one day I wouldn't be there to stop it.

So, I didn't tell her everything. Everything would trigger her customary avoidance. But I told her some. Then I waited hopefully and anxiously for her response.

"How did she react to this news?" Theo asked now.

Well, she made the first move, that's how she reacted. She walked up to me, laced her hands behind my neck, and kissed me. That...I didn't expect. Not at all. It's rare someone can surprise me, but that surprised me. I stood there dumbfounded for a moment. She pressed her soft, warm lips against mine and waited. So maybe I didn't respond instantly. And maybe I wasn't the smoothest guy on the block. And maybe we still had a long way to go before she completely trusted me. But, in that moment, with her familiar smell of pomegranate shampoo filling the air around me, and her fingers massaging the back of my head, and the realization she was opening her heart to me even a little, I did exactly what I'd been dying to do for years. I slid my arms around her waist, pulled her to me, and kissed her back. Her breath caught for a moment. Then she sighed and relaxed into my *arms.*

"She seemed," I smiled at Theo's question, *"receptive to the idea."*

I'd always known kissing Samantha would be sweet. She was passionate but playful, confident and delicate, warm and open and welcoming and all female, if and when she trusted you. I'm amazed I ever let her go. I feared I wouldn't. If I ever have her in my arms again, I may not. Eventually, thankfully, clarity returned. I remembered the dangerous position being with me put her in. I pulled back to rediscover my control and get her back on topic – namely, her training. If we were ever to be together, she had to be prepared, ready, and knowledgeable on how to protect herself. This was paramount. This was critical. This was what I successfully focused back on, until she agreed to meet me tomorrow after her girl's night with Sarah so we could talk about her training…if I kissed her twice more.

"We've had our first kiss," she'd said tonight. "Now we'll need two more to reach three." She'd been leaning against her backyard table with her long, bare legs crossed at the shin. Her face was still flushed from that first kiss and that untamed hair of hers blew tendrils across her swollen lips.

It took everything I had to keep my feet firmly planted and my hands to myself.

"Is there something special about three?" I'd asked.

"Three is a sacred number, Jackson. The ancient Greek philosopher and mathematician Pythagoras believed three to be the noblest of all digits. We should never be dismissive of nobility."

That flirtatious spark in her eyes was nearly my undoing. I'd felt a sensation around my heart, very nearly like pain. But good pain. Satisfying pain. Pain that spurred a deeper breath, a flexing of strength, an innate fighter instinct, a clearness of thought and purpose. I rubbed my hand against my chest as I crossed my arms.

"I see."

"You can get started on two now"–she'd tapped her cheek where the moonlight brushed it–"and fulfill your remaining quota tomorrow. If you want this conversation, these are my terms."

I loved Samantha Addison. There was no doubt about that. I couldn't remember a time not loving her now. But I also just really liked the girl.

She made me laugh. Sometimes on purpose. Sometimes not. Always, though, she delighted me. It was the only way to explain what I felt when she was around: delight. She should know that. I should tell her. And I will…as soon as she stops avoiding me.

As for her terms, they sounded reasonable. But, in my opinion, nobility should never have to wait. So, I fulfilled my quota tonight. The second kiss was smacked playfully on her cheek. The third kiss was my turn to play offense. She seemed all *too proud of herself for catching me off guard. This time it was my turn to be in the lead.*

Threading my hand into her curls, I tugged her to me, held her as tight as I dared, and kissed her until her bones turned gooey.

Game score: tied.

Theo glanced at me over the rim of his bottle. "Man," he took a swig, "you've got it bad."

~

I woke up from that dream/memory in a gasp. Prowling through a person's mind could be considered impolite, especially when they're thinking about you. In that unguarded state, Jackson might think things he'd never want me to know about. Not bad things, necessarily. But personal ones. Or thoughts he wanted to share with me on his time.

Then again, what if it is in his control?

I'm assuming this dream/memory walk trick of mine was under my control, but what if it wasn't? What if he was sharing specific memories with me as a way to communicate something? As a way to talk to me when he couldn't talk to me?

I mentally reviewed the dream/memories in search of a pattern or message.

So far, I'd seen the day Jackson discovered his ability when Theo fell out of a tree and Jackson carried him to help. Was that his way of sharing his backstory?

The next dream/memory had been when he ignored his father's advice and ended up running into a clothesline. Was that his way of relating to my perpetual bruises?

The next dream was the night Senator Chad McBride died, and Jackson rescued me on the roof of the Oklahoma Now building. Was that his way of connecting me to the night we met?

The memory after that had been the discussion with Jerry about keeping an eye on me seven years ago. Was that his way of opening up about his history with me?

Lastly, he shared the conversation with Theo on the night of our first kiss. Was that to show me how much he cared?

One curious comment in that memory I didn't understand. Theo had mentioned there being a "deadline" and a person named "Hal."

What was this deadline? And who the devil was Hal?

In front of me, Doc sipped on a cup of coffee that materialized out of nowhere. We listed this way and that on a two-lane road that looked a heck of a lot like the road to Jackson's neighborhood. He trained his eye to some dark spot in the distance.

"Hey, you there." I tapped Doc on the shoulder. "What's your name?"

He swallowed his coffee and smacked his lips. "Hal."

That was a surprisingly easy mystery to solve.

"Where are we going, Hal?"

He sipped his coffee.

"What do you want from me, Hal?"

He peered out the window.

"Should I be afraid, Hal?"

He sipped more coffee.

"Are you always this forthcoming, Hal?"

Cheekbones drove obediently and silently along, while Trudy described the scenery out the window for Kyle. The two new pals had finally stopped arguing over whether strawberries should be dipped in milk or dark chocolate.

"It's not far now," Trudy told Kyle, as we pulled into the entrance to Jackson's neighborhood. Instead of going straight, Cheekbones turned left into a narrow asphalt road largely overgrown and hidden with tree limbs. I'd never noticed it before. As far as I could tell, this road led to nothing and nowhere.

"We're surrounded with trees that are all bald now, but still alive and peppered with long, healthy limbs." Trudy's voice was clear, but with a hint of intimacy their earlier arguments didn't hold. She was acting as Kyle's eyes, which was sweet. "The moonlight is pouring through the shadows, and we're driving through their blocks of light. It feels like we're passing through frozen ice cubes."

She was no writer, but her descriptions weren't bad. Not sure about the ice cube reference, though. To me, it looked more like passing through filmy, bone-white curtains draped over the trees, each using the gauzy light to hide their knotted limbs until spring.

"Ice cubes, huh?" Kyle was impressed. "Good visual description."

Sure, if you go for that blunt, clear, precise style.

"Up ahead," Trudy continued, "the road is opening."

As we moved forward, the trees shuffled away from the road.
"You can see a small pond. It's completely still."
We drove past a still, small pond.
"You can make out the clouds and other trees in the pond's reflection."
The water mirrored the back-lit clouds above it and the brotherhood of trees beside it.
"The rain has stopped, finally," she continued. "The air is clearer now, so the trees are easier to see without the drizzle."
The wet camouflage lifted.
"Now, we're curving back to the east, and you can see a two-story, big log cabin at the end of the driveway."
She was spot-on there. It was a big log cabin.
Trudy took a deep breath as if summoning inspiration. "There's a faint light on inside, which is casting a soft yellow glow through the windows."
A soft, buttery glow.
"On the north corner of the cabin, three four-wheelers are parked. And that's always a welcome sight. It means the family is home," she sighed.
"Family? Home?" Kyle echoed my thoughts.
"Well"–she grinned self-consciously–"more like a second home and a family by choice."
In the front seats, Cheekbones put the Cutlass in park and climbed out. Hal opened the door, put his feet on the ground, turned sideways to look me in the eye, but didn't climb out.
Done playing the rewrite game in my head, I took his stern – bored and stern – look without flinching. I wasn't scared of this guy. No one named Hal was going to intimidate me.
"Addison, to answer your earlier question if you should be afraid…" Hal paused, in no hurry to finish his sentence. Instead, he sucked air through his teeth in quick succession while mulling over the answer. Finished contemplating the world's greatest mysteries, he passively nodded once. "Yes."

14

The very moment you expect everything is wrong, everything is off, and the chances of anything working out are not in your favor, things may actually be working out in your favor.

After Hal gave his answer, he strode into the buttery, lemony light from the log cabin. Taking off the borrowed raincoat and leaving it inside, along with Fred's envelope, I dragged myself out of the Cutlass to follow suit but couldn't find the motivation to put one foot in front of the other.

If he'd answered my question with a "possibly" or a "likely" or even a "probably," I would have felt mildly pacified. Encouraged, even. I've faced worse predictions than that. But "yes." The simplicity of the word, the unyielding meaning of it, the lack of additional syllables, it sounded so final. As if the end of this story had already been written, and it was a tragedy.

Jackson obviously knew Hal. He and Theo both did. And, not to overstate the obvious, but we were at a massive log cabin at the edge of Jackson's property. Somehow, Hal, Cheekbones, and Trudy were part of the sidekick crew. We were all on the same side, although my side needed to stop locking me in vehicles.

All of us being part of this big, happy, dysfunctional, semi-violent family meant Hal was giving me a pre-warning of what was coming. While locked in the trunk of the Cutlass last night, I'd known this was the start of something dark and dangerous.

For me, the unceasing Friday night of racing for answers and running from Jackson hadn't ended. Me getting shot, Jackson healing me, the Widow McBride driving away, Jude lying unconscious on the floor, it had been the final scene before intermission. Not the finale. The story paused for three days and revved back up again.

I knew this. I knew it even before the sun set Saturday night with Jackson unconscious and me at his bedside. Being with him in the hospital offered security, as if we'd escaped into a cocoon where no one could touch us or separate us again. Even with Jackson in a coma, at least we were together. And being together was all that mattered. It meant we won. The bad guys lost. Isn't that when the credits roll?

That wasn't our story, though. The Widow McBride wasn't going to disappear off camera. And the mysteries surrounding Jackson weren't going to be edited out, either.

Like, Lucian.

Who was he? The Widow McBride said he was behind her husband's lucrative offers if he sabotaged his own gubernatorial election. The man or power Senator Chad McBride tried to tell me about when he fell off the Oklahoma Now building seven years ago. The power player no one says "no" to and lives to tell about it. The man with a pocket full of copper pennies.

The night he died, McBride likened Lucian's influence to the coins used to shift the time on Big Ben.

"What if you were the man with a pocket full of copper pennies? And you could place them here, remove them there, make...insignificant changes all over the world that could create ripples...that grew into tidal waves. What would that make you? God, Miss Addison. It would make you god..."

To McBride, we were all coins in Lucian's pocket, all nudged to buy, sell, live, act, vote, believe what we saw in the news, watched in entertainment, heard from favorite celebrities, or passed around on social media.

I trusted all the mysteries surrounding McBride, his widow, and Lucian would eventually be revealed. Was that what Hal was referencing? Or was something else coming? Something even darker? Why did Hal believe I should be afraid?

Lost in my own thoughts, I hadn't moved from my spot next to the Cutlass. I hadn't looked up to survey my surroundings, either. When I did, the rest of the gang had already gone inside the cabin and left me alone in the dark all by myself. Except for the broad, looming, masculine silhouette of the man standing in front of that buttery, lemony light.

∼

My mouth fell open. I would have said something. Or moved. Or blinked. Or swallowed. Or breathed. But the sight of that familiar, beloved, brawny shadow disconnected my brain. Nothing kicked on upstairs until I heard a woman's voice, thick with emotion, cry out.

"Jackson?!"

The voice was mine.

The silhouette took one measured, calm step toward me and into an ice cube of moonlight. Every curve, line, and dimple in his face came into view.

Jackson Christy stood thirty feet away. Alive. Awake. Safe. And here. He didn't move close to me or further away. He stood his ground and let me work through all the emotions crossing my face like a flipbook.

I couldn't believe it. All those hours waiting to see him open his eyes, to hear his voice, to feel his life and strength and awareness return. Now, he stood as tall as ever, as broad-shouldered and sure-footed as ever, with the heaviness of his own agonizing wait pooling in the blue of his eyes.

I felt a single sob escape, and then I ran to him, which lasted two steps until I tripped on a tree limb. Before my knees, nose, or teeth made contact with the ground, Jackson grabbed me around the waist.

We stood facing each other, arms around each other, blinking back at each other, and lost in the moment where death was no longer wedged between us.

"Hey there," Jackson spoke softly.

"Hi." My throat tightened.

We stood in the silence, neither moving or speaking for longer than I realized. I should have grabbed on to him and not let go. Or smothered him in kisses. Or burst into sobs. Or anything other than stand there awkwardly in his arms doing nothing. But I felt paralyzed, either with relief or joy or both.

"You look...better. You look"–my hands rested on his chest–"good."

"Thanks." His face was inches from mine. "You, too."

"I meant," I rubbed at the sweatshirt material under my fingers, "healthy. You look healthy."

He nodded, more focused on the movement of my mouth than the words they formed. That look made my pulse race, and my pulse racing made my mouth keep going after it should have shut up.

"Not that 'good' couldn't also mean other things beyond healthy. Because it could. Like stylish. Or handsome. Or sexy."

Jackson focused back into the conversation. "You were saying I look sexy?"

"No. I mean, I could have. But I wasn't. I was saying 'good' to mean 'healthy.'"

Amused, his hands relaxed at my waist. "I see. So, you don't think I look sexy," he teased.

"No, that's not what I'm saying."

He wrinkled his brow as if once again reassembling the puzzle pieces to make a complete Samantha picture.

"What I'm saying is"–I tried a new approach–"you look healthy. Which is sexy," I quickly added. "A healthy sexy. Hexy."

What was I saying?

I didn't know how to feel. The man was willing to give his life for me. Who does something like that? How was I supposed to talk to him now? I felt so much, wanted to say so much, but I didn't know where or how to start.

His eyes burning at a high-level blue intensity messed with my head, too. When did he start looking at me like that? I don't remember him looking at me like that before. Did he always look at me like that?

I couldn't think. All I wanted was for him to hold me. Could I ask for that? Had our relationship reached that level? We went from not dating, to dating, to him dying for me, all within a twenty-four hour'ish timetable. We skipped several dating thresholds, like that awkward moment at the end of a first date, that awkward dinner with each other's friends, that awkward conversation about past romantic relationships. Now that he was back, did we start at the beginning? Take it slow? Jump ahead?

I really wanted him to hold me right now.

His warmth was everywhere. His woodsy scent, too. I couldn't believe he was standing there, awake and alive and looking at me with, of course, a quizzical expression.

To end the weirdness, all I had to do was reach out and pull him close. But I didn't.

"This is awkward," I admitted. "I don't know how to…" I motioned my hand between the two of us. "You know?"

"I see." He considered the situation. "I have an idea that might help. You want me to…?" He motioned his hand between us, mimicking me.

I shrugged. "I guess that would be okay."

"It would go something like this." His arms wrapped around my waist and lifted me off my feet. He buried his face in my neck and held me as close as he could.

He was right. That helped.

I closed my eyes and lost myself in the safe, untouchable world inside his arms. This was exactly where I wanted to be. And, I didn't even have to ask! Now that I was here, good luck getting me to leave.

"Never leave me again, Samantha," he spoke softly in my ear. I could feel his heart beating against my ribs. "Seeing you shot nearly killed me."

He had that right. It nearly did. And all because he took the hit himself, nearly bleeding out in my arms. I didn't even know he was dying until he lost consciousness.

How do you ever get past a shock like that? One minute, you're kissing your new boyfriend and thanking him for saving your life. The next minute, you're sitting in a pool of his blood. That can never happen again. Next time he's dying, he bloody well better tell me.

He would. Wouldn't he?

That would never happen again. Right?

There's no chance he could be bleeding out right now. Is there?

I tapped on Jackson's shoulder. "Hold that thought. I need to check something."

He set me back on my feet, and I did a cursory body scan, but that moonlight ice cube wasn't living up to its hype. I skipped the visual inspection and went for the physical one.

Slowly at first, a little hesitant of what I might find, I pressed my palms against Jackson's shoulders and ran them down his sturdy arms.

I checked my hands. No blood.

I ran my hands down the broad front of his black hoodie. Checked my palms again. No blood.

This wasn't going to cut it. That sweatshirt material could absorb liquid like a sponge.

"Here, help me with this," I pulled Jackson's hoodie up to expose his torso. A circular scar, but no bandage, stretched over his left rib area. The flesh, still pink and tender, stood out in stark contrast to the rest of his tan, hairy chest.

I ran my hands over it, checked my palms, and did a secondary inspection of running my hands over his chest again. You want to be thorough with these things.

"Uh, Sam? You want to tell me what you're looking for? Maybe I can help."

Nope. I could handle this assignment all by myself.

"Almost done." I moved to his back, lifted the hoodie, and ran my palms across his muscular shoulders, down his spine, and along his firm obliques. The boy always ran warm, but his skin felt nearly on fire. Was he feverish? Or maybe…

Jackson inhaled sharply. "You do know your hands are freezing, right?"

Yep, that's what it was.

"Just a few more minutes."

I placed my palm over the horizontal scar on his back. It was the exit wound, or exit tear, as Hal described it yesterday. I'd take that scar back in a heartbeat if I could. I'd take back every second of pain and every drop of blood I've cost him.

When I pulled my hand away, no blood. I leaned forward, placed my lips on the jagged-edged scar, and kissed away the hurt it brought.

In response, Jackson cleared his throat. But didn't interrupt me.

Good boy. I wasn't finished, yet.

Satisfied with my upper body inspection, I moved lower and ran my hands down each leg. I checked my palms and continued to the ankles.

"Raise your right foot for me, please."

He did it, but not without grumbling. "You want to tell me what's going on?"

I checked for any stream of blood leaking from his boot. Then moved to the left.

"Shh. You're distracting me. Next foot."

"Sam?" He didn't like it, but he cooperated by lifting the other foot. "This is getting ridiculous."

Satisfied there wasn't any gushing blood, I checked his neck for nicks or scratches near the carotid artery.

"How is it possible that whatever you are doing is getting weirder?" Jackson complained while I ran my hands along one side of his neck and then the other. No blood.

Relieved, I took a deep breath until I questioned whether I had been thorough along his chest. Probably not. I should check again.

When I slipped my hands under his hoodie to check the wound area again, Jackson had had enough. He took both my hands and held them in his. They warmed instantly.

"Okay, this has gone on long enough. On any other day or under any other circumstance, you are welcome to run your hands over my chest anytime you want. But this doesn't seem healthy. Though still kind of fun." He tipped my chin up so I'd look him in the eye. "What's going on?"

"I was just checking." I eyed the hem of his hoodie. How could I get my hands under there without him noticing?

"Checking what?" When I didn't answer, he repeated himself. "Samantha. Checking what?"

I shrugged. "I needed to know you weren't bleeding, okay? That you weren't injured, and I didn't know about it. Like last time. That you weren't dying right in front of me, and I was completely oblivious." I held up my palms. "Do you know how long your blood was on my hands? I couldn't get it off. It stained my cuticles. And I was glad it did. I wanted that constant reminder that you were there in a coma because of me."

He squeezed his eyes closed, "Ah, I see." With a deep breath, he rested his hands on my shoulders. "Samantha, listen to me. It was my choice. I didn't have to do what I did. I could have let you die, but"– he ran his fingers down my cheek–"my heart couldn't take it. I couldn't live with that. Taking your place was my choice. Mine. I did it of my own free will, while fully aware of what I was doing. And, if I had to live that moment all over again, I would make the same choices."

I pressed my face into the palm of his hand and let go, shaking my head. "How can I ever repay that? How can I ever make amends?"

"I'm not asking for repayment."

"Then what do you want?"

Jackson started to move, then stopped. "What do I want? Here. Let me make that clear." He pulled me to him and covered my mouth with his.

~

There are few moments of purity in life. Of being purely vulnerable and purely open. Purely defenseless and purely protected. Purely content and purely loved. Purely passionate and purely alive. In this moment, with this kiss, I was all of those things. And a few delicious more.

Jackson's mouth claimed mine as if it no longer belonged to me. I handed it over. His lips were all softness and awareness. He kissed me like a man returning from war, gone too long, desperate for that long-awaited touch, and thankful to not only be alive but be fully living. He pulled me into that moment until I forgot there was a world outside of us, forgot my fear, forgot all the pain in the waiting and wondering. All that existed was him and him alone. If time can be reversed and pain redeemed, it happened in that kiss, in that touch of his lips against mine, in our breaths mingled together, in that letting go of individual me and individual him and becoming only us.

He pulled away, only to hold my face in his hands and kiss me again softly, tenderly, until the tears I hadn't realized I'd been crying finally stopped.

"All I want, Samantha, is to love you." He kissed me again, gently, barely a whisper of his warmth. "That's all." He smiled. "And I wouldn't hate it if you loved me in return."

I pulled in a shaky breath. Love him? How could I not?

I placed my hand on his face. "I can do that."

His hand covered mine. "Is that so?"

With another breath, I got the better of my emotions. Squaring my shoulders, I wiped my face and flashed him a confident smile. "Piece of cake." I winked.

Jackson threw back his head and laughed. Oh, how I'd missed that laugh. It was all male, all open and deep and intimidating and fearless and masculine. And hexy.

While he was distracted laughing, I slipped my arms around his neck and pressed up against him. He stopped laughing to look down at me.

"Just so we're clear," I spoke with as much seriousness as I knew how to speak, "I don't know exactly when I fell in love with you. But I love you now so desperately, so impossibly, that you can never, and I mean never, put yourself in harm's way again for me without my express and possibly written permission. No more healing of Samantha unless Samantha says so. I lived through three days of waiting to see if you lived or died. I can never go through that again. Understand?"

Jackson rested his hands on my hips and, sensing my seriousness, only nodded.

"Secondly, no more keeping me in the dark about anything. I want to know what's going on and, while we're at it, who the bloody blue blazes are Hal, Trudy, and Cheekbones?"

"Cheekbones?"

"Hal's muscle."

Jackson stifled a laugh. "You're calling Gabriel, Cheekbones?"

"He never introduced himself and, honestly, there are so many unnamed people pursuing me these days, I have to give them nicknames to keep them straight."

He nodded seriously. "I'm sure he won't mind being called, 'Cheekbones.'"

I tightened my hold. "I'm not done with my demands."

"Right." Jackson kissed me quickly. "Continue."

"This may sound crazy but after the last three days I've had, I think it's a reasonable request."

"Okay, what?"

"You are to keep your eyes open at all times."

"Huh?"

"No closing them again. Not ever. I never needed someone to open their eyes so badly in my life. Now that they are, I want them to stay that way."

Jackson thought that one over. "What about sleeping?"

"You've rested enough."

"Blinking?"

"Use eye drops."

Jackson squeezed my hips affectionately. "You realize that sounds crazy, right?"

"Yes. But pretend you'll try anyway and humor me."

"Sure. Why not."

"And finally, my last demand. Now that you're whole again…" I paused, "you are, aren't you?"

"Yes, baby, I'm whole."

"The wound won't come back?"

His brows furrowed. "Come back?"

"I don't know how this healing thing works. Once you're better, you stay that way, right? It doesn't return from time to time like a recurring rash, does it?"

"No. It won't return."

I let out a breath. "Good. Then here is my final demand."

He raised his eyebrows.

"We need to celebrate."

Jackson pulled me in tighter. "How should we celebrate?"

"I have an idea that might help," I repeated his line from earlier. "You want me to…" I motioned my hand between the two of us.

Seeing where I was going with this, Jackson smiled. "I guess that would be okay."

I settled in closer, moving until my lips nearly brushed against his, and then held there. "It would go something like this…"

15

When your boyfriend returns from the dead, it's customary for people to give you time to catch up, make out, and be left alone. That's in a normal universe with civility and etiquette rules. That's not the universe I lived in now.

"Sorry, love birds. Hal sent me to fetch you," Trudy stood in the log cabin doorway being bathed in obtrusive, rude, canary yellow light. "The alone time needs to push pause."

She disappeared back inside, leaving Jackson and I grinning at each other with conspiratorial overtones.

"The kids are getting restless," he motioned his eyes toward the cabin.

I ignored them. "They're fine. Besides, I have a better idea than going inside."

"Oh? What's that?"

"We run away," I threaded my fingers through his stubbly hair and massaged the back of his neck. "I hear Aruba's nice this time of year."

His hands laced behind my back. "I was thinking Maine. All that snow."

"I'll need a toothbrush."

"And a fresh pair of socks."

"A neck pillow for the flight."

"And hats for when we arrive."

"So, no one sees my bed hair."

"I was thinking more about keeping our ears warm. And, you don't have bed hair. It's adorable all hours of the day."

"Even in the mornings?"

"Even then."

"That's a lie, but it's a beautiful lie." I snuggled into him. "So, it's settled. We're running away."

He agreed. "Far, far away."

I gave him another thorough kiss, lingering in the moment, and sighed. I could have stayed like this forever. Why can't reality ever get gone and stay that way?

"We're not actually going anywhere, are we." It wasn't a question, it was resignation.

"Yes, we will. I'll take you on a vacation, a real one, soon. But first." Jackson nodded toward the cabin. "We have to go in."

He laced his fingers with mine, and I let him move me toward the door.

"I still want that hat," I told his back.

"It's yours."

"And the neck pillow, too."

"Consider it done."

"And for you to never leave me again."

Jackson stopped and faced me. "Sam, you know I never left, right? It may have felt that way, but I was still there. Still with you. Even when you couldn't see it. Even when you thought I wasn't listening. I was. Which brings up a point. We need to discuss last night's boyfriend quiz score. C? Really?"

My jaw dropped. "You heard me?"

Jackson pressed his lips against my knuckles. "Every word."

He never left me? How comforting. How romantic. How…oh, wait.

"Every word?"

Jackson nodded. "Mmm hmm."

"From the entire time you were in a coma?"

He looked up at me while turning my hand over to plant a kiss in my palm, then on the pulse point at my wrist, then on the soft skin above it. "Yep."

Uhhh…

"Do you," please say no, please say no, "remember everything you heard?"

A knowing grin slowly turned up the corners of his mouth. "Mmm hmm."

Oh, crap.

I never actually thought he could hear me. I mean, I wanted him to, but I didn't believe he did. So, I didn't filter my conversation topics or content. A few things I said and did may prove embarrassing, like, when I drooled peppermint-flavored spit on his arm. In my defense, I frequently passed out from physical and emotional exhaustion with little warning. Like…while sucking on hard candy.

The nurses would have forgiven me, even after cleaning pink, sticky drool off his arm, my face, and the sheets, but later that same day I nodded off again while chewing gum.

There were also a few other things I said and did I'd prefer he didn't remember…

Like oversharing: "The thing is," I told him on coma day one, "tomato paste gives lots of people hives. So, I'm not alone there."

Or being too needy: "Should I cut my hair shorter? Or just add more layers? Which hairstyle makes my thighs look thinner?"

Or being too honest: "Jerry is such a good cook. I don't know how she can get chili so wrong."

Or being too open: "On average, I'd say I dream about you once a month. Since I met you about seven years ago, that's 84 dreams to date. And, coincidentally, you're always bare-chested."

Or being too sensitive: "Did you hear that? The new nurse told me I should get some fresh air. What's that supposed to mean?"

Or being too ridiculous: "Here are my top picks for our couple name. We could go long form with Jackantha or Samackson, or short form with Jam or Sack. Actually, Sack is terrible. I'm nixing Sack."

Jackson watched me mentally review all the stupid things I've said over the last three days. "Hey, where did you go?"

What other humiliating things did I say? I needed to make a list.

"Sam?"

Later. I needed to make a list, later. "Here. Was lost in thought for a minute."

I'm probably overthinking this. He says he remembers every word, but he probably missed more than he realized he missed. I talked a lot. He couldn't have been tuned in the whole time. Don't coma patients sleep?

"You okay?" He smoothed a strand of hair away from my face. "Ready to go in?"

I surveyed the outside of the cabin, contemplating what awaited inside. "This is it, isn't it? We're starting my training now."

"Not starting. That happened last night at 9 pm."

That was about the time Hal locked me in the trunk of a 1980s Cutlass. I still had a lot of confusion about the last 24 hours that needed clarified.

"What happens now?"

Jackson tugged at my hand. "You'll see."

Inside, maybe what waited were answers. Answers that would help me understand my ability to "borrow" the gifts of others, like Jackson's speed, Jerry's precognition, or whoever can talk to coma patients, animals, and speak languages they've never learned. How I did it, how to control it, whose abilities I was picking up on, all of those things would supposedly come through my training. And the time was now upon me.

I felt anxious, but excited. I'd put this off for long enough.

"Okay." I sounded resigned. I didn't want to appear too excited or Jackson would think he finally won this argument. "Let's get it over with."

Jackson chuckled, as if he knew exactly what I was doing. And, because it was Jackson, he probably did.

"That's the spirit." He laced his fingers with mine and turned toward the heavy cabin door. "Oh. Before I forget to tell you. My pick is Samackson."

Jackson led the way inside, and I followed obediently behind. Instead of paying attention to the cabin, I paid attention to Jackson in motion. I call it "action poetry." He has an agreement with gravity not to let it get in his way.

Besides, I'd been dying for any small finger twitch or eyelid flutter or toe wiggle for days. Watching him move was my top priority for the foreseeable future.

Once inside, I tore my eyes off the shifting muscles in his back and looked around.

The inside gleamed. When seeing the cabin from outside, it looked broad, old, but sturdy. A rustic porch, lining the front, socialized with two wooden rocking chairs. High and wide windows broke the continuity of the log pattern and opened the facade to a sense of breath and interaction with nature. It was from those windows the sometimes buttery, sometimes canary, light faintly seeped outside.

Overall, the cabin was charming, but not too charming. Functional and earthy. Those were my initial impressions. Inside, I altered my impressions.

The outside door opened immediately into a great room. And I do mean great. The ceiling reached the full two floors in a peak where mammoth cedar logs met and shook hands. Hazelnut-stained wood covered the floor. Bone-colored rock and stone covered the fireplace. Floor to ceiling windows took the entire far wall, reaching all the way to the peaked ceiling and reflecting the bluish black of the night outside.

Overhead, a rustically elegant chandelier sparkled and stretched down from the ceiling as if grown, not hung. What looked like tree branches curved and intertwined around the lighting fixture, while pale crystals attached to each limb cast delicate globes of white.

Below it, a faded patterned rug of muted greens and blues warmed the floor, while floor lamps and three overstuffed couches sat semi-circled around the crackling fireplace.

On the far right, a broad staircase circled into the ether above. Before reaching it, two double doors off to the side opened to what appeared to be a dining room of multiple small tables currently in shadow.

Most appealing of all, the entire place smelled like Jackson when he's black-hood guy: fire. I sucked in a noisy breath, exhaled, and breathed it in again. Now, I knew why he smelled the way he did. It was this place. This rugged, manly, fire-scented place.

Although predominantly masculine, the interior also had a soft, intimate feel. It was comfortable, homey, even romantic.

I let out a low, appreciative whistle.

Jackson watched my face as I took it all in. "You like it?"

I nodded. "Your handiwork, I take it?"

He smiled, the chandelier light playing with the deep blue depths in his eyes. "A remodeling job. I didn't build it. The old cabin came with the property. But it was mine to restore. So, I gave her some new clothes."

"Well, nice threads."

He squeezed my hand.

We walked to the crowd lounging around the fireplace with their coffees and coco's and Jerry with her beer. All the lively chatter from the group quieted down. I stood with Jackson and visually connected with each one. I nodded at Gin and Angel, who sat facing the fireplace. They had previously been in a deep discussion with Theo, who sat perched on the coffee table.

They were what I thought of as my alpha sidekick crew. It'd been ages, or roughly four days, since our hours of captivity in that warehouse. Everyone but Jackson came through it without a scratch, except Gin. He got a cough from breathing burning plastic fork fumes.

I still contend my escape plan was brilliant. Though, admittedly, a tad suicidal.

Moving on, I made eye contact with Jerry, who sat farthest from the door and raised one quizzical eyebrow at me. Jackson must have already told her about the chili.

Next, I gave a brief nod to Trudy, who smiled and returned it. She sat next to the fireplace with Kyle, who returned my "what's up" head nod and is quite possibly not actually blind.

Meanwhile, Cheekbones haunted the back windows, and Hal smoked a cigar while leaning against the fireplace mantel.

Give everyone glam wear and an expression of self-importance and we'd have a Vogue cover.

Now that we were all together, I looked at Jackson for direction of what came next. He nodded to Hal, who slowly released a heavy puff of gritty smoke. It twisted out of his lips, curling upwards in serpentine strands along both sides of his face. For the briefest of moments, as the smoke spread, he appeared headless.

Then his mouth appeared. It was turned up in a grin. Not a warm grin. Not a friendly one, either. A grin of power. A grin of command. A grin not for anyone's amusement, except his own. A biting grin. A grin I didn't want to see from a guy who always got the better of me. A most unsettling grin.

"This," he finally spoke, plugging the cigar back into the corner of his unamused mouth and biting it between his teeth, "is going to be a lot of work."

~

Hal may have unsettled me, but he didn't have that effect on anyone else. I took that as a sign he wasn't diabolical, unless everyone was diabolical.

Jerry watched me as if reading my mind where I stood. She was a strong case for the latter.

Jackson leaned down. "You look freaked out."

I observed Hal and his devilish exhales and glanced back to Jerry and her evil eye. "Me? Freaked? Nah."

"One day at a time, okay, Sam? It's all going to be fine."

I leaned into him and turned my face partially away from the curious eyes. "What, exactly, is going to be fine? And what exactly is going to be a lot of work?" I spoke quietly, while not moving my lips. "Those are the parts I'm hazy on."

"I know." He gave me a quick, little kiss. "You're about to find out."

I grasped Jackson's hand and hid behind his arm. The staring reached the creepy phase.

The Samantha trance lifted and the group chatter resumed. Gin stood up to get everyone's attention. "I have an important question."

Gin looked less stylishly homeless than the last time I saw him. He came to visit Jackson at the hospital on Sunday. Afterward, he stayed away because Beatrice, his van, had broken down again, and Angel, his girlfriend, wouldn't give him a ride anywhere until he trimmed his beard.

His ginger facial hair now matched his ginger haircut. Both short, trimmed, and well-groomed. You could actually see his face now, which made having him here all the more heartening. When you're in uncomfortable, unknown situations, having childhood friends close feels safer.

Whatever Gin was about to ask, I knew it would set a good, productive, and informative tone for the rest of the gathering.

"What's your question, Gin?" Jackson asked.

"We've all been discussing Sam's unique ability. You know, the way she can absorb someone else's strength or what have you. And we're wondering," Gin got nods of solidarity from Theo, Angel, Jerry and Trudy, "would a good superhero name for her be The Human Sponge or Super Paper Towel?"

I let out a single, hard laugh. Like a bark. Seven pairs of unamused eyes and one pair of unamused tinted glasses rested on me before returning to Gin.

"Or," he ignored my outburst, "what about Lady Mop?"

I snorted.

Angel spoke up, "I like 'sponge' better."

"But is that really what she's able to do?" Trudy, the lover of all questions, asked. "I've wondered if she isn't absorbing others' talents but reflecting them. Wouldn't a better name be, Moon Girl or The Incredible Mirror?"

I snickered, but I was the only one.

Theo jumped in. "I knew a guy in Tallahassee who could mimic a person's voice and mannerisms to perfection. He did a great stand-up routine at this dive bar off west Tennessee Street."

Jerry held up her hand. "He has a point, everyone. Give him a minute. What's your point Theo?"

He shrugged. "No point. I just thought he did an incredible Tom Cruise. His Jack Nicholson was decent, too." He snapped his fingers. "Oh, and what about The Human Mime?"

All mimes are human.

"Wait," Theo corrected himself, "I've got a better one. Dangerous Duplicate."

That's horrib...wait. That's not bad.

"Or," he kept going, "Miss Facsimile."

And we're back to being horrible.

"If Sam can copy people, why not Xerox?" Kyle, who had no idea what they were talking about, wanted in on the game, too. "Or Replica?"

Trudy offered, "SheClone."

Angel suggested, "Diva Doppelgänger."

Cheekbones took a turn. "Double Trouble."

Gin, whose ideas were the worst, proposed, "The Gift Thief."

I looked at Hal, who continued smoking and squinting and watching me for some kind of reaction. I looked at Jackson, who had no facial expression but his skin looked unnaturally pink.

"That one fits, Gin." Jerry inserted her take. "She did take a ball gown that has yet to be returned."

"Excuse me. That's unfair." It was fair, actually. "I didn't steal it. I borrowed it." And had no intentions of returning it, which could be considered stealing. "You were the one who insisted I wear it, remember?"

I looked around the room for some semblance of sanity. And found none. What kinds of stupid names were these?

"And enough of these names. They're all horrible!" I thought about SheClone again. And Replica. They were so bad they were almost good. "Mostly horrible."

Everyone had stopped talking and sat, stonily, listening.

"Super Paper Towel? You can't be serious. The Incredible Mirror? Will I be putting on a magic show, too? These names are flat. Lifeless. And, honestly, embarrassing…for you guys. Lady Mop." I shook my head in disgust. "I'm not sure I want to know you people anymore."

No one said a word. When I glanced at Jackson for support, he continued that pink-tinted expressionless look, but he squeezed my hand in support.

Intense annoyance radiated from the group. Maybe I should have started my new role by being a tad less honest.

"But, I mean, the effort was there. So that's…" I had nothing, "something. And, besides, naming stuff isn't important. Right? Why don't we just stick with Sam for now." Still no response from anyone. "Or, I don't know, I guess Xerox isn't bad."

With that, everyone burst into laughter. Even Hal and his cigar smoke looked diverted.

Great. I'd been punked and fell for it.

Jackson, whose face had turned back to a normal shade after he also burst into laughter, dropped his arm around my shoulders. "Sorry, babe. They wanted to welcome you properly."

Gin, whose face was now red all over, stepped out from the group. He hadn't stopped laughing, but he was trying. I'd give him points for that.

"Sorry, Sammie. You're always going on and on about how we don't name stuff around here. We wanted to show you that we heard you. And we're going to do better. Starting with you."

When he cracked himself up again, I removed his points.

I turned to Jackson. "Just hilarious."

"An initiation of sorts. A way to make you feel part of the group. You're not mad, are you?"

I watched all of them laughing, smiling, happy, carefree, slapping each other on the back, repeating some of their lines, and congratulating each other on keeping me going for so long.

So, this was my new family, huh? These people would be my inner circle? The people I could trust with my life? Who I could turn to for support? This group of ridiculous yahoos?

Watching their self-congratulations and overwhelming pride at their prank, I burst out laughing. "Jackson, I already love it here."

16

If there's such a thing as a happiness hangover, I had it.

When I woke up the next morning in my room on the second floor of the log cabin, my eyes were scratchy from not getting enough sleep because the night had been too good to end. My voice was hoarse from laughing. My face was flushed with anticipation for the day ahead. I needed to sneeze, but that had nothing to do with happiness and everything to do with someone wearing a vanilla-scented perfume in here.

Blinking up at the slanted ceiling, I stretched, rubbed at my eyes, and turned on my right side. Laying in the next half bed was a young woman in her late 30s with hair so shockingly white it blended with the bed sheets. The morning sun, only now turning the indigo sky to an azure, caught the flutter of her eyelashes as she lay there blinking at me. When our eyes met, she smiled warmly.

It was too early to make new acquaintances, so I offered an awkward smile and turned over on my left side.

I get friendlier as the day goes on.

On the half bed to my left, another woman sat crosswise, watching me and scribbling notes in a brown leatherbound book. Her short legs dangled over the side of the bed while her back rested against the wall. She wore off-green cargo pants with zippered pockets on the thighs, a basic grey scoop neck T-shirt, and beige crocs on her feet. Her thick black hair was pulled back in a ponytail with a chunk of it shockingly red and hanging across one eye. The other eye kept darting from me to her notebook to me again. She looked like she'd been up for hours. If she was one of those absurdly early morning people who hit the ground running, I'd need to switch beds with someone else on the other side of the room.

When our eyes met, she scribbled more in her notebook.

I turned once again on my back and blinked at the ceiling. So, this is why fish stuck in bowls hide inside decorative rocks.

All of us ladies were sleeping youth-camp-style in an oversized room with six half beds in the second floor of the log cabin, but we weren't crowded. Even fully occupied, there was still room for a choreographed dance number by the seven Pontipee brothers and their seven brides.

I didn't even bother looking around to see if the other ladies in the room were watching me. Of course, they were.

Last night, Jackson had warned me to expect unfamiliar faces and an uncomfortable amount of attention. My training had officially begun, he said, and reinforcements were arriving to participate. It was a sidekick hoedown all in my honor.

"You're going to be the center of attention for a while," he'd told me last night after escaping the group to enjoy a few hours alone. "But it won't be negative attention, only…knowing you, more attention than you'll be comfortable receiving. And from a couple people you have yet to meet. But you'll love them."

This part didn't excite me. "Will I?"

Jackson had laughed. "Eventually."

After working up an appetite with their little prank last night, the sidekicks moved like a cloud of locusts into the dining room. Waiting inside were crock pots of hot chicken enchilada soup. All heated, ready, and prepared by none other than Jerry.

Usually, Trudy handled feeding the mob, I was told. As the group's master chef, as well as a professional caterer, delicious food was her gift. The normal, mortal kind. The kind that takes years of training, sweat and effort, hard work and long nights, and a passion to keep going even beyond the failures.

Instead of fixing dinner, she'd been assigned to babysit me all day. That left Jerry with kitchen duty, which ingratiated me to her even more.

"I've been boiling chickens all day, Samantha Eloise," Jerry told me last night, while everyone milled around the great room before dinner.

"Sorry?" I started to pat her consolingly on the shoulder but thought better of it. "Why was it so important for Trudy to be with me? What's her supernatural ability?"

"She's an encourager," Jerry headed back to the kitchen to finish meal prep, but not before grumbling, "and apparently you needed it."

When Trudy walked up to chat, I told her 'encourager' was not the ability I would have guessed for her. "You're inquisitive for a cheerleader."

She'd given me a mischievous look. "Am I?"

Hardy har.

"The questions were to help you think," Trudy explained. "Also, I really am a freelancer with *Oklahoma Now*, and I really do have to write an article about you, which I'll let you do for me. 850 words. Due Monday." She sipped on an iced tea with mint leaves mixed in it. "Make me look good."

She had a piece of mint stuck to a front tooth. I didn't tell her about it because I decided it made her look good.

"So, your ability. Basically, you have the power of positive thinking?"

She found the mint and swallowed it. "You really know how to mock a thing, don't you?"

I really did.

"I'm trying to understand, Trudy." When she gave me a suspicious look, I held up my hands in defeat. "Honest. Explain the encouragement thing to me. I won't mock."

Maybe.

"It isn't about positivity. Not positivity for positivity sake, anyway. That's too flimsy. Too weak. And only lasts as long as you can stay emotionally high and avoid reality. Hard things happen, Samantha. Horrible things. Illness, violence, loss, defeat, disappointment, loneliness, betrayal, you get my point. Being positive won't last long when standing on its own. It needs reasoning, support, legs."

I wasn't getting it, yet, and my face must have shown it.

"Okay, think of it this way," she continued. "When you feel defeated or overwhelmed, what do you need more than anything else to get through it?"

"Wine."

She gave me a dirty look.

"Sleep?"

She waved me off. "Hope, Samantha. People need hope. Real hope. Hope with teeth. And that's what I help them find."

I thought about being locked inside the refrigeration truck earlier today with her. Trudy believed I would eventually break the zip ties, but I didn't. All I remembered was the cold and the ache and the sharp sting every time I'd raise my arms, slam them into my hips, and the zip ties didn't break. After three tries, I was done. I didn't want to try anymore. It hurt too much, and it wasn't working, anyway.

But Trudy, somehow, convinced me to try again. And I knew, I just knew, this time it would work.

I looked at her with new appreciation. "You did your little hope mind warp on me today with the zip ties, didn't you?"

Trudy casually pushed her flaming hair away from her face. "Is that the only time?" She raised one eyebrow, smiled, and walked off.

Oh, she's good.

Jerry opened the dining room doors and yelled out a "come and get it while it's hot and don't spill any on the floor" from the threshold.

The sidekick crew surged forward. They were all buzzing with energy and excitement. More sidekicks were coming tonight. Getting everyone together didn't happen often, according to Jackson, so this was as much about my training as it was an excuse for a long weekend party with friends.

While they grabbed bowls, ladled their fill, and buzzed about the dining room to push tables together and toss around old stories, Jackson walked up to me and spoke quietly. "You hungry?"

I shrugged, taking in all the comradery. The family dynamic was obvious, including signs of dysfunction. They moved about as if they'd eaten together in this room and in this manner hundreds of times. Even Kyle found the group's rhythm and easily fell in step.

I wondered if this is what it looks like when you have unity of purpose and brotherly love.

"You want to go in?" Jackson asked, while we both haunted the threshold. "Or…"

I glanced at the heavy rose-colored women's sweater grasped in his hand. "Or?"

He motioned for me to follow him, then put his finger on his lips for me to stay quiet. I did exactly that because I'm great at taking direction.

Moving away from the doorway, he crossed the great room to an outside exit behind the staircase. Here, Jackson paused with his hand on the door handle.

"We're going to be surrounded by people for days. How about hanging out with just me tonight?" He looked me in the eyes. "You game?"

All I had to do was smile, and we escaped into the night.

Outside, he closed the door on the muted laughter, and we breathed in the vibrant, chilled air of freedom. The thunderstorm had passed, which meant the clouds had cleared out and left behind plummeting temperatures. Jackson draped the sweater over my shoulders, and I laced my arms inside.

As a balm for the now bitter breeze, the stars polished their light and started their evening show.

Instinctively, Jackson and I stood side-by-side and took the silence and calm and solitude in. We had so rarely been alone while both of us were conscious or one of us wasn't avoiding the other. The long-awaited truce had a sweet taste. We'd already crossed a lot of hurdles for these simple moments and more hurdles were coming.

But not yet. Right now was simply about being together.

"You up for a walk?"

"Mmm hmm." I smiled at the prospect. "Is this one of those super-fast excursions where I'm taught how not to run into trees? Or are you actually wanting to walk like normal people at a normal pace?"

Jackson clasped his hand with mine. "Neither. I think we should take it nice and slow."

∼

True to his word, Jackson slowly led the way.

Outside of the cabin's back door, the earth curved delicately down before leveling off, briefly, on a dirt path. It had the width needed for a four-wheeler to cruise comfortably and the tire tracks to prove it.

Solar-powered dim blue lights, dimpling the darkness like depressed lightning bugs, marked the outside edge of the path. They didn't give off enough wattage to illuminate much, other than the lack of ground on their outside perimeter. Stay on this side of the lights and we had a shadowed but solid walking path. Get on the other side of the lights, and you'd feel the wind in your hair as you plummeted off a steep decline.

At least that's what Jackson said. All I could see at this hour was another hill in the distance and a black hole between us.

Hand-in-hand, we heeded the lights advice and meandered along the tire ruts into the tree line. Once we crossed into the shadows and out of the moonlight, the cliff's edge eased into the night, the woods crowded around, and those solar-powered lights felt more soulful than mournful. They glided through the thick, slumbering terrain, marking the path like Tinker Bells wandering through the woods.

We walked along, quietly, letting their pale radiance draw us into the solitude of the night and the entrance into a new adventure. This time, together.

Wherever we were going, I didn't care. I only wanted to be where he was so here, there, or anywhere suited me fine. For Jackson, however, I sensed this wasn't solely a romantic walk through the woods. It was time for a talk, maybe one he didn't know how to start, so I let him work it out in his own time.

After a few minutes of listening to the wind squeeze between the trees, smelling the heightened earthy scent after a hard rain, feeling his heartbeat thumping in his fingertips, and knowing he would speak when he was ready, I heard Jackson clear his throat.

"I know you have a lot of questions." He continued before I could respond. "And rightly so. I have a lot to explain, a lot I want to tell you, a lot you need to know."

I nodded. "That's a lot of a lots."

"I'm going to do my best to give you whatever information you want. You've been patient, sort of."

"Hey."

"And I think it's time you knew...whatever you want."

"Thanks."

"Is there anything you want me to answer first? Or should I just dive in?"

I thought about that as the leaves crunched underfoot. The dense tree cover, though mostly barren, had obstructed the rain from soaking the ground. Outside the wooded area, the wetness covered everything.

You could smell that moist earth here, but not hear it. Instead of the slush and suck of mud at our feet, we crushed twigs and brittle leaves. The snapping, cracking, crumbling kept me company while I thought about his question.

What did I want to know? What was the most important mystery I needed solved? What information did I need so badly I'd gone through a ridiculous amount of risk and spent a ludicrous amount of energy in search of over the last month? What corner of the wrapping paper did I want to rip off, first?

Of all the unknowns, there was really only one thing that mattered. If he could answer that to my satisfaction, I didn't even need to know the rest.

Well, okay. Need, no. Want? Yes.

"Here's what I need to know more than anything else."

Jackson guided me around a broken limb. "Okay. What's that?"

We walked through scraggly tree shadow to scraggly tree shadow, "Is this the end of the secrets between us?"

Jackson didn't hesitate. "Yes."

"The end?"

"Yes."

"No more secrets?"

"None."

"Is that a promise?"

Jackson stopped and faced me. The low-watt lighting placed one half of his face in bluish light, the other in bluish shadow, while both of his eyes were inky bluish pools.

"You have my word, Samantha. No more secrets between us. You can know everything. I am, and will forever be, an open book to you. Whatever you want. I'll hold nothing back." His thumb caressed my cheek. "This is important for me, too, okay? I don't want anything between us anymore, either."

"No more secrets," I repeated.

"Never." He tugged at my hand to pull me in closer. "Here's what I need to know from you: will you promise the same?"

"Me?"

"You."

"Keeping secrets?"

He raised a skeptical eyebrow.

I knew where he was going with this. I was good at keeping certain types of secrets. Well, maybe not good. Good is a relative term. I was well-versed.

I didn't withhold secrets like the origins of my superpower, why I'd built a compound for sidekicks to come and feast on chicken enchilada soup, or what I'd been doing since waking up from a coma while the love of my life hunted me down, but I did frequently keep other information hidden. Information like my feelings, my failures, and my vulnerabilities. That's what he was talking about, and I knew it, and he knew I knew it.

"Sam?" Jackson sounded less than patient. I'd spent too long weighing out the answer. "This isn't the kind of question you mentally debate. It's a yes. Or it's a no."

"Right. That."

"Sam." He had that paternal tone in his voice. I hated that tone. He was going to make me stand here, face him, and share stuff. That tone made my legs fidgety. It made me want to stretch, limber up, and run away. Or, in cases where I couldn't, it made me want to tell a sarcastic joke, wait until he was distracted, and then run away.

I released his hand and took a step back. "I was thinking–"

He took a step forward. "I know you were."

I took another step back. "Now, wait. Let me finish. I was thinking, but not about what I wanted to hide from you."

He took another step forward. "Yes, you were."

I took another step back and ended up on a log. "Don't make this a trust thing."

He stepped up taking all the ground left. "It is a trust thing, and you know it."

"Hmph." Know. Who says I know anything? Sometimes, I can be a real dingbat.

Maneuvering around him, I continued down the path, leaving him behind while I considered all the ways to weasel out of this.

"I'm not keeping secrets." I threw over my shoulder. "Not your kind of secrets anyway. Actually, they aren't really secrets at all. They're more like…" Insecurities? Fears? Weaknesses I didn't want him to know about?

Yeah. That. Just little old weaknesses he didn't need to know about. Nothing big. Nothing important.

I ran into Jackson's chest.

"Hey!"

Slamming into immovable him threw off my balance. He grabbed my arms to steady me.

"How did you…never mind. You super jettisoned yourself into my path, didn't you?"

Jackson released my arms. "Yes."

"Why did you do—"

"So you'd look me in the eye," Jackson answered. "When you want to avoid a question, you avoid eye contact."

That's true. I do that. So, in keeping with tradition, I stared at his chest. Then, because I have no impulse control when it came to him anymore, I laid my head on it.

He gently rubbed my back. "You done rationalizing your issues, yet?"

So, he knew. Dang.

"No."

"It's time to stop running, sweetheart. You can't keep reverting to emotional avoidance every time you get scared." His low voice, heavy with deep vibration, tickled the top of my head.

"Besides, there's nothing to fear with me. You aren't the one protecting your heart anymore. That's my job, now. And I'll never betray you, Sam. I promise."

I believed him. I really did. I never believed that kind of physical and emotional safety existed in the world, but he had proven me wrong. Jackson Christy made me believe in true love. Not the swooning, butterflies in the stomach, kind. Although he did that. Not the passionate, can't keep my hands to myself, kind. Although he did that, too. But the sacrificial kind. The love that motivated a person to live their life in service to another or, if needed, to give their life for that person.

Sighing, I wrapped my arms around his waist, breathed in that smokey scent, felt his warmth soak into my bones, and held him as tight as I could.

"Okay," I squeezed my eyes closed, "I promise, too. No more secrets."

The walk from the log cabin to Jackson's house, in a normal walking pace, might take fifteen minutes. It took us an hour and a half to walk there and back. We stopped and talked and walked again. We ambled and rambled and meandered again. We strolled and told and sauntered again.

I channeled my inner Trudy and quizzed him. He answered dutifully, though briefly. The guy wasn't hiding anything. He was just a guy. He answered in dude speak. So, details were generalized, and thoughts were summarized. But I got the gist.

One thing that surprised me was that the sidekicks were far more numerous than previously thought. How many there were I could never get a precise number from him.

"Hundreds?"

He shrugged.

"Thousands?"

He considered it.

"You don't know?"

Mr. Popular passed it off. "I don't count my friends. Do you?"

"Some days, yes."

However many existed, more than the modest number chowing down on chicken enchilada soup, two more were headed here to partake in my training. Because my talent was mimicking the talents of others, Hal wanted to test and try the possibilities. He was the guy in charge of training everyone, which now included me. He was the Mickey to my Rocky. If Hal said to work out with a string tied around my ankles, I was expected to tie a string around my ankles.

"Do you know how much I love it that you used a Rocky reference? You might be my undoing, Samantha Addison."

I winked at Jackson. "Women weaken legs."

As for Hal's methods, I'd take that up with him at some point. He needed to explain his obsession with locking me inside vehicles.

He, along with Gabriel, aka Cheekbones, and Caroline, aka Jackson's stunning and brilliant hacker who acted as his Fred, had been busy doing reconnaissance from the moment Jackson fell into a coma. When Jackson woke up in the hospital last night, he immediately reached out to Hal for an information update and to find me. I'd disappeared from his hospital room and, since the date and time of my official training had been set by Hal weeks prior, Jackson knew Hal had something planned.

"So, you wake up from a three-day coma, make a call, and disappear?"

Jackson dismissed my incredulity. "I had things to do."

His 'things,' he explained, was getting to wherever I was so he could keep a watchful eye on me. Hal already had me locked in his trunk and was escorting me out of town to test my problem-solving skills. Apparently, he'd been testing my 'good judgement' skills when he'd talked me into accompanying him – a stranger at the time – to the parking garage. Then, he tested my observation skills when he'd had Gabriel walk up behind me, unnoticed, and shove me into the trunk.

Shockingly, I scored poorly in both categories.

"I talked him into letting me help you escape the trunk," Jackson pointed out, as if that made any sense at all.

"What are you talking about? I did that all by myself."

"You did," he agreed, "after I told you what to do."

Jackson's voice in my head, giving me ideas on how to escape, turned out to actually be Jackson's voice on speakerphone, broadcast from a cell Hal positioned in the back window.

"You weren't my imagination?"

He playfully squeezed my side. "I told you I wasn't."

Humph.

I asked Jackson what Hal had found out about the new thugs, Opie and Mr. Clean, and the old thugs, the twins, and how all four showed up in Eugene Percy's neighborhood this afternoon.

According to Hal, the twin thugs were still employed by the Widow McBride. The other guys were unknowns who, unbeknownst to Kyle, followed him back to me. No one knew who they were working for, yet, or their end game.

"What did you call them?" Jackson asked.

"Opie and Mr. Clean."

"You'll have to explain those nicknames to me later. So, Opie and Mr. Clean have been hired to grab you. It's obvious they weren't there to kill you, or they would have gotten to know me far better."

"It was obvious? Trudy had a bullet whiz by her head."

"By 'by' you mean a good four feet high and six feet to the right, landing squarely in the mass of a tree trunk? It wasn't even close. Mr. Clean also only fired once. If he'd wanted you dead, you would be. Well," he corrected, "no, you wouldn't be because I'd end him first. But he didn't know that. He could have attempted to take a another shot and didn't."

I stopped. "You were there?"

"Of course."

"Then why hide?"

Jackson grabbed both of my hands and held them. "I promised Hal I wouldn't interfere in his initial assessment…much. At the very least, I'd stay out of sight. He wanted 24 hours to evaluate you without me in the way. I gave him 20, and I never promised I wouldn't watch."

"Have you been around all day?"

"Yes."

"The casino?"

"Yes, I was there."

"Pickpocketing my phone?"

Jackson nodded.

"Do I even have to ask why?"

Jackson motioned for us to keep walking. "I knew what Hal was evaluating. I wanted to give you a clue."

"Which was?"

"Call someone. Get help coming. Don't try to outwit and outrun the situation on your own. You, of course, did exactly that." He squeezed my hand. "But you do look great in a cowboy hat."

We talked about who might be behind Opie and Mr. Clean, but he didn't know.

"Someone worse?" I asked. "Could there be another villain out there?"

He didn't need to consider the question before answering, "Sam, there's always another villain."

17

Becoming a superhero's sidekick wasn't for the faint at heart. This, I discovered before breakfast. Training entered stage two, and stage two, I quickly learned, was fun for everyone but me.

Hal gave me exactly ten minutes to shower, change, and get in the Cutlass. When I explained that curly hair does not yield in ten minutes, he responded with kindness and consideration.

"Ten, Addison. Ten." Hal stomped back down the stairs. "Wear a ballcap."

I didn't have a ballcap. What I did have was a backpack of my clothes Trudy had packed, unbeknownst to me, while we'd stopped at my house yesterday. She'd rummaged through my belongings while I'd been in the shower removing twigs from my hair.

The clothing selection was decent. She'd managed to grab at least two pairs of my favorite jeans, a few sweaters, and enough underclothes to last me until the return of Haley's Comet. My knee-high boots paired well with a grey long-sleeved undershirt and a fuzzy pink sweater that always reminded me of hydrangea petals.

The hair went into a ponytail, with curly tendrils throwing little fits around my head and down my neck for rushing them into the day.

I met Hal in the Cutlass, where Cheekbones…er, Gabriel, sat behind the wheel and Gin sat in the backseat.

"So, you're the first sidekick guinea pig, eh." I'd teased Gin.

"That's me, Super Sponge." His beard looked dusted in Tang in the morning light. "Get in."

Jackson explained last night that my first phase of training – the assessment – was complete.

"Assessment. Is that what your people call locking me in a trunk? Trying to run me off the road? Pursuing me through a casino? Kidnapping me outside of a hospital? Locking me in a refrigerated van? And sending a spy to tag along with me all day?"

Jackson gave me one of his slow smiles. "Yes."

The second phase involved field tests. Basically, I was assigned a sidekick, given a challenge, and expected to emulate their ability. Gin was up, first. And, according to Hal, the challenge was to help Gin on morning playground duty at West Fillmore Elementary School.

"Playground duty? Really?"

Gin was an elementary math teacher, which was news to me. I thought he spent all day tinkering with his van and growing facial hair. His ability, which was to calm mobs of people, basically equated to crowd control. On a playground of third and fourth graders, that shouldn't be too hard.

"Keep an eye on the kids," Gin's own eyes continually roamed, "and make sure they're staying safe and getting along. That's it. It's pretty easy."

Gin told me this while we stood in a grassy section of the school playground where kids tossed one thing or another over, next to, and beside our heads.

"Keep an eye on." I nodded once. "Got it."

I focused on one kid and visually followed him from the big toy to the monkey bars to the tether pole and down the slide, all within three seconds. Watching bullets ricochet took less eye movement.

An hour later, Hal, Gabriel, and I arrived back at the cabin. Gin stayed behind to teach his math class and to clean up the mess I made.

When we pulled into the cabin's gravel driveway, Hal turned around in his seat. "Are you still depressed? Because you look depressed."

"I'm not depressed."

"You sure? Rafael told me you were depressed."

"Yeah, well, Rafael is a real gossip for a fourth grader."

Hal clicked his tongue and exited, followed by Gabriel.

I stayed in the Cutlass for a minute alone. The first field test hadn't gone well, but no one was perfect. And, really, how bad was it? Kids cry all the time.

What I wanted to do was call Jackson. To tell him about what went wrong. For him to tell me it wasn't that bad. But I reconsidered. He had a busy morning of playing coma catch-up at work, and I didn't want to distract him. Thankfully, Karen, his assistant, had visited him every evening at the hospital to give him an update on the day's work. At the time, I thought it was pointless. Sweet. But pointless. Unbeknownst to me, he heard every word.

Karen was really good at her job.

Jackson also had to drop off that manila envelope of Fred's I burgled from Eugene Percy's house yesterday. Also, there was a certain raincoat I'd borrowed from a certain garage that Jackson was going to return today without, hopefully, getting caught. And, lastly, he promised to check in before noon to see how everything was going.

He was a busy boy.

What I wouldn't do was disappoint him, yet. So, I didn't call. Maybe the next field test would go better.

With that in mind, I hunted down Hal and found him in the dining room drinking coffee with Jerry.

"Addison, come in." He motioned his white head toward a chair. "Have a seat. Jerry's your next field test."

Sorry, Jackson. Disappointment is a sad fact of life.

~

"Samantha, you aren't concentrating."

I was, though. Sort of.

"How do you know, Jerry? Can you tell a person isn't concentrating simply by looking at them?" I drew hearts in a dusting of spilled sugar on the table.

Her mouth twisted. "Yes."

I dusted off my hands. "Fine. I stopped concentrating ten minutes ago. We've been at this for over an hour. Maybe you can force your visions to happen, but I can't. My déjà vu flashes come when they want and not when they don't."

Jerry settled against the wooden-backed dining room chair to study me. Her little chin stuck out from her soft, fleshy face, but that was nothing new. Short, white curls curved this way and that, some around her face, some around her ears, some around a figment of its own imagination. She looked toasty and overly holidayed in a red sweater with Christmas trees embroiled down the sides. It was early in the season for ugly sweaters, which I told her while not realizing she wasn't wearing that sweater ironically.

"Let's try one more time, okay? Then, we'll take a break." Jerry waited for my nod. "What am I going to serve you for breakfast?"

I perked up. "I'm going to get breakfast?"

"Yes. After you tell me what it is."

For over an hour, Jerry and I had been watching Hal and Gabriel play cards on the other side of the window. They sat on the porch, with a footstool between them, drinking coffee, betting with and eating oatmeal cookies, and playing poker. We sat in the dining room and fogged up the glass.

For three games, Jerry asked me to concentrate on the game and see what future plays I could call. Plays I could "see" in advance. It turns out that I couldn't "see" anything, but I could guess that Hal was good at bluffing, and Gabriel favored four of a kinds.

Those cookies looked amazing. "I would love some breakfast."

"Then, let's try that. Imagine I'm bringing out a tray. I'm setting it in front of you. What can you see?"

I concentrated on that visual. I imagined Jerry walking through the kitchen door carrying a tray. I imagined that tray stacked with food. I imagined the smell and warmth of that food.

"Nothing."

She knocked on the window, signaling to Hal and Gabriel the test was over.

Hal hollered back, "In a minute." He held his cards, while never breaking eye contact with Gabriel. "Gabe's about to give me back my cookies."

Jerry turned back to me. "We'll let them finish up. In the meantime, how about that breakfast?"

My stomach growled a yes.

She disappeared into the kitchen and returned with a tray burdened down with a slice of ham and cheese quiche, a bowl of melon squares, and hot peppermint tea in an adorable white cup with a gold-painted rim. She slid it in front of me.

"Eat up. You've got a long day ahead of you."

I grabbed a fork but hesitated. As empty as I felt, the pit in my stomach got more attention.

"Jerry, something is bothering me."

She perked up. "Oh?"

"I don't want to disappoint Jackson."

"Oh that." She perked back down.

"So far, I'm failing. Gin's field test was a disaster. Who knew kids didn't like scary stories?"

"Everyone."

"All children love R.L. Stine."

"Apparently not."

"And now my second field test has tanked. My déjà vu flashes, or visions, as you call them, are usually only one thing: my impending death. Not that it isn't handy, but rather useless for everyone else. You can see other events. Things happening to other people. How do you do it?"

Jerry stirred her hot tea absentmindedly. "It's a discipline, Samantha. It's about training your mind to think about others. Not only about yourself."

"Ouch."

"I don't mean that harshly."

That's a first. "No?"

She smiled, enjoying herself. "Not this time." She set down her spoon, clanging it on the saucer. "It really is about directing your mind outside of your viewpoint. Outside of your experiences. Outside of your concerns. Outside of yourself."

"And you can do this at will?"

Jerry hemmed and hawed on that one. "Once upon a time, yes. I'm getting older, though." She smoothed down her Christmas sweater. "I know I don't look it, but I'm not as young and feisty as I once was. It's time for someone new to fill this role. I think that someone is you."

Maybe. If it didn't involve poker.

"You never had the eye twitching, though, did you? My eyes always twitch before a vision."

Jerry shook her head no. "No eye twitching. I got cramps. Be thankful for the twitching."

"Brutal. Do you still?"

"No. They go away as you get more comfortable with the visions.

It's a sign your body is fighting the unknown. The more you relax, the more you grow confident in your gift, the less they'll appear."

I picked up my fork again. "Cramps. That sucks."

"Truly." Jerry smiled, sipping at her tea.

It occurred to me this was the first time she and I had carried on a conversation that wasn't laced with hostility. Or competitiveness. She wasn't trying to outsmart me, and I wasn't on guard with her. We'd crossed into amiable territory. What a huge relief. If no other progress came out of this day, I could at least tell Jackson his grandmother and I had a breakthrough.

I cut into the flaky quiche crust, sent a silent appreciation to Trudy for her skills and to Jerry for her kindness, and took a bite.

Hmmm. Weird. My chewing slowed. This didn't taste right. Had it spoiled?

"Jerry, this tastes funny…"

The next moment, I found myself still sitting in the Cutlass outside.

~

"You did what to my food?!"

I paced in front of the dining room table where Hal sat drinking coffee, Jerry sipped her tea, and Gabriel kicked back with a cookie. When I walked inside, that's where I found the three conspirators, and that's where they'd remained while explaining how I'd passed my second field test.

"You had a vision of the quiche. So, that's a win. But the fact it was the quiche, that's too bad," Jerry said, right after telling me the quiche had been poisoned.

"Why are you always slipping things into my food, Jerry? It's not normal."

"And yet here you are perfectly fine." She flitted her hand at me. "But still whining."

"Hal, you want to jump in here? Did you approve of the poisoning? Speaking of," I turned back to Jerry, "what was in the quiche? More Ambien? A dash of valerian root?"

Jerry shook her white curls. "Solanine."

"Solanine?!"

At this angle, the morning light spilled through the broad pane of the dining room window and backlit Jerry's white curls. She looked like an angel. Of death.

"Jerry, that's poisonous!"

Jerry looked at Hal. "She's smart, but also slow."

Hal set down his mug. "Addison, we've tried other avenues to goad your talent into activating. Encouragement. Freedom. Guilt. Sense of duty. Only fear works. Now, why is that?"

I crossed my arms. "Could it be that my life has been a nonstop nightmare for over a month? And I'm running on pure adrenaline?"

Hal skipped over my response. "Jerry spent an hour…or, planned to spend an hour…coaching you before resorting to the breakfast question. Correct me, if I'm wrong, Jerry."

"That's right, Hal. The quiche was the last resort. If she ended up with the quiche, that meant I'd exhausted all other motivators to spur her into action. If she got the pancakes, that meant she'd succeeded at least once."

I pivoted in my pacing and stomped back. "What was in the pancakes, Jerry?" I raised my eyebrows. "Ricin?"

She sipped her tea. "Blueberries."

"Addison, we don't like that fear is your prompt, but we have to work with what we're given. You've got to be trained, and this is what lights a fire under you."

"How about bribes? Have you tried offering me large sums of cash? Because I'm thinking that'd get me going."

Gabriel snickered and dug into another cookie.

"Samantha," Jerry lasered her cloudy blue eyes on me, "if you don't like it, change it. No one is forcing you to only focus when you're threatened. Stop making that choice."

I tapped my foot on the floor and the tapping increased. "I liked the you in my vision better."

Jerry opened her mouth, thought better of whatever biting response she'd planned, and exhaled. "Look, Samantha, I know this feels harsh. But I'm trying to protect you and Jackson and anyone else who might be involved one day down the road. Your visions…"

"Flashes."

"Whatever you want to call them. They're dangerous. You're only seeing immediate threats. Not final outcomes. You're acting on those threats," she held up her hand to stop my retort, "understandably, but without any idea of the secondary repercussions you could be causing. It's risky. And unwise."

I stopped tapping my foot and uncrossed my arms. This sounded important. "What do you mean by 'final outcomes'?"

"Final outcomes. The end results." Jerry thought it over. "Okay, let me explain it like this, let's say you get a flash that you're about to hit a deer in the road. What do you do?"

"Slam on my brakes."

"Right. And that keeps you from hitting the deer. But what else does it do?"

I didn't understand the question. "It..." I had no idea, "stops me from hitting the deer. I don't know what you mean."

Jerry twisted her cup half a turn on her saucer, then half a turn back, as if the answer was kept inside a safe, and she was rehearsing the combination.

"You've just introduced a new variable into the timeline. You've changed what was going to happen to what you decided should happen. You don't get to make that decision and then ignore the ripple effect. So, you slam on your brakes and..."

Jerry knew I had no clue, and now I knew I had no clue, too.

"There are all these variables you have to consider when you mess with possible futures, Samantha. What if, when you slam on your brakes, a vehicle behind you slams into you killing the driver. You've saved your life, but now taken theirs. Or you slam on your brakes and spook the deer, who runs into oncoming traffic, causing someone else to hit it, instead."

Considering all the times I've already acted on a flash, did that mean I could have hurt someone already with this ripple effect?

"Samantha, sit down. You've turned a ghastly pale color." Jerry impatiently pointed to a chair, which Gabriel jumped up and slid behind me.

"Let her off the hook, Jerry," Hal prompted. "You're making the girl panic."

Jerry shifted in her chair. "There's another 'or,' Samantha. So, relax. Or..." she dragged out, "you slam on your breaks, the deer runs into the woods, and you continue down the road without mishap. My point is that you could set other bad events into motion, not that you have."

"Have I?"

Jerry shook her head. "No." She blotted her mouth on a napkin. "I wouldn't let you. As long as I can protect you, I have and I will. But my time for all this is coming to a close." She held up her hand to stop me from asking when. "Not immediately, but eventually. And you've got to be ready to handle this. You've done amazingly well so far."

I raised my eyebrows in shock. A compliment from Jerry.

"You've adapted. You've reacted quickly to your visions. You've saved Jackson's life and Gin's, too. I'm impressed."

My mouth dropped open.

"But you've been playing with fire without knowing it burns. And it's time you knew." She reached over, placing her bony hand on mine. "If you don't learn to control this ability now, you're going to burn the house down." Her hand squeezed mine. "Possibly the neighborhood, too." She patted my hand twice and pulled back. "And maybe start a forest fire."

Goodbye, again, breakthrough.

18

Pain does not require a corresponding visual to be pain. That's why no scratch, cut, bruise, or abrasion will ever look as bad as it feels.

"It doesn't look that bad."

Trudy squinted at me from her perch on the couch because moving closer would require effort.

I pulled the collar of my sweater up and plopped the ice pack back on my shoulder, all while glaring at her.

"Shouldn't you be in the kitchen frying up some hash browns with hemlock?"

My first day of hands-on training was officially at a close. I was starving. And a little broken. The heat in the great room's fireplace relaxed my muscles and melted my ice pack. I couldn't decide which element helped more, so I let them duke it out.

"I don't think Hal plans to poison your food again. He likes to keep things unpredictable." Trudy curled her legs under her and swirled a glass of red wine. She looked content and completely unconcerned about my slow starvation.

"Great. So, about that food again. Isn't that your area?"

Trudy sipped her wine. "We're having a baked potato bar. It's all set. Only waiting on the potatoes to finish in the oven."

My stomach responded with more grumbling. "And that would be?"

"Soon, Samantha." Trudy checked her watch. "Another twenty minutes and we can eat."

Twenty minutes. No problem. I could hack not eating for twenty more minutes. I'd hacked not eating all day.

After the poisoning at breakfast, I'd passed on any offers from Jerry to fix me a fresh breakfast. Poison in my food makes me lose my appetite.

"How about some scrambled eggs? Something simple," she suggested earlier. "It'll be perfectly safe."

For some completely unfounded reason, I didn't want her touching my food.

"Thanks, but I'm fasting."

I left Jerry in the dining room and went in search of food elsewhere.

Jackson came by to check in and left again. He walked in about the time Hal and Jerry were wrapping up field test number two and explaining how part of my training would involve overcoming my fear of death.

"Huh? How do you overcome such a thing? It's the fear. All other fears sprout from that one," I explained.

Hal, who was on his third cup of coffee and fifth cookie, spoke between grabbing bites. "Maybe 'overcoming' isn't the right way to explain it. It's more about accepting it as a possibility."

"During training?"

He sipped his coffee. "Unlikely."

"Unlikely, Hal? I was looking for an 'of course, not.'"

Hal reached for the last cookie, then stopped to offer it to me. I waved him off. I wouldn't be accepting any food from him, either.

"Addison, you've got a decision to make now. Living this life, being with Jackson, it won't be safe. That's the reason he's been pushing so hard for your training. He knows the risks. The question is, now that you're getting a glimpse at those risks, do you want to move forward?" He leaned back as if this wasn't the worst question anyone had ever asked me. "Because you can back out now. There's no obligation here. We'll help you with this little Mrs. McBride problem." Little? "And you can go back to your normal routine. You can choose the safe life."

"You mean, if I walk away from Jackson."

Hal tipped his head in agreement and popped the last cookie in his mouth. "Now's the time to decide. If you've got doubts, voice them now."

I stared at my fingernails. Hal needed an answer. Here was my out. I could walk away. Go back home. Snuggle into my comfortable life. Take up a new hobby. Even meet another guy. Live quietly. Peacefully.

Without concerning myself with the state of the world, the people victimized, or the precious few fighting to make a difference.

There wouldn't be any more field tests. Or failures. No more abilities to mimic or assassination plots to survive. And all I had to do to be free of it all was walk away from Jackson.

"Okay, Hal."

Hal watched me over his coffee cup. Jerry, who'd been sitting quietly during the exchange, stopped fiddling with her tea. Gabriel, who never said anything, grew even quieter.

Hal set down his mug gently. "Okay?"

"Okay," I took a deep breath. "Here's what we're going to do." I looked him, Jerry, and Gabriel in the eyes. "We're going to stop sitting here stuffing our faces and get to my next field test. And you will never, ever ask me this again. If I have to accept the risk of death to be with Jackson, so be it." I leaned forward to make sure they understood. "I will never leave him. Never. Do we understand each other? He is my life. So, if we're done here, go toss some strychnine in my lunch and let's get back to work."

Jerry slid lower in her chair, relaxing all her muscles. Gabriel winked at me. Hal looked past me and said, "You get all that?"

I turned around to find Jackson, back in his jeans and polo, this one the color of mint leaves, leaning against the dining room entrance. He looked like he'd been there a while. His arms were crossed. His shoulder rested against the frame. He looked casual, until you reached his eyes. They reflected a deeper end of the ocean than I'd ever seen before. And they never left me.

"I heard," he answered Hal.

As soon as I saw him, I scooted back my chair, crossed the room, and threw myself in his arms. He held me tightly, while dropping his face into the crook of my neck.

Behind me, chairs scraped on the floor. The general rustle of movement told me everyone was on their way out of the room.

Hal walked past us. "I'll give you guys a minute." He left to prepare whatever mayhem came next.

With everyone gone, I snuggled into Jackson and sighed. "They've been watching too much 'Arsenic and Old Lace,'" I mumbled into his shoulder. "Wait until you hear what was in the quiche."

"Samantha?"

I pulled back to look at him. Jackson leaned down and kissed me urgently, but briefly. His mouth was hot and demanding and then gone.

Bummer. I wasn't in the gone mood.

Jackson spoke with a breathiness in his voice I'd never heard before. "Samantha, I love you so much I'm"–he clutched his heart–"crazy with it."

Gently, I touched his cheek. I understood exactly what he meant.

"Babe, considering this house of fruitcakes, crazy will blend right in."

~

Jackson promised to return by dinner. After he was gone, I found Hal by following the smell of something cinnamony and nutmegy and buttermilky into the study behind the fireplace. It was an oblong area with the three outside walls taken entirely by one window and one long, cushy window seat topped with solid grey, rust, and turquoise pillows. Under the windows, Jackson constructed built-in bookshelves stuffed with every reading genre. And by the bookshelves were two wingback chairs. And by the two wingback chairs was a floor lamp. And by the floor lamp was a table. And on that table was a basket of muffins.

Yum…muffins.

"Addison, come over here and meet your next assignment."

Hal stood at the end of the room chatting with the 30-something dark-haired note-taking girl, who'd been watching me sleep this morning. The red chunk of hair I'd noticed earlier was now threaded into a thick French braid.

"Addison, this is Lauren." Hal made introductions. "Lauren, this is Samantha. Get her ready. She's…" He held out the 's' unsure what word came next. "Sssspecial."

That's one way of putting it.

Hal turned back to me. "See how well you do mimicking her ability." Before strolling out of the room, he threw over his shoulder, "You're going to need it."

I sat down on the window seat near Lauren, who sat cross-legged with her notebook in her lap, a drab olive green bookbag next to her thigh, and a half-eaten muffin in her hand.

I couldn't take my eyes off the muffin.

"Well, mold me and make me, Lauren. What's your ability? And where do I start mimicking?"

Lauren reached into her bookbag, pulled out a softcover book, and handed it to me.

"Here. Read this." She took an oversized bite from the muffin.

I salivated over what I imagined that muffin tasting like and asked if she planned on finishing it.

"Yes."

"Are you sure? Because I could finish it for you if you're full."

I don't usually eat after people I just met, but this was an extenuating circumstance. What if the muffins in that basket were tainted with nicotine poison? What if it was another test?

"I'm not full." Lauren popped the remaining muffin in her mouth. "Now I'm full."

I remember being full once. About a thousand years ago.

I looked at the book she'd handed me. "'The Oklahoma Wilderness Survival Guide: How Not To Die in Rural America. Volume forty-seven.' There needed to be forty-six previous volumes? How dangerous is this state?" Lauren didn't answer. "I'll get started on this tonight."

She shook her head. The movement dislodged her heavy black eyeglass frames from the bridge of her nose, causing them to slip lower. "You need to read it now."

Lauren had a confidence about her that made you feel like obedience was your only option. She wasn't flashy or loud or stern. She seemed pragmatic, as if once she decided to say something, it was truth, and once she decided to do something, it was done. She was a woman with her own mind, and that mind, churning away behind those unblinking green eyes, wanted me to read that book now.

"You want me to read all of it now?"

Lauren delicately pushed her frames back into position. "Yes. Now."

"Right. Okay." I cracked it open. "This could be interesting. For someone. Who cared about this topic. Probably."

Her green eyes narrowed. "Hal said you weren't good at taking instruction."

I snorted. "Oh, I take it. I take it and shove it where…" I caught myself, "...it's easily accessible for future reference. Like on a bookshelf. Or a handy coffee table."

Was she buying this?

"Anyway," I moved on, "let's get to reading this fascinating book you've chosen. Should I read it out loud? Or silently to myself?"

Lauren's unblinking eyes finally blinked. "You're a peculiar kind of special, aren't you?"

∼

Peculiar didn't quite cover it. Then again, I wasn't the one wanting to electrocute me. Lauren was.

"Now, fair warning, it could stop your heart."

From her book bag, Lauren had pulled an AED, abbreviated for 'automatic external defibrillator,' or, as I like to call them, electrocution on the go, and decided to use it on me. I'd been reading the book for an hour with no appearance of mimicking happening, and she believed this would jump start the show and tell.

According to Lauren, her super ability was basically "knowing stuff." And after reading four chapters, I should know stuff, too. I should also be able to recollect every factoid I'd ever consumed throughout my entire life and, despite her continual asking, no I could not name all the state capitals.

"If you could do it in the fifth grade, you should be able to do it now. If, that is, you're picking up on my ability, which you obviously are not."

Lauren remembered everything she read, saw, and heard. I asked her if that meant she basically had a photographic memory, and she said, "Yes, if you could get a doctorate in photographic memory."

I don't think you can.

So, I read, and she periodically quizzed me about what I'd read. I did remember patches of info, which meant I didn't have a super ability, but I did have basic reading comprehension.

"Keep going," she'd told me earlier, and went back to scribbling.

"Chapter Five," I started reading where I'd left off. "It was the best of times, it was the worst of times, it was the age of wisdom, it was the age of foolishness..."

Lauren looked up from her notebook. "It doesn't say that."

No kidding.

"Lauren, I think we both know this isn't working. Is there something more you can tell me about your ability? Or maybe you have an idea of something we can try? I'm open to ideas."

She closed her notebook. "I didn't want it to come to this, but there is something we could try."

She placed her hand on the top of my head and rubbed it vigorously. In response, my hair came out of the ponytail and stretched out with static electricity. A few strands stuck to the side of my face, while others crackled as Lauren removed her hand.

"Lauren, let me amend"—I fought against my hair with my two hands but my hair had a bigger army—"I'm not open to all ideas."

She gave me a minute to smooth my hair down and cinch it back into a ponytail. Then, the questions started again. "What's the state capital of Minnesota?"

I was done with this.

"Honolulu." I snapped the wilderness survival book closed. "Explain to me why you messed with my hair, and then tell me what you aren't telling me. Because you obviously aren't telling me something."

Lauren set aside her notebook. "From the data Hal collected and provided me on your ability, I've concluded it requires high doses of energy to engage."

"Data?" I snorted. "What, did Hal provide a spreadsheet?"

She blinked. "Yes."

Oh. Okay.

"Now, instead of manipulating your bpm, I wanted to attempt an external recreation to spare the extra workload on your heart by not increasing myocardial oxygen demand or causing vasoconstriction."

"Right. Of course. We wouldn't want that." I'm assuming.

"So," she shrugged helplessly, "I gave static electricity a shot. It was unlikely, but the hypothesis needed to be tested."

"It's always good to test those hypothesis'es. Hypotheses? Hypothi."

Lauren shook her head, disappointed.

What she said sounded similar to what Jude Likow...Wiklok...Kozliv...What's-His-Name said when he swapped my pain pills for Viagra. Did she know about that? Had it been included on Hal's spreadsheet?

"Lauren, this feels familiar. Did you hear about the Jude guy who did his own unsanctioned test on me Friday night?"

She said she didn't. "What's his last name?"

"He didn't have one." I told her the whole story, including how the pills worked for a while but mostly gave me a temporary high where I heard David Bowie singing in my head.

When I started the story, Lauren had resumed scribbling down notes. When I mentioned Bowie, that caught her attention.

"Cool. Like, 'Fame?' And 'China Girl'?"

"Well…"

"And 'Let's Dance,'?"

"Um…"

"Oh, and 'Space Oddity,'?"

"Sure. Why not. The point, Lauren"—we needed to get back on track here—"is that manipulating my heart works, but it's short-lived. Scaring me half to death had a bigger impact than drugging me."

Lauren wrote that down. "Tell me about that. This Jude person tried scaring you, too?"

I told her about how he ran far ahead of Theo and I at the park and we lost sight of him. Then, without warning, he ran out of the woods screaming like a madman. At that point, I hadn't needed pills or static electricity. I bolted.

"I see," she scribbled more. "And that burst of fear kickstarted your ability. Did it stick around longer? Or seem easier to access afterward?"

Come to think of it, yes. While being held with the other sidekicks in that office building, I'd used my déjà vu flash to see one of the twin thugs shoot Gin. Then, I'd used my speed to beat the crap out of them. Two abilities accessed back-to-back. I couldn't remember ever doing that before.

"I guess it did."

"Great." Lauren rummaged in her bookbag and pulled out the defibrillator. "Now, this might hurt a little."

∼

I didn't believe she'd really use that thing on me, until she turned it on, and the automated verbal instructions started. "Begin by removing all clothing from the patient's chest."

"Uh, Lauren, I think this might be taking it too far."

"Cut clothing if needed. Look carefully at the pictures on the white adhesive pads," the female defibrillator voice instructed, while Lauren adeptly removed the white adhesive pads.

"Seriously, Lauren, I'm not open to this idea."

She held the adhesive pads up and moved in closer. "Lift your shirt please. The pads have to be adhered directly to your skin."

I scooted back as far as the window seat allowed. "This is crazy, Lauren."

"I think we've given your ability long enough. It's time to get proactive. Now, are you going to cooperate, or do I need to call Gabriel in here to assist me?"

"He wouldn't."

Lauren didn't blink, but I did.

"Okay, strike that," I swallowed, "he would."

"Lift the shirt, please. This will only take a minute, if it works."

"But Lauren, what if–"

She cut me off. "Stop worrying. I know CPR. If you flatline, I can bring you back. Just don't go toward any light, okay?"

I pulled my knees into my chest protectively. "Saint Paul!" I remembered. "The capital of Minnesota is Saint Paul."

Lauren stopped. "What about Vermont?"

"Montpelier."

She stopped moving toward me, but didn't put down the pads. "Arkansas, Delaware, Iowa?"

"Little Rock, Dover, Des Moines."

"Maine, Maryland, Michigan?"

"Augusta, Annapolis, Lansing."

The floor lamp flickered, buzzed, and popped, leaving the study lit with only natural light.

Lauren noted the electrical interference with a "cool." She pulled back. "Now, what are some helpful tips in preventing a scorpion sting when outside?"

My mind flipped through the first four chapters of Lauren's book. Slowly, the pages stopped flipping, and the information appeared as clearly as if I'd been handed a photograph.

"Scorpions dig out burrows under rocks, logs, wood piles, and piles of leaves or other organic debris, so exercise caution when lifting up old tree bark, wood, rocks, or anything that has been on the ground for even a few hours. They're nocturnal but can be disturbed during the day. If one stings you, it's best to wash the area with antibacterial soap, apply ice and hydrocortisone cream, and prepare yourself for the coming pain, numbness, swelling, and stinging sure to follow. Unless it's a striped bark scorpion, then prepare for hell."

Lauren sat back with nearly a smile on her face. Or a close facsimile thereof.

"See?" She packed the AED and placed it back in her bookbag. "That wasn't so bad, now was it?"

I wanted to strangle her with her French braid.

"You wouldn't have really used that thing on me, would you?"

Lauren didn't blink again, but, again, I did.

"Never mind."

Finished packing it away, Lauren returned to her corner of the window seat, placed her notebook back in her lap, and scribbled more while talking to me.

"I wouldn't have because, unfortunately, an AED automatically analyzes the heart rhythm to determine if, and how much, of a shock is required. So, unless you really were having a cardiac arrest, you were safe." With her free hand, she rummaged in her bookbag and pulled out a stun gun. "This, however, doesn't have any such restrictions."

With that, the stun gun was shoved back into her bookbag. There was no telling what else she held in that bag, so I kept my distance. We sat in silence, me combing through my mind for forgotten factoids, her writing feverishly until her hand instantly stilled, as if crossing a hard-fought finish line.

"You still seem freaked." Lauren rested against the pillows with her notebook safely tucked against her breasts. "Aren't you happy?"

"Happy?" I grabbed a rust-colored pillow the size of a small child and hugged it to me. It would serve as a good shield should Lauren attack again. "What should I be happy about?"

Lauren furrowed her forehead, confused. According to her calculations, I should be elated.

"Your ability worked," she stated plainly. "We kicked it on. You mimicked my ability. These are all good outcomes for a field test. Why wouldn't you be happy?"

Well…let me think.

"To get that 'good outcome,'" I air quoted, "you threatened me with electrocution, Lauren. That seem like a win to you?"

"But it worked," she pointed out.

"I don't think I'm making myself clear here. Let me try again: fear is not a positive." I over enunciated the last five words. "This is not how I want this to work. So, every time I'm in a situation where my ability is needed, I'll need to crank the handle of a jack-in-the-box to get going? Who wants to live in fear?"

Lauren assessed me with those owl-like green eyes of hers. "Yes, Samantha. Who would?"

19

Time may not wait for anyone, but when you're hungry it may loiter before dinner.

"You're sure it hasn't been twenty minutes, yet?"

"Yes, Sam. I'm sure," Trudy glanced at her watch. "Still seven to go."

We were still in the great room before dinner, and I was still starving.

"If you took the potatoes out of the oven seven minutes early, would it be that big of a deal? How important is seven minutes to a potato?"

Trudy went back to sipping her wine. "If you're that hungry, go into the kitchen and grab a snack. Don't sit there making yourself miserable."

"I'm not miserable." I was. "I can wait." I couldn't.

No one was stopping me from eating, but I preferred to eat what everyone else was eating while everyone else was eating it. Hal and Jerry hadn't intended to scare me off food, but I wasn't ready to trust a déjà vu flash to protect me from overdosing on belladonna.

"Hey, Samantha," Trudy glanced behind her, making sure no one else was around, "can I ask you something?"

I choked on my own saliva. "You're kidding, right?" All this woman ever did was ask me somethings.

"I'm serious," she glanced behind herself again, then slid off the couch and sat next to me on the fireplace hearth. "I wanted to know about…"–she looked around and lowered her voice–"Kyle."

Ah.

"What about"–I gave the same surreptitious look around the room–"Kyle?"

Her eyes narrowed. "You're not going to make this easy on me, are you?"

I shook my head. "Doubtful."

She flipped her red hair off her shoulder. "Fine. Have your fun. I'm just not sure what to make of the guy."

"What's got you confused about him?"

Trudy settled in, leaning toward me so she could keep her voice low. "Well, he's different. Very stubborn, but I don't mind that, actually. I like a man who can hold his own. And opinionated, but I don't mind that either. If you haven't noticed, I can be opinionated, too."

"Hmmm," was the only answer I gave. "So, what's the problem?"

"Well, I think we have a connection."

It looked that way to me, too.

"But I'm afraid learning about my"–she searched for a description–"extended, uh, family and our special, um, talents might freak him out, you know?"

I clarified her question. "So, you're worried that being part of an oddball group of misfits with heightened abilities on the superhero spectrum, who like to get together at their super-secret clubhouse in the woods will scare him off?"

She halfheartedly shrugged. "Yeah?"

I dismissed it. "Nah."

She silently contemplated.

"Besides," I added, "what man wouldn't be drawn to a woman with the superpower of pep?"

She slanted her greens at me. "Must you?"

"Look, this is a lot to take in. It's a lot for me, and I'm one of you oddball sidekick people. Kyle got dragged into this by being my friend. Nothing more. So, yeah, it might seem like a lot to take in all at once."

Trudy slumped, understanding it but still disappointed.

"However," I added, "Kyle is a weird dude, too. The guy may not have a particular super ability, per say, but he's bizarrely talented. Do you know anyone else who can identify the make and model of a vehicle by the sound of the engine?"

Trudy shook her head. "No."

"Or name the individualistic smells of a house while walking past it?"

Trudy shook her head again.

"Or navigate by the creases and potholes in the road?"

"He can do that?"

"Or memorize the layout of a building he's never been in before, never visibly seen, by walking through it only once?"

Trudy, Jackson and I had given Kyle a walking tour of the log cabin last night before we all retired to our rooms. It was to help Kyle get a sense of where he was being held against his will.

"That really was incredible." She considered all the evidence. "Do you think he's annoyed we won't let him go home? I mean, he understands we can't for his own safety, right? Not with those two guys…"

"Opie and Mr. Clean," I filled in for her.

"Yeah, those guys, having followed him yesterday to get to you. If we took him home, it could be dangerous for him. Until we can take care of this Widow McBride woman and these other weird dudes working for her—"

"Or someone else."

"Or that," she agreed. "Until this situation is handled, Kyle isn't safe to go home, either. Do you think he understands?"

I took a moment to consider her question. "Do you want to know something else he's capable of doing?"

Trudy leaned in. "What?"

"Sneaking up on people without making a noise." I motioned with my eyes for Trudy to look behind her where Kyle was standing there listening.

She saw him and immediately turned her anger eyes on me, while silently mouthing, 'You knew?'

Kyle sat down on the rug in front of us. "No, she didn't notice me either, Trudy."

If a strawberry cupcake can look astonished, Trudy did.

"You want to know what else Kyle can do?" I asked Trudy. "Freak people out."

~

While waiting for the potatoes of great repute to finish baking, Kyle stretched out his legs, got comfortable, and said, "It's time for that talk, ladies."

Trudy and I exchanged glances. What could we tell him? What was I allowed to say? What would put him in danger if he knew? How did I explain my sidekick role to a friend? I hadn't even told my brother and sister-in-law, yet. Would he find it creepy? Fantastical? Impossible? Would he be weirded out and no longer want to be friends?

I didn't know how to start this. I looked at Trudy, and she gave me the exact same look. She didn't know how to start, either.

While we were busy swapping facial expressions, Jackson walked in from the kitchen. He'd gotten back about an hour ago, saw me holding my shoulder funny, and grabbed an ice pack. When I'd shushed my growling stomach, he'd excused himself saying he needed to "take care of something" and would be right back. He returned carrying two small water bottles and a cloth napkin stuffed with something.

Jackson sat beside me on the hearth, passed over a water bottle, and opened one corner of the napkin so I could see hot, buttery croissants inside.

Maybe the way to a man's heart is through his stomach, but it's also a good detour to reach a woman's heart when she's hungry, too.

I took one look at those croissants and one look at him. "You're the handsomest man I've ever seen."

"Thanks." Jackson offered the bread. "But that could be your low blood-sugar talking. Eat. Then you can tell me how handsome I am again, later."

I grabbed a croissant, kissed him on the cheek, and chowed down.

"Hey Kyle," Jackson did one of those guy head nods. "How are you adjusting to this place?"

Kyle's raised one eyebrow so that it hovered higher above his tinted glasses than the other. "This place? Or these people? Or this whole secret society thing you've got going here?"

Jackson chewed on a croissant. "Yeah, all that."

Kyle started to speak and hesitated. "What are you guys eating?" He sniffed the air. "Croissants?"

Jackson passed the napkin of goodies to Trudy who offered them to Kyle. He took one, inhaled the warm yeasty smell, and took a bite.

Swallowing, he said, "Were these coated on the outside with egg prior to baking?"

Trudy took one and passed the napkin back to me. "Yes. Why?"

"Because they're perfection." Kyle took another hungry bite.

After all their arguments over food recipes in the last 24 hours, his comment – in my opinion – said two things: I'm not angry that I'm stuck here, and I want another croissant.

I tossed one at him, and he caught it.

"Now, as far as the other topic, this entire gig is strange. But, after hanging out with different people today, I'm getting the gist of it." Kyle held up a finger, indicating now was not the time to interrupt. "Correct me if I'm wrong. Everyone here possesses some kind of extraordinary talent, which they are using to help Sammie become better at her extraordinary talent. It's a collaborative meeting of savants. Like the U.S. Festival of '82 when Fleetwood Mac, Santana, Tom Petty and the Heartbreakers, the Police, and the Talking Heads all played in San Bernardino over Labor Day Weekend."

Trudy looked at me and raised her eyebrows, as if to say 'what's your take?'

I glanced at Jackson, who pursed his lips and nodded.

"Yep," I jumped in, "that's it exactly, Kyle."

"Also," Kyle continued, "whatever it is you savants do together has made some enemies. And from what I can gather, they all hate Sammie the most."

He's a perceptive guy, that Kyle.

"Yep," I said less enthusiastically, "that's it exactly, Kyle."

Jackson squeezed my knee consolingly.

"Because I'm Sammie's friend, I'm now a target, too. Either to torture for information or use as bait. So that means I have to stick around and lay low until the coast is clear." Kyle spun his finger in a circle. "And that wraps up what I've gathered so far, ladies and gentlemen."

Well, I couldn't have explained it better myself. "Are you annoyed? About being stuck here?"

"No, Sammie. Not if you give me the last croissant."

Crap. He was right. There was only one left.

"Fine." I tossed it to him and took smaller bites of the only croissant I'd be getting. For about five more minutes.

"How much longer, Trudy?"

She held up three fingers.

Okay, for three more minutes.

"Kyle," Trudy watched him with enough admiration to melt the butter on my pastry, "that was…I'm impressed that you…you really are…"

Kyle, the guy who never laughed and rarely smiled, slowly grinned. "You, too, Trudy."

The chemistry crackled between the two of them. I looked at Jackson to see if he was noticing what was going on between them, and he winked.

Kyle got his head cleared first and changed the topic. "So, Sammie, how did that day of hiking go? That's where you were headed when I ran into you, right?"

Right. Hiking. A word that can also mean a backwoods, redneck safari into the land of untamed wilderness.

Kyle meandered into the great room this morning after I finished with Lauren. My third and final field test for the day had me paired with two sidekicks, both crazy in their own way. They were tasked with taking me on a nature walk and an outdoor picnic lunch. But I knew better. This place was a personalized Samantha death trap. And I needed to prepare accordingly.

Before leaving for our jaunt into the Oklahoma wildlands to discover the elements, insects, animals, and plant life capable of snuffing me out, I requested a brief recess. Jerry loaned me hiking boots, and, as I explained to Hal, those take a while to lace up. Plus, I explained to him, I'd need a hat. And a bathroom break.

He passed it off with a "get to it, Addison" and I'd waited until he went outside to breach the pantry for supplies.

Grabbing a backpack, I shoved in three individually wrapped granola bars, a water bottle, a package of unopened bologna from the frig, a paring knife, a package of wet wipes, a small box of Band-aids, a handheld flashlight, a box of matches, and a can of bug spray. Now, all I needed was a roll of duct tape. Don't ask me why. I needed to be prepared for anything, and duct tape seemed like a given.

I emerged from my scavenging, feeling triumphant, prepared, and super sneaky for not getting caught. Then, Kyle walked into the great room and caught me.

"Right, Sammie? A hike? That's what you'd said when I saw you this morning, although you were carrying around enough supplies in that backpack to launch a small offensive."

"It was a hike," I assured him now. "Into the vicious lands of a peeved and blood-thirsty Mother Nature, who thought today would be a good day for me to die."

Trudy bought into the drama more than Kyle, who gnawed on the last croissant while oblivious to how I yearned for it. Jackson listened quietly, while gently tugging me against him so I could lean back.

"What in the world happened?" Trudy set her wine glass down. "Theo said you hurt yourself when you fell out of a tree running from a squirrel."

He would see it that way.

"I wasn't running from a squirrel. I was running with one. And I didn't fall out of a tree, I fell into it."

Kyle and Trudy responded with a "huh?"

"It's a long story and we've only got"–I questioned Trudy, who raised two fingers–"two minutes before I focus on eating. So, here's the short version, but don't say I didn't warn you when the nightmares come tonight."

∼

Theo had one part right. I did hurt my shoulder when I connected with a tree. But he is omitting the fangs and claws and eyes, oh those eyes, that were chasing me at the time. You never forget eyes like that. And he misrepresented my relationship with the squirrel. That little dude was my friend.

It all started when I met up outside the cabin with Hal, Theo, and the 30-something Greta. She was the other bunkmate from this morning, the one with the white-blonde hair that hung down like a willow tree, the pale complexion of a trumpeter swan, and the gangly body that listed with the wind like a foxtail.

She was also the reason animals sometimes love, sometimes hate me. Why reptiles may congregate at my feet. Why I can speak Spanish even though I don't speak Spanish. And why comatose patients chat me up.

Greta was a communicator. That was her ability. I thought of it like a gift of tongues. She could exchange words, thoughts, and feelings with nearly anything.

"No insects, though," Greta clarified. "I still can't get those pesky things to listen."

"Pity," I told her, while fanning away a gnat that had, so far, survived the winter.

Hal said my "refreshing hike and carefully prepared lunch" with Theo and Greta would be my chance to test my mimicking abilities "in the heart of God's country."

"'Carefully,' Hal? Why was lunch prepared carefully?"

As we headed south along a well-trodden path, I asked Theo about lunch because Hal had ignored me.

"Little sister made it," he patted his own backpack. "So, it'll be tasty."

Little Sister? Was that a nickname for Jerry?

"No, Raggedy. My actual little sister, Trudy."

"Now that you mention it, I can see the family resemblance." They didn't look anything alike.

Not far from the cabin, we came to a one-story metal building, much newer than the cabin, constructed in the dense trees.

Painted a neutral beige, the building blended easily into its environment. There was nothing flashy, nothing decorative. Three windows along both sides gave it less of a storage building look and more of a multipurpose building look. A single white wooden door led inside, although Theo and Greta made no move to go in.

"What's that?" I asked them.

Greta smiled at the sight of it, as if recollecting a treasured memory. "That's our training center."

"That's where you'll be training with Gabriel tomorrow." Theo marched beside me. "You'll love it, Raggedy. He'll push you to your limit and then keep pushing."

"I'll love that?"

We walked past the structure and continued in silence. Well, Greta and I were silent, that is. Theo told his tales the entire time.

He dived into more of his escapade stories, like that winter he worked as a firefighter in California and how the mountains turned to piles of burning embers, that spring in Missouri when he drove for a storm chaser and how the tornadoes up close appeared to breathe in and out, and that summer in Houston when he volunteered with local fishermen during a flood and how the water roared like a beast in its death throes.

I listened, while taking in the peaceful, sunny atmosphere. The air was clear. The chill manageable. Leaves crunched under our feet in hushed, sleepy tones. Other than the sound of our breathing and the listless wind and Theo's nonstop chattiness, there wasn't another noise. Not a car horn. Or train. Or plane overhead. No other voices. No need to speak. No one asking me questions. This wasn't such a bad field test. Maybe my favorite.

As we veered off the path and into more rocky, unmarked territory, I noticed a squirrel overhead jumping from limb to limb and tree to tree, keeping pace with us. We wound along on no particular path or trail, turning one way and then shifting to another. Only moving thicker and thicker into the unknown.

The squirrel kept pace. He was a committed little fella.

After a while, I nudged Greta and pointed to him. "One of yours?"

She smiled up at the little guy, who twitched and climbed down closer.

"Not me." She nudged me back. "He's here for you."

"It can't be me. You're the squirrel whisperer. Besides, my mimicking always happens when I'm scared or stressed, and I'm neither right now."

Greta smiled into the wind. It kicked leaves into my chest, while gently feathering her hair with a caress.

"Always?"

"Yes, always." Actually, come to think of it. "No, not always. It can also activate when I've been drugged with Viagra. But I always know that's happened because I also hear David Bowie in my head."

Greta took it all in. "Groovy. When was the first time that happened?"

"Last Friday. It showed up while I was resting in the hospital room of this comatose patient."

"Someone you know?"

"Not at the time. But we've become friends since."

While we watched the squirrel watch us, I told her about Mr.

Portelli, the pills, the Spanish-speaking mother and daughter, the dogs in Angel's neighborhood, and the snakes at the park.

"Everyone and thing responds to me differently. Sometimes friendly. Sometimes angry. Sometimes a minute apart. That's a temperamental ability, Greta. Does it work that way with you, too?"

She tipped her head to the side and the wind returned to smooth out her hair again.

"Of course. But that's the nature of communication. Exchanging thoughts, ideas, opinions with any living being is unpredictable. Who knows what they think? Or feel? Or believe? And why? It may seem so foreign to us and our experience that we struggle to relate. But so what? So, our ideas get stretched. Or challenged. That's the beauty of it, and the ugliness." She leaned toward me. "Listening isn't for sissies, Sam."

Greta took in a deep breath, filling her lungs with the wind before it threw more leaves at me and sauntered off. "I love it," she confessed. "Even when it goes all wrong. It helps me step outside of myself and my limitations. And I become…more. Seeking to understand others will always make us more, Sam."

"More what?"

She raised her bony shoulders and dropped them. "That depends on what's being communicated."

For a woman whose ability meant dealing with one of the most turbulent activities known to man – communicating – she had impressive inner calm. When I mentioned that to her, she gave me a piece of advice.

"Sam, when it comes to communicating, we will nearly always get back what we give. If you want people and animals to respond to you with anger or bitterness, be angry and bitter. Carry that around with you everywhere you go. Snap at people. Take offense. Get easily annoyed. Lose your patience. And you'll get all of that in return. But, if you want consideration and understanding, be considerate. Give understanding. If you want kindness, be kind. Personally, I want peace. So…" She held out her palm as if to conjure peace and the wind gave her a high five.

"So that's why the dogs in Angel's neighborhood changed? They started out angry and threatening, then they turned docile, happy, and even protective of me. But that all happened because I changed?"

"That'd be my guess," Greta wiggled her nose at the squirrel. "Do you remember what you were thinking about when they approached you?"

I did. I'd taken a walk to work the turmoil, doubt, and fear after seeing those faux Jackson pictures of a black hoodie character committing crimes. "Yes. I was deeply upset."

She shrugged as if to say, 'There you go.'

It made sense. Later in the park, it had been the same with the snakes, alligator, and coyotes, all aggressive from my frustration to get my speed back.

"You're blowing my mind right now, Greta. It's clicking. But why did your ability come so easily? I have to work so hard with everyone else. With you, it's—"

"Natural?" she interrupted. "Maybe because, Sam, you're naturally a communicator. Right, Lois Lane? You only need help polishing it." She winked. "A little."

~

Greta squeezed my shoulder and walked away. The squirrel stayed with me while I considered what she'd said. "So, I'm a natural communicator." I looked at the squirrel. "That sound right to you?"

The squirrel twitched.

"Are you here because you need to talk to me? Has the sad lack of acorns got you down? Are you here hoping I've got unshelled pecans in my pockets?"

The squirrel jumped to a lower limb.

"Well, no pecans. But I do have," I pulled off my backpack and rummaged in a side compartment, "granola bars. Cyanide free. You want?"

The squirrel ran down to a limb directly over my head.

"You can have some, but you've got to share."

I unwrapped the granola, broke off a piece, and held it out. The squirrel's tiny black button eyes looked at me, looked away, at me again, away, at the food, at a limb, at its feet, at me, at the food, over his shoulder, at a limb, at the food, and then snatched it with its mouth and held it there with his tiny five-fingered paws.

"You're terribly adorable for a rodent, but you knew that, didn't you?"

I popped a bite of granola in my mouth and broke off another piece for the squirrel, primed and ready this time, who snatched it with less fidgeting, while I surveyed the area.

Where did my hiking companions go?

"Greta?!" No one responded. "Theo?!" I heard no chattiness. "Hey, squirrel, where did everyone go? Did they not wait on me?"

He kept chewing.

"I can't believe they didn't wait. Did you at least see what direction they went?"

If he did, he wasn't saying.

Not knowing this area, I needed to catch up. We'd curved and turned and shifted so many times since leaving the trail, I wasn't sure which way was what. Besides, we'd been walking for nearly two hours. It was way past lunch, and Theo had the food.

"So, I'm thinking…"

The squirrel leapt onto my head and clung to my hat. I stifled a shriek, opting instead to make a little squeak sound.

"What the…? Why are you…? What's going…?" I tilted my head, and the squirrel dug in. "Okay. This is invading personal space, buddy. You can't sit on my head anytime you feel like it."

The squirrel didn't budge.

I didn't feel comfortable manhandling the little guy. If I tried, I wasn't positive he wouldn't bite me. And, for some reason or another, that squirrel desperately wanted on my head. I didn't have the heart to toss him to the trees, but I couldn't stand there all day while Theo and Greta got further away, either.

"Okay, here's the deal. You can stay there until your emotional crisis passes. But we aren't going to make this into a 'thing.' Understand? It's a one-time event. And, as soon as Theo and Greta come into view, you jump off. I don't need anyone knowing about this." Who hasn't had a squirrel riding on their head at some point? "Also, don't get granola crumbs on my hat." It was actually Jerry's hat, a royal blue knit cap crocheted from the softest yarn. She loaned it to me along with the boots, and I wasn't giving either of them back. "It's new."

Now, to find Theo and Greta.

I scanned the area. With no obvious trail, they could have gone anywhere. Each direction looked the same. Nothing but hibernating oaks and elms and black walnuts. Chunks of sandstone and shale and limestone. Strings of downy brome, henbit, and mouse-ear chickweed.

All I saw was brown, brown, and brown. Beige, beige, and beige. Blonde, blonde, and blonde. Sickly green, pasty orange, and dirty cream. And, nestled in amongst it all, a pair of eyes.

"Squirrel, we have a problem."

20

Get back what we give, Greta said. Communicate, Greta said. Well, I wasn't giving out hostility, but I was getting it back.

With the squirrel holding onto my head like a desperate passenger on the roof of a speeding car, I cleared my throat and spoke to the watchful eyes. "I'm not hungry or aggressive right now," I spoke calmly. "So, I'd appreciate those same sentiments back."

The eyes moved closer until the head cleared the dry brush. It appeared to be a bobcat. Too small for a cougar, too big for a kitten. With grayish-brown fur and dark spots, it blended seamlessly into the terrain making its outline difficult to distinguish. Pointed, feline ears stuck up from its face, which maintained a skeptical, curious expression. With my juicy self now topped with a delectable squirrel, I probably looked to it like a red meat shish kabob.

Done watching from its stealthy hole, the bobcat emerged from the weeds to give me the first full view of its height and weight. Its size wasn't as intimidating as a mountain lion, but there weren't many dog breeds that could emasculate it, either.

That bobcat was on the move, and the direction was me. It took slow, halting, deliberate steps by lifting a paw, holding it in mid-air, then putting its weight on it in a surge of prowess, all before taking another slow, measured step.

Each shift of its shoulders, tilt of its head, movement of feet, happened as if illustrated on a single sheet of paper and then flipped to the next illustration, and the next, and the next, creating a halting but forward movement. I didn't know if that's how bobcats behave when they're coming over to say a friendly "hello" or how they behave when they are coming over to eat you.

"Squirrel," I quietly addressed my little friend, "I now get why you've attached yourself to my head. But I don't think that did either of us any favors."

If I was going to get out of this without puncture wounds in my neck and the squirrel devoured as an appetizer, I'd need more info on bobcats. In a typical human/bobcat interaction, I didn't even know who was the predator and who the prey.

But I could find out.

Somewhere in my brain was that knowledge. Lauren put it there.

In my mind, I opened the forty-seventh volume of "The Oklahoma Wilderness Survival Guide: How Not to Die in Rural America" and flipped to the section about bobcats. The pages appeared as if right before my eyes.

I skimmed quickly, picking up facts like how bobcats are usually frightened of humans and run away when spotted, which was good. Then, I noticed how this bobcat wasn't frightened and wasn't running away, which wasn't good. I also learned they were strict carnivores, usually feasting on rabbits, rats, birds, mice, possums, deer, and, yes, squirrels.

"Sorry, dude," I whispered to Squirrel.

If a bobcat does attack a human, the survival guide said it was unusual but probably meant the bobcat was rabid. That was when humans needed to start worrying. The survival guide put it this way, "This is the moment you want to stop focusing on prevention and start focusing on whatever you can do to protect yourself."

Optimistic suckers.

I mentally flipped back to the prevention page, where they were still rooting for you to avoid bloodshed and read the instructions on how to react when confronted.

First, back away slowly.

I took two steps backward, and the bobcat leapt out of the brush and landed weightlessly into a clearing.

Second, make noise.

I snapped off two dried limbs from the squirrel's tree. Then I banged them together while yelling, "Good Morning, Vietnam!" The cat's whiskers flicked, but, otherwise, it wasn't affected.

Third, don't feed them.

"How do you feel about granola?"

I'd dropped the granola bar the squirrel and I had been munching on when I spotted the bobcat. It now sat on a pile of leaves at my feet. I kicked it toward the bobcat, who wasn't intrigued. Even strict carnivores might be tempted by honey-sweetened whole grain oats if I could sell it.

"What you may not know is that oats, when toasted, taste just like rabbit."

The bobcat wasn't buying.

I added more visuals by pulling out the last two granola bars and tossing them toward the bobcat. They plopped in the dirt and stayed there.

"Those are poison free. I checked the integrity of the wrappers myself."

The bobcat didn't bother even smelling them.

"Keto only, huh?"

Fourth, don't run.

When at all possible, the survival guidebook says to avoid running away because that could trigger a pursuit response. I didn't want to trigger anything in this bobcat, but, by the growl and fang display, not running wasn't at all possible.

"Hold on, squirrel. It's about to get bumpy."

Super speed is more impressive in open territory with fewer obstacles and a clear path from A to B. Running at high speeds through the woods was a skill I hadn't yet mastered. There were too many twigs and rocks underfoot, too many trees and boulders in the way, too little room for maneuverability. I could move fast, but I couldn't navigate as quickly. It was a running, halting, slowing, running mess.

Behind me, the bobcat pursued relentlessly. It knew this territory. It had a lithe body designed for rapid woodland pursuit. Where all I could do was run, it could also climb and pounce. Eventually, one of us would wear out. With the bobcat hunting in its element and me with a single bite of granola as fuel, I was betting I'd be the one.

"Squirrel, I think we're in real trouble here."

I pushed myself and the squirrel forward. With no familiarity of the area, I was at a loss to know if we were moving toward civilization or away. I didn't even know if we were heading toward Theo and Greta.

Weren't these field tests designed with a safety net should something go wrong?

"Jackson"—I puffed out between breaths—"what would you do in this situation?"

I know what he'd do, he'd run with pleasure. Even in the most hair-raising situations, Jackson could still rejoice in his ability. He didn't war with it, like I did. He enjoyed it. He enjoyed himself. He delighted in being who he was. Not arrogantly, but honestly. Gratefully. Joyfully.

I, on the other hand, stressed out. And strategized.

Speaking of strategy, I pulled the bologna out of my backpack and tossed slices behind me. That strict carnivore instinct kicked in. The bobcat snatched up one slice, then ignored the others. Without mayo and two slices of bread, bologna has a hard time selling itself.

That singular pause gave me and the squirrel breathing room. Time to expand it.

As I raced around triplet trees twisted and intertwined with no space to pass through, my right hiking boot landed on a sandstone boulder, pushed off, and catapulted me airborne until I landed hard on my left leg. The move shifted the squirrel, whose tail drooped over my eyes as it scrambled for a better perch.

"Squirrel! I gotta see!"

He wiggled around up there, whipping his tail free and then not free, clear and then not clear, out of my sight and back into my sight. When he finally found his footing, the tail moved, the trees cleared, and the ground dropped away into nothingness.

At the speed we were moving and my sight temporarily obstructed, I didn't see the cliff coming until we were over it. It was too late to stop. Too late to pivot. Too late to keep us from flailing through the air.

I screamed until the impact knocked the oxygen out of my lungs. We hit hard, but it wasn't the ground. The squirrel and I found ourselves caught in the bony limbs of an oak tree.

The cliff we'd leapt off was more of a steep decline than a vertical drop. It marked the edge of this hill cluster, which descended sharply into a ravine far below, before ascending with enthusiasm into the next hill cluster.

Oklahoma hills don't jut, they roll.

If given enough time, I could have climbed down the hill by holding onto tree limbs and resting on protruding rocks to offset gravity. It could have been done without even a rope or climbing gear, but not done quickly.

At my torqued speed, I propelled myself and the squirrel off the ledge and into the side of a sturdy oak. When we landed, I struck my shoulder on the trunk and my ribs on a bough. Both ached, but, otherwise, I'd gotten off easy.

The shock took longer to process than the pain. Not so for the squirrel, who landed on a thin branch and kept running. Reaching the tree trunk, the squirrel twisted its head to look at me, at the trunk, at its hands, at the cliff, at me, at the trunk, at me, either wanting me to follow or deciding whether or not to abandon me. I gave the little guy a clear conscience.

"Go ahead, Squirrel. I'll catch up when I can."

Once that bobcat followed us into the tree, I might get cut and bit and clawed but survive. The squirrel was dinner.

He scrambled to higher branches, leaping to another tree, and flitting off in search of pecans. The more distance he made between himself and that bobcat, the less fear I felt. It drained away at the speed of his twitchy, prancing run toward freedom.

With him now out of sight and safe, I felt remarkably at peace. The fright that had gripped me upon seeing those eyes now felt like a child's nightmare. A horror easily dissipated by flipping on a light switch. Or observing the situation from the eyes of an adult.

Not that rabid bobcats aren't frightening, but, if nothing else, I could and would fight back. The earlier panic, as I considered it now, felt more like how a squirrel might feel about a bobcat. As if, instead of projecting my calm on the squirrel, I'd absorbed the squirrel's fear. Then communicated that to the bobcat.

No wonder that feline saw me as prey. I communicated like one.

Now, with the squirrel safe, I focused climbing out of this tree and finding a heavy enough log to fight off the bobcat.

I shifted my weight on the massive branch and surveyed my options. Getting down wouldn't be too difficult. Solid branches shot out of the trunk until nearly ground level. I hadn't climbed a tree since grade school, but the same rules applied. Don't stand on branches that give with your weight. Don't change your foothold until you have a solid handhold. Move along the trunk where the branches are their thickest. When climbing down, don't bump into a bobcat climbing up.

As soon as I felt my arm brush against fur, I glanced over. My brown eyes locked with the bobcat's yellow ones. In spite of getting my fear under control, that freaked me out. The bobcat and I both screamed.

Before the screams stopped echoing in the valley, the bobcat clawed up the trunk with no more effort required than a woman speed walking on level ground. For a bobcat who'd chased me fearlessly through the woods, it now skedaddled away as if I'd become the embodiment of the boogeyman.

Sighing with relief, I resumed my climb down, careful not to lose my grip as I gingerly picked my way through the branches. As I neared the ground, I saw a glimpse of movement in the corner of my eye.

A bulbous, brown, burly shape mulled around below with little to nothing to do. The new visitor ambled toward a rock, stopped to feel the breeze, strolled over to the tree, sniffed the air unceremoniously, and scratched its back against the trunk.

As soon as I realized what I was seeing, I shot the bobcat a dirty look.

"You couldn't have given me a heads-up about the black bear?"

One of the things I've learned about mimicking this particular ability is that it made any forays into the natural world crowded. There was simply no way I could hang out in the woods, at a park, and maybe even my backyard anymore without feeling I'd never be alone again. There was always some warm- or cold-blooded creature out there feeling misunderstood and needing to communicate. Or feed. It was as if the entire animal and reptilian kingdom had become that obnoxious neighbor who shows up at your front door any hour of any day, expecting you to drop everything, so they can shoot the breeze.

"No," I told the bear, who dug its claws into the trunk to climb up, "I'm putting my foot down. This tree is already crowded. There simply isn't room."

It watched me while breathing through its mouth.

"You're...what? Three hundred pounds? Three fifty? You stay where you are. I'm coming down and, as long as you don't eat me, we can talk."

Reprimanding a bear wasn't one of the recommendations in the forty-seventh volume of "The Oklahoma Survival Guide: How Not to Die in Rural America." But I'm an improviser.

What the book did recommend was not climbing a tree: too late. Not running away: not possible. Making noise, which I tried. But "Good Morning, Vietnam!" was now "O" for two.

Besides, I was too tired to be afraid anymore. The earlier "running for my life" tapped me out. Now that I'd gotten over my fear of being eaten by a bobcat, I wasn't in the mood to fear being eaten by a bear.

Even anxiety needs refueling from time to time.

Besides, as I got a good look in his beefy face, my newest visitor had that stupefied expression frequently on the face of Yogi Bear. It made him look harmless and gullible and like a cartoon. I could talk my way out of a cartoon.

As I climbed down, the bear sauntered over to another tree, it's big bottom swaying under all that fur, and started scratching his back again.

While he took care of a hard-to-reach itch, a familiar voice called to me from across the valley.

"Hey, Raggedy, is that you?"

To get a better visual of the other hill, I climbed back up a few limbs where a gap offered a clear view. That's when I spotted Theo and Greta, her white-blonde hair acting as an easy focal point among all that brown and beige.

From what I could make out, it looked as if they were picnicking on a boulder among a gaggle of other boulders on the side of the adjacent hill. One boulder hung over them, one under. If I had to pick a good place to recline out of the elements, that would have been mine, too.

"Where have you guys been?!"

Our voices carried easily across the valley as long as we yelled at each other at the top of our lungs.

"Waiting on you!" Theo waved. "How's it going so far?!"

He had to be kidding. "How's it...! You guys left me! I know squirrels who are better hiking companions than you! Right now, I'm stuck between a bobcat freaking out on a limb above me and a bear scratching himself against a tree below. How do you think it's going?!"

Theo's laugh bounced off the hills. "Sounds exciting! Do you want us to come to you?!"

"Do you have any food left?!"

"Yes!"

"Then come!"

He and Greta packed up what was left of lunch and disappeared into the shadows. While they trekked back down the hill, through the valley, and back up to me, I climbed out of the tree. It was time to have a chat with a bear.

While the bear puttered about, I climbed down and sat on a lump of sandstone. Knowing I couldn't outmaneuver a bear on this incline, my best bet for survival was finding why the bear had been attracted to my location in the first place.

The bear ambled over, stood facing the wind, and plopped down on his butt. He "humphed" in place as if too glum to go any further.

"Okay, bear, what's going on? Are you depressed? Because you look depressed."

We hung out in that same spot for the twenty minutes it took Theo and Greta to hike back. In the meantime, I talked to the bear about how it was lonely being the biggest boy on the playground.

"Am I getting warmer? Huh, big guy?"

The bear sat there staring off into the distance, bobbing his head from side to side, and sniffing the air.

When Theo and Greta found us, I'd moved on from therapy to comedy and was rehashing episodes of Yogi trying to escape Jellystone Park.

"But, then, Park Ranger Smith caught him." I laughed. "I don't know what he was thinking. You can't dig an underground tunnel out of the park."

Without so much as a cautionary pause, my two lousy hiking companions walked up. Most people would have approached slowly, but they were both insane.

Greta, without saying a word, instantly mimicked the movements of the bear by staring off into the distance, sniffing the air, and shifting her weight from foot to foot, as if swaying to a song in her head. With her and the bear connecting on a deeper level, I turned to Theo.

"Hey there Boo Boo, what have you got in your pic-a-nic basket?"

21

The trick to convincing people you're an amazing cook is not feeding them until they're starving.

"That's not what I was doing." Trudy loaded a glass into the dishwasher.

Dinner was over and now came the cleanup. As the rookie in training, I was awarded the honor. Jackson stayed to help. Trudy stayed to protect her kitchen. Kyle stayed to eat croissants.

For dinner, we scarfed down potatoes loaded with cheddar or pepper jack or goat cheese, topped with chicken or pulled pork or bacon, embellished with grilled corn or roasted peppers or avocado, drizzled with salsa or marinara or barbecue sauce, seasoned with fresh chives or fresh basil or ground cumin, alongside a side salad and croissant, and then we sat back and complained of eating too much.

By the end, no one could take another bite and everyone loved Trudy, fulfilling her devious plan all along.

My first dinner with the entire sidekick crew felt Walton'esk. We sat at tables of four, but the conversation carried across the entire room. It entailed a lot of laughter, retelling of tales, others jumping in to retell those tales better, and a general sense of brotherly affection. There wasn't a single sourpuss in the bunch. Even stony-faced, quiet Gabriel joked.

Throughout dinner, Jackson smiled that boyish smile of his. When I asked him why he kept doing that, he said, "Why am I smiling? Because I'm too happy not to." Then, he gave me a quick kiss and went back to eating and laughing and adding to Theo's tale about the time the two of them saved this teen from his own Fourth of July fireworks show.

"I've never seen a fire engulf a vehicle that fast. I told him, 'The next time you shoot off a roman candle, don't do it while driving.'"

Afterward, everyone broke into different areas for the rest of the evening. Lauren, Greta, Gabe, and Theo gathered around the outdoor campfire pit to make S'mores, which prompted a groan from everyone else at the idea of eating more. Jerry retired early to her room. Gin and Angel chatted with Hal over a bottle of wine by the living room fire. And Jackson and I cleaned up the dinner mess with Trudy and Kyle.

"Dinner really was amazing," I told Trudy. "I'd probably feel that way, even if I hadn't been starving."

Trudy leaned against the wall in the dining room while pointing to tables that still needed wiped down. "Why were you starving? I packed you a good lunch - a turkey tomato on rye, potato salad, and a homemade brownie. Didn't you eat it?"

I wanted to eat it. I planned on eating it. I even fantasized about eating it. But the bear was so forlorn, he'd turned to food as a crutch. When he smelled what was in Theo's backpack, he no longer held any interest in communicating with me. He ate everything left, which was my share.

"In my imagination, I ate it." I wiped the last table. "And it was delicious."

With the kitchen and dining room restored, Trudy and Kyle joined the wine drinking with Gin, Angel, and Hal. Before leaving, Kyle let me know my hiking story from earlier wasn't at all scary.

"The suspense wasn't there for me," he said, "because I already knew you'd survive. Besides, the situation didn't sound like that big of a deal."

"Glad you feel that way," I patted his arm. "I've arranged for you to be chased through the woods by a bobcat and bear tomorrow."

Kyle didn't roll his eyes. If he had, you wouldn't pick up on it behind his tinted glasses, anyway. Instead, he rolled his head back with his mouth open. "Geez. You're so super sensitive sometimes, Sammie."

I returned to the kitchen where Jackson, dressed in his heavy boots, jeans, and a navy cargo coat buttoned up over his broad chest, was pouring hot liquid into a thermos.

"Where are you going, Hero?"

He screwed on the lid. "Grab your coat. You're going with me."

"Outside?" I hugged his free arm and watched him finish his task. "Outside gets crowded with me. You willing to risk it?"

"Trust me." He turned me in the direction of my coat and smacked my butt. "And hurry."

We exited out the kitchen door to avoid running into the wine drinkers in the great room or the s'more eaters around the campfire. Outside, Jackson climbed onto one of the four-wheelers and shoved the thermos into a black bag attached to the fender.

"We're taking that thing at night?"

Jackson started it and smiled flirtatiously back at me. "Uh huh. Come on, kid."

I threw my leg over the back and slid onto the seat behind him, wrapping my arms around his waist. "I'm only going because you always know what you're doing. Otherwise, I'd be out."

Jackson laughed, released the brake, and told me to "hold on tight."

He gunned it out of the camp and hit the trail. I held tight like a squirrel on a head. We followed my path from earlier. Traversing it at night didn't hold the same angst as the day. Maybe because I wasn't waiting for a death-defying test. Maybe because I wasn't carrying a heavy backpack. Maybe because I wasn't walking. Maybe because I could enjoy holding onto Jackson, whose scratchy coat pressed against my cheek as I hugged his back.

So far, this was my favorite way to travel.

In three bitterly cold minutes, we reached the training center. Still dark. Still empty. Jackson cut the engine. "Come on." He retrieved the thermos, fished a key out of his pocket, and unlocked the door. "It's warmer in there."

Jackson flipped on a light switch and hustled me inside.

A tight grey carpet on the floor softened the noise we were making. Doors on both sides of the entrance were marked men and women's, which were locker rooms, he said. Ahead was a double-door and darkness beyond.

Jackson walked through the double doors and disappeared into the black hole. Seconds later, lights came to life one after another. Each buzzing with the effort.

The main room stretched farther and reached higher than it appeared from outside. Open and spacious, a blue wrestling mat took the center. Smaller wrestling mats ran the walls. Free weights rested their weightiness in one corner. Stability balls balanced precariously in another. Two punching bags hung ghostly undisturbed from the far wall. Kettlebells sat silently behind them. The unheated air smelled like rubber and lemons.

"The infamous training center." I bounded on my feet to feel the cushiony floor underneath. "Why are we here?"

Jackson tossed a wayward basketball into a corner storage cart. "Come here, and I'll show you."

∼

The hot chocolate from Jackson's thermos heated the air. Or only my insides. Either way, I felt warmer. We sat in the center of the mat – him with legs stretched out, me cross-legged – and sipped the sweetness from styrofoam cups.

"You really know how to romance a girl." I snuggled into my coat. I was warm, but not that warm. "This place isn't romantic?" he teased.

"No. Not. But it's quiet. No one is demanding I perform right now. Or trying to trick me. Or scare me. Or sit on my head."

Jackson shot me a quizzical look and then remembered. "The squirrel."

"What I mean is, it's nice here." I leaned toward him. "It's always nice where you are."

Jackson smiled a slow smile, grabbed my coat collar, and pulled me to him. "Now that's romantic."

His lips, warmed by the hot chocolate, pressed against mine and lingered. He tasted sweet and minty and familiar. His breath caught in a "mmm" as the kiss deepened and I no longer felt any cold, not even from areas on the mat my butt had yet to warm. As he released me, he changed his mind and pulled me back in for another slow kiss before letting go.

I smiled into his eyes. "Yes, I definitely like it here."

Jackson shook his head, grinning to himself. "Oh, Sam. What oh what to do with you."

I shot my empty cup out toward him. "Pour me more hot chocolate, that's what." With a refill warming my hands, I sighed as the fattening heat scorched a path to my thighs, where it would attach itself and remain for all of time. "This is, by far, the best part of my day."

Jackson laid on his back, laced his hands behind his head, and looked as comfortable here as anywhere else. It reminded me of the night of the mugging when he drove me home and invited himself to stay.

"Remember the night you crashed on my couch?" I nudged him with my knee.

He turned his head toward me. "I remember, especially the part where you snuck into your living room to watch me sleep."

He was never going to let me live that down.

"Keep plugging quarters into that machine." I moved on. "What I remember is how you reacted when you caught me."

When I'd walked into my living room after two fitful hours of sleep, Jackson Christy sat up on my couch, head back, arms at his side, chest rising and falling on each breath, and the moonlight toying with the contours of his face. I reached out to touch that moonlight, and he woke up. Before I could scream, he'd yanked me onto his lap and held me there.

"You were supposed to be asleep," I reminded him now.

"So were you," he pointed out.

"Then you grabbed me."

Jackson congratulated himself. "That I did."

"You're such a guy, you know that?"

He grinned wider. "Thanks."

I tugged my coat tighter. "Why did you?"

Jackson raised an inquisitive eyebrow. "What? Grab you? It was an act of pure self-defense." He winked. "That, and you were so adorable, all sleep tousled and wide-eyed. You looked so vulnerable and a little bit afraid. I couldn't help myself. I had to hold you."

How sweet.

"Even if you did elbow me in the gut," he finished.

How Jackson.

I crawled next to him, lay on my stomach, and leaned on my elbows. "You want to know what got me about you that night?"

He propped his head on one arm and dropped the other around my waist. "Sure."

"How comfortable you were in my house."

He laughed. "Really?"

"You were just so…at home. Around you, I always felt awkward and off-balance. And there you were, uninvited and on my territory, and you still acted more comfortable than I did. It was intimidating. And infuriating. I wanted to bother you like you bothered me. Even a little."

Jackson squeezed my side. "Samantha, sweetheart, you bothered me all the time. You still do. Does that make you feel any better?"

It did, actually. "Still?"

Jackson gave a husky laugh, nearly a growl. "Yes, still."

He took my hand and placed it over his heart, which pounded like galloping hooves beating the ground. Jackson raised his eyebrows as if to say 'see what I mean?'

"Because of...?" I pointed at myself.

He nodded once. "Because of."

~

We stayed for another hour at the training center, mostly to avoid everyone else. I ended up drinking three cups of hot chocolate, which should have made me wired but instead knocked me out. I rested my head on Jackson's chest, while he retold his day of playing catch-up at work.

While his voice rumbled beneath my ear, I drifted. Jackson talking in the background acted like a homing beacon tethering me so I didn't drift too far. But, visually, I was in a lavish room of exquisite dancers. Couple by couple, they twirled by. Only shapes, really. Blurry blobs of color. There then gone. A man in a pin-striped suit blocked my view. Then he disappeared. A woman in red walked by. Her legs and hemline visible. She disappeared. A violinist played in the darkened cold. He disappeared. Each new image flipped in and faded out. A collage of time snipped into two-second reels. The violinist turned into a waiter. The waiter poured amber liquid. The waiter disappeared. My hand reached out and faded away. Glass windows burned with blinding, unfocused light. Here, then gone. No more light now. Only a rusty metal beam. A white owl perched on a branch. A car door. Headlights. Black shoes. A cane. A shadowed man in a business suit. All snapshots. Flipping through. Here, then gone. All fade. Fire. So much fire. It's everywhere. There's nothing but red now. Only red. And a woman shrieking in terror...

I jerked awake.

"Sam?" Jackson's arms tightened. "You okay?"

I sat up, looking around the room to orient myself. The training center. We hadn't left. The lights burned overhead. The darkness pressed against the windows. No sounds but the listless, ignored wind running up and down the walls.

There were no flames, no screams, no elegantly dancing blobs.

"Did you have a nightmare?" Jackson rubbed my back. "You drifted off twenty minutes ago. I didn't have the heart to wake you, yet."

"So much red." I leaned into him. "I guess it was a nightmare." I rubbed at my forehead, willing all that red away. "Or a Stanley Kubrick film."

"You want to tell me about it?"

I wiped my hands on my jeans, working to rid my skin of a filmy foreboding. "I couldn't describe it if I tried. It was random images. Nothing, exactly, frightening. Except for the screaming. And all this red. Not a normal red, either. Not uniform. It was blotchy." I painted the air with my hands. "Black and yellow areas. Orange. But also red. Deep red. Liquid red."

Jackson pulled me close. "What did you think it was?"

I buried my face in his neck. "I don't know. But this helps."

He stood up, pulling me to my feet. "Come on. You've had a big day. I think it's time to call it."

I dusted myself off and picked up our cups. "Okay, but I want to hear the end of your story. I nodded off where you were talking about what was in Fred's yellow manila envelope."

"Oh, you'll love this. It was a photo of his buddies from their college days."

While Jackson shut off the lights and locked the building, he recounted the part of his day when he dropped off the envelope at Fred's and learned the story behind Fred's errand.

"On Monday, the photo will be flashing on a digital billboard somewhere in Tacoma, Washington."

Jackson climbed onto the four-wheeler, and I climbed on behind him.

"So, it was all for a stupid college prank?"

"A stupid college prank going on for more than three decades. And next week is their reunion. But yes."

I snuggled into Jackson. "Fred owes me now. That's a good feeling."

Outside, the air had that sinking cold feel as it tried to sneak down a few more degrees without anyone noticing. I tried to dislodge that woman's scream from my head as the motor roared, the tires whirred, and the wind swished.

The woods grew stiller as the nighttime sank in, and all the littlest creatures snuggled into their holes. I wondered where squirrel was tonight and if he'd found that elusive pecan. I wondered if bear had eaten bobcat. I wondered if, after today, my brain was on overload, and the red nightmare was its way of saying, "Back off!"

Back at the cabin, everyone continued their festive mode. Laughter from the s'more eaters drifted in as the engine died. Peeking through a window, I saw Trudy, Kyle, Gin, and Angel around the fireplace inside, playing card games. Hal had disappeared.

After securing the four-wheeler, Jackson motioned for me to follow him. At the side of the cabin was a set of exterior wooden stairs that led to an upstairs entrance. He, of course, had a key. We gained entry, making as little noise as possible, and Jackson walked me to my room. With my female bunkmates still downstairs, I motioned for Jackson to enter quickly, then I shut and locked the door behind him and used my body to block it.

He crossed his arms, eyeing me suspiciously. "What are you doing?"

"Buying us time." I kissed him quickly, then stripped off my coat and kicked off my boots. On my way to put them in the oversized closet, I told him, "Get comfortable. I'm not ready for you to leave, yet."

Jackson leaned against the door. "Let me know when I'm dismissed."

Finished, I came back and plugged my arms inside his open coat and around his waist. "Thank you for a nonlethal evening and a tour of the training center."

He smiled down at me. "You're welcome. I hoped you'd enjoy that. I wanted to give you a positive experience of the place before you train there tomorrow."

That sounded ominous.

"Because tomorrow won't be a positive experience of that place?"

Jackson shifted, buying himself a moment. "That's not exactly what I meant. Tomorrow will be great. Gabriel knows what he's doing, and I trust him."

"But?"

"But…it won't hurt that your first memory of that building was good."

That still sounded ominous.

"Jackson, exactly how bad is tomorrow going to be?"

He brushed his fingers across my cheek and tucked a curl behind my ear. "Not bad. Only…not easy. And very real."

22

There are places on the human body most people will never feel comfortable grabbing, kicking, or gouging. I was one of those most people.

"You've got six seconds before you lose consciousness. You need to make your move."

Gabriel pressed me against a wall with one hand around my throat. His fingers grasped but didn't squeeze. Yet. This was practice. Eventually, he told me, we'd be playing for reals and I either stopped him or he hurt me.

I wasn't sure I liked Gabriel.

To counter the attack, he taught me a move called the brain tickler.

"This isn't a fight with rules, Samantha. When someone comes for you, it's amazing how quickly they can unleash pure violence. You are going to be harmed, maimed, assaulted, or killed, unless you fight back with a willingness to do more violence than your attacker."

It was my third hour into the self-defense portion of training and my fourth choke hold. So far, Gabriel criticized my upper body muscle mass, knee strength, core tightness, and killer instinct.

"You're not nearly mean enough." He said it like that was a bad thing.

It was shaping up to be a peach of a day.

We started the training after breakfast, another meal available to everyone but me.

"With the physically demanding day you're about to have, you'll only end up throwing it up," Hal told me. "So why waste the food?"

After everyone else ate, Gabriel and I speed walked to the training center. Hal, riding a four-wheeler, followed behind with a toothpick clamped in his teeth.

We speed walked because that's as fast as I can move without using super speed and, as Gabriel explained, "While training with me, super abilities are not allowed. You must learn to defend yourself without them. Thinking you've got the upper hand in a situation because of your ability will only get you locked in a trunk."

I opened my mouth to argue, but Gabriel raised one eyebrow daring me. I shut my mouth.

"I'll be ready for you next time."

"Yes, you will." He picked up the pace. "I'll make sure of it."

So far this morning, I've died twelve times. Two broken necks. Five head traumas. Two suffocations. And three strangulations.

"Six seconds Samantha. Six. In a choke hold, you start losing consciousness and strength by second one. You're already on your way out by second two. If you don't fight back instantly, you're done by second six. When the lights go out, you're dead or mutilated or brutalized. Six. Understand?"

"I liked you better when you were mute," I croaked.

Using both hands, I struck his arm on opposite sides to hyperextend his elbow. That's what he called "the pop." I jabbed the middle and index fingers of my right hand to his eyeball. In real situations, my fingers would jab through his eye to his brain. Thus, the brain tickler.

For now, it was all rehearsed in slow motion to start creating muscle memory with proper form.

"There." I pulled my hands back. "Brain tickled."

All I got out of Gabriel was a snort and a "better" followed by an "again."

While I learned all the ways to dismember a person with my bare hands, Hal sat on a nearby lifting bench, alternating between sipping coffee and chewing his toothpick. I still wasn't sure what the guy actually did, other than bossing me around.

Meanwhile, Gabriel drilled me on moves when someone grabs me with their left hand, grabs me with their right, chokes me from the front, chokes me from behind, grabs with one hand, grabs with two. I feigned poking his eyes out, breaking his trachea, shattering his nose, snapping his arm, twisting his neck, and kicking him in the groin over and over and in no particular order.

By the time lunch rolled around, I felt meaner, less naive, and extra sad. The physical training part of being a superhero always looked fun in the movies. You broke things, like boards. You did a decent amount of gymnastics. The kicking resembled a hip hop dance routine. The arm movements looked like Tai Chi. Even the punching seemed like a great way to decompress.

Instead, Gabriel was teaching me what action to do to protect myself and the consequences of that action.

"If you fail to connect with the eyeballs, you can jab your two fingers above their eyebrow, sending their head back and exposing their throat," he demonstrated on me during one practice move. "This sends their nose toward the sky, which naturally tightens their exposed throat. Feel it tighten?"

I was standing with my head back, mouth open, and Gabriel's fingers pushing into my forehead.

"Uh huh," was all I could get out.

"Then, with your body at a 45-degree angle, you use a half fist and put your body weight behind the punch." His hand slowly connected with my throat. "That's like driving a sledgehammer into two-inches of cartilage. It crushes their trachea." He stepped back, so I could straighten my neck. "Then, they suffocate, basically."

Gabriel said they'd lose bowel and bladder control, thrash around on the floor, make horrific noises, and die an agonizing death.

"It's a move that often traumatizes the person who uses it, too. Even when it's necessary. The death will be slow and violent and acute. So only use it when necessary but be prepared to do it when it is necessary."

With every passing hour, I understood why Jackson brought me to the training center last night. Today was everything he warned – not easy and very real. He knew the memory of our hot chocolate date here would be a comfort. And he was right. Every time Gabriel taught me a new way of disfiguring someone, I'd check out for twenty seconds to remember some happy moment from last night.

Gabriel chose one of those moments to hit me in the shoulder with a basketball.

"Ouch!"

"Samantha." He retrieved the basketball as it rolled across the floor. "It's time to talk environmental awareness."

At lunch, Gabriel went outside to eat his food in the fresh air. I stayed inside to avoid running into bear. This turkey and tomato on rye was mine.

Hal, surprisingly, pulled a bench over to my eating spot on the floor and ate with me. Today, he wore a washed-out navy ball cap on his pristinely white hair, along with jeans, a light maroon sweatshirt, and his customary boots. He still looked worn and roughened by the wind or genetics or life. My first impression of a man who achieved what he was determined to achieve had been confirmed over the last couple of days. Whatever project he took on would be completed to his satisfaction, and, at the moment, I was his project.

"How do you think your training is going so far?" He bit into his sandwich, chewing twice before swallowing it whole and taking another bite.

I, on the other hand, ate like a civilized person by chewing four times. "Isn't that your area?"

He wiped his mouth with a wadded-up napkin. "Yes, but what's your take?"

I took a swig from my water bottle. "I have no idea. Personally, you all seem like happy, intelligent lunatics. So becoming more like you is a mixed bag. I want my training to go well, of course, but what does that look like? So far, it means being nearly poisoned, threatened with electrocution, abandoned in the woods, chased by animals, and becoming skilled at causing a compound fracture. I'm not in a position to say how it's"–I air quoted the next words"–going so far."

Hal popped a corn chip in his mouth. "That's fair." He rummaged in his little chip bag for another. "Is there anything you wished was going differently?"

I considered that while digging into my container of potato salad. Trudy had packed the exact same lunch as yesterday since, according to her, it was delicious, and I needed that experience.

"Not really," I spoke around a mouthful of potato salad, heavy on the dill. "I only wish Jackson could be here, but I know he's got to work."

I needed to work, too, but I took two personal days. Delaney responded by texting me a notice that she'd changed her employee policy last year to erase all accrued vacation days on January 1 and forgot to tell me. I responded by texting her a screenshot of Oklahoma Administrative Code, section 380:30-1-5 guaranteeing my ridiculous amount of accrued vacation days were safe. She'd texted back with, "Enjoy your days off."

"He does have to work," Hal crinkled his chip bag. "But, also, I asked him not to be here."

Of course, he did. "Why would you do that?"

Hal smiled at snagging the final chip and, for the first time, I noticed the whiteness and heaviness of his teeth. Like pearled paperweights.

"Because you need to work out your fears, Samantha."

I plopped down the potato salad. "Are you kidding me, right now? You poisoned my breakfast yesterday morning, remember? Fear is supposedly my sole reason for living, according to you guys. You've planned my entire training regimen based on stoking that fear. Now, you want me to work it out?"

Hal went back to fishing out more chips. "I never said I wanted you to be afraid. Fear is never a strength."

I shook my head. "I'm so confused."

Wadding up my trash, I left my brownie and water bottle on the floor and tossed the other wrappers into the trash can. It gave me a minute to take a calming breath. When I turned around, Hal was unwrapping the cellophane from my brownie. "You didn't want this, did you?"

"Well…"

"I just assumed, with your big evening planned, you wouldn't want a heavy lunch."

The big evening Hal was referring to was dinner with Jackson, which did not require pre-date fasting.

"You assumed wrong, Hal."

He took a big bite and spoke with a mouthful of my brownie. "Did I?" He took another bite. "Look, I know you're frustrated, but just because you're choosing to make fear your motivator doesn't mean I support your decision. I'm only acknowledging it."

"Hey"–I shoved my finger in his face–"I'm not choosing fear. That's not what I'm doing."

"Sure it is. You don't trust what you've been given, yet. You don't trust what you have or who you can be. So, you fear what you can't control. And that becomes your motivator."

Whatever Hal's job was, he sucked at it.

"You're getting it all wrong, but"—I dusted imaginary lint from my workout pants—"that's fine. I don't see why this should preclude Jackson from being here, though."

Hal crumbled up the empty cellophane wrapper. "Because Jackson has become your safety net. You relax with them. You trust him."

That's true. I did. "You got one thing right. I do trust him."

Trust was a topic Jackson and I had danced around, dug through, grossly dissected, and thoroughly shredded. He demanded it, rightfully so. And I, being a person of monumental personal growth, had evolved into a healthy person who gave it.

Hal wiped his mouth with the back of his hand. "You do. Except, of course, when you don't."

He was back to being bad at his job again.

"I do, too. I trust Jackson completely. And, for saying that, I should make you cough up that brownie."

Hal didn't back down. "You trust him with your fears?"

"Of course."

"Your faults?"

I hesitated. "Sure."

"Your weaknesses?"

Um… "Most of the time, yes."

"Your failures?"

That was pushing it. "I'm…leaning more that way…I think."

Hal wasn't impressed. "There's still something holding you back, Addison. A fear of something. What, maybe you don't even know. But it's there, and it's primal." One of his white eyebrows raised conclusively. "That's why fear continues to be your motivator. And, at some point, a life with Jackson will require you to come face-to-face with it."

～

"You look terrible."

Trudy, her hair pulled back in a red highlighted ponytail and her green eyes squinting with judgement, greeted me in the great room at the end of the day.

Gabriel and I spent the afternoon with him attacking me and me fending him off. He took it easy on me, he said, because I wasn't ready for full-on no-holds-barred fighting. When I asked him how long before I was ready, he laughed.

I'd shoved him. "How is the answer to my question laughing?"

Gabriel said today wasn't even the beginning of my self-defense training. It was a preview of the beginning. My self-defense training started now and continued until the end of time.

"If this is going to take a while, then how about we end early today? I have a date tonight and need time to shower and get ready."

It wasn't just any date. It would be Jackson and I's first. Before leaving my room last night, Jackson had asked what I thought about going on an actual date with him.

I wasn't sure I'd heard him right.

"A date date? Like a normal couple? Without an entire brood of people around who are strategizing their next test of my physical and mental boundaries? That kind of a date?"

Jackson nodded. "That kind."

"And you'll be there?"

He tilted his head, watching me as a smile crept in. "Yes, I'll be there."

"Then, yes, I want to go."

Our relationship had skipped a few basic milestones, like a first date. When you considered the seven years he'd been watching me from a distance, the year of working together, the three weeks I'd avoided him, the three days he'd been in a coma, and all the time in between where we never could get the timing right, going on an actual date was a milestone.

I wasn't about to let today's self-defense training interfere. Yes, I had bruises on my hips from throwing Gabriel off me in a floor hold and soreness around my ribs from being rammed with a boxing pad, but I wasn't bleeding and no joints were dislocated.

I was in a glass half-full kind of mood.

Gabriel had grumbled about the early quitting time. "You need two hours?"

Hal smacked him on the shoulder. "There are battles we're not trained to face, old friend. Wave the white flag and call it a day."

Now was prep time. Jackson said last night not to worry about what to wear. Trudy, yet again, had been tasked with making a run to my closet. One day, that girl would make a wonderful lady's maid.

"Look, Trudy," I told her now, "what I need from you are helpful comments and suggestions. Do you think you can do that?"

Trudy pointed to the stairs. "Go. Shower. Then meet me in our room. We only have two hours to get you ready, and we'll need every minute."

By "we," I took that to mean me and the clothes she'd chosen. When I entered my room after showering, I found "we" meant all the women. And I do mean all.

Trudy and Angel unloaded items out of bags, while Jerry, Greta, and Lauren sat on my bed eating popcorn.

I stood in the entrance with wet hair and dressed in my robe. "What's going on?"

Trudy walked up with a hairdryer and hairbrush. "We're here to get you ready."

"All of you?" I eyed Jerry, who grinned suspiciously back, but said nothing. "Ladies, it's a date. Not a crowning."

Angel held a semi-formal gown of deep-emerald lace. "Girl, are you sure about that?"

Seeing what they expected me to wear, along with the flushed faces of every woman in this room, I wasn't so sure.

"You did not pick that dress up from my house because I've never seen it before."

"I bought it," Trudy brushed it off, "using Jackson's credit card."

"Does he know that?"

Trudy shrugged. "Sure."

"Should I believe you?"

Trudy pointed to a chair in the middle of the room. "Sit down. You can cross-examine me while I fix your hair."

After I sat down, Angel rolled over a table with a full spread of eyeshadows, eye liners, blushes, lipsticks, powders, creams, and what looked like the squashed corpses of several spiders.

"What in the world?"

Angel pulled up a stool. "Those are fake lashes..."

"I don't think..."

She shushed me. "We got you, girl. Trudy's taking care of your hair.

And I'm handling the make-up. For tonight, leave it all up to your fairy godmothers."

I looked at the three stooges – Greta, Lauren, and Jerry – getting crumbs all over my bed. "And what are the three of you here for?"

Greta and Lauren looked at Jerry, who dropped more popcorn on my comforter. "We're here for the show."

"And moral support," Greta added.

"And research," Lauren pointed out.

This could go wrong in so many ways. Did Jackson know all the ladies were involved? And one was freely using his credit card?

"Ladies, Jackson never mentioned this date being this formal. This may be overdoing it."

Angel opened a container of cream. "It's not."

"I think it's sweet. He wants to make your first official date special." Greta passed the popcorn bowl to Lauren, who agreed.

"It's a calculated strategy to heighten the romance." Lauren munched on a kernel. "Well played. It increases his chances of meeting the objective."

"Which is what?" I asked.

"He's hopeless," Jerry took the popcorn bowl from Lauren. "Don't make him regret it."

"Regret what?"

No one would explain. They were focused on me and ignoring me at the same time.

"He's not hopeless, Jerry," Greta said dreamily. "He's in love."

23

The perfect romantic evening rarely includes defusing a bomb, but everyone's love story is different.

Our romantic evening got sidelined with a boom, but it started out typically. All the men congregated in the great room, drinking scotch, while all the women congregated upstairs, playing dress up.

Lauren, who periodically spied on the men to report back, said they hadn't noticed I was running late.

"It looks like a Glenlivet commercial down there. Lots of male bonding going on so, as long as they stay distracted, we've got time. But not much."

Angel and Trudy were on their second round of fixing my hair and makeup. The first round ended in shame for all involved. No one realized how overboard Trudy and Angel had gone until I stood in front of the full-sized mirror.

Greta, Lauren, and Jerry, finished with their popcorn, moved in for a closer look, while Trudy and Angel hung back contemplating what went wrong. I stood in front of the mirror wondering how much weight in eyeshadow the eyelid could reasonably hold and how much weight in bobby pins the neck could reasonably support.

The whole effect wasn't bad, just overblown. If I'd been going for the guy-in-drag look, they'd nailed it.

When no one said a word, Trudy jumped in with explanations. "Maybe it's the lighting right there."

Angel agreed, "It is casting a weird shadow."

"A weird shadow that makes me look like a raccoon?"

Lauren switched from writing about me in her journal to sketching me in it.

"I wouldn't go with 'raccoon'." She tapped her pencil against her lower lip. "I think you look more like a bandit."

Greta's inner Pollyanna feverishly searched for the positive. "But a cute bandit."

Jerry snorted. "A bandit with a beehive."

"Okay." Trudy guided me back to the chair. "We can fix this, Samantha."

Angel agreed. "Absolutely. Maybe we do a little—"

"Less?"

She patted my knee. "Yes, less. Something elegant, sultry, but understated, which is more like you. Trust us. Trudy and I know exactly what to do."

Did they, though?

Trudy and Greta removed the bobby pins, while Angel wiped away enough make-up to recreate Gene Simmons. Two varying-sized curling irons smoothed the frizz into bouncy 1940s-reminiscent waves. Instead of putting my hair back up, Trudy let it fall in curled layers and swept it to one side with only three bobby pins, which my neck could handle.

Meanwhile, Angel kept the fake lashes, which she assured me weren't too gauche, and created a dramatic upsweep of my lash line with liner, blending shadow, and a whisper of glittery green along the edges. A matted rose plumped my lips, and she declared it "perfection."

This time, I stood in front of the mirror in my deep emerald-green gown, and all the ladies oohed and aahed. The hair over one shoulder played up the straight neckline of the lace bodice, which scalloped the edges across my shoulders and around my wrists. The make-up, dramatic but sensitive, paired well with the long, flowing fit of the gown. The coverage, which started at the collarbone and ended at the floor, hid the bruises on my legs, while the shapely cut created a dramatic glamour girl silhouette.

The ladies discussed whether or not to add jewelry, but there was no clear consensus. Trudy thought my hair and dress should do all the visual talking, while Angel thought added sparkle around my neck would make my eyes pop.

Jerry offered to loan me a pair of diamond stud earrings, if I promised to return them. That woman would never learn.

In the end, Greta, the super communicator, presented a nuanced take that determined the outcome. "What makes you feel more vulnerable?" Her lanky frame swayed with her words. "Wearing jewelry or not wearing jewelry?"

Was that a thing? "I don't think jewelry–"

"Just answer the question, Samantha."

"But I'm not sure jewelry can–"

"Which one," she interrupted again.

"What you're saying is–"

"Choose, please."

"What if I–"

"Stop debating and pick."

Greta was soft-spoken and motherly, but she was no pushover.

"Not." My answer didn't surprise me, the fact I had an answer did.

She blinked once, slowly, as if relieved to finally move on.

"Good. Now...." She picked up Jerry's earrings, held them in one hand and held nothing in the other, and held both hands out for me. "Choose. Who do you want to be tonight with Jackson? Do you want to be more careful, more cautious?" She raised the hand with the earrings. "Or do you want to be more open, more vulnerable?" She raised the empty hand.

When I hesitated, she added a last thought.

"Whether you wear jewelry or don't won't matter to Jackson. He'll find you beautiful either way. What will matter to him, Samantha, is whether or not you're willing to let him into your heart and your life…without fear. Now's as good a time to decide as any."

The quiet drive into town soothed any first date jitters. Perry Como sang about some enchanted evening, while the highway lights passed reassuringly, rhythmically overhead, and life passed serenely, securely outside.

Everything around us felt like a blur, as if we were the only two objects in the world in perfect focus. We rode in companionable silence, simply enjoying the moment, the peace, the evening ahead, the crisp air, the nearness, the warmth of our hands clasped together. He raised my fingers to his lips, pressing them softly against his mouth. In the sedating blue of his SUV's dashboard lights, I smiled and watched his eyes dance in return.

Neither of us wanted to speak. Words felt intruding. Unwanted. Unnecessary. Only Como could break the silence but not the magic. So, we rode, side by side, and followed the headlights wherever they led.

This moment was a far cry from the boisterous scene we'd left behind at the cabin.

When it was time to come downstairs, the ladies made a thing of it. They insisted on going down to join the men and announcing my entrance. I threatened to send a swarm of attack squirrels if they did. So, we compromised. The women trickled down casually, none indicating when or if I'd ever be ready. In return, they were allowed to freely stare at Jackson the entire time so they wouldn't miss his reaction when I entered.

What they didn't know is that I had no intention of walking down those stairs like a beauty pageant contestant. It was too much pressure. There was only so much anxiety I had to spread around, and all of it was directed at our actual first date.

It wasn't a typical first. It was more momentous than that because of all that we'd shared, faced, and overcome together to be here.

To calm my own nervousness, I'd chosen a sneaky entrance. I'd slip outside from the upstairs exit, creep down the outdoor staircase, and slip unnoticed into the great room with everyone reoccupied watching Jackson. It was one of my brilliant, perfect plans. And it would have worked, too, if someone hadn't engaged the lock on the upstairs exit, which I did not have a key to unlock.

I squeezed my right hand into a fist and hissed through my teeth. "Jerry." Her precognition was a pain in the butt.

Out of options, I disappointedly headed for the inside stairs.

The noise of conversation, laughter, and glasses clinking drifted up the stairwell. I took my first step down, feeling every centimeter of my three-inch heels. The wood creaked underfoot. Holding onto the banister with one hand and lifting the hem of my dress with the other, I crept down until reaching the landing where the staircase curved, and I could see the room.

The fire blazed, giving all the minglers a soft buttery glow. Everyone huddled in small groups. In the midst stood Jackson, his body facing the stairs, as his best friend regaled everyone with a story. He hadn't noticed me, yet, which gave me a moment to notice him.

Dressed in a classic black suit with a white shirt, wine-colored tie with pinprick dots, and a matching handkerchief, he took my breath away. While Theo told another tale of adventure and adrenaline, Jackson smiled and laughed with one hand naturally dropped into his suit pants pocket, the other around a water bottle. He looked so happy, so comfortably content.

Over the last year of our working relationship, I often noticed a sobriety about him. Like he walked through life with a stone across his shoulders. He carried an unseen responsibility I never knew about until the night of the Durant Ball.

Now that I knew about his responsibility, I never wanted him to carry it alone again. If I could help somehow.

Theo ended his funny story, and Jackson threw back his head and laughed. His teeth looked shockingly white in the firelight. He closed his eyes. When he opened them again, his eyes landed on me in the shadows of the stairwell.

The smile fell from his face. His focus shifted to me, and my mouth went dry. Slowly, he set his water bottle down on the end table and stood as if frozen.

I managed a nervous smile, but Jackson only shook his head as if clearing it of some thought or another. At his reaction, the rest of the room shifted their gaze in my direction and the room hushed.

Blood pounded in my head. Was he happy? Was he dismayed? Should Trudy and Angel go for a third make-up and hair reboot?

I ran my hands down my sides to smooth my dress, as if that accomplished anything.

Jackson lifted his hand and placed it over his heart.

It was the simplest of gestures. No one else might even notice. But I knew exactly what he was saying. Last night, he'd done the same thing with my hand. His heart hammered so hard then that I could still feel it beating against my palm now.

In understanding, we exchanged a slow smile.

He liked the dress.

I headed down the last section of the stairs. Distracted as I was with his eyes on me, I forgot to lift the hem of my gown. On step one, my shoe snagged, and I stumbled.

Gasps rippled through the room. I scuffled with the banister for a solid grip. Slipped. And fell right into Jackson's arms. Just like a cheesy rom-com. He'd bolted to the stairs and caught me before I ruined my second hairstyle for the night. I would have laughed the embarrassing scene off, but the moment shook me. Instead of pretending I was fine, I took this opportunity to enjoy the strength of him. I rested my hands on his chest and breathed.

"Thank goodness," Greta said.

"That was close," Hal added.

"Nice one, brother," Theo chimed in.

"What did I miss?" Kyle asked.

The clamor of the room returned as conversations cranked back into gear and we were forgotten.

I rested my forehead against Jackson's cheek, took a deep breath, and straightened back up. "I don't know why, but I'm always clumsier when you're around."

Jackson leaned in, his freshly shaven cheeks brushing against mine, and whispered in my ear, "Lucky me."

~

Music drifted like a providential fog, rolling in rhythmic waves down the stone steps, across the sidewalk, through commercial vehicles parked in the unloading zone, over the road, and found me and my better half standing on the sidewalk.

Street-performing musicians under the Centennial Tower's colonnade strummed, bowed, and wailed the 1980s R&B song "Just The Two of Us," adding melody to the downtown district's Saturday night atmosphere. What made the 17-floor monolithic office building such a hot spot this evening wasn't the black granite and glass architecture that gave it that multilayered chocolate cake look. It wasn't the palatial pedestrian park to the north where couples sought a romantic moment and smokers sought lung cancer. It wasn't the Chestnut, a five-star restaurant on the Centennial's first floor, where opulent bread was broken and gilded glasses were raised. It wasn't even the musicians, who were making a purely instrumental version of the popular ballad into a classic.

What was so special about the Centennial Tower tonight was the fact it was located across the street from the Durant Hotel, and the Durant Hotel was our evening's destination.

We would go inside eventually, but we were enjoying the foreign pleasure of standing together, listening to live music, and not dodging bullets. When we came around the corner of the hotel and heard the music, we paused, and paused we remained.

Across the street, pedestrians meandered up the Centennial Tower's steps, lounged on the cement planters along the walkway, and generally congregated. Over here, we had the sidewalk to ourselves. Still closed, the Durant Hotel didn't attract any foot traffic other than those passing through. Once it did open, this little spot of real estate would turn into a revolving door of guests and drivers. Until then, it was ours for the standing.

"These are the best seats," I slipped my arm through his. "You spoil me."

He winked. "That's the plan. One free concert at a time."

On our walk from the parking garage, Jackson had explained why he brought me downtown for the evening. "The Durant's lobby is finished. You've been so involved in the project, I hoped you'd want to see it."

Want? Try passionately long.

Getting to see the Jackson Christy Construction remodeling project of the Durant Hotel over the last year had been a personal dream. I'd been in love with the romance of the place since my gangly teen years. Spouting tidbits of Durant Hotel history had been one of the things Jackson teased me about when we worked together.

As much as an Art Deco structure can be a matchmaker, the Durant Hotel had been ours.

Coming here now felt like destiny, but a disquieting destiny. As much as I loved the chance to see the renovation progress, I also hadn't been back since the Durant Ball. The night Trevor dangled from the rooftop. The night I learned black-hood guy's identity. The night I discovered my own running-like-lightning ability, as well as the impressive durability of a corset.

Now, as the musicians busied themselves building castles in the sky, I craned my neck to get a glimpse of the roof. From here, I could make out an undefined line of the building's shadowed edge across the night sky.

"Thinking about the night of the ball?" Jackson asked.

"Yes." I pulled my eyes away. "Do you ever think about it?"

He gently pulled my hand further through the crook of his arm. "Of course."

I snuggled in tighter to his side. The brisk temperature took a bite as the wind passed.

"What part do you think about the most?" I studied his profile "Holding on to Trevor, right? Not letting him fall? I can't even imagine the strain of that."

Jackson turned to me. "No, that's not what I think about."

"DeLuca? He came so close to shooting us."

Jackson shook his head. "Not that either."

"Me figuring out your alter-ego? Black-hood guy was fun while he lasted."

Jackson raised an eyebrow. "'He,' huh? We're back to talking about me like I'm not here again, I see."

He always got jealous when I talked about him to him. It was adorable. "Oh, you know. I just miss the guy sometimes, is all."

Jackson shook his head and ignored me.

Across the street, the musicians wrapped up the musical tribute to Bill Withers and moved on to a musical tribute to Lionel Richie and Diana Ross' "Endless Love."

"So, back to my original question. What do you think about the most from that night?"

Jackson moved in closer. "There is no 'most.'" His arm wrapped around my waist, the other grasped my right hand. "This is the only thing I think about when I remember that night." His grasp tightened and, in one swift motion, he lifted me off my feet. I dangled in his arms until my tiptoes connected with the ground.

He'd moved so quickly, all I could do was blink back at him.

Him holding me like this was how we'd danced at the Durant Ball. If I had to trace the exact moment I fell in love with Jackson Christy, that was it.

"Yes," my voice quivered, "this does feel familiar."

24

Superheroes aren't known for being romantics. Maybe, if they had less crime to fight, they'd find the time. Superman might have written love poems in Lois Lane's reporter notebook, if Lex Luther had taken more vacations. Spiderman might have made Mary Jane a playlist of love songs, if the Green Goblin had taken up marathon running. But there are only so many hours in the day.

Jackson, even while playing catch after his coma, had still managed to plan an entire evening designed to keep me swept off my feet. Who knew how he found the time.

"Do you want me to put you down, now?"

I wrapped my arms around his neck. "Eventually. But two things first."

Jackson raised his eyebrows.

"If that move was to throw me off my game because I teased you about black-hood guy, well played. I won't talk about the crush I had on you anymore."

"Had?"

"We're not talking about it, remember?"

Jackson grumbled. "Is there no winning with you, woman?"

"I'd imagine not." I settled into him. "And, secondly, since I'm here, you should kiss me. But make it snappy, man. There's a tour waiting for me inside."

Jackson brushed a kiss on my bare earlobe. His rough whisper rumbled in my ear. "Let it wait."

The friction of his face against mine as he took the long way home convinced me he was right. Tours can be rescheduled.

In the background, the 80s-themed street performers had switched to an instrumental rendition of "Nothings Gonna Stop Us Now" by Starship.

Jackson wasn't concerned about Starship at the moment, and I found myself caring less and less. His lips parted over mine, sinking us both into a place disconnected from all others. Even as my toes stretched toward the pavement, I could feel the ground slipping further away. It receded until I floated in nothing but space.

Whether or not the rest of the human race continued to exist in that moment, I'll never know. I couldn't sense them anymore. Nothing seemed to exist outside of his kiss and his touch and the heavy sighs between us. Monuments have been erected for events with less impact. Small monuments. Local monuments. Monuments denoting a historic event of little consequence. But, still, monuments.

He spoke to me through caresses. About his adoration…as his lips brushed mine. About his promise to protect me…as his arms tightened. About his desire to love me like no other…as his breath caught on an inhale.

I clung to him, knowing this teasing kiss had matured into a moment of one heart, open and defenseless, seeking the openness of another. And I would never again leave his heart wanting.

I murmured against his mouth. "I love you, I love you, I love you."

My heart lurched. Deep, bottomless, abysmal. Sharp, shocking, poignant. It thumped with fury, with agony. I gasped. A heat surged over my skin. Not from the inside out, but the outside in. It seared, it burned. Flames licked my arms and neck. And not in a good way.

Mixed in with the pleasure of the moment was a foreign pain. An undefinable hurt. I stiffened. An element of our tender moment felt briefly alien, as if it'd been part of a different time, different moment, that didn't belong here.

I jerked back, staring wide-eyed at Jackson, who set me back on my feet.

Around us, the world formed again, bringing with it all the noise of the passing vehicles, mingling pedestrians, and indefatigable Starship.

"What was that?" I placed a cool hand against my cheek.

"You're shaking."

He was right. I was. And, sadly, not from desire anymore.

"How did you do that?"

Jackson looked puzzled. "Do what?"

"Make me feel…" I considered how to say this, "…an intense…wave…of heat."

He laughed. "I'm not sure how to answer that. But thank you?"

I smacked his arm. "Stop being a guy for a second. I mean heat literally. As in burned. You didn't feel that?"

He smiled pridefully. "Oh, no, I felt that."

For pity's sake.

I tabled the topic. I didn't understand what I'd felt with enough clarity to explain it to Jackson, even after he stopped teasing and honestly asked.

Whatever I'd felt, it had been beyond wonderful until the last three seconds. Maybe the training mind games caused my brain to misfire. What lousy timing.

Jackson led me inside the Durant Hotel and, as soon as I saw what he'd planned, I forgot it all anyway.

"What is this?"

A singular table, draped in a cream-colored tablecloth and two wine glasses, waited in the center of the empty lobby. There were no more saws and sawhorses, scaffolding and ladders, sanders and equipment, nor any dust. Glass lamps along the mezzanine cast a filmy light below. Pinprick white lights, like glittery shawls, wrapped around the stairway banister.

Behind the mahogany bar, the shelves stocked dark and light glass bottles, thin and regal or squatty and stout, offering warmth to all who decanted. Three bottles of deep-set red had been uncorked and left to breathe.

Over the sound system, Frank Sinatra sang about flying to the moon and playing among the stars. He had nothing on us.

I stood for several awkward moments with my mouth open. I hardly recognized the place. So many days I walked this space between the elevators and Jackson's office. Never knowing what this place or the man beside me would come to mean. At the time, I didn't understand how badly I needed someone to show me a future out of the shadows.

I understood now.

Jackson pulled out a chair, and I closed my mouth.

"She's stunning. And so alive. You did it."

I brushed my hand across his cheek and sat, which signaled a waiter. Dressed in black slacks, black vest, black jacket, and white shirt, he emerged from the kitchen's swinging door with a chilled bottle of champagne. Efficiently, he uncorked and poured, giving our glasses an inch of liquid and letting the bubbles fill the rest. While he concentrated on our drinks, a waitress in the same uniform flourished a tray of hors d'oeuvres like a magician unveiling the rabbit.

"Mini crab cakes with pineapple-cucumber salsa." She had a voice trained to awaken hunger.

As quickly as they appeared, they vanished, leaving only the swinging kitchen door as proof they'd ever been here at all.

I fingered my champagne flute and eyed Jackson from across the table. "What's happening here?"

He smoothed his hand over the tablecloth, as if placing the final touches on the evening. "I wanted a night out with you. And Chef John wanted a practice run with his staff before the Durant opened to the public. We came to a mutually beneficial agreement."

I was loving this idea. "We get to sample the menu tonight?"

"Are you up for it?"

I dropped the cloth napkin across my lap and picked up my fork. "Are you kidding? I skipped dessert for this."

Over the next half hour, the wait staff emerged time and again with a new eating adventure:

"Caramelized figs with smoky bacon."

"Cayenne deviled eggs with green olives."

"Caviar and creme fraiche tartlets."

"Cheese stuffed mini squash."

"Sweet pea pesto crostini."

"Hot crab pinwheels."

"Mushroom and parmesan elephant ears."

Each hors d'oeuvre was a mouthful, but no more. That meant the waitstaff could keep serving, and we could keep eating. Eventually, my stomach would run out of room, but not yet and not for a while.

While we devoured a toasted ravioli puff, Chef John emerged from the kitchen bowels to greet me and shake Jackson's hand.

Chef John was a rotund fellow with straight black hair that hung limply around his head like a crocheted doily and cheeks so rosy you wondered if someone had slapped them recently.

He informed us the main course – ducklings stuffed with oranges or maybe it was oranges stuffed with duck – would be served later. He believed palates needed time to be cleansed.

We took the opening for Jackson to give me the long-promised tour. Unbeknownst to us, we had seven minutes left to live.

∼

Jackson's on-site office still had those flat pencils sitting around. And a draft desk with blueprints marked up with colored highlighters. And a bound notebook with measurements, dates, and order numbers filling each line. And a coffee-ringed mug empty but waiting.

We came here first so Jackson could grab a set of elevator keys. The tour would start in the rooftop bar and move down. I didn't have the heart to tell Jackson I'd rather skip that part. After two harrowing rooftop experiences, I'd become a ground-floor kind of girl.

While he rifled through his desk drawer, I stood at the window, watching the well-dressed bodies dining and dancing inside the Chestnut on the Centennial's first floor.

Soft notes from the street performers slipped through the sealed window cracks. Although the concert was muted, 80s music is distinctive enough to recognize through any sound barrier. They were playing Cyndi Lauper's "Time After Time."

I could hear them, but not see them. A flower delivery van parked in the unloading zone blocked my view. I didn't mind. It wasn't possible for a woman to ever get annoyed by a flower delivery van.

Under the lights of the Chestnut, diners toasted at tables along the glass walls while couples moved in unfocused forms on the center dance floor. Unless I was watching ghosts. Or mere tricks of light that weren't real at all. From here, they were nothing but blobs of color and shadow.

Something about the dancers felt familiar, but I couldn't put my finger on it.

The night of the Durant Ball, I'd stared out this window. The roaming shadows I'd watched that night had been quivering reflections from the patrol cars' emergency lights.

What I knew that night, and every hour since, was that my life and my heart were gone. They'd been taken. I couldn't get them back, and I didn't want to try. Jackson and I belonged together, and I'd never feared anything like I feared that.

"You're not here"–Jackson stood next to me at the window, the keys now in hand–"so, where are you?"

I smiled, so ridiculously happy just to have him near and conscious. "I was thinking back to the Durant Ball when Det. Casey interviewed me in here after they took DeLuca away."

Jackson leaned a shoulder against the window. "You haven't been back here since that night. I just realized. Is that why you've been haunted by it all evening?"

"Maybe." I wasn't sure. "Maybe not."

Jackson squeezed my hand. "You want to talk about it?"

"Maybe." I wasn't sure about that, either. "Maybe not."

What was disturbing me most was a nagging feeling I was missing something right in front of my face. And I do mean right in front. Like half an inch from my nose. Just outside the reach of my eyelashes. So close it bounced my breath back at me when I exhaled. And I couldn't see it because I couldn't train my abilities to kick in until I was in a do-or-die situation.

"I think"–I weighed how to say this–"it has more to do with something Hal said to me today."

Jackson crossed his arms, waiting for me to continue.

"He said," I took a settling breath, "the reason my ability shows up when I'm afraid is because I'm choosing fear."

Jackson considered it. "Are you?"

"It's not impossible." I ran my finger along the groove in the divided-light window, feeling the chill of the glass and the vibrations of Lauper's 'time after time' on repeat. "He says it's primal or something."

"Do you think he's right?"

I dropped my hand, fighting off a sense of defeat. "Probably. The guy is annoying, but he does know his stuff. I think. He appears to know his stuff. I'll give him that. And his exercises have successfully goaded me into action a couple times."

I returned to watching the blob dancers. Each a smeary shadow unburdened with things like superhero powers.

Jackson wasn't one to leave a problem seeking a solution. "So, what do you want to do about it?"

Nothing. Something. I was undecided. "Ignore it?"

"Or..." he prompted.

"Or...ignore it?"

He raised an eyebrow. "Or..." he pushed.

"Or..." I dropped my hands listlessly. "I don't know 'or.'"

I turned my back on the blobs and leaned against the window. The chill from the frigid glass tiptoed down my spine. That's what I told myself. I wondered if that rawness soaking into my marrow wasn't the cold outside but a cold inside. Coming from a realization I didn't want to admit: Hal was right. At some point, I'd have to come face-to-face with whatever it was I feared the most. This great, distending unknown. I didn't know what it was, what it looked like, why it had power over me, but I could feel it creeping in even now. Inching in. Slinking in. Prowling closer. Nearer this second than the one before.

Jackson took my hand and rubbed his thumb over my fingers.

"What if I offered you an alternative?"

"To irrational, nameless fear? Sure. Why not, if you've got one." I eyed him skeptically. "Do you?"

He nodded. "Mmm hmm."

I shifted away from the window and the eighty-seventh chorus of 'time after time' and turned toward him. The lamp over his desk was the only light on. Outside, the warm glow from the Chestnut shouldered its way into our space without asking. It caught Jackson's face in patches, one across his eyes, the other across his mouth. The rest of him in grey, grainy darkness.

I leaned into him, pressing my free hand against his chest. "Okay, Hero. What's your alternative?"

He brought my fingers to his lips. "Love." He pressed his mouth against my knuckles. Then, opening my fingers, against the palm of my hand.

"Love, huh?" I fought for sobriety, feeling intoxicated by the man. "Like...a general 'love of all mankind' kind of love or more specific. Say...love of a spa day. Or...love of puppies."

Jackson shook his head.

"Love of baseball?"

He pressed my hand against his heart, the rhythm so familiar to me now my own heart matched it.

"More than that. Love that never leaves you. Never hurts you. Never," he took a breath. "Never fails you. Love that will always forgive you anything, if only you'll ask." He exhaled, as if relieved to say it. "That's the love I'm talking about."

I didn't have a joke to tease my way out of that one. Jackson Christy could always shut me up when he wanted. It was infuriating, really. Right when I'd get my heart into a safe space with the guy, he'd pierce it straight through with sincerity and devotion I never saw coming.

I didn't know how to accept love like that. Or how not to want it with every breath in my body.

"Oh," my breathlessness betrayed me, "that kind of love. Well, sure. I mean, when you put it that way." I leaned into him, smiling into those piercing blues. "Did you mention where I could find it?"

He pointed to himself. "One place only." Then he returned my smile, and my knees went a little wobbly. "There's no room for fear with my love, Samantha. No room at all."

He tipped my chin up to meet him. His lips brushed against mine once, twice, then sank in as his arms slipped around me and Lauper finished her final 'time after time.'

I sighed.

Then the Chestnut exploded, killing us both.

25

Death is an experience you only want once. Repeating it is unpleasant.

The instant the windows shattered, sending the glass cutting through our tender flesh, and the heat rolled in, sucking out the oxygen with a lethal hot, I stiffened and screamed.

Instantly, Jackson set me on my feet, and I found myself alive, unsinged, and standing on the sidewalk outside the Durant with Starship playing in the background.

The night was calm. The wind cool. The Chestnut pristine. We were neither on fire or dead. We didn't even smell like smoke.

Jackson scrutinized my face. "What's wrong? What happened?"

I hated déjà vu flashes. I really, really hated them. Freakin' Jerry.

I sucked in the cold air.

Longer flashes were hell on the body. Until the flash yesterday about my poisoned breakfast, glimpses into my death only lasted a few minutes. Sometimes seconds. That food poisoning flash had been half an hour.

Afterward, I'd found myself still sitting in the Cutlass gasping for air like I'd run a seven-minute mile. This flash, however, had been even longer. Maybe an hour or more. My heart raced so rapidly it took a moment to hear Jackson over the pounding in my ears.

"Are you okay?" He looked helpless, concerned, confused. He reached out to touch me, then pulled back and waited. What else can a guy do when his date hyperventilates?

"I'm fine," I finally got out. "For now. But I saw something."

"Saw?" Jackson scanned the area.

"Not out there." I tapped a finger on my forehead. "In here."

He instantly got it. "Tell me."

Quickly, I ran down the last few moments of my flash. "I can't say for sure when it will happen, but we had enough time to eat nine hors d'oeuvres. And, if we live through this, tell Chef John to toss the tartlets but keep the pinwheels."

Jackson pulled his cell phone out of his jacket pocket and hit a speed dial.

"What are you doing?"

He held up his finger in a 'give me a minute' gesture and started talking rapidly into his phone. "Caroline, we've got a bomb near or in the Centennial building. An hour or less before it detonates. Contact the authorities. Notify the Chestnut. Tell them whatever you have to tell them. Just make sure they evacuate the entire block, as well as the one to the north. I'll call back when I have more."

He clicked off and turned to me.

"Now, you." He fished his keys out of his pocket. "Take my car. Go back to the cabin, and I'll be there as soon as I can."

"What? You can't be serious."

"I'm deadly serious, Samantha." With that scowl, he looked it. "Don't argue with me. I want you out of here."

"But..."

"Don't argue."

He glanced toward the building, still brimming with affluent diners. A fire alarm pierced the harmonic tones of the street performers. Caroline must have hacked the security system.

Slowly, leisurely, Chestnut diners rose from their tables, glanced around, gathered their things, waved to others across the room, chatted as they strolled toward the door, none looking even a little worried.

If there's no smoke, there's no panic. Nothing else in their view sent them scurrying for escape.

Outside, even with the pulsating alarm, the street performers were determined nothing was going to stop them now, which was taking Starship's lyrics too far.

Jackson's face tightened. People weren't evacuating fast enough. The police, fire, and bomb squad would still be minutes away. We had about an hour before it detonated, but there was no way to time it precisely. Jackson needed to get those people out of the area, and I was the perfect sidekick to help. I'm great at bossing people around.

"Jackson"—I touched his arm—"I can help. Let me. This is what I'm training for, remember?"

His eyes turned back to me and focused. "Someday, Samantha. When you're ready. But not before." He watched the diners slowly meander outside, laughing and talking and congregating to hear the band. "This isn't happening fast enough," he muttered under his breath, before noticing me still standing there. "Samantha." I knew that tone. That tone never worked out for me. "There is a command structure to all this. Guess who I am."

"Four-star general?"

"Try Commander-In-Chief. Guess who you are."

I rolled my eyes. "Infantryman. Okay, I get it…sir. But you need me, you know."

His thumb brushed my cheek. "I do know. Now go."

With that, Jackson ran across the street, up the stone steps, and weaved into the exiting crowd. I watched until I couldn't differentiate his well-dressed, broad-shouldered shadow from the other well-dressed shadows.

"You'll miss me. You'll see," I told Jackson's disappearing outline. "I'm great with crowd control." I wasn't. "I've handled situations like this before." I hadn't. "I know exactly what to do." I didn't. "But, fine. Pull rank. I didn't wear the right shoes for this anyway."

I stood in place for a moment longer to exert my independence, but a good partner knew how to defer the lead, too. Jackson asked me to go, and I would respect that.

I pivoted on my fancy shoes, turning toward the parking garage, and a ball of fire consumed me again.

∼

The second time I came out of the flash from being burned alive, the scream was twice as intense.

"What's wrong? What happened?"

Jackson set me on my feet, but I wouldn't let him go. I held on, shaking and gasping for air while Starship continued never stopping. My heart pounded in my neck, my fingers, my chest, my toes. The dizziness screwed and unscrewed my head.

Not waiting any longer to find out what was happening, Jackson swept me up in his arms and took me inside the Durant.

"Grab the chair, will you Matt?" Jackson spoke to, I assumed, the male waiter.

I heard the chair being dragged across the polished floor. "What happened?"

"She's had a scare." Jackson sounded calm to anyone who didn't know him. But I knew him. He was worried.

He lowered me into the chair and knelt beside me, getting a glimpse of my face. I must have looked decently disturbed because Jackson ordered me a drink.

"Would you grab her a bourbon?"

I sucked in a shaky breath. "Brandy," I croaked out.

"Make that a brandy," he corrected, taking off his jacket and wrapping it around me. Then he held my hands and rubbed the warmth back into them.

Matt returned quickly with a glass of brandy, which I downed. Then I asked for another and Matt took off again.

Jackson pulled up the other chair beside me, sat on the edge, and leaned forward so he could get a good look into my eyes. "Can you tell me what happened now?"

I nodded, finally getting my heart rate under control. The second brandy from Matt didn't hurt either. He put it in my trembling hands and disappeared again.

"I had a flash, Jackson. Something terrible is going to happen. It's already happened twice."

I told him about the Chestnut bombing, how it happened an hour from now in the first flash and only minutes from now in the second.

"We've got to get everyone out of this area." Jackson reached for his phone.

I stopped him. "You already called Caroline for operational support. She triggered the building alarm and contacted the authorities. It didn't work."

"Okay"—he considered what to do next—"then I'll sound the alarm and get them out myself. You stay here. I'll be back as soon as I can."

I shook my head. "You already tried that, too. It didn't end well for anyone. But I have an idea."

"What?"

I took off his jacket and handed it to him. I downed the second glass of brandy and handed the glass to him, too.

"Hold this."

I grabbed the hem of my dress and speed walked outside, across the street, behind the never-going-to-be-finished-unloading flower delivery van, through the concert attendees, up the stone steps, and toward the street performers. My shoes click, click, clicked across the asphalt and concrete and stone until I came to a stop at the street performers.

As the female violinist played through the "nothing's going to stop us now" line from Starship, I grabbed her mic and screamed, "Bomb! There's a bomb!" which actually did stop her now. People ran in all directions, making a commotion of the whole evacuation affair.

If I could get one group to panic, I could get more. I dropped the mic and ran for the Chestnut.

Meanwhile, Jackson weaved through the panicking crowd, while helping a woman up who had tripped and stopping a guy from knocking a cement potted plant on top of two teens. He was trying to reach me, I knew, but I wasn't ready to go, yet. And the crazed crowd needed him more than I did.

I bolted for the Chestnut.

When a well-dressed woman walks into a restaurant and releases a blood curdling scream, followed by, "Bomb! There's a bomb!" people don't meander. They scatter through every egress they can find, while knocking over tables, chairs, and each other. I would have preferred a calmer, more civilized evacuation, but they'd already been given that chance and blew it.

"Bomb! There's a bomb!" I screamed again in case anyone was left wondering. I pulled the fire alarm. The more noise and ruckus, the faster people exited and the farther they ran. If I'd had a tambourine, I would have been striking it against my leg.

Jackson fought his way through the doors.

"This was your idea? Total anarchy?" He spoke over the ruckus, while moving an overturned table out of the way for an older couple struggling through the chaos.

I watched the crowd flooding out all three exits. "It's working, isn't it?"

Jackson grabbed my arm. "Let's go. You're getting out of here, too. Now." He noticed the pride on my face and bit back a laugh. "Are you proud of yourself?"

I blushed uncomfortably. "You say that like it's a bad thing."

We exchanged a secret smile on our way out the doors as the Chestnut exploded.

~

The third time I emerged from the death-by-fireball flash, I fainted.

Jackson must have carried me into the Durant. When I woke, I was lying on two chairs pulled together. I blinked at the inlaid ceiling overhead and knew exactly where I was. I bolted upright.

"What did I miss? What's burning? Where's Jackson?!"

Jackson sat on the floor next to me, my hand in his. "Hey, baby," he spoke sweetly. "I'm right here. Right beside you. Everything's okay."

It took a moment before my hand registered the warmth of his. I squeezed.

I dropped my feet to the floor and felt the room spin. "It isn't okay. Not even close. I have to tell you something," the words rushed out in a slur. "But, first, I need your phone. And a drink."

He handed it to me, while speaking to someone behind me. "Hey, Matt, would you bring her some brandy?"

I glanced behind me at Matt and back to Jackson. "Why brandy? Why not bourbon?"

"Do you want bourbon?"

"No. I want brandy. But why didn't you order bourbon?"

Jackson and Matt exchanged confused looks.

"I'll bring a glass of both." Matt chose the democratic option and disappeared in a way only Matt can disappear.

Jackson now perched on the end of the chair beside me. He still looked fresh and unwrinkled and gloriously male. "Now, what do you need to tell me?"

"I'm going to tell you and Jerry at once." I hit her speed dial number. "It'll save time and we don't have much of it. Or, we have an hour. I have no idea."

Because I used Jackson's phone, Jerry picked up on the first ring. Instead of 'hello,' she went with "What did she say?"

Matt reappeared with two glasses, placing the brandy in my hands and handing the bourbon to Jackson. He dematerialized again. I swallowed the brandy in one cheek-bulging gulp.

"Jerry, it's Sam." While I spoke, the liquor caught a stiff wind and sailed into my stomach. I liked brandy. "What did I say about what?"

"Samantha? Why are you calling me on Jackson's phone?"

"He's okay, Jerry. He's here with me. I need to talk to you, and I don't have much time. You know those 'final outcome' flashes you said I should be having? Well, it isn't going well."

I quickly ran through the Chestnut blowing up, the three flashes, the two extreme timelines, what we'd tried so far, and how I had no idea what to do next.

"I see." She remained quiet longer than we had time for quiet.

"I can't see how to stop the bomb. We can't save anyone. And I can't even get the flashes to stop. Unless I have, then Jackson and I may have only a few more minutes left to live."

"Hmmm, interesting." She was no help at all.

"Jerry! You understand the situation here, right?"

"I do." She paused. "We'll need to create an action plan. But, first, I need you to answer a couple of questions."

"Ask. Quickly."

"Where were you when the first flash happened?"

"Outside the Durant. Standing on the sidewalk across the street from the Chestnut."

"Where were you when the flash ended?"

"Inside Jackson's office, standing near the windows."

"Hmmm," was all she said.

What was the relevance of this? "Why does this matter?"

Jackson leaned his elbows on his knees. Relaxed but listening. Our eyes met, and he shook his head. He didn't know the point of these questions either.

Jerry's matter-of-fact voice came back on the line. "What were you doing when the flash happened? Were you talking about anything in particular? Looking at anything specific? Tapping a foot? Humming a song? Anything."

I looked at Jackson and shrugged. I'd have to tell his grandma we were making out. He knew it and shrugged back.

"I was kissing Jackson."

Jerry replied with a surprisingly non-quippy, "I see. What were you doing in the flash when it ended?"

Jackson looked at me for the answer, not knowing himself, and my cheeks flamed.

"Um...kissing Jackson again."

His mouth lifted in a lopsided, prideful grin.

I nudged him and whispered under my breath, "Will you stop that?"

He winked and the grin went full mouth.

"Why does it matter what I was doing, Jerry? We're in the blast radius of a ticking bomb. Time is limited."

"Actually," Jerry sounded less concerned than she should, "time is the one thing we've got on our side."

The woman never made understanding her easy. Napalm or not. "Jerry, I love you. I honestly do. But I'd strangle you right now if my hands would reach."

"Look, there's always a catalyst that puts a vision on a loop. And it isn't the explosion. You don't get unlimited tries to alter the future, not even to save yourself, Samantha. Usually, you get one. For your mind to be operating at this level, a significant personal event had to have happened when the bomb went off. It did, didn't it?"

I looked at Jackson, whose eyebrows questioned me.

"Yes," my voice sounded small and alien even to me, "you could say that."

"What happened, Samantha?"

Jackson covered my hand with his and whispered, "Tell me."

That moment between Jackson and I had been intimate, not for others' ears, not for replay, and not easy to share. It was too fresh, too precious. Even to tell Jackson. He had the right to own his words. To decide when or if to share. To say what he wanted when he wanted.

But bombs change things.

"Jackson and I were talking about my training today and how Hal said I choose fear."

"Which is true," Jerry piped in.

I will strangle her if given the chance. I really will. "Jackson said he could give me an alternative to fear..." I looked at him and could see it on his face. He knew. "And that the alternative..."

"Was trusting my love," he finished.

I nodded once. "Yes. Exactly that." What he said was the most wonderful thing anyone had ever said to me, and it was too personal to share while on speaker phone with Jerry. I touched his cheek and moved on. "And that's all I'm going to say about that."

Jerry broke in. "That explains it then. Love is powerful. Far more than fear. Your vision isn't actually about saving you this time. It's about saving Jackson. Your mind is spinning through visions until you find one that accomplishes the job. This could work to our advantage."

I gripped the phone tighter. "How?"

"Well, for starters, you need to die again."

26

What you don't know can't hurt you, unless what you don't know is a bomb. Bombs will always hurt you. You don't even need to see it coming.

I knew about the bomb. Jackson, however, soon wouldn't. Everyone but Jackson agreed to keep it that way. He thought not knowing was lousy.

"You can't honestly think I'll go along with this," he told Jerry and I. "It's foolhardy. A plan that is too dangerous to risk. Samantha," he had that stern, blue-steel look, "I want you to leave. Take the SUV. Go back to the cabin. Get out of here."

I waved him off. "I know. You've told me this before. I don't end up leaving so let's skip ahead."

For our plan of saving everyone to work, Jackson couldn't know about it because, if he did, he'd never go along with it. Like he wasn't going along with it now.

"Plan overruled." Jackson interrupted Jerry and I's conversation periodically to insert his displeasure.

We were all in his office, mapping out our strategy, where the wait staff couldn't overhear. It also gave Jackson room to pace while Jerry and I ignored his protests.

I'd never seen Jackson pace. He stalked the length of the room like a prowling lion. Powerful, controlled, with the capacity for overwhelming violence at the exhale of a breath. Without his blessing, I didn't know if I had the courage to go through with this plan. And, to save everyone, I had to go through with this plan.

"This might work, Jerry. If I can pull it off."

I'd taken over Jackson's desk and one of his flat pencils so I could sketch out the plan. It looked...certifiable. But I would do it.

"I'll know. Even if you don't tell me, I'll know, Sam." Jackson found a spot near the window and halted all pacing. His stillness scared me more than his movement. Stillness denoted obstinance. I couldn't win against Jackson's obstinance.

"He may be right about that," I told Jerry. "He knew about the brandy."

Jerry sounded interested. "What about the brandy did he know?"

"That I wanted it. He didn't know that the first time."

"Now that's interesting."

Jackson wasn't in the mood to be interested. Instead, he'd stopped talking to Jerry or I and only offered one pinched mouth and one annoyed eyebrow in response.

"He's giving us the silent treatment, Jerry. But is it possible? Could he be remembering a flash?"

She dismissed the idea. "How can he remember something that hasn't happened?"

"But he did."

"He can't."

"And yet he did."

"And will again," Jackson threatened.

I smiled at him from across the room. "You're adorable."

"Focus people. Now, Samantha, remember you cannot let your guard down around anyone. We have no idea who is behind this or who is involved. So, you've got to sell it at all times." Jerry sounded more excited than worried, which helped with my nerves. Jackson looked unyielding, which didn't.

"I'll do my best, Jerry."

Because it's Jerry and mercy isn't her thing, she added, "You do better than that. Make this happen. You have no other choice."

Pep talk over.

With the plan in place, I told Jerry I wanted to hang up before we died again so I could talk to Jackson alone.

"There are only about ninety-seven choruses left to this song, so I need to go."

I'd opened one of the south-facing windows in Jackson's office in order to hear when Cindy Lauper returned. And she was back. Time would only happen after time so many times before time stopped.

"You aren't actually dying, Samantha. You're seeing a glimpse of a possible future where you die. In reality, you're still in front of the Durant, making out in public with my grandson."

Right. That.

"Thank you, Jerry. That last unsupportive comment really helped."

We hung up, and I turned to Jackson, who leaned his back against the windows, crossed his arms uncooperatively, and stared me down.

"I can see that you're mad." He didn't argue. "And I understand why." Still not a word. "But you have to let me do this. Please understand. It's the only option left. You understand that, right?"

The shadows, as they had before in this room and at this approaching moment, picked and chose what part of Jackson to highlight and what part to cast into utter darkness. His naturally broad-shouldered form appeared even more unyielding than usual.

Jackson didn't break form, but he did speak, "This isn't how things are going to be between us anymore, Samantha. No more keeping me in the dark. No more facing the world alone. We work through challenges as a team. You and me. We talked about this two nights ago. No more secrets, remember?"

I stood but didn't dare move closer. "I remember."

"Did you mean it?"

"Of course! Only…in this circumstance—"

"In every circumstance," he punctuated. "Not only the simple ones. When things get messy, Samantha, when the problem is too great, we still decide together. And, when the issue involves your life, or the lives of others, then I'm in the lead. You don't have to like it, but I am asking you to respect it."

He had every right to be angry. Even hurt. I would be. Approaching it any other way, though, meant a high probability of failure. I couldn't let that happen. It was up to me to save his life this time, and I would not fail.

"I do understand that, Jackson. Your experience, your ability, your role, it places you in a position to see things I don't."

He raised one eyebrow as if to say, 'So, what's the problem?'

"But I already know how you're going to react to me helping. I've seen it. You send me away. Or try to drag me away. I know it's because you want to protect me, and I adore you for that, but you have to let me do this. It's our only chance."

Jackson had yet to uncross his arms, but he powered down the stare and directed it out the window. That was an encouraging sign.

"Jerry thinks this is the best course of action, too," I reminded him. "And she's been right so far."

The bomb hadn't gone off in minutes, like the two times prior, but had lasted until Lauper. Jerry believed the reason for the two wildly different timelines was due to the evacuations. That had been when the bombs detonated in both early timelines. Whoever was behind this, most likely, had the bomb on a timer or at least a planned time to detonate, along with a remote detonator. Seeing the crowds disperse must have prompted them to act earlier. They wanted a high body count.

That was the theory, anyway.

If we couldn't evacuate anyone without triggering an early detonation, then we kept everyone in the dark. That 'everyone' included Jackson, who would never let me execute Jerry's plan if he was allowed to know it.

Done thinking, Jackson turned away from the window and crooked his finger at me. I wanted to go to him, but I hesitated.

"Come over here." His crossed arms dropped to his sides. "You're standing across the room as if there's something to fear. Even when you're infuriating me, Samantha, I will still always want you close. Besides, we only have a few moments left, right?"

I nodded, having counted forty-two 'time after time's so far. He opened his arms. "Then don't waste them."

I made short work of the distance and slipped into his arms. When I'd been dying from the gunshot to my stomach last weekend, this was where I'd preferred to do it. In his arms.

Jackson pulled me in close. His steady heartbeat thumped against my ear. His sandalwood scent calmed my mind. His warmth lowered my shoulders as the tension eased. I squeezed my eyes closed and focused only on the here, even though it wasn't the now.

"Sam," he spoke quietly, "when this thing starts all over again, will you remember something for me?"

"Mmm hmm," I murmured against his chest.

"Whether or not you tell me is not Jerry's decision to make. It's yours. I'll let you decide. All I ask is that you trust me to do what's best for everyone, whatever that is. Even if you don't agree, trust me,

Samantha. My love for you will never fail."

~

The fourth and, hopefully, final awakening from the flash happened in a slow, almost soothing, speed. I didn't gasp, even though my heart hammered in my chest. I didn't scream, even though I felt the fury of death a moment earlier. I stayed conscious, alert, nearly serene, as I realized it was time to look the man I love in the eyes and boldface lie to him.

Jackson's lips left a final, tender kiss on my neck and eased me back down. We were back to the beginning, back to the sidewalk, back to pre-destruction.

My weight settled on my feet, and my guilt settled into my stomach. Not five seconds ago in my head, he'd pleaded with me to believe in him and not do what I was going to do. So, out of respect, I would make sure he never knew he didn't want me to do what I was going to do.

That should take care of it.

Jackson brushed his hand down my arm. "Okay, sweetheart, how about it? You ready to go inside for that tour now?"

All that blue steel only moments ago was gone. His eyes were unguarded. His shoulders relaxed. To solidify my shame, his smile curled around the razor-wire guarding my conniving heart.

I wanted to tell him. To let it all gush out like the splatting of a water balloon over his beautifully trusting head. But I couldn't because I knew we had only one chance left. All the tokens had been played. This wasn't another flash. This was real life, real time, real consequences.

The loop had closed and sealed our fate to whatever walked through reality's door in the next hour.

I knew this because I knew it. Exactly like how you know when you're no longer dreaming, but awake, even though you thought you were awake while dreaming.

Inside a flash, everything feels real, authentic, and solid, no matter how bizarre. Outside of a flash, reality is clear. It has more weight, sharper margins, harsher shades and smells and sights and sighs than a flash. Reality follows the rules. It's even more tedious to breathe here, but the struggle feels natural.

I never remember the experiential difference between a flash and reality while in a flash. I only remember when I'm on the outside. When I'm awake. When the flash is no longer guarding it's kingdom from discovery.

That's how I knew this was real. And how I knew what I had to do about it.

I smiled my most beguiling smile at Jackson. "I'd love that…but." I darted my eyes toward the Chestnut. "What do you think about grabbing a pre-tour drink and dance at the Chestnut? I've never been inside. Do you mind?"

Jackson glanced at the shimmering warmth of the Chestnut and back at me. Our private dinner, catered by Chef John, waited inside the Durant. I remembered the delight on Jackson's face when I'd seen the table, and the champagne, and the wait staff, and the first hors d'oeuvre. He would be so anxious to unveil the surprise, while also wanting to indulge my whim simply to make me happy. And I was using his giving nature to get my way.

Saving lives should feel more noble than this.

"We can walk over, if that's what you want." He didn't have a note of disappointment in his voice. He made feeling good about deception so hard.

I slipped my hand into his. "Great!"

Together, we stepped into the street. An SUV passed slowly by. Followed by a sports sedan. Across the street, the flower delivery van rested in place, one of the few vehicles parked on the street and not in the six-story parking garage beside The Centennial.

Soon, all puttering traffic dissipated once again, and we moved across the narrow two lanes separating the Durant from the Centennial.

Under the Centennial's colonnade, Jackson paused to enjoy the boobidy bops and ziggidy zaps and screechidy scraps of the cello, saxophone, and violin. I smiled, sucking in air through my teeth. Hurrying him along would seem out of character for a carefree couple out on a Saturday night. Whoever had their finger on the trigger could not detect anything amiss. Or the cookout came early. So, the musicians kept musicing and Jackson kept listening and I kept teeth air sucking.

Nothing was going to stop Starship. Not now. Not ever.

Jackson smiled down at me, squeezed my hand, and motioned toward the bar entrance. There, we could grab a drink and, with a little luck and a whole lot of deception, I could ditch him.

His arm went around my waist, and he moved us toward our salvation or our end. The night was still too young to tell.

~

Inside the Chestnut, surrounded with spotless glass, toasted lighting, blingy guests, and the soulful sound of Etta James, we'd arrived for the monumental moment. It was time to either live or die.

Whatever happened, one thing I knew: it would only happen once.

As the fiery notes moved dancers into slower paces and tightened embraces, Etta James perfectly captured my mood. At last, we were inside. At last, this nightmare would end. One way or another. At last, it was time to stop a bomb.

Without the options of evacuation or notifying the authorities or having enough time to identify the bomber, all our hope was left to me executing Jerry's plan. And, as far as plans go, it was the worst I'd ever heard.

Bad plans were my specialty, but I couldn't take credit for this monstrosity. It was Jerry's. If it went horribly wrong, even though that meant I'd be dead, I took comfort in knowing no one would blame me.

For the plan to even have a chance, however, meant Jackson had to vamoose. Jerry agreed there was no use putting Jackson's life at risk and that, if he knew about the bomb, he'd spend too much time arguing with me to leave.

Honestly, I think she doubted her plan would work and wanted him clear of the blast radius. I didn't blame her. He was her grandson, after all.

Now came the part that would embarrass us all. I had to use my feminine wiles, crank up the high-maintenance, and charm Jackson out of here. When we'd discussed this part of the plan, Jerry and Jackson both believed I couldn't pull it off. But they both underestimated my passion for proving people wrong.

"Oh, Jackson," I turned to him, pressing my hands on his chest and tilting my head down but my eyes up to appear as helpless and distraught as possible. "I forgot about my evening wrap." I held up the thin, shimmery moss-colored fabric draped across my shoulders. "I've still got it. I'm such a silly goose." Cringy phrases are always an indicator I'm manipulating someone. "I can't dance wearing this."

The tricky part at this point was striking the perfect vocal note of disappointment, sadness, and hope. Go too far and I'd sound whiny.

"You can't?" Jackson looked genuinely baffled. As he should. There was no reason in the world I couldn't dance with my wrap.

"Oh, never mind me. I'm being so fussy. I can. Of course, I can. I was only worried it'd be too hot." It weighed the equivalent of tissue paper. "Or that I might trip on it." I can walk and chew gum at the same time. "It's so delicate, it might rip if I did." It's sturdy enough to be used as a tourniquet. "Or someone would take it if I left it in a chair." That was actually possible. "But it'll be fine. I should have left it in your car, but I can carry it."

Jackson studied me with a mixture of confusion, suspicion, and masculine delight. He wanted to save my day here, he didn't understand why my day needed saving from a strip of fabric.

"Is it bothering you that much?"

I pulled off an Academy Award-deserving embarrassed look. I've perfected it over the years by repeatedly embarrassing myself. "I don't know why I said anything. Please, ignore me and let's enjoy our night. I'm being ridiculous."

I turned away, studying the dancers as they swayed. This had to work. I didn't know how else to get Jackson out of here if it wasn't on some kind of errand for me.

"I'll tell you what," Jackson touched my arm so I'd release the wrap, "I'll run it out to the car for you. How's that? Then you won't have to worry about it."

I flashed him my brightest, most admiring smile. "Oh, would you?! Thank you! I'm so sorry to ask, but it'd be such a huge relief!" I kissed him gratefully on the cheek and pressed the wrap in his hands.

"Wait right here, okay?"

I pointed to the floor. "I won't move from this spot." As soon as he could no longer see me through the windows, I would move from this spot.

Jackson turned to leave, then turned back for one last glance. The look in his eyes could have been a bourbon-to-brandy thought. I couldn't be sure. In response, I smiled and waved easily. He shook his head, exited the bar door, and made his way down the stone steps outside.

It was time to make my play.

When I turned back to the room, I bumped into a broad-jawed blond fella in a pinstriped Ralph Lauren drinking with other pinstriped Ralph Laurens. They looked relaxed and wealthy and already buzzed. There's no end to the confidence of posh, inebriated men. A fact I could see clearly in his grey eyes as they focused on me.

"Excuse me. Coming through." I attempted to squeeze out of the pinstriped crowd.

"Well, hello there." He moved into space that didn't exist, which put me with the bar in my back. "Where did you come from?"

"Tupelo, I think. Or Tallahassee. One of those 't' towns. I'm on my way back there now," I motioned toward the exit, which his previously broken nose followed to conclusion.

"You can't leave, yet. I still have to buy you a drink."

Drunken men were so inconvenient. "Do you, though?"

Pinstripe tossed back his head and laughed. The recessed spotlight backlit his blond eyebrows, turning them into porcupine needles. If he didn't get out of my way soon, I would tweeze every one of them out.

"One drink. You wouldn't leave a guy to drink alone, would you?"

His buddies, who had turned back to their comradery, overhead his joke and laughed. Slapping him on his pinstriped back and leaving him alone again with his game.

I didn't need to become this guy's challenge for the night. I needed to slip out of the room without melodrama.

"Look, I came with someone," I told him, giving him my 'bummer' smile.

He placed his hand on the bar to stop my exit, "So, what excuse should we give him when you leave with me?"

Whatever I did to the guy from this point on, he now deserved.

"Well, now that you've put it that way…"

Pinstripe smiled, his teeth as confident as their master. "What would you like? How about a Cosmo? Or something more fruity?"

"Hmm. What are you drinking?"

He held up his copper martini glass. "A Manhattan."

"I'd love a sip of that. And a whiskey."

Pinstripe raised his porcupines. "A woman after my own heart." He leaned over me to speak to the bartender. His alcoholic breath pressed hot against my neck. "Can I get a whiskey for her? And a refresh on my Manhattan."

I rubbed at my throat and spoke to the bartender. "And add some lemon and honey to mine, please."

I covered my mouth and coughed once, causing Pinstripe to stiffen. Then I added two more juicy coughs, which had him stepping back.

"Sorry, I seem to be coming down with something." I cleared my throat and coughed again. "There's this nasty flu going around at the office. I'm sure it's nothing serious. It's not like I've got COVID or something." I laughed, then sniffed. "Do you have a tissue?"

Pinstripe looked as sober as I'd seen him. He shook his head 'no.'

"I'm going to run to the bathroom for one, then. Don't you move, though. I'll be right back for my drink. And a sip of your Manhattan."

27

Bad plans are not the end of the world. Unless they accidentally set off a nuclear holocaust. Then, they are, by definition, the end of the world.

That was not the kind of bad plan we were dealing with here. This was your typical, garden variety kind of bad plan. A bad plan that wouldn't end all human life, only threaten some of it. A bad plan with the likelihood, but not the guarantee, of collateral damage. A bad plan that, yes, could cause my death. But, also, might not. So, a laterally bad, bad plan.

Even if it was Jerry's fault a bad plan was all we had, she didn't need to get defensive about it.

"This couldn't possibly be something I'd support."

"Support?" I whispered harshly into the phone. "You did a lot more than support. You wrote the crappy thing. It's your brainchild."

"Highly unlikely."

"Totally likely, Jerry. I was there."

We didn't have time to argue, but we were doing it anyway. I'd called Jerry after ditching the pinstriped brigade to inform her of the bomb, the loop, and what we decided to do about it. Calling her had been step three of the plan, right after inconspicuously entering the Chestnut and ditching Jackson. Step three wasn't going well.

"You said you'd help me."

"I will help you, Samantha. I'm not going to let you be blown to bits. But I'll never believe this was my plan. It sounds more like one of your harebrained ideas than mine."

She wasn't wrong.

"It was your idea. Can we move on? If you think it's rotten, then

I'm back to having no plan again. And no time to come up with a better one."

Jerry grumbled, "It wasn't enough of a plan to mourn it."

"Jerry! Please, focus. The bomb!"

Behind me, a woman gasped. I turned to see a middle-aged, fair-haired woman in a circular-skirt red dress and a coordinating circular red mouth. The former curved from pleats. The latter curved from shock. She'd stopped in her tracks on the way to the ladies' room and gave me a horrified look that hungry bears invading campsites would recognize.

We were both drawn to the low-lit hallway at the back of the Chestnut but for different reasons. She wanted access to the bathroom. I wanted access to the Centennial lobby, available at the other end.

Seeing her struggle to swallow, I smiled to disarm her. I moved my left hand like a mouth, indicating I was on the phone with a talker, and rolled my eyes.

"No, no. The Keto fat bomb," I feigned impatience.

Jerry on the other end offered a simple, "Huh?"

"That's the recipe I want. Did you use crunchy or creamy peanut butter with that?"

"Samantha," Jerry wasn't amused, "what are you talking about?"

The ruse worked. The woman's mouth returned to a soft, curved line. She eased past me, her red skirt waving around her legs, her citrusy perfume following her like a shadow, and whispered, "Those are delicious."

I took note to control my language. No one in this building could afford anyone starting a panic. It'd kill us all.

"Samantha?" Jerry tried again. "Are you losing it?"

I walked further down the hallway and lowered my voice. "Ignore that. What's the plan?"

Footsteps padded over the speakers. She was on the move. "I'm working on that. Give me a minute, and I'll get back with you."

We clicked off, and I paced. When the red dress reemerged, she smiled and waved, while having no clue her life and mine hinged on a return call. I couldn't tell her she might die tonight, but I could tell her she had lipstick on her teeth. So I did.

My phone buzzed. "What have you got for me?"

I could hear a cacophony of arguing voices in the background. Jerry had assembled the sidekicks.

"We haven't come up with anything promising, yet."

"Nothing?"

"We're still working on it. Gin wants to know, if we can't evacuate everyone out of the building without this bomber triggering the device, what about moving them somewhere else inside the building?"

"How is that not evacuating?"

"Hold on. He can tell you."

Gin came on the line.

"Hey, Sammie." The sound of my childhood friend's voice tightened my throat. "What about moving everyone into a more fortified area? If you can't get them out, what about moving them further inside? Further away from the blast epicenter?"

"Right. That." I cleared the fear from my voice. "Good thought. But I don't know the specific location of the blast epicenter. What if I moved them closer to it? Besides, even if I did, how could I get everyone to move without telling them why? Whoever has orchestrated this would notice when everyone started filing into the back of the building."

"You don't know who it is? Or where they're watching from?"

"No clue."

"Okay, I'll keep brainstorming. Here's Lauren. She had a different idea."

Lauren's reassuring, no nonsense voice came on the line. She would have a good plan, unlike Jerry's.

"Hi Samantha. It's Lauren. Jerry told me about your plan."

"It was her plan."

"It doesn't really matter who came up with the plan."

"I think it does."

"The important part is that you don't, under any circumstances, do it. It was bad. Taking into account the high probability of failure, how could you even consider it?"

"In my defense–"

"Let's not waste time finger pointing. Here's my idea: if you could locate the bomb, maybe I could walk you through defusing it."

Would that work? "You've been trained in how to defuse a bomb?"

She paused. Pauses weren't good. "Not precisely."

"But you've studied it."

"Well…"

"Watched a YouTube about it?"

"Not so much. But I have watched all seven seasons of 'Burn Notice' and can recall several techniques Michael Weston and Fiona Glenanne employed. If this bomb is structured anything like one of those, I could take you through the steps to disarm."

"'Burn Notice,'" I repeated. "The television show."

"If I knew what kind of bomb it was and had time to research it online, I would. But we don't. And those shows use experts for consultants. So, all I'm saying is it's an option."

I rubbed three layers of skin off my forehead. "Please put Jerry back on."

"Of course. Glad you didn't go through with your original plan, though. That would have been a disaster."

She handed the phone back to Jerry.

"Theo and Gabriel are on their way there, Samantha."

I leaned against the hallway, pressing my panic into the wall. "They'll never make it in time. And, besides, what can they do? Crush the bomb's trachea? No one has any ideas, Jerry. I'm out of options and Lauper will eventually come."

"Who is Lauper? Never mind. Let's talk about your options. So, you have none." She needed to sound more disturbed than she did. "What do you do when you've done all that you know to do?"

Quit? No, not quit. Cry? Got that covered. Panic? Check. After that? I rewound through all the times over the last month when circumstances looked hopeless. What did I do? I got help.

"I need Jackson. I need him, Jerry."

"Okay. What's the problem?"

"He's not here. I sent him away. Step two, remember? After I ditch him, you send him on a brief, but urgent, assignment out of the area. That's step four. It was a huge part of the plan working."

Jerry sighed. "Really stupid plan. Good thing I didn't know about it."

I wiped at my face. "I told you about it when I called a few minutes ago."

"Oh, right. You did. Well, then it's a good thing I didn't follow it."

I took in a shaky breath. "What do you mean?"

"I mean I did call him, but I didn't send him on an errand. As soon as I hung up from you a few minutes ago, I called and told him what's going on. He should be back there, oh, about..."

Under the recessed lighting, the Centennial lobby door opened. The cool, blue light followed Jackson down the hallway.

"...now."

~

Jackson pressed his steps against the floor until the floor gave up and lay there. Shadows in the creases of his face fell like lost puppies down a well. If the blast had happened in that moment, the purposefulness of his stride would have pushed it back.

"Don't cry, Samantha. Everything's going to be okay."

Without pausing, he grabbed my hand and pulled me into his current. I fell into step behind him and off we went toward possibility.

"I have an idea," was all he said and said no more.

We emerged out of the hallway and back into the swirling couples and celebratory tables. The notes of "God Only Knows" by The Beach Boys fell like solid drops of promise, each one tapping me on the shoulder, splashing around my ankles, and blowing across my neck. "God only knows what I'd be without you..."

Jackson maneuvered us through the swaying crowd, some from dancing, some from drinking. As the human shapes spun past, and a waiter pivoted by with champagne-filled flutes, and the lights crossed my iris in a fuzz of pink and white light, it hit me. The familiarity I sensed earlier. This was the red nightmare from last night.

The blurry dancers. The pinstripe suit. The red dress. The explosions. All in my dream. But there was more to come. An owl. A metal beam. A woman's scream. A man with a cane. What did all those images mean? What was coming that I still couldn't see?

Keeping a controlled, casual pace, Jackson took us through the bar to the side exit. As we passed through, Pinstripe caught my eye.

I pointed to Jackson and mouthed, "Feeling better."

Outside, we moved under the colonnade, past the street performers and around the lounging crowd.

Someone had finally stopped Starship. The musicians had moved to Chris De Burgh and his obsession with a "Lady in Red." That meant we were one more song closer to Lauper.

Walking past the Chestnut windows, crowded with hobnobbers cheering their status in life around private stables, I zoned in on another red dress. Tailored and persuasive. A brunette. Diamonds on her fingers.

I blinked and she was gone. All I got was an impression of a woman who knew she was the strongest magnet in the room.

The tilt of her head caught my attention more than anything. I knew that tilt. It was the tilt of the vivacious she devil terrorizing my life. But that couldn't be right. The Widow McBride wouldn't be here. Not at ground zero. The dark power that causes the storms does not get caught in one.

"What's wrong?" Jackson felt my steps slowing. I glanced over my shoulder. "I may be losing it, but I saw someone through the window who looked exactly like the Widow McBride."

"Looked like her or was her?"

"I can't be sure."

Jackson led us through a group of millennials energetically discussing the hardships in their life, while snapping selfies of four-dollar coffees on their multi-camera smartphones. We moved past the flower delivery van to the edge of the street. Paused. Then crossed.

Once we got out of everyone's earshot, Jackson rundown his plan.

"Jerry told me about the flashes. The different detonation times. The area affected. Something didn't click for me."

He kept his voice low, but still in a conversational tone. His eyes roamed the area, but with only casual outward interest. His walk maintained an undaunting pace, but no more than a couple might if headed to their vehicle or attempting to get out of the cold.

From all outside appearances, we were enjoying a romantic evening.

"What didn't click?" I looked up at him, noting the lines and shifts in his face as headlights from a passing sedan touched his cheeks. We reached the curb and headed for the Durant's front door.

"The blast radius. You're sure the bomb was inside the Chestnut?"

"Yes." I answered first, considered it second. "Maybe."

"Think about it for a minute. Did you see the blast originate from inside the Chestnut? Being certain of anything you experience in a split-second would be difficult but try to focus on that detail alone. Are you sure?"

If I'd experienced the explosion once, he'd be right. I wouldn't have much detail. But I lived through it four times. After four times, you pick up on stuff.

"All I can say for certain is the blast came from the direction of the Centennial, while taking out the front of The Chestnut and the front of the first floor of the Durant. Why? What are you thinking?"

We approached the front entrance to the Durant.

"I think a blast radius of that magnitude or reach, if originating in the Chestnut, would require a tremendously powerful explosive. One hard to hide."

"So, what's the alternative possibility?"

Jackson pulled his keys out of his pocket. "That it's not located in the Chestnut, but somewhere between there and here. Move the center of the blast closer to the Durant, and you'll get that same impact with less explosives."

I glanced back at the Chestnut. The twirling shadows from earlier, which had shifted into flesh, were now back to only shadows again. I scanned the colonnade, the patrons coming and going, the historically narrow road. There was nothing there. Where would a bomb be hidden if not inside the Chestnut?

"But where? There's nothing between here and there. Only a few people, no bulky backpacks among them, a staircase, a couple concrete planters, a flower delivery truck..." My mouth dropped. "A flower delivery truck."

Wide-eyed, I turned to Jackson.

He nodded once. "That's what I think."

"Is that why we took the long way back here? So you could walk past the flower delivery truck?"

He nodded once.

I looked behind me at the floral, boxy thing. The painting of blue skies and field of flowers on the side now looked ominous. Even mocking. The bright sun painted up in the sky looked angry, scorching, mean and hurtful. The curly-cue writing advertising – "Flowers Everywhere. 24/7 delivery. Say it in a way they won't forget." – now felt like a threat. A flower delivery van had accomplished the impossible: it had become the enemy.

"Jackson"–if chests really do heave, mine did–"what are we doing to do?"

He opened the door to the Durant and motioned me inside. In the entryway, our whispers echoed in the lobby, bouncing back at us in a continual "s" sound. Like a kitchen sink left on full blast.

"If we can't get the people away from the bomb," Jackson explained, "we get the bomb away from the people."

I leaned in closer. "But how? We get close, and they'll detonate it."

"We need to interrupt the signal so they can't." Jackson motioned toward his office.

"You can do that?"

"Yes. In theory."

I followed Jackson to his office, while waving at Matt who stood behind the bar waiting for us.

"Hi Matt." I called out his name before remembering we hadn't met, yet. The look on his face said as much. "Or whoever you are."

I hurried to catch up with Jackson, who closed his office door behind me and opened up a cabinet drawer. What he pulled out looked like a black walkie-talkie, only wider, a little thinner, and with five blunt fingers on top.

"What is that?"

"It's a portable cell phone jammer. It'll interrupt the frequencies of cell phone signals and block them from connecting to a cell tower." Jackson saw the question in my eyes and shrugged, as if embarrassed. "I use it to create a dead zone when I'm needing to protect sensitive information. Periodically. Anyway, it isn't legal. It also won't affect anything unless it's in range."

"What's the range?"

"75 feet. Give or take. It should work to keep any wireless attempts at detonation from activating the bomb."

"Should?"

Jackson stuffed the jammer inside his jacked. Nothing looked out of place. Per usual with him.

He looked me in the eyes and slowly smiled. If I'd had a football, I would have tossed it to him for the winning touchdown. "Trust me, Sam. This is what I do."

For a guy racing against the clock, he looked so serene. Not relaxed, necessarily. But focused. In tune. This was Jackson in his element. The savior, fulfilling his life's mission. I wanted to take a picture of him or paint him like this on a large canvas. To mix turquoise into the blue waters of his eyes so that the light behind them shimmered like ocean waves in the sun. To add a bottomless blackness to the line of his shoulders so that all light, like all worry, was absorbed not deflected. To capture with a color not yet created the authority in his stance that took dominance over the circumstances.

More than all of that combined, I wanted to never be a reason any part of who he is ever dimmed. Like by not trusting him. Or needing him and not letting him know how much.

I stepped up, smoothed out his lapel, and buttoned one button. "This, my love, is what we do. Remember?"

His wrinkled brow said he didn't.

"Oh, right. You haven't said that, yet. Previous flash. Wish you could have been there." I rested my hands flat on his chest. "Well, you will say it. Eventually. Some day. Here's the short version: we do things together, now. You and me. No more solitary heroics. So, superhero, we have three eighties love songs left before that thing goes boom. What's your plan? And where does your lovely sidekick come in?"

28

Historically, sidekicks always get left behind, forgotten, overlooked, and underestimated until they save the hero, who then saves the day. What usually follows is a hearty pat on the back and an understanding they'll be left behind, forgotten, overlooked, and underestimated again tomorrow.

And, yet, even during their greatest frustrations, I'm doubting Robin, Jughead, Kato, or Woodstock were ever assigned the task of faking a broken shoe strap.

It felt beneath my talents.

Jackson and I emerged from the Durant with champagne glasses in hand. We toasted under the awning, sipped lavishly, laughed loudly, and clumsily waltzed our way across the street.

Nearing the flower delivery truck, my celebratory and faux inebriated-self stumbled with a shoe malfunction.

Right on cue.

I limped the final two steps toward the delivery truck, leaned on the driver's side door for support, and examined my shoe. Jackson knelt down to examine my ankle, using the angle to scan the area for anyone coming or watching. As soon as he stood up, I leaned against his arm with the street to my back and laughed loudly again.

All these ridiculous cackles were part theater, part signals. It was the sign to Jackson I was ready to hold out my arms and adjust my evening wrap.

While planning this strategy, Jackson had fetched my wrap from his vehicle to use as a good visual blockade. He'd handed it over with a warning to never manipulate him with feminine wiles again, except in rare cases where I thought he'd enjoy it.

"It was unexpected. And unsettling. And adorable." He recounted earlier, while mapping out our new plan. "I knew I was being used, but I enjoyed it too much to call you on it."

"Told you I could pull it off."

"You did?"

"In another life. Yes."

Now, it was show time.

While I adjusted my wrap, Jackson used the temporary cover to slip a slim jim in the driver's side door and unlock it. Usually, that would take a minute or so. With Jackson, it took a half second.

With the door unlocked, my role was to take the champagne glasses and run back to the Durant, locking myself inside.

Let it be noted that I never agreed to that part of the plan.

"I'm going with you."

Jackson's stern look said 'no.' He followed that up by saying, "No."

"Yes. Or, by the time you have the van hotwired I'll have broken the back window, unlocked the door, climbed in, and done it all using my own speed and this."

I opened my hand to show Jackson his brass-handled center punch, which I'd lifted from his toolbox.

Jackson growled, opened the door and motioned me inside. I slid over the driver's seat, dropped the champagne glasses, my wrap, and the center punch into the passenger seat, and slipped into the back.

From the outside, the fresh paint and advertising hid the age and usage of the van. On the inside, no one cared to hide anything. The vinyl seats lacked stuffing. The dashboard lacked a radio. The shelves lacked flowers. All of it I registered in the corner of my eye, which was solely transfixed on red glowing digits.

Resting without any fanfare in the dark, the numbers dropped lower and lower and lower per second. Lower and lower. Lower and lower. They spun down to the grave as the timer nestled in a configuration of wires and clay. The threatening contraption attached neatly to a five-gallon blue bucket, which was sandwiched between two other five-gallon ominous blue buckets full of what I feared to guess. All three buckets, wearing a thick black belt, were buckled against the wall.

"What do you see?" Jackson busied himself knocking a screwdriver into the ignition with a hammer, all equipment he'd hidden under his suit jacket.

The plan was to drive the van to an abandoned parking lot in the warehouse district. Nothing around there would be open this time of the night. We couldn't stop the explosion, but we could reposition it in a part of town where it wouldn't cause harm. All we needed was the time to get there.

With the screwdriver wedged deep enough into the ignition, Jackson turned the handle, started the van, and unlocked the steering wheel.

Before he threw it into drive, I yelled to stop. "How long will it take to drive there?"

"Three minutes."

"We don't have three minutes."

Outside, the street performers were wrapping up "Eternal Flame" by the Bangles and firing up "Lady" by Kenny Rogers. As iconic of an 80s love song as that was, Rogers didn't belong. He never made an appearance in my flashes. Lauper and her ninety-seven choruses were next, but something in this timeline had altered the playlist. In this timeline, the timer was also missing two minutes.

Jackson pivoted in the seat. "How many minutes do we have?"

I couldn't take my eyes off the glowing red numbers. "Less than one."

Jackson threw the van into drive, burned rubber out of the unloading zone, and took a hard right into the parking garage.

"51 seconds. What are you doing?"

We swung into the parking garage under its low entrance warning, bottomed out, and hit the ramp heading up. Parked vehicles and musty lighting passed by one after another out the side door windows.

"If we can't get the bomb away from the crowds horizontally," Jackson gripped the wheel, "we'll go vertically."

"44. Make a left."

Our tires screeched around the curves, the squeal echoing in the enclosed space.

"Got it."

"42. Left again."

To counter the inertia of the turn, I jammed one foot against the side door and another in a lunge position and both hands grasping the back of the passenger seat.

"Sam, sweetheart, left is the only option. I got this. Just try to breathe. And keep that thing still." He gunned the accelerator as the lot straightened before another curb. "And hold on"

"38. Okay." I had the seat in a death grip. "36. How far are we taking this?"

Jackson maneuvered the van around another unforgiving turn. "To the top."

We wound up floor after floor. Screamed past vehicle after vehicle. The higher we went, the fewer the vehicles. We passed SUVs, and sedans, and trucks, and economy cars, and each slung with precision or madness between two yellow lines. Numbers in empty spaces ticked up while the numbers on the timer ticked down.

The garage had no end.

We kept going, and the spaces kept coming, and the tires kept shrieking, and we were spinning ourselves into heaven. Literally. If we didn't get out of here soon.

"29. I'm sorry about ruining your special evening. The Durant looks amazing, by the way. And Chef John's pinwheels are the best."

"You saw the dinner?"

"25. Appetizer only."

"Did we try the crab cakes?"

"23. Yes. You thought they needed more sauce. So I ate yours."

"You must have liked them."

"21. I liked everything about tonight that involved you. We had a really nice time."

"I'm glad."

"18. We should do it again soon. Maybe make it all the way through dinner?"

"I'd like that."

"15. We're not going to make it, are we?"

"Almost there."

"14. Time is up."

We shot out of the lower floors and onto the roof like a geyser. The van bumped and sparked as the back wheels grabbed pavement.

It was darker outside at the top of the parking garage than down below inside it. And, yet, the open space, the yellow-tinged city-lit sky, the quieting isolation, lent itself to a momentary sense of hope before the red glowing numbers caught my attention again.

"9"

There were no vehicles up here. Only space and empty yellow lines seeking companionship.

"7"

Jackson slammed on the brakes, throwing me sideways across the back-passenger seat.

"5"

Nearly upside down, but I could still see the numbers.

"4."

Jackson rocketed out of his chair, grabbed me, and exploded out the van side doors.

"3!"

He didn't take time to see if I could catch up, but, instead, grabbed me and launched.

"2!"

He moved with such speed we may have taken flight. A ferocious roar painted the world in the reddest red, a red's red, a kind of red that made other reds feel pink.

The impact clawed Jackson in the back. We flew forward. Red's red everywhere. Then blackness.

~

I woke in a state of groggy discomfort. Something wasn't right with my arms. Or my legs. Or my eyes. My tongue rolled through my mouth, seeking moisture. A salty bitterness overpowered the lingering sweetness of champagne. I turned my head and turned it back again, unable to fan away the roar of bees in my ears. Cleansing tears rolled down my cheeks. Stinging smoke clung to my eyes.

Blinking in the sooty blackness, I made out the line of a broad-shouldered man standing over me. When I tried to speak, a "moo" came out. There's no telling what I meant.

Gruffly, the man pulled me up into a standing position. My legs dipped, wobbled, then held. The man's arms kept me from toppling back to the ground again until I could bear my own weight.

I murmured, "Jackson," feeling lifeless and limp.

The male voice, close to my ear, gave a single, "Nope."

Silly. Of course, it was Jackson. Who else would it be?

With a tug on my arm, which still wasn't working right, he led me away from the bonfire. The flower delivery truck sparked and raged on, unaware no one was in the mood for its theatrics.

I wobbled alongside the man. My shoes were back there in the smoke. Left behind as debris. Underfoot, the pavement cooled as my unsure steps took me further from the blast radius.

The breeze pushed back the curtain of soot and unveiled my male companion. He had the broadness of Jackson, but that's where the similarities ended. His bald head squatted on an overly thick neck, which had been scribbled on with an irregular tattoo of a war scene. Or a duck. It could be either. Beneath the blue-inked attempt at a Franz Marc painting, his bulky frame had been hardened in a brutal way. He had the look of a man who'd lifted weights until his body became uncomfortable to live inside.

It was Mr. Clean.

I didn't know who he worked for or what he wanted, only that he had some beef with me. But, these days, who didn't?

"Ma, ma, moo," I blathered, selling a still muddled mind, while stumbling over my own feet.

His hand kept a tight hold on my bicep. I tugged at my wrists realizing what was off about my arms. They were bound behind my back. That could pose a challenge when it was time to make my move, but it wouldn't stop me.

Hanging my head down, letting my hair fall partially over my face, I wildly scanned the parking lot for Jackson. He had to be around here, somewhere. The fog of burnt air, coupled with the twisted parking lot light it'd destroyed, dropped the area into a deep shadow. The lights from the surrounding buildings, dimmed though they were, acted more as an impediment than a help. The faint glare deepened the rooftop darkness.

Where was Jackson?

I scanned quickly, not wanting Mr. Clean to catch me acting too lucid. There was no sign of Jackson from what I could make out, but I could only look in one general direction. The mass of muscle fibers, connective tissue, and steroids beside me blocked my view.

Up ahead, a black Chevy Impala idled with the headlights off.

The passenger door opened, and Opie stepped out. He looked as Ron Howard'ish as ever, even without a director's chair. He spoke on his cell phone, his voice juicy and deep, which disturbed the whole

Opie persona. When he clicked off, he slipped his cell phone into a pocket and exchanged it for a gun. Instead of pointing it at me, which he should have since I was about to take it away, he aimed it at Mr. Clean.

An odd tactic.

Opie's eyes scanned my body as if expecting a second head or third arm. "This is to keep you cooperative."

He overestimated my concern for Mr. Clean's welfare.

"Do as I say, and I'll let him live."

Still not seeing the motivation.

"I don't have to kill him. Shooting him here would complicate the story, but I will if it's necessary."

Story?

"As long as he doesn't interfere, he can live. For now. If, that is, he's still alive."

What was he talking about?

I took a half step back to look around the bulky Mr. Clean. Along the blast perimeter, lying next to the crumpled door of the delivery van, was a face-down Jackson. At this distance and lighting, I couldn't tell if he was breathing. A black sludge oozed down his face. He was bleeding from the head and unconscious.

I instinctively sprung forward to go to him, but Mr. Clean held onto my arm, and Opie tsked. "Nope. Like I said, cooperate and I won't shoot him." The gun hadn't been pointed at Mr. Clean, but slightly past Him at Jackson. "Try to run or fight back, and you might be able to stop me. But I'll get a shot off first." He took out his handkerchief and dabbed at beads of sweat on his upper lip. "You can roll the dice and see if I lose. But I'm an excellent shot."

Cocky, scrawny guys like him are never excellent shots.

"I really am."

It was doubtful.

"I wouldn't doubt me."

I could take him.

"You won't stop me in time." His head tilted, as if raising an ear to the sky helped him hear my thoughts better. "But you're welcome to try."

I watched Jackson's still form and considered my options.

"He's one of the good guys, isn't he?" Opie smirked. "Pity."

I couldn't, I wouldn't, risk Jackson's safety.

I cleared my throat, attempted to speak, and coughed up part of the delivery van's exhaust pipe. "What do you want?" I asked in a voice this side of sandpaper.

Opie motioned toward the vehicle. "We're going to take a little ride."

He nodded at Mr. Clean, who tugged me toward the back of the vehicle. Instead of opening the door, he pushed a button on his keyring and popped the trunk.

"You've got to be kidding me."

Mr. Clean pushed open the lid. The trunk light automatically switched on. Inside was a brunette in a red dress. Her make-up flawless. Her hair impeccable. Her eyes so wide that white rimmed the green. It was, most definitely, the Widow McBride.

I blew out a frustrated breath. "You've got to be kidding me."

∼

Stuffed, as we were, in the trunk of a Chevy Impala with her in her red dress, me in my green, I felt like one-half of a holiday themed package of Hostess snack cakes.

"Samantha, I know I'm the last person you want to see right now."

Or maybe Little Debbie.

"But, if we work together, we can get out of this."

She only said that because we were handcuffed together.

"Agreed? You and me? Partners?"

Her kumbaya would have been easier to believe if, upon first seeing me, she hadn't released a string of expletives so severe it'd turned Mr. Clean's head pink. She hated me. She'd been trying to kill me for a month. She shot me in the stomach last weekend. Working with her was unthinkable. Trusting her was out of the question. Partnering with her was a death sentence.

"Sure. Why not." I wiggled for more room. "Now, zip it. I'm trying to do something here, and your lies are distracting me."

McBride huffed. Her breath still smelled like perfume. The alcohol-based, allergen-inducing kind.

"I knew you couldn't get over our past."

I strained against my constraints. "It was last Saturday."

When Mr. Clean had tossed me into the trunk, he'd handcuffed our hands together but didn't remove my zip-tie restraints. The overkill meant these guys were threatened by me.

I would exploit that later.

"It wasn't personal." McBride wrongly assumed I cared. "It was business. You're in the way. Personally, I think you're interesting for a common sort of person. In different circumstances, we might have been friends."

"You said that last weekend, too. Right before shooting me in the stomach."

"Did I? I must believe it then."

She didn't.

To get out of this, I needed to attack one problem at a time. First, the zip ties. Getting those off wouldn't free me of McBride, but it would free one arm. One arm was a good start.

"You need to get as far away from me as possible. Give me as much room as you can," I instructed.

"Hey, darling, we're both stuck here against our will." Her southern accent, the one she tried so hard to hide, strengthened under duress. "Let's not bicker over space."

"Just scoot. I'm working on something over here."

We were in total darkness, which didn't help my nerves. If she had a knife or blunt instrument in her free hand, I wouldn't know until it entered my gut.

She moved back. "What are you doing?"

"Something." I didn't elaborate.

Stretching my arms back like I'd done in the refrigerated van with Trudy, I slipped my intertwined wrists over my butt and down my legs. The move prompted a grunt and "Ouch! My arm!" from McBride.

She should have that looked at.

With my hands now in front, I activated step two. Raising my hands, I checked the space above my head. McBride's arm came with me.

"You need to tell me what's happening over there."

"Downward facing dog. Do you mind? Yoga relaxes me."

She scoffed. "If you think you can get out of this, by all means. Try."

I lifted my hands again, pushed my hips up in a half bridge pose, and struck down. Unlike the refrigerated van, I didn't have space. The strike against my hip bone needed to be an explosion. Fast and hard.

I tried again. And again. And one more time. Each hit shoved the metal handcuff into my left wrist. Twice my fists connected with the hood. A few more tries and I would have successfully kicked my own butt.

McBride, less encouraging than Trudy, offered loud sighs. "Whatever you're doing isn't working. And it's jerking my arm. A lot."

McBride wanting me to stop buoyed me to keep going. One try later, the zip-ties shattered.

"Ha! I'm free!"

McBride tugged at the handcuffs, which tugged at my left arm. "Not quite, sugar. If you got your hands free, super. But we're still handcuffed together, remember? And, not to bring up the most obvious problem, but how are we supposed to get out of a locked trunk?"

I rubbed at the cuts on my wrist. "Oh, that's the easy part. We pull this glow in the dark trunk release lever."

29

Not everyone has a right to their opinion. But, if I'm wrong here and they do, they don't have the right to make me hear it.

"We can't jump out of a moving vehicle," McBride argued. "That's not a plan."

It was the best plan in these circumstances. Simple. Possible. Ready now.

"You can come, or you can stay here. I don't care."

McBride jiggled her arm. "You can't go anywhere without me."

She had a point, but I wouldn't let her know that. "To get away from you, I'm willing to gnaw off my hand."

Outside, the Impala clicked along. We'd left the city. Using Kyle's vibration technique, I also knew we were on a well-paved road with decent curves and no stop signs or lights. We never paused. We didn't slow. The outside noise was nothing but wind. No car horns. No traffic. No signs of life outside this suffocating blackness.

Once we got to wherever we were being taken, I was certain we wouldn't be left to hitch a ride with a lonely, citrus-loving dragonkin. So, I told McBride what I thought would happen when the vehicle stopped, and she appreciated the brilliant insight.

"We are not going to be forced to dig our own graves."

She didn't know that for a fact.

"Look," she sounded calmer than she should, "I have an idea of how to get out of this."

I stilled my free hand on the trunk release lever.

"Does it involve you firing a bullet into my belly because, PS, you've already done that."

She huffed. "Do you want to hear it or not?"

That wasn't a 'no.'

"You've got thirty seconds to sell me on it, then I'm popping this trunk, jumping out, and taking your arm with me."

McBride sighed into the void. "Listen, I know who is behind this. Behind what's been happening to you, what's happening to us both right now."

"You are what's been happening to me."

"It doesn't end with me, Samantha. I'm as much a victim of circumstances as you are."

"No, you aren't."

She gave a soft laugh. "Okay, maybe that's taking it too far. But I can help us both. I can talk to the man pulling all these strings. I can reason with him. He likes me."

He had her stuffed in a trunk.

"I think you're misreading his signals."

The friction of wind silenced. Gravel popped under the wheels. McBride and I pressed against the door. The wind picked up speed again. We'd turned onto another road.

"You need to trust me, Samantha." McBride pushed herself back into position. "I can get us both out of this."

I didn't trust she could or would. The woman wanted me dead. The only moral problem she had with this situation was that it included her.

"I doubt it. What I know about you is that you like to shoot people at close range and hold their friends hostage in a room full of unhealthy snack options."

McBride exhaled with forced drama. "I wasn't going to hurt your friends. I only needed to borrow them for a few hours."

"You do not borrow people, McBride. That's not how being a human works."

"Well," she fidgeted with the handcuff, "I let them go, didn't I?"

"No, they escaped. By breaking a second-story window. And jumping out of it."

She huffed. "Well, whatever. They're fine. No harm done. I only needed to get Jackson's attention, and I did. Besides, grabbing your friends wasn't even my idea."

"Oh?"

"Look, I wanted to meet Jackson. Jude told me all about him after

I sent him to do a little reconnaissance on you."

"And find out why I wouldn't die," I finished for her.

"He told me about Jackson's speed. And," there was a lascivious smile in her voice, "all the man's obvious physical prowess. He sounded intriguing. I wanted to meet this man of steel for myself. To see him in the flesh." Her tone made me want a shower. "And what a sight, I must say."

I couldn't argue with her there.

"So," she toyed with something making a crinkly sound, "I told Jude to make it happen. And Jude always makes what I want happen."

The thespian liar. How could I forget. "Right. Jude What's-His Name."

"It's Koslowski." She misunderstood my sarcasm, but everyone always does. "I told Jude to make sure Jackson was there with you when I arrived. And he made it happen. If I had to guess, he probably told Chris and Francis to grab a couple of Jackson's friends, and they went overboard. They're always doing that."

She spoke as if the guys grilled too many hamburgers for a cookout, not kidnapped an entire group of people.

"Chris and Francis." I'd never heard these names mentioned before. "Is that the twin thugs?"

"Twins? They aren't twins." She stopped messing with the crinkly thing. "I don't think they're even related."

"They look exactly alike except with different hair color."

She dismissed it. "I don't see it."

"They both have a hulky build with stubby legs."

"Yeah, so?"

"And droopy cheeks with boxed chins."

"I guess."

"And meaty shoulders that curve forward."

"Hm. Never noticed."

"And heavy chests with short torsos."

"Maybe."

"And faces like cereal boxes."

"They have some physical similarities. What's your point, Samantha?"

I didn't have one. It only surprised me we couldn't agree even on this.

"Forget it. The point is, I don't trust you to tell me the truth because you're a she devil. And she devils always lie."

She clicked her tongue. "See? This is the kind of attitude that can fester when you hold on to the past."

I rolled my eyes. "Again, it was Saturday."

∼

"Look, Samantha, the truth is, like it or not, we're in this together."

I didn't think that was the truth, actually.

"And," she continued, "we need to work together to get out of it."

We really didn't.

"So, if we can at least agree on that…"

We couldn't.

"…I'll tell you what I know, and we can come up with a plan."

I let those words hang in the air as we rode in silence.

There had been a day not all that long ago I would have believed her. The sincerity in her voice. The dire circumstances we shared. The belief most people were inherently good. I would have been persuaded, while hoping she felt remorse for her actions.

But that was then. This was now.

Now I knew, deep down, way down there, at the very core, people were selfish. We're born that way. We could, however, choose to change. But McBride hadn't. This was why I was doing my best to pick the handcuff lock without her hearing it.

"Fine," I begrudgingly broke the silence. "Tell me about this person who likes you so much they shoved you into the trunk of a car." I fished a bobby pin out of my hair. "But talk fast. Or I'm out of here."

"Glad you're finally coming around." McBride wiggled in her space, as if turning toward me for a more intimate atmosphere. "Here's what you need to know about this person. Our steamy relationship started about seven years ago…"

That's when the true discomfort of my situation reached its peak. I did not need to hear about McBride's sexual exploits, but she told me anyway. I distracted myself by bending the bobby pin open with one hand.

When Trudy restyled my hair earlier, she removed thirty bobby pins and left three. One was all I'd need.

The Impala hit a hard pothole and turned into a rough gravel road. The trunk bounced, sending McBride and I airborne. We landed with a thud and an "ugh" as the air knocked out of our lungs. Once we recovered, McBride picked up her story where she left off, and I picked another bobby pin out of my hair.

Okay, so two was all I'd need.

"We were crazy about each other. In the beginning. We couldn't keep our hands off each other. Oh, the deliciousness of a new romance. It's so thrilling. So fresh and unknown. So electrifying. Every moment together is about pleasure. It's all so intoxicating. You know what I mean. All you can think about all day is…the man. The smell of him, the heat of him, the feel of–"

"I get it. Please, for the love of all that is good and holy, move on."

She sighed. "All I'm trying to say is that he's a fabulous lover."

"And Don Juan's name is…?"

"I'm getting to that part."

She didn't get to that part. Instead, she talked about how her extramarital affair strengthened her marriage.

"We're still talking about the husband you poisoned, right?"

While she babbled on about "delectable chemistry," I worked on bending the tip of the bobby pin into an s-curve. This you could do by inserting it into the keyhole and using the edge to bend it backward. Then, all you had to do was reinsert the pin and release the teeth.

It's an easy trick. One I remembered – thanks to Lauren's doctorate in photographic memory – from my third-grade obsession with David Copperfield. Performing it, however, was easier when you could see the lock. And, if not see, find. Between the cuffs bouncing or being tugged when McBride moved, and the entire trunk vibrating on a gravel road, inserting a tiny pin into a tiny keyhole while blind was more difficult than making the Statue of Liberty disappear.

Time ticked down. The Impala slowed. And, McBride, who was still obviously stalling, was still obviously stalling.

I tried one last time to refocus her attention, while I kept mine on unlocking my handcuff. "McBride, out of curiosity, why does your Latin lover want me dead?"

She resituated her legs. "I never said he was Latin."

"Never mind."

She exhaled in false melodrama. "Okay, fine. I guess there's no point in hiding the truth from you now. He thinks my husband Chad told you something the night he died that could connect back to him."

"Told me what?"

"Who knows." She sounded bored. "He's the paranoid one. Not me."

That final conversation with Senator Chad McBride on the top of the Oklahoma Now building had replayed in my head every day for the last seven years. He had said nothing that could identify anyone to me. Except maybe…

"Lucian? Is that who's behind all this?"

Suddenly, the Impala braked hard, scattering gravel and it's two trunk passengers. McBride pushed into me, I pushed into the wall, and the wall pushed the second pin from my hands.

Okay, so I'd need three.

~

The great thing about super speed is, of course, the speed. You can move faster than anyone else. You can take people by surprise. Instead of letting them open a trunk, for instance, you can pop the trunk release lever early. Then, you can shove the lid of that trunk upward with such unexpected speed it dents when connecting with a man's head. And you can do all of it with one arm handcuffed to someone else.

The bad part is that, at that level of speed, you have to consider the blunt force when you stop. Unless you have super strength, you may suffer the periodic bruising of the legs from trees and the periodic breaking of the hand on a man's skull.

With Mr. Clean dazed but still on his feet, I'd followed the blunt force of the lid on his head with the blunt force of my fist on his face. You could actually hear my bones crack.

Originally, my plan had been to pick the handcuff lock, jump out, and run until I hit Seventy-First Street. When that didn't work, my second plan was to take out Mr.Clean and Opie with Hal's braintickler technique, pick the handcuff lock, jump out, and run until I hit Seventy-First Street.

My plans never live up to their hype.

Mr. Clean now sat on the ground, staring up at the stars as if counting little birdies circling overhead. Meanwhile, I leaned halfway out of the trunk, moaning in pain and cradling my hand.

Opie, approaching with his gun drawn, looked like a violent prone Academy-Award-winning director. "What did you think that would accomplish?"

I sucked in a breath while trying to wiggle my fingers. "I don't know." I blinked as tears slipped down my cheeks. "Thought I'd try it and find out."

Opie remained fifteen feet back. "Live and learn." He bobbed the business end of his pistol. "You can get out of the trunk as fast or as slow as you like. Makes no difference to me."

I crawled out, followed by McBride. We both took in our surroundings.

We were in the middle of a decrepit, single-lane metal bridge in the middle of nowhere. Parallel wood planks, covered in dirt and gravel, connected the end of the road to the beginning of the road. Corroded, arthritic beams crisscrossed overhead, giving the sense we'd parked under a game of pick-up stix.

The ramshackle bridge, wedged between two hills, extended roughly three car lengths. It was one of those mini-structural finds secreted away in the forgotten rural lands and left to rust and wait.

Underfoot, wood planks scratched against the soft spots on my bare feet. Under the planks, lost in the darkness of mellowed moonlight, rushed a muddy river. I couldn't see it, but I could hear it. The mud part was assumed.

"A bridge," I groaned under my breath. "Of course, it had to be a bridge."

It would be impossible for this to happen on the ground floor. Or on a flat, level plain.

Beyond our man-made, man-neglected bridge, the area belonged to the four-legged and two-winged beasts. This was their playground, their night club, and we didn't have reservations.

In the recesses of the surrounding blackened hills, curious, displeased eyes watched with wariness. Something, or many somethings, were out there. All possibly sensing my fear.

From the trees, a barred owl echoed back with its eternal, eerie questions, "Who cooks for you? Who cooks for you all?"

Beside me, McBride smoothed out her dress, her hair, her brow.

The bosom buddy persona had ended, replaced with a confident cockiness. This woman, without a doubt, was in control of her circumstances.

"I get the feeling you're less kidnapped than me."

She smiled politely and returned to smoothing herself out. She was, obviously, done playing her role. She'd completed her job of anchoring me in the trunk. I could run fast, but not while dragging another person.

"So," I watched Mr. Clean lean open-mouthed against the bridge, and Opie lean into his gun stance, "we're waiting for whom, exactly? And are they usually this late?"

No one answered. All they had to do was wait. And ignore me.

I assumed the mystery villain, this Lucian person, was the part of McBride's performance that held an element of truth. Not because I trusted her but because she acted like she was waiting, too.

Whoever Lucian was, if he felt threatened by me, he sounded weak. And weak people didn't scare me...unless they hired goons with guns. Then, yeah, a little scared.

I wanted to end this. I'd had all the kidnapping and trunk stuffing and gun pointing I could take for the month. And now my hand hurt.

Vehicle lights in the distance punched holes in the wooded darkness. The end had finally come.

Bounce by bounce, the headlights threaded through the trees along a road we'd previously traveled. Behind Opie, who'd been dabbing sweat off his lip with increased fidgeting, the full-sized SUV stopped at the entrance to the bridge and settled.

The lights remained on. Bright and blinding.

McBride looked impatient. Opie looked damp. Mr. Clean looked dazed. And I looked at the lights.

A vehicle door squeaked open. McBride and I shaded our eyes until the brights dimmed. Behind the softened glow, I could make out the outline of two legs attached to the upper half of a male body. The silhouette glided forward. The natural bob and step of his walk couldn't be made out in the glare, giving the impression he stood on an airport conveyor belt taxiing him to a terminal. The only movement to break the illusion was the swing of his arms moving in and out of the headlights.

He walked through the shroud of dust particles and gnats. Through the breeze tossing dirty shrapnel. Through the distance between us. And, finally, stopped in front of me.

Relaxed, dressed to kill, stood media mogul Robert Maessen. My old boss. The man who gave terrible Christmas bonuses. The guy I originally suspected, then didn't, then felt ambivalent about.

"You're not Lucian." I sounded disappointed. "Where's Lucian?"

Maessen walked over to McBride and planted a kiss on her upturned cheek. "What is she talking about?" he asked her.

"I have no idea." McBride ignored my "you've got to be kidding me" response and spoke with Maessen. "The boys said you needed help getting her here. You owe me you know. I had to ride in the trunk with her. And this is a new Jovani." She smoothed her hand along her trim hip. "What are you going to do with her?"

"Yeah, Bob," I echoed her question, "what are you going to do with her?"

Before he answered, a door opened on Maessen's SUV, and another figure emerged. The man walked with a cane, his click, step, click, step marking his progress until he reached the bridge and the 'clicks' turned to 'clomps'.

From what I could tell, he appeared younger than Maessen. The shadow of his shoulders still retained that broadness of prime life. The headlights struck the tips of his hair. I could make out a white shirt under a darker jacket before I could make out his face.

Then the chin came into view. The outline of the nose. The set of the eyes.

I knew that face. And this was the last place I wanted to see it again.

"Hi, Sass," my old editor, old flame, old mentor who taught me how to fight for the voiceless, stood next to his father.

"Hi, Trevor," I breathed out.

30

Edgar Allan Poe once said you should "believe nothing you hear, and only one half that you see." I wondered if Poe had ever been held captive on a lonely Oklahoma bridge by an old boyfriend and his disapproving father.

Trevor took in my evening gown, my messed hair, my swollen hand. "It's good to see you." His eyes were unreadable pools of ink. "That's a pretty dress."

I opened my mouth and shut it. What was he doing here? How was he mixed up in all this? And what the bloody blue blazes was going on? Wasn't there a Lucian person coming?

"Thank you," I muttered before I could stop myself. I'm southern. Those words will happen no matter how hard you try to stop them. "How's the, uh, how's the knee?"

I needed to think fast. Whatever was happening here didn't make sense. A dark, faceless, threatening figure I knew how to respond to. A friend, a teacher, a confidante, I didn't know what to do with that. It couldn't be real. Trevor Maessen would never hurt me. His father? Maybe. If he found the guts, and it was expedient for him. But Trevor? Not Trevor. No way.

"It's getting stronger. Doc has me in physical therapy." One hand leaned on his cane, the other ran his fingers through his hair.

I'd seen him do that thousands of times. When on a tight deadline, Trevor would rake his fingers through his hair as if finding additional minutes woven in there somewhere. Instead of making him look tired, it increased his appeal.

He had that way about him. That Robert Redford ease, a natural comfort and confidence in his own skin. It made you relax when around him, unless you were being held captive on a dark, rural bridge with a sweaty Ron Howard pointing a gun at you.

"Been there," I said. "I get it."

His mouth turned down, struck with an out-of-character sadness. "I know you do."

A month ago, Trevor had been willing to fall off the roof of the Durant Hotel if that freed me to escape. I could still see the image of him from that night. His face red and strained. His arms grasping onto the ledge. His hands slipping. Him urging me to run while I could and save myself.

That's when I decided to take Poe literally. He said to only believe half of what you see, so I chose to believe the Robert Maessen half.

"So, what's the plan here?" I asked the general audience. "Will McBride and I be digging our own graves?" I held up my swollen fingers. "She should go first. It's going to take me longer."

McBride puffed out a soft, dismissive laugh. "Robert, get the handcuff keys for me, will you? I've got drinks later at the Penvenens, and I need time to freshen up, first."

She wasn't quite getting it.

I looked at Trevor, then Robert. "Who's going to tell her?"

Neither responded, while the corner of Trevor's mouth twitched in amusement.

McBride ignored me. "Gentlemen? Now would be good." She lifted her cuffed arm, which lifted mine and jiggled it. "Unlock them or cut them. I'm done helping."

No one made a move, as I expected.

What I knew that McBride didn't was that she had been in the blast radius tonight. I'd got a glimpse of her in the window of the Chestnut. Maessen may want me out of the picture, but he apparently wanted her to go with me.

With no one else ripping the Band-aid off for the woman, I jumped in.

"Look, McBride, Bob here is cleaning up loose ends." I tugged at our cuffed hands so I could scratch my nose. "And you seem pretty loose to me."

She did a laugh snort, which isn't a good look on anyone. "Don't be ridiculous."

The men made no coordinated moves to help her or contradict me.

"No one's going to tell her?" They each fiddled convincingly, so I turned back to her with a different tactic. "Do you see anyone jumping to unlock your cuffs?"

She looked from me, to her hand, to Maessen, to her hand again, to Maessen. Her eyes narrowed. "You can't be serious, Robert."

I leaned toward her. "I told you jumping out of the trunk was a good plan."

∼

While the love birds argued, I went back to strategizing a way out. With my fingers swollen, picking the cuff lock now would be impossible, even if I could do it without everyone watching. As long as McBride and I stayed attached, I stayed stuck. My second option was running and dragging her behind.

I eyed her lean frame and posh dress. It was a thought.

Whatever I could do, I would, but I wasn't depending solely on me anymore. Not this time. I'd been through the fire too many times not to expect Jackson to walk into the flames. He would show. He always found a way, and he'd find one again.

I grew so certain of this, I stopped stressing about escaping. Let the freaks fight it out. The longer they attacked each other, the more time Jackson had to wake up, get up, and get here. I didn't know how he'd find me, but he would.

"I never told you to kill her, Marilyn. Now, don't put that on me," Maessen sounded like every politician, always publicly washing the blood off their hands. "I told you to manage her. You took it too far and made it into a spectacle. I'm about to announce my candidacy for Senate, Marilyn. I can't afford any spectacles."

I mouthed the name 'Marilyn' as a question to Trevor, who nodded surreptitiously back. So that's her first name. I was never going to remember that.

Maessen put his hands on his hips to scold her like an old schoolmarm. "You know I don't go along with killing people."

"Except when you do," I mumbled.

Trevor, who was the only one listening to me, looked amused again.

McBride, not amused, laughed. "Except my husband. You went along with that."

Maessen pointed his finger at her. "I didn't know about that until it was too late. You always take things too far, Marilyn. I tell you to make sure Samantha Addison can't connect those bribes to your husband back to me, and you post a contract hit on her. And link my office to the posting. What were you trying to prove?"

McBride casually dusted the side ruffle of her dress, even though it wasn't dusty. "You shouldn't have been ignoring me, and I wouldn't have needed to get your attention."

He rolled his head, galled at her answer. "Oh, you got attention alright. You had the mayor's attention and the police chief's attention. Everyone is hearing about this old employee of mine..."

"Former employee," I corrected.

"...former, whatever, wreaking havoc. People were anxious. Questions were asked. We did everything we could to downplay the events in the paper. But even the governor called after he heard Trevor was questioned in connection to the drive-by shooting. You could have cost me his endorsement."

I'm guessing that's what McBride wanted. If she hated politics enough to kill her husband to escape them, she hated them enough to also frame her boyfriend in hopes of ending his campaign. Maessen should be thankful she hadn't yet resorted to poison.

McBride tried crossing her arms, but mine wouldn't stretch that far. "Why do I always get involved with politicians? Huh? I'll never learn. And you'll never learn. I told you, Robert, real power isn't in the public eye. Have we not had a good run of it? Look at what we've been able to do behind the scenes over the last seven years. You and your control of the information. Me and my ability to convince people..."

"Threaten them," Maessen corrected.

"...persuade them to see things our way."

"Threaten, harm, and evil kill," Maessen added.

She wasn't deterred or embarrassed. "That's what it takes to alter elections, grow the right companies, destroy the wrong ones, move people into power, and shift public funding, darling. You've always had a delicate stomach when it came to getting the job done. That's why you've needed me." She jutted her hip out in stubbornness, "And why you need me still."

"We've been planning my campaign for years, Marilyn."

"You," she corrected. "You've been planning it. I hoped you'd wake up. Politicians are paper tigers, Robert. All their babbling and soundbites and begging. It's pathetic."

For a worldly-wise woman, she wasn't too perceptive. Maessen's entire reason for being was glory. Whatever the two of them had been cooking up behind the scenes, he had done it all to position himself as a powerful power player among power players. Even I knew that.

If she hadn't shot me in the stomach last Saturday, I would have told her. But she did, so I didn't.

McBride elongated her neck, lifted her chest, and plopped a hand at her tiny waist. She knew her assets and was using them. "You do this, Robert, and I'm leaving you."

Trevor and I exchanged a confused look. She still wasn't getting it.

I tipped my head up at Maessen to get his attention. "I explained the situation to her the first time. Now, it's your turn."

~

I needed a chair. And a sling. And a snack.

While Maessen and McBride talked out their relationship woes, I mouthed a 'can I go home now?' to Trevor. He only smiled in return, but it was an easy smile. An unstressed one. The more his father and McBride talked, the more at ease he looked.

The situation deflated quickly once they started working out their relationship problems. McBride and I were still handcuffed, but the general mood had calmed. Even Opie wasn't holding the gun on me anymore, but standing by Mr. Clean, chatting about some football game.

All in all, this was the dullest finale death scene in history.

Not that I'm complaining. My anxiety storehouses were full.

Now that I knew how this whole mess had come about, I could finally make sense of it. From what I could piece together from Maessen and McBride's conversation, I'd been dragged into the middle of a Fatal Attraction meets Wag The Dog situation.

Apparently, this dynamic narcissistic duo had fallen in lust seven years ago when Maessen approached Senator Chad McBride, offering him a bribe to step out of the gubernatorial race. The senator, a glory hound, refused. His wife, however, was interested.

Marilyn hated politics and loved money. After overhearing

Maessen's pitch to Chad and Chad's refusal, she approached Maessen with a plan. And it worked. Instead of a flat bribe, Chad received private job offers from faux "Lucian," which caused Chad to sit up and listen.

"But why?" I asked. "Who's Lucian?"

Robert and Marilyn exchanged a bored look.

"A ghost," Marilyn said.

"An urban legend," Robert offered.

That night on the roof, Chad seemed terrified of the guy. "He doesn't exist?"

"Doubtful," Robert shook his head. "Maybe he did, once. His name is tossed around in certain circles when a sure deal goes bust or a preferred candidate tanks or a foreign power unexpectedly changes direction or when anything goes against the tide."

"'Against the tide.' Meaning, not doing what you and your pals want."

Trevor pointed his finger and clicked his tongue. "Bingo. When Dad and his pals and his pals' pals can't explain how some election or narrative or movement can't be manipulated in the way they want, they blame it on 'Lucian.' It's an inside joke."

"More like an expletive," Robert corrected. "I have no idea how it started."

A joke? A freaking joke?

"Why would Chad take it seriously, then?"

Trevor adjusted his weight on his cane. "Because not everyone thinks it's a joke. Some believe Lucian is real."

"Like Chad," I filled in.

McBride rolled her eyes. "He was a true believer. As if there's some faceless person behind the scenes with the power to manipulate outcomes." She grinned, seeing the irony. "Unless it's me, of course."

I thought back to that conversation with the senator before he fell. "He seemed so certain."

"Oh, he was," McBride confirmed. "He used to tell me this story about Lucian having all these pennies..."

I pinched the bridge of my nose. "Big Ben in London?"

She looked amused. "So, you've heard it. See how easy it would be to manipulate him by simply dropping that name?" She huffed, as if disgusted. "It was almost too easy."

"Murder apparently is," I paused, "for some people."

McBride didn't appreciate my comment. "Honey, get stuck in a tedious marriage with a prenup and let's see how you get out of it."

"Not with poison."

She lifted her chin, pleased with herself. "I thought the solution was quite elegant."

I looked at Maessen. "You really know how to pick 'em." I turned back to her. "If Lucian's name was only used to manipulate Chad, why mention him again on Saturday to Jackson? You gave Jackson a message for Lucian. Something about a 'business proposition,' I think. It's hard to remember much before you put a gun in my stomach and pulled the trigger."

She flitted her free hand in the air. "You've really got to let that go. You're fine, aren't you? And your man's back to being healthy and magnificently masculine. Now, that's an interesting topic. Let's talk about that. How did he do it?"

I looked in that devilish face of hers, at that dark curiosity, and wanted to say, 'Love like that can work miracles.' But she would get nothing useful out of me. "He gets plenty of rest. Drinks lots of water. Eats his greens. And takes an excellent multi-vitamin."

McBride's mossy eyes softened, while a smile of malevolent admiration tugged at her reddish mouth. In that moment, I knew we'd reached an understanding. Marilyn and I were to be forever at war.

～

"Lucian," Marilyn continued, "was a red herring. A wild goose chase. A smoke screen. A fool's errand. A diversionary tactic. A false flag. A Quixotic ques—"

I stopped her with a gesture. "I get it. It was a lie."

"It was a diversion," she sounded so proud. "Jackson would, of course, be upset after you died."

A wee bit. "After you killed me."

"And I needed a way to keep that virile man of yours chasing after phantoms and not chasing after me. Him, I would never hurt. He's too pretty and too..." she took a deep, tingling breath, "mysterious to damage."

She also hadn't yet decided how or if he could be of use, if I had to guess.

"So, you throw out a name that, in the past, has proven useful to get your desired reaction. And, before that, you have Jude dress like Jackson and commit crimes and get his picture captured on surveillance cameras, as a way to frame Jackson."

She couldn't have been more impressed with herself. "A girl's got to have a back-up plan to protect herself. In case he became a problem, I needed a way to manage him. A modern woman such as yourself understands this."

"I don't, of course, but I'm not darkness personified."

McBride snickered. "So defensive when it comes to your boy toy, aren't you? If it makes you feel any better, the pictures disappeared nearly as fast as we posted them. He's got a good support team behind him. So, he isn't easily victimized." She patted my arm. "Now, doesn't that make you feel better?"

It was definitely time to gnaw off my hand.

"Then, all I have is one last question for you and Bob there. And then you're free to resume reconciling and scheming and being a general blight on mankind. Why me? Why did you ever go after me, in the first place? The online hit? Jude kidnapping me? Opie and Mr. Clean over there, pursuing me?"

Opie and Mr. Clean both spoke up with a "who?"

"Now this?" I motioned to our current location. "How am I a threat? I have nothing to do with either of you and I'd love to have even less."

"That was Robert's idea," McBride said, while Maessen answered simultaneously, "That was Marilyn's doing."

This was giving me a headache. "You guys know you're in a toxic relationship, right?"

McBride rubbed Maessen's arm and squeezed. "Let me answer this one, babe." She turned to me. "Robert is paranoid."

"What?" The paranoid guy sounded it.

"He thought Chad blabbed to you about Robert offering him a bribe. That you'd connect him to Chad's untimely death. And use it against him. Robert thinks you don't like him."

I met his eyes. "Oh, well, that's true. I don't like you. The rest, though, is paranoia. But, even if he had told me about your earlier bribes, so? I wouldn't have any proof. And I thought Chad's death was an accident until last Saturday when Marilyn told me differently. Besides, that was seven years ago. Don't you think if I knew anything or even suspected anything, I would have done something about it before now?"

Maessen dropped his hands into his pockets in a show as close to discomfort as he would ever allow himself. Behind his shoulder, two pinpricks of light punctured the black blanket. Another car was coming.

I took a deep breath and let my fear ride away on the next gust of wind. It was Jackson.

Ignoring, or not seeing, the lights, McBride jumped in to answer, "Robert thought you were keeping it secret until he announced his Senate campaign. He said you used to be a hell of an investigative journalist. He thought you were sitting on his political demise. That you'd be able to link him to the offer letters and eventually Chad's death. He asked me to get rid of you before he made his announcement."

"To 'manage her,' I said," Maessen corrected.

McBride fluttered her hand, dismissing his comment. "I knew what you meant."

"So, managing to you," I was speaking to Marilyn, but interrupted myself to direct the next comment to Maessen, "which would mean 'kill' to a killer, and you knew it," I turned back to McBride, "was posting a hit job on a public forum and creating a murderous free-for-all."

She smoothed her hair as the wind breezed by. "Random acts of violence do happen every day, Samantha. It seemed like a tidy solution at the time."

Someone not with a broken hand should smack her.

Behind Maessen, the lights bounced closer, and with them my freedom. This whole situation would be wrapped up in a little bow soon. I would be free. McBride and Maessen would be arrested, along with their meatheads. Trevor would explain his role to my satisfaction. Theo would transport everyone to jail. Jackson would have leftovers from Chef John, and we'd picnic under the moonlight, right after I took painkillers for my hand.

The joyful thought of all that was coming made my face flush. Then, I looked at Trevor, who spotted the approaching vehicle, and the blood drained back out again.

"What?"

Trevor pushed against his cane to move closer. He leaned in, feigning a kiss on the cheek, while whispering in my ear, "We have to get you out of here, Sass. Jackson isn't going to make it in time."

31

Nothing can prepare you for a moment of unconditional, absolute, no holds barred trust like a thousand itty-bitty moments of uncertain, mediocre trust. You can't soar from here to there without clocking the required hours in the cockpit.

I didn't know if all my times with Jackson, once added up, equaled absolute trust now. All I knew was that, while hanging precariously off the side of the bridge, it was my only option.

My bare feet peddled in the open air as if craving a cycling class. I was desperate to connect with a solid object and knew I wouldn't. I dangled in the nothingness, not falling, not rising, only swaying. This way and that. This way and that. Lost in the uncertainty of the moment.

"Hurry, Jackson." I mouthed the words more than said them. "Please hurry."

My circumstances went topsy-turvy the moment Jude What's-His-Name arrived. I'd been hoping for Jackson, instead I got faux Jackson, the lying thespian who didn't seem to like me much. He climbed out of the newly arriving vehicle, followed by Chris and Francis, the unrelated twin thugs.

Right before that, however, things weren't half bad. Marilyn and Robert were rediscovering their mutual enjoyment of corrupting others for personal gain, while making out in front of everyone.

The lessening tensions had Opie giving Mr. Clean, who wasn't himself tonight, a pep talk. They were discussing the 1991 NFL game between the New York Giants and the San Francisco 49ers where Joe Montana got sacked by Leonard Marshall. "Even legends have off nights."

Everyone was ending the murderous evening on a good note. Then

Jude pulled up and the mood – for Trevor and I – shifted. No one else seemed to care.

"I texted Jackson our location." Trevor stood protectively beside me, while whispering low and talking fast.

I matched his subdued volume. "You have Jackson's number?"

"Yes. We've been talking. Not important right now, Sass."

It kind of was. "When did you text him?"

"After we arrived. Found out Dad's plans for," he glanced at Marilyn, "about an hour ago. Rode out here with him to talk him out of it. He never mentioned you. When we pulled up, I saw you. I waited until Dad exited the vehicle. Then, texted Jackson."

"Any response?"

"Not yet."

It didn't matter. "He's coming."

"But maybe not in time." He spoke so softly I could barely hear. The words came out in a rush. "I'm sorry about this. Really sorry. Didn't know Dad was part of what's been happening to you. He's unreasonable, lately. Think"–he slanted his eyes toward Marilyn again– "has him panicking."

"How long have you known something was up with"–I motioned my eyes toward his dad.

"You mean how long have I known he's an ass? Forever. How long have I known he got in over his head by having a long-term affair with a psychopath? A while. Listen, this Jude guy. He met with Dad, recently. I don't know what's up between the two of them, but I know he's dangerous."

I watched Jude's long walk toward us. The broad shouldered, slim hipped build that once looked similar to Jackson's, now looked off balance. Wired wrong. Too top heavy or bottom light. Too left-leaning or right-justified.

"He is," I confirmed. "We tussled last week."

Trevor kept his eyes on Jude's approach. "That's an interesting story, I'm sure. For later."

"Off topic here. But on a scale of one to ten, how uncomfortable is it to have your dad making out in front of you?"

Trevor didn't answer, which meant a ten. "Focus Sass. I fear this isn't going to go well, so stay behind me. Understand? I'll find a way to get you out of this."

"Do you have any peanuts?"

Trevor shot me a sideways look.

"Jude's got a bad peanut allergy." I brushed it off. "Never mind. That probably wouldn't work a second time."

Trevor's grip tightened around his cane as the trio approached.

Beside me, Marilyn and Robert whispered villainous nothings in each other's ears. Neither appeared concerned, while Trevor and I hummed with it.

Chris and Francis didn't worry me as much as Jude. I'd danced with those meatheads before. And I lead. Jude, however, had always been hard to peg. He used and discarded personas like daily renewal contacts. Wear them. Toss them. Start fresh the next day.

It made it difficult to know his boundaries or limitations. Anything I deduced about the man could casually be peeled away, flicked into the trash, and left to dry out while he transformed into someone new. The unknowns about him concerned me more than the calculated coldness in him I already knew about.

"Everyone looks cozy." Jude addressed the four of us huddled shoulder-to-shoulder.

In all their slobbery reconciling, Maessen and McBride hadn't bothered to remove the cuffs. We were standing in a tight group because my arm only stretched so far.

"Hello, darling," McBride called out, coming up for air. "You're just in time! We've been reminiscing about some of your best work. Remember that night you presented those offer letters to Chad as a 'representative,'" she air quoted with her cuffed hand, making it jingle like a bracelet, "of Lucian's. You were perfection. Or those pictures we staged with you as Jackson? A masterpiece of physical theater."

Jude grinned broadly, waving her off. "You're making too much of it."

"I'm not. You were glorious! Even Samantha thought you were Jackson."

"Well, I," she wasn't wrong, "wasn't sure."

Jude thought about his performance. "That was some of my best work. You have to get the posture just right or it ruins the believability."

"You were a marvel," she gushed.

He feigned modesty but not well, which made me reconsider his acting skills.

"Thank you for coming all the way out here," she practically purred. "But I won't be needing a ride to the Penvenens after all. Robert and I made other plans."

Maessen, not meeting Jude's eyes, gave him the casual "thanks, anyway" brushoff. "I'll give her a ride home."

Maessen acted…what's the word? Guilty.

"You sure?" Jude asked Maessen, not McBride.

She didn't seem to notice, instead running her red nail down the side of her lover's neck.

"Yes. I'm sure." Maessen was clearly giving Jude a signal. "I'll drive her. You are no longer needed." He stressed the last word.

Everyone was picking up on this, right? Jude worked for Maessen, now.

"You and the boys can take the rest of the night off," McBride spoke to Jude, while planting a tiny kiss on Maessen's mouth, "right after you take care of her." She tipped her head in my direction.

I wiggled the fingers of my cuffed hand. "Hey there."

"Samantha Addison." Jude said my name as if diagnosing a fungal infection.

I looked him up and down, noting the dark jeans, black shirt, plain brown leather jacket, and overly gelled hair. Yet again, he looked plain. Threateningly plain, actually. His glasses, an accessory that deceptively showed weakness, caught a sliver of moonlight and ate it.

I nodded an acknowledgement and echoed his greeting, "Jude Krakow…uh, Kosmat…mm, Kowal–"

Jude held up his hand. "Let it go."

"Works for me."

"Marilyn, before you leave, I need a moment. Could we?" He moved away from the group and leaned against the bridge railing.

She patted Maessen's cheek affectionately. "Be right back, lover."

When she walked off, I walked with her. I didn't have a choice.

"We need to get these cuffs off me, now." McBride held up her arm to show Jude how we were attached. "I think they've lost the key. Do you have one?"

Jude tenderly moved McBride where her back was against the railing so he could hold the cuff up to the headlights. "Yes–" he examined the lock–"I can take care of this for you."

He lowered her arm gently before slamming both his hands against her shoulders and shoving her off the bridge.

Like all McBrides do when falling from a great height, she took me with her.

∼

In perfect unison, we screamed. At last, Marilyn McBride and I found something to agree on.

As she tumbled over, I instinctively hunkered down and shot all my weight backward to counter her fall. The tautness jerked us both. It might have helped yank her back, if she'd grabbed the railing instead of my arm.

With her weight yanking against my momentum, I tipped forward. Not falling, yet, but precariously uncentered. Jude shoved at my back and gravity won.

Marilyn fell backward, while I followed headfirst.

Being dragged down with a McBride I've done before.

While she tumbled into the air, I grabbed at the railing. All I needed was one secure grip. My fingers hooked the edge but didn't hold. Determination couldn't will strength back into broken fingers.

My nails clawed the metal as it whizzed past my hand. With the rail out of reach, my free arm flailed in the open air for anything else to grab. Any other metal pole. Any hanging tree limb. Any spiderweb that might do more than expected.

All I found was air. Scads of it.

Trevor screamed my name, along with a surprised "No!" from Maessen. I hoped hands would grasp my waist or legs or feet. I hoped someone would stop us from falling before it was too late.

Then, it was too late.

McBride and I descended into another world, one you didn't remain in but only passed through. It was made of darkness and wind and screams and heat that seared your chest like a hot poker covered in Tabasco.

As we fell, McBride never released my hand. She held on as if I was her last dying hope.

The descending quickly started and quickly stopped. The brutal halt knocked another scream out of us both, while slicing into our wrists, yanking our joined arms over our head, and slamming us into each other.

We headbutted. Then we dangled. Hanging by our handcuffs.

The chain connecting us had snagged on a metal bolt sticking out of the bridge's bracing beam. We weren't saved. We weren't dead. We were pausing right in the middle.

"Grab the beam, Marilyn." I reached for it, too.

The chain wouldn't support our combined weight for long. The bridge's bracing beam would hold us if we could get a good grasp.

With my broken hand, gripping anything was out, but I could throw my free arm over the beam in an aggressive side hug. Surprisingly, that placed the top of my head at street level. It felt like we'd fallen further, but McBride and I were still savable with a little outside help.

A clear image of Jackson snapped into my head. It was him, black-hood clad, leaning over the balcony of the Oklahoma Now building seven years ago and grabbing my hand. I'd never remembered that moment with this much clarity before. I could see and feel everything – the kindness in his eyes, the roughness of the ledge, the strength of him pulling me back from the nothingness. The memory was so vivid I could smell his smoky, campfire scent.

"Hurry, Jackson," I whispered. "You've got to hurry."

Marilyn clung onto the beam with a wild intensity. The woman had decent flexibility. She threw an ankle over the beam. Without a higher slit in my dress, that option was out for me.

Bolts and rivets along the edges pressed into my arm. The pressure, increasing the pounding in my swollen hand, ignited the pain to a new, unmanageable level. Tears spilled down my face.

"Jackson," I squeezed the water from my eyes, "please get here."

Above us, Maessen and Trevor reached the railing. The father looked down, too paralyzed to move. The son had no such issues.

"Grab my hand," Trevor reached toward me.

I had no hand available. One was supporting my weight. The other was snagged on a bolt and attached to McBride.

"Help her. Try to get our handcuff chain free," I directed him. "I can't let go of this beam."

She would be easier for him to reach, anyway. Using her legs, she'd managed to push herself up until her free hand could grab the lowest rung of the railing. That woman always knew how to take care of herself.

"Dad, help me." Trevor glanced at his father. "Dad! You are not this person. Do not have a hand in Marilyn's death. Snap out of this and help me."

For the first time, Maessen's face took on a human form. He shook himself out of a daze. Together, he and Trevor grabbed McBride by the free arm and lifted.

That's when Chris or Francis, whichever one it was, struck Trevor in the back of the head. He dropped unconscious to the ground, Robert dropped his grip, and McBride dropped from the bridge railing.

∼

The sounds were deafening, like the "no, no, no" from Maessen as he fought to hold on. The meaty slap of Marilyn's arm as it struck the metal beam when she slipped. The metallic snap of the handcuff chain as it broke. The final sucking in of air as she fell into the darkness.

She held my eyes while clawing the air. I watched her fall until the darkness took her. My last clear image was of Marilyn McBride puffing out her cheeks in preparation of submerging underwater. Just like her late husband. Who fell into a Buick.

It was possible Marilyn survived the fall, but unlikely. Even if the impact of the water didn't snap her neck, the current would suck her under. At this height, once you started to fall there was no second chance.

I sucked in a hysterical breath and threw both arms over the beam. The hard edge bruised my armpit but stabilized my hold. It wasn't great, but it was improvement.

Jude's consoling voice drifted down in an aerosolized bioweapon. "It was for the best, Maessen. We talked about this. She was unstable. It'll be cleaner for you this way."

Maessen wasn't convinced. "I had changed my mind."

"You weren't thinking with your mind," Jude blurted. "But don't take it personally. She seduces men to get what she wants. And she is...was good at it. Now, let's finish the job. Samantha is still down there. I heard her grunting."

I shifted to get a stronger hold and took a hard-fought breath. "I'm not," grunting, "grunting."

"I don't know about this anymore, Jude." Maessen's humanity woke up. "I've never been comfortable with this. There's got to be a better solution."

"We're almost done here, Maessen. You hired me to take care of your problem. This is taking care of it. When she falls, everything falls into place."

"But what if people start asking questions?"

"They won't. I'm good at what I do. That's why you hired me, remember? All the details will be covered. Authorities will find a murder-suicide note in Marilyn's townhome. I'll plant it when I leave here. Her computer already has evidence linking her to the online hit targeting Samantha last month. That'll convince authorities of her guilt. There are surveillance photos of Samantha in her desk. All of which, I took at her behest. All covered in her fingerprints. I'm telling you, the narrative works. Marilyn will look obsessed with getting revenge for her late husband. She kidnapped Samantha. Drove out there. Jumped off the bridge and took Samantha with her. Add in her nonprescription medication, which I won't even have to plant, and it's an open and shut case."

Maessen said nothing.

"Before you announced your campaign, you wanted to crush your skeletons into powder. This is how you do it."

"I don't know…"

"How about this, Maessen. We'll agree to do nothing. She can't hold on forever. You can leave. Chris and Francis loaded Trevor in your vehicle. He'll be fine. He'll have a headache when he wakes up, but he'll be fine. You drive away. When he wakes, tell him you tried. You did everything you could. You weren't able to save her."

Would he leave? If he did, would it matter?

Jude omitted the most pivotal event of the night. Of course, he would. He'd failed miserably. Well, I wasn't dead, yet. If I couldn't take him out physically, I could at least damage his criminal reputation. Maybe cost him a raise.

"Bob, ask Jude about the," I took a breath, "bomb."

∼

"Tonight. At the Chestnut. He doesn't have everything," sucking in, "under control. Don't believe it."

Maessen leaned over the rail. "What are you talking about?"

Lifting my head to catch a glimpse of him caused sweat to run into my ears. I motioned my head in a I-can't-talk-right-now-ask-Jude-about-his-colossal-screw-up way.

"What is she talking about, Jude?"

As self-important and greedy as Maessen is, he was also weak. A bit of a fraidy cat, really. He didn't get his hands dirty. He got a manicure. Even though he wanted me dead to safeguard his reputation, he wasn't gutsy enough to order a straightforward hit. He hinted. He alluded. He assumed Marilyn's extremist temperament would give him the result he wanted, all without the guilt. And he'd been right.

Knowing that, I had a hard time believing he knew anything about a downtown bomb. All that death. The carnage. The pain. The mess. Even Maessen wasn't that evil.

Jude, however, was.

If Maessen knew what Jude had attempted earlier tonight, I wasn't sold he'd go along with it. And, if Maessen blinked, maybe he'd help a girl out.

"Jude, you know," saltiness seeped into my mouth, "you have to tell him."

Above me, Maessen asked again. And, Jude, like I knew he would, answered.

"Maessen, I'll admit my first strategy had been to clean up all three of your problems - Marilyn, Samantha, and Jackson - all at once by placing a small explosive device inside a vehicle at their location."

I took in a ragged breath. "It wasn't," grunting, "small."

"You what?!" Maessen yelled.

"She's exaggerating. It was sized according to the need," Jude corrected me. "Nothing too extreme. Light structural damage only of two nearby buildings. Some windows and such. Only people within a small radius would be affected."

"Killed." I gritted my teeth against the shakes. "Maimed."

"It was completely under control, Maessen."

"A bomb? A bomb!" Maessen was a beta, but even betas can get loud. "Are you insane?!"

"Consider the opportunity." Jude sounded insulted. It's hard when people mock your plan. I get it. "All three of your problems – Marilyn,

Samantha, Jackson – in the same place. All three removed, and authorities looking elsewhere."

"What do you mean, elsewhere?" Maessen's clipped words held curiosity.

"A militia group I located two hours south of here. I had enough set up to cast reasonable suspicion their way. With the help of your publication pushing the narrative, stoking calls for revenge and swift justice, they wouldn't stand a chance. And then you, Robert Maessen, could be the people's candidate, galvanized by this horrendous act to bring an end to domestic terrorism."

You could hear it in his voice. The nut job still considered it a good plan. When my plans implode, I, at least, admit it.

Maessen paced to the edge and looked down at the space McBride last occupied. "How in the hell did Marilyn not find out about this?"

"She has never been big on micromanaging." Jude stood next to Mason. "She trusts me to finish the job."

I barked out, "Trusted. And look what it got her, Bob."

Jude ignored me. "I told her about Jackson planning a romantic evening for Samantha tonight at the Durant. My guys tried to grab Sam earlier this week, but the timing was off. When we couldn't locate her, I had them hitting her and Jackson's known connections and gathering intel. I found out about the dinner tonight and reported to Marilyn my plans to grab them both. Then we'd dispose of them after. Did she want to watch? She did, of course. So I recommended she get a table by the window and wait. When it didn't work out due to a minor glitch…"

I interrupted. "The van carrying the bomb," breathe, breathe, breathe, "got jacked."

Jude acknowledged it. "Like I said. Minor glitch. So, I went with Plan B."

I snorted. There was no Plan B. This was Jude feverishly working to cover his incompetent ass.

"I texted Marilyn and asked her to play the fellow kidnap victim role to get Samantha here. And then called you. I told you that you didn't need to come."

Maessen gripped the rail like a man who'd lost a grip on his own soul. "I couldn't…without seeing her, without talking to her before…" He left the blank spaces to be filled with a truth too ugly for him to speak. "I thought maybe…"

"You," my chest wheezed, "never would've gone through with it, Bob. Jude," sucking in, "forced your hand."

I fanned the flames of animosity between them. I could do nothing more.

"When you view the plan objectively, Maessen, I think you'll see the value in it."

Jude failed to read the room. Maessen breathed so loud the force of it drifted down to me and blew my gown around my ankles. That's when the shouting started.

I tuned out the ruckus. It sounded like Maessen screaming in rage, Jude yelling in defense, Opie and Mr. Clean refereeing, and the twin thugs snacking on pork rinds. Whatever happened up there now, it was too late to benefit me down here. My arms were done.

"Jackson." My muscles rattled. Tears streamed down my cheeks. "Please…"

A gust of wind spun up from the river. Moist cold slithered its fingers under my hair to slow walk across my neck. The earthy perfume of rich, rotting vegetation panted out its foul breath. I turned my face only to find it again. Heavier than before. A close talker with garlic on the tongue.

No sign of hope anywhere. No headlights in the distance. No black-hood-guy in the shadows. No Jackson. No one but me, alone in the battle.

"Damn it." Jude leaned over the rail. "She's still here. I need something…the cane. Where is Junior's cane, Francis? This is taking too long."

Thug shoes kicked at the gravel under foot until the dirt shrapnel – ping, ping, ping – dropped on my head, stung my arms, and bounced off the beam. Other shoes returned.

"Thanks Chris. This will work."

He stood directly overhead cradling a milky brown boulder the size and shape of a watermelon. He lifted it. He stopped and held it there, while the moonlight created an Atlas silhouette with the world suspended over his head.

"I am sorry about this, Samantha. You seem kind of interesting for a common sort of girl."

Killers are always saying that.

I knew what was coming. He would drop that rock, and the blow to the head would end me instantly.

As Jude positioned the boulder, I realized what I had to do.

The night of the ball, I'd released Trevor and trusted Jackson to catch him. Now, it was my turn. I had to practice that faith in Jackson for myself. Wherever he was, he would reach me in time. He had to.

The image of Marilyn's face sinking into that black hole came to mind. I would not end up like that. I wasn't going down into that darkness. She'd chosen a path that led to death long ago. I wanted a life in the light. Standing next to Jackson. To do that meant I had to trust him completely.

Now.

Right now.

I sucked in a petrified breath. My fingers relaxed. My arms settled. The tension seeped out. Jude breathed out a sigh of relief. "Don't take it personally." His hands released the rock as my hands released the rail.

In a symphony of bursts and yells and grit and fear and hope, I screamed, gravity attached, and the rock shattered on the beam and burst into dusty shrapnel.

I didn't feel the debris hitting my face or neck. All I could sense was the air against my fingers as they reached high. Jackson had to grab them now, or it would be too late. His warmth and strength had to connect with me, now, or I wouldn't survive. He had to save me. Or I wouldn't be saved.

He had to be there.

But he wasn't.

The moment came. The moment went. And gravity took its prize.

Air whizzed past my ears. My gown whipped in the wind. My body dropped into the dark. All I could feel was the emptiness in my hands, the nothingness below, and the wind vibrating between my fingers as I fell.

As the bridge rose into the sky, I knew I was lost to this world. Dead already, but with a two-second delay. That black hole that swallowed Marilyn was opening its mouth wide.

How could I have been so wrong? Wasn't that what all this had been about? All the near misses? And unanswered questions? All the moments of facing down death? Of running through that cycle of doubt and trust? The weeks of hunting down my gift? Of Jackson in a coma? The hours by his bedside? All the scratches and bruises? All the pain? All the unshed tears? And the shed ones? Hadn't this, from the time Jackson saved me even years ago to now, been about giving Jackson my complete trust and that trust rewarded with salvation?

His love was never supposed to fail. But what was this?

The blackness passed by in a solid block of wind pushing from against my back. I dropped into death with nothing to stop me. No hope of survival at all. I'd plunge into that murky, cold water and be sucked down into the afterlife.

Hal had pegged me all along. I did have one crippling fear. That Jackson would fail me when I needed him most. That he couldn't be all he promised. That I'd finally trust him without question and that's when I'd meet destruction. Hal said I'd face my greatest fear, but he never said the fear would win.

I sucked in a deep breath, my cheeks puffing out in preparation to submerge underwater. Darkness blurred beside me. The world closed the curtain. And my heart shattered before I broke the surface of my watery grave.

32

Death doesn't always come quickly. For some, it pulls a snag in our life until we unravel in one, long, single thread. It's an excruciating way to go. It takes time, but we're no less dead in the end.

I hit the water hard but survived. Dazed but conscious. The churning undercurrent, rippling over drowned logs and rocks, aerated the water enough to keep it nearly bubbly. The effect meant an easier entry, but not an easy exit.

I slipped into the inky mass. The cold fingers of the current slithered around my ankles and tightened. The smothering blackness was everywhere and nowhere. It covered me completely, but it couldn't be grasped. I flailed and bucked against the bulk of it, but it was weightless. Punching, then dissipating. Landing blows, then formless. The current would do what it wanted, take me where it wanted, and never concern itself over my oxygen levels.

At first, I didn't miss breathing. I didn't give it much thought. The river flipped me over and over, taking me further and further, and I was in the thick of war. You don't have time to think about things like breathing when you're on the battlefield.

Until you do.

My lungs got my attention with a beginning ache. Then a tighter ache. Then a tightening, twisting ache. Then the ache turned into a scream. God himself had his hand on the screwdriver. With each turn, my lungs creaked.

I couldn't take much more.

Whether any tears wiggled out against the tide, I'll never know. They would have been snatched away by the same current plummeting me downward. What I did know was that I never expected it to end like this. And this was the end. The one death I never saw coming was always destined to be the one that succeeded.

The cold, spinning, furious current felt miles away now. I'd been dragged down into the lower, somber, patient current. The current in the deep bowels moved unseen by the naked eye. The current conducting its business unimpeded by the world above. The current that carried carcasses and corpses to the muddy floor and wedged them under an unoccupied rock.

My panic passed in, through, and out me. I wasn't fighting anymore. I wasn't connected enough to my body to feel it. My soul was doing that swelling thing again, like it'd done in the conference room last Saturday.

Death had taught me last weekend that dying wasn't about shriveling. It was about expanding. Not a decrease but a release. The body was such an uncomfortable weight to lug around. Once shed, your soul would never fit back into that cramped space again. Mine had grown so large even the current couldn't touch it anymore.

Before I went wherever I was going, I sent one final thought out into the world. Maybe it would find its way to the target.

I love you, Jackson. Even now. Even though. I'll never stop.

~

"We have to get you out of here, Sass. Jackson isn't going to make it in time."

I popped open my eyes to find myself dry, alive, and standing on the bridge with Trevor whispering in my ear. Behind him, headlights bobbed until the vehicle stopped. It was Jude, who was only now arriving.

I'd had a déjà vu flash. A damn flash!

"Bloody hell!" I yelled before I could stop myself.

Trevor jerked in surprise, so I put my hand up.

"Not you. I was thinking about this old woman I know who gave me a gift I can't return."

The flashes were going to give me a heart attack, one I will see coming so I can experience it twice. I hated this superpower. The more flashes I had, the more real the experience. My chest still ached from lack of oxygen. My heart still hammered from suffocation. Between my fingers, I could feel wet, muddy water.

No wonder Jerry was ready to share her treasure. Misery loves company.

I bent over to catch my breath and get my head straight. What I needed was a good cry and a strong drink.

"Sass, you okay?" Trevor patted me consoling on the back.

I sucked in two shaky breathes, which were real, and then switched to open mouth breathing, which was not. Escape Plan B would require an award-winning performance. "I don't know. I think I'm going to be sick."

That got Marilyn's attention. "Don't even think about throwing up while handcuffed to me."

I continued mouth breathing, while pausing for dramatic swallows. "Then you better get the cuffs off..." I gagged, "...because this passenger is about to deplane."

"Get the keys! Quick!" Marilyn was wearing a new Jovani, remember. "Hurry!"

Behind me, Opie hustled up and grabbed the cuffs. While he worked the lock, I threw in more gagging. He worked faster, while shooting me nervous glances fearing an eruption.

"What is wrong with you?" Marilyn snapped. "Can't you keep it together?"

I arched my back in pre-vomit body language. "Car sickness."

She tapped a foot impatiently. "We got out of the car ten minutes ago."

I gagged. "Retroactive car sickness."

"That's not a thing."

Finally, the click signaled Marilyn's handcuff release. Mine still dangled as a bracelet, but it wasn't tethered to another human anymore.

That was my cue.

I straightened, sucked in a cleansing breath, and smiled at Marilyn. "And...," I gave a half bow, "end scene."

Her eyes narrowed. "Oh, no, you don't."

I winked. "Ah, but I do." I took off.

Running at super speeds is unpleasant on the feet when you're not wearing shoes. The gravel, the limbs, the uneven dirt road. It stabbed my softer underfoot parts, but nothing compared to drowning in water ripe with bacteria.

When I zipped past Jude's vehicle, I gave a little wave. Whether he could see it at these speeds and in the dark, I had no idea. But I was raised by a southern mother and there's no cause to be rude.

I pummeled the ground until only the woods remained. The shadowed lines of limbs smoothed into a solid wall of black as they smeared past. Foot up, foot down. Gown whipping wildly behind. I'd hitched it above my knees with my one working hand, while the cuff rat-a-tat-tatted against my thigh. Even the evening air didn't bother getting my attention. I had one objective and one objective only: get the hell out of here.

I wanted as far away from that flash as possible. No more bridges for me. No sir. No rivers either. Maybe no heights of any kind. Or wooded areas. Only ground floor urban life from here on out. Single-story concrete jungles and flat desert plains. Everything else was a death trap.

Within a minute, I reached a two-lane paved road. From here, I might luck out and hitch a ride with a griffin, a golem, a centaur, or any other folklore out transporting produce.

Underfoot, the asphalt slapped back. I slowed to a normal, leisurely pace. All the elements caught up with me. I ambled down the road under the star-dimpled night sky. A musk-free breeze caressed my cheek. The swish of my dress around my legs set a rhythm to my walk.

What a nice evening it turned out to be. Chilly, but not biting. Refreshing, really. I smiled to myself at the chaos I'd left behind. Then, I laughed. I thought about Marilyn and Jude and Bob and laughed more. What a bunch of ninnies!

I strolled my barefoot and battered self down the road and whistled the tune to *The Neverending Story*. Who wouldn't want to be a luck dragon?

Speaking of needing a ride, I wonder where Jackson was about now. And if he knew where Chef John stored his leftovers. Specifically, the pinwheels. Maybe a crab cake or two. I was famished. And my feet ached. And my hand throbbed.

Geez, this was a crap first date.

The longer I walked, the quicker the adrenaline surge petered out. Dying is no picnic. Discovering you didn't skyrockets your endorphins. Survival high, however, can't last forever. Eventually, your broken hand reminds you it's broken, your bare feet remind you why people wear shoes, and your conscience reminds you that you can't let a woman die.

"Bloody hell."

~

The heated confrontation on the bridge reached peak finger pointing. And peak teeth grinding. And peak arm waving. With the vehicles' headlights overexposing every wrinkled brow, the three main characters resembled dramatized theater actors putting on a production of Shakespeare In The Park.

I watched from a safe distance behind a dense entanglement of shrubs on a nearby hill. Camouflage I didn't have, but a green cocktail dress I did. Tomato, to-mah-to. Unlike the amateur cast down there, I also had the shadows, more dilated pupils, and box seats. Invisibility might be my next superpower.

I plopped down on a grimy stump and decided to watch until intermission.

"You are out of your mind," Marilyn growled.

Jude backed her up against the bridge with Robert frozen at his side. Trevor, as previously foreseen, lay on the ground unconscious. Destiny demanded he get conked on the head, apparently.

"You left me lying on the floor of that warehouse, Marilyn." Jude leaned in, his mundane, blasé expression hardened. "How did you think I'd respond?"

Last weekend, Marilyn shot me but abandoned Jude. Between the two of us, I had more reason to want revenge. But, if I had to guess, Jude suffered from jealous lover syndrome. He must have thought he and Marilyn's story had been more Romeo & Juliet than Macbeth.

"They will never let this stand." Marilyn leaned in confidently, too confidently. The kind of confidence that doesn't know you're about to be tossed off a bridge. "You know better."

They? Ohhhh. Now, that's interesting. Who was 'they'?

Robert impatiently waved a "stop" motion to Jude. In the headlights, his arm cast a dragon-like shadow puppet diving overhead. I got a sudden craving for a grapefruit.

"Who's 'they,' Marilyn?"

Yeah, what he said.

She ignored the question. Her and Jude stood eyeball-to-eyeball. I hoped one of them would suddenly sneeze.

With no answer, Robert tried a different source and an increase in volume. "Who's 'they,' Jude?"

Jude kept his eyes on Marilyn. "It's nothing, Maessen. She's messing with you."

"You didn't tell him?" Marilyn raised an eyebrow, which sometimes makes me sneeze. "A miscalculation, Jude, dear."

Robert's blood pressure darkened his fake tan. "What are you two talking about?"

Jude brushed him off. "It's a trick, Maessen. There's no 'they.'"

Marilyn acted unimpressed by the exchange. It gave her an air of believability when she turned to Robert and said, "You'll find out soon enough, darling."

Dang, I needed popcorn. And a tangerine.

That was the last straw for Robert. He jerked his arms as if buzzed by a bee. His dragon-like shadow shot into the air and dove back into the earth, bashing it's snout against the gravel. "Enough. This has gone too far. I was never going to go through with this, Jude. I only wanted to teach Marilyn a lesson. So let it go."

That's not exactly accurate. He did go through with it in a different timeline. Then regretted it horribly. But Robert loved to massage the truth so let the man oil up his hands.

"I've let this go too far."

I'd read enough Shakespeare to know the guy who thinks he's in command is never in command. Also, he usually gets stabbed a lot. Robert needed to wise up and get out of there before they ad-libbed Julius Caesar.

"Now I'm done with this nonsense. Marilyn, I'll take you home. Jude, we'll review our continuing relationship tomorrow."

They weren't listening. Marilyn and Jude faced off. One with a twitching mouth. One with a twitching first.

I scooted to the end of my stump and chewed on a strand of hair. Any minute the tension would force one of them to knock over the first violent domino.

"Do you hear me?" Robert stomped a foot. "Both of you. Stop this."

They snapped in unison, "Shut up, Bob!"

I threw back my head and laughed.

Oops. Didn't mean for that to be out loud.

The actors on stage broke from the scene and scanned the blackened hills.

"She's here." Jude called to his twin thugs. "Back there somewhere. Go check it out."

Well...poo. Now I'm going to miss the rest of the show.

"She, who?" Robert's head swiveled back and forth, scanning a forest he couldn't see. "Who's out there?"

Marilyn patted his arm. "Samantha, dear."

He threw up his hands. "I don't understand any of this."

She gave him a pitying expression. "I know."

Chris and Francis stomped my way. I could take them out relatively easy. Easier if I had an Encyclopedia Britannica. First, them. Then, Opie. With his gun out of commission, I would be approaching the finish line. Mr. Clean was no longer a problem. Marilyn wouldn't resist. And Jude I could shoot.

Overall, not a bad plan. One I could finally complete tonight, which offered its own satisfaction.

"One thing before I forget," Jude turned to Marilyn and shoved her over the railing.

Never mind. New plan.

33

I caught her by the Jovani.

While Marilyn tumbled backward, while her arms flapped, while her mouth widened, while her vocal cords vibrated, I ran between the thugs, across the bridge, over Trevor, around Jude, past Robert, and grabbed her designer dress shoulder strap.

Before her weight took us both down, I linked my arm around the rail so my elbow, not my broken hand, took the strain. It hurt, but it worked.

As thin as her diet and drugs kept her, Marilyn was still dead weight. Her poundage slammed me against the rails, her against the bridge, and tugged us toward the afterlife. But my grip and her dress held. We were alive. As far as this evening was concerned, that was progress.

"Grab a hold!" I instructed.

The shock hadn't worn off enough for Marilyn to register what had happened. Falling from great heights to your death causes the human brain to hiccup. I understood it. I expected it. I just didn't have time for it.

"Marilyn! Snap out of it! Grab the rails, put your foot on the support beam, and climb up!"

Behind me, the other halfwits were processing. I could hear the wet, meaty slap of Robert's tongue against the roof of his mouth while he tried to speak but couldn't. Beside him Jude chose a breathless "damn it!" Somewhere back there Chris and Francis exchanged a, "How is she here?" with a, "That chick's a freak," response. Opie fiddled with his gun, while Mr. Clean was the only one to see what was coming next.

"There's a bird circling my head."

This time, it was true. There was a bird. Several, in fact.

"Owl!" I yelled. "Now!"

If one lesson throughout my crime fighting experiences stuck, it was that you never confront murderers alone. Muggers, maybe. Kidnappers, possibly. Petty criminals, no problem. Murders, never.

They sat at the top of the darkness food chain. Every one of them itched to pull the trigger, plunge the knife, or drop the boulder. Even when they convinced themselves, like Jude, that killing was a means to an end and brought no pleasure, they were lying. Mostly to themselves. They wanted to believe they were more than blood-thirsty savages, but every killer is a blood-thirsty savage. Some simply have better PR.

You never faced that kind of evil alone. So, I brought a friend. And she brought a few more.

"What the–!" Jude yelled as Owl swooped low and buzzed his head. Followed by one of her winged pals. And another. And another.

A flock of birds, swarming in frantic patterns, squawked and screeched over, around, and in between the men. The sound of war had come. Their sirens stabbed the ears in piercing, icy flesh wounds. Claws drew blood across faces. Winged bodies dive bombed in rapid succession. The whir of their flapping blades disoriented retreat. All the while puffs of carefree, AWOL feathers hovered in the pandemonium before falling like shrapnel on eyelashes.

Hitchcock couldn't have written a more chaotically poetic scene.

Earlier, before returning to the bridge, I'd stopped in the woods to chat with Owl, who'd been shadowing me for miles. Greta believed I communicated emotions to animals, so I told Owl about rage. Then, I pointed my fingers and flapped my arms in the general bridge direction. Birds weren't half-bad at charades.

She gathered some friends and hung back waiting on my signal. I wasn't positive "Owl! Now!" would cross the species divide, but it did. With the men distracted, shrieking, ducking, frantically clawing at car doors to get inside, and firing off wild shots in the air, I turned my attention to Marilyn.

She grabbed at the rails, but her hands kept slipping. "I can't get a good grip! There's lotion on my hands. You grab me instead!"

I only had one hand and it was already engaged. "With what? I'm giving you all I've got to give here, Marilyn. Some things you've got to do for yourself."

She grunted, jerking and slipping, each movement scrapping my hips against the railing. "I need help! Robert! Robert, help!"

I glanced over my shoulder to see her knight in shining armor trampled by four deer, spooked by the commotion, running like wild beasts across the bridge. Hey, it's rural Oklahoma. These things do happen on their own.

"I had nothing to do with that!" I yelled at Robert, who lay in an unconscious bloody heap in the gravel. I turned back to Marilyn. "He's got problems of his own, Marilyn. Now wipe your hands on your dress, get a grip, and save yourself, woman. I can't hold on all day."

I couldn't hold on for another thirty seconds, actually. But she didn't need to know that.

"And hurry!"

Marilyn wiped and gripped, wiped and gripped, until she had a strong enough grasp to pull herself high enough for a toe hold. Her weight on my arm released. I kept a grip, but she had taken back the burden.

I let out a heavy exhale, almost a sigh. I was changing the outcome of tonight for us both. Thank goodness! I'd feared this flash would be particularly stubborn to rewrite.

As Marilyn stepped on the bottom rail, Jude ducked Owl, ran up, and shoved Marilyn off the bridge again. And Marilyn, like Marilyn always does, took me with her.

I hate heights.

∼

I give up. I just give up.

Marilyn had already sunk below the darkness and I was back to dangling alone from the bridge. Nothing I'd done had changed anything. Not a single thing was different, if you didn't include the birds back to circling overhead, while Robert drooled into the dirt and the thugs hid inside vehicles.

"You shouldn't have come back," Jude leaned over the rails. "Why did you?"

I gripped the support beam like before. "Because I'm interesting for a common sort of girl."

His nostrils, from my vantage point, flared. "What are you talking about? You're always making jokes that no one gets but you."

I grunted, feeling the strain set in. "Never mind. You had to be there."

Jude pressed one hip against the rails and tilted his head toward the moon as if crowned night king. He couldn't have looked more satisfied if he'd lit a cigarette. Then, he lit a cigarette.

"You know, Samantha"—he exhaled grey soot—"I do find you more challenging than most. So, take that as a compliment."

I adjusted my grip.

"Funny. I was thinking the same thing about you."

Jude turned back to his cigarette and contemplated the meaning of it all. The sickly fog drifted down until it braided with the oxygen I managed to suck into my lungs.

"I still don't understand how you can do what you do." Smoke, like synchronized belly dancers, twisted out of the end of his cigarette. "Take the birds, for instance. Or the dogs in that neighborhood. Or the alligators in the park. How are you communicating with them?"

I shook my head at the cigarette smoke as if it'd get the hint and gyrate away. "Charades."

Jude snorted. "It's weird. Amazing, but weird. Who knew animals could be controlled so easily."

My body trembled at what was coming. So, I focused on the here and now.

"Not all that different than controlling weak men." I coughed twice, caught a breeze, and pulled in fresh air. "You should have asked Marilyn how she did it."

Jude puffed, each drag crackling as the paper curled. "Well," he grinned, "it's a moot point now." He flicked the cigarette into the nothingness below. "Don't hang around on my account. If you want to let go, I won't judge."

I ground my teeth as the muscle shakes started. "I'm fine. It's a great spot to watch the sunrise."

Jude leaned over the railing to eye the drop and whistled. "That'll be a fall, all right. Lots of time on the way down to think about what's coming. But, a quick end, I'd imagine."

Alive people know nothing about death.

"Not so quick." I adjusted my grip.

"You might be right. Poor Marilyn. You can chat about your shared experience when you get to heaven or hades or wherever women like you go."

"The day spa." I took a shaky breath. "Women like me go to the day spa."

Jude straightened, stretched, and yawned. "Well, it's time to wrap this up. This is isolated." He scanned the area. "But you can never be too careful."

Right. Witnesses. If only. I could hang here until the Fourth of July and only Owl would take note. Not that I had the strength to keep hanging here. I'd lost all feeling in my fingers. My arms still gripped the support beam, but blood flow stopped somewhere around my wrist. Still, I held on. I knew what awaited if I let go. Death was a good motivator.

To keep Jude from getting proactive, I tried distraction.

"I'm sorry Marilyn used you like that."

Jude ignored me, while scanning the area for a box of books, kettle bell, or that boulder he was destined to find.

"That's painful. I get it. No wonder," I pulled in a breath, "you pushed her off a bridge. Many have done…felt like doing…the same," another deep breath, "when their heart is broken."

Except those many aren't violent, egomaniacal lunatics who go through with it.

Jude snorted, finally reacting. "She didn't break my heart. She disrespected our arrangement."

"By abandoning you."

He continued scanning the area, as if in the Secret Service, but I had his attention. "It's bad for business."

"Right." I smothered a groan from the muscle ache. "Business."

Annoyed, he pivoted back to me. "What are you trying to say, Samantha? That I killed her because my feelings were hurt?"

I would have shrugged if I'd had the strength. "You're saying you didn't?"

"You don't get it. She messed up. Big time. She got emotionally attached to that preening, self-important clown." He motioned his head backward, I assumed toward Robert. "He was a means to an end. That's all. A useful tool. And she fell for the guy."

The ache in my arms reached the nauseating level. Where could a girl go when dangling off a bridge for some privacy to vomit?

"Maybe," I swallowed the thick, gritty gel that had once been saliva, "you were the tool. Not him."

Jude squatted down to speak to me as close to eye level as possible. "He was the mark," Jude stressed. "His newspaper ownership makes him useful or I'd retire him, too. Once he runs for office and wins — and he will win, we'll make certain of it — he'll be even more so." He took a breath, satisfied. "If they'd found out she was trying to talk him out of running, they'd have sent me to end her anyway. So, all I did was speed up the process."

'They' again. So, there was a 'they.'

"Who's 'they,' Jude? You and Marilyn are working for someone?"

Jude pulled back. "I never said 'they.'"

"Yes, you did."

"There is no 'they,' Samantha."

I adjusted my grip, again. "You're really bad at lying for a liar."

Jude stood up and dusted himself off. "This is taking too long. I need something heavy."

~

Falling is not a liberating experience. You do not dance to Cheryl Lynn's "Got To Be Real" while plummeting downward. There is no transcendental high.

Skydiving might be different. Maybe you can experience all that free fall delight with a stopping mechanism strapped to your back. Without a parachute, however, you can't enjoy the experience of falling because of your dread of landing. It's like asking a person deathly allergic to shellfish to enjoy their lobster before the anaphylactic shock kicks in.

That's where I was again. Back to the excruciating fall.

My heartbeat turned into a single, uninterrupted thumb. I screamed, but the friction of the air sucked it out of my mouth. My arms and legs flailed without purpose. Panic contracted all my major muscle groups until it felt like a whole-body charley horse. And…my hair was in my mouth.

I was miserable. And, I wasn't even in the water, yet. That's when the real misery began.

The thought shot another scream out of my mouth and the wind, once again, grabbed it away. I couldn't even have that. No saved Marilyn. No avoiding the flash. No screaming all the way down.

This sucked.

I stilled my mind for the inevitable slow, breathless goodbye and sent out a final prayer, 'God. Help.'

A blur to my right struck hard enough to knock the piety right out of me. The force shifted the wind from a below direction to a side direction. Arms locked around my waist and I heard Jackson yell, "I've got you!"

We hit the ground like a tuning fork. My bones, I learned, play the A above a middle C note. When the vibrations ended, I laid on my back and breathed. The dead leaves beneath me rustled with each expansion of my lungs. Pain throbbed in my shoulder, but it was my left side. The opposite of my broken hand. So, now I felt even.

Beside me, Jackson performed his own deep breathing. He'd leapt off the east bank, grabbed me in mid-fall, and landed us both on the west bank. The ravine was deep, not wide. For a superhero with a running start, it could be traversed. Landing, though, wouldn't be pretty for any mere or advanced mortal.

Jackson had managed to clear the river, hit the opposite bank, and drop us against a section of earth with bulging roots threading in and out of the dirt. Hitting those roots was like walking barefoot on lush carpet sprinkled with Legos. Except it wasn't your feet but your back. Not carpet but dead leaves. Not Legos but wood. Not walking but falling after slipping off a bridge.

"Are you okay?" He asked without moving.

I wasn't drowning. So, yes. "I will be." I breathed hard enough it came out in squeaky wheezes. "That's a better outcome than the last time."

"A flash?"

"A bad one."

"You should tell me about it."

"I will."

We both said, "later." And left it at that.

"How about you?"

He grunted. "I'll survive."

Jackson absorbed the brunt of the landing, I knew. He'd cushioned my fall as best he could by positioning most of my body to land on his. And him landing on his back. It mostly worked. I'd landed halfway on him and halfway off. Then, rolled onto my back next to him. I hurt, but, thanks to him, I had no additional broken bones.

After a full minute of nothing but silence and breathing, my lungs returned. Jackson needed less time but left me alone until I'd recovered. Laying side-by-side under the tree shadows, listening to the hushed gurgling of the water below, not being circled by birds or threatened by boulders or drowning in muddy water, this moment ranked in my top five for the night.

"You're never going to take me out again, are you?"

Jackson worked a kink out of his neck, rotated a shoulder, and rolled onto his side. He propped his head on his hand and looked down at me. Dried blood, likely from the flower van explosion, marked a red smeared line across his neck and over his scar. More colored his collar. Dirt and soot browned the whiteness of his shirt. His dinner jacket was gone. No tie. He looked exhausted. And relieved.

"How about tomorrow?"

I smiled, laughed, and burst into tears.

Jackson gathered the mess of me into his arms and held tight. "Okay." He rubbed my back. "Monday then."

I sobbed until the tears stopped, which took about thirty-seconds before I grew disenchanted with them.

"It's been such a horrible night." I mopped my face with his soot-stained shirt. "I lost count how many times I've died. None of my plans worked. I lost faith in you. And my dress got dirty."

Jackson kissed my forehead. "I'm sorry, baby. It's been a rough couple of hours. But you're alive and with me, now. Your plans did work because we're together. How's the faith in me coming?"

"Restored."

"Good. And I'll buy you a new dress."

"And shoes."

"A package deal."

"And take me out to dinner again."

"Anytime."

"Let's give it a day or two."

Headlights sliced the ravine and a truck roared onto the bridge. Jackson sat up, then motioned for me to follow.

"What's happening?"

Jackson smiled, dropped his arm around my shoulders, and pointed to the truck. "The night just got better. That's Theo and Gabe."

Exhausted, I leaned into Jackson's side. "What are they going to do?"

On the bridge, we heard the sound of metal against metal.

Jackson listened, nodding along with approval. "Sounds like they took out a vehicle." More metal wailed and glass shattered. "Make that two vehicles."

We sat in our shadowed hideaway and watched from a distance. At this angle, we couldn't see the activity. The crashing and yelling, however, gave a decent picture.

"Do Theo and Gabe need our help?"

Jackson smiled. "Nah. I feel more sorry for Jude and his hired muscle. Theo's been wanting to punch that guy in the face for a week."

"I wouldn't mind another round, myself."

Jackson agreed. "Ditto."

While we listened to a brawl above, Jackson told me about getting the text from Trevor after waking up from the explosion and finding me missing. Once Theo and Gabe arrived, he jumped into Theo's truck and rocketed out of the scene as the authorities arrived. When they exited the highways, Jackson went on foot.

"I could move faster through the woods than Theo could on the roads. And that's how I saw you fall."

"Nice catch, by the way."

Jackson squeezed my shoulders. "Sorry about the landing."

I was alive. I didn't drown. Bruises were toy things.

"So, you and Trevor. When did you guys become best buds?"

Jackson listened to the ruckus on the bridge, looked satisfied, and continued. "When he was in the hospital. I went to visit him, and we realized we shared a common goal."

"Which was?"

"Finding who was responsible for threatening your life and ending them."

According to Jackson, Trevor had been working with Caroline and Hal since the Durant Ball to identify who posted the online hit. Then, last weekend, Marilyn showed up at the warehouse. When Hal told him about her, Trevor wanted to believe his father wasn't involved with his girlfriend's scheme. So, he dug into his dad's financials, phone records, home office, and found shady business dealings with Marilyn as a benefiting partner.

"That's when he knew his dad was involved. He asked me to give him a couple of days to try talking his father into turning himself in. It, apparently, didn't go well."

I snuggled into his side, while careful to baby my broken hand. "I told you the guy never liked me."

"You did."

"And, that he was behind this."

"You did that, too."

"So now you'll concede that I'm always right even when you don't agree."

Jackson's mouth twitched. "Well, you're always cute, anyway. Right or wrong. Isn't that enough?"

I leaned my head on his shoulder. "For now. I'm too tired to be unreasonable."

Jackson said Maessen planned on announcing his run for Senate in January, which made sense why he'd be tying up loose ends now.

"I'm going to tell everyone about his lousy Christmas bonuses."

Jackson squeezed my knee. "As you should."

While the action film continued on the bridge, Jackson tore off the end of his shirt, snapped a couple sticks for stabilizers, and made an impromptu cast for my hand.

When he was finished, I pulled him close and pressed my lips against his until our breathing synchronized. We sank into the kiss, allowing the fear of nearly losing each other to fade away. I didn't pull away until my head went lightheaded.

Jackson blinked wide-eyed at me. "What was that for?"

"You're alive. I'm alive. Why not? Also, you saved me. Again. And I'm grateful."

Jackson smiled through the dirt streaks on his face. "I've always been a fan of your gratitude."

34

Dating is a dangerous business. You're gambling with your heart, sure, but even a good date might include explosions, killers, kidnapping, and the occasional tossing off a bridge.

I could accept that if they all ended up like this: Jackson and I hanging out watching a good show together.

"Who's that, do you think?"

We'd been sitting in our leafy spot for ten minutes while additional vehicles came on the scene. After Theo and Gabe arrived, Gin and Angel pulled up in Beatrice. Then, Trudy and Kyle in her catering van. Now, the Cutlass.

"Has to be Hal. Probably bringing Jerry, Lauren, and Greta."

The bridge was getting crowded. Trudy parked on the side of the road to set up tables.

"What is she doing?"

Jackson watched for a few seconds. "Looks like she's going to feed everyone."

"A picnic? At a crime scene?"

"Well," Jackson scratched at his evening facial growth in amusement, "you're hungry, aren't you?"

Come to think of it..."I have been craving citrus fruit for the last hour."

"There you go. When the cops and rescue workers arrive, they'll be hungry, too. It'll keep everyone from getting grouchy. And maybe earn us some goodwill. This is going to be a mess to explain."

Good point.

When we heard sirens in the distance, Jackson and I decided to join civilization. He clawed our way back to the road with me holding on to him. Once again on level ground, we walked hand-in-hand onto the bridge to find the entire sidekick crew there with extra cast members.

Trevor, awake and hunched over, had received that promised headache. He and Kyle sat on the bumper of his SUV. As a long-time Maessen Publishing Group employee, Kyle had known Trevor since they were both in college. Now, they spoke in low, somber tones, breaking only to nod at us and continue their private conversation.

Beside them rested a metal contraption of Impala parts intermingled with Jude's SUV. The vehicle amalgamation dripped fluid into a streaming puddle. With the shadows settling into the unnatural new twists, and if you turned your head to the left, the metal structure resembled Jabba The Hutt.

Robert Maessen sat in its shadow, bloody and far less attractive than Princess Leia in that same position. He spoke in loud tones to his criminal defense attorney, while shooting me a look of pure exasperation.

I smiled and waved. "Feels good to be alive!" I called. "Thanks for asking. Isn't this evening's weather delicious? Bummer about those deer. That looked painful."

Jackson slipped his arm around my waist and lifted me off my feet until he moved us past a pile of broken glass. Then, he sat me back down again.

"Was that to stop me from antagonizing Bob or because you like to show off and have me swooning?"

Jackson laughed. "It's because you don't have on any shoes."

"And, you like me swooning," I finished for him.

He winked in response.

Chris and Francis, the unrelated twins, didn't find our flirtations amusing. They grimaced from their restraints as we walked by. Both were fastened to the railing and bleeding from dissimilar wounds. It was now the best way to tell them apart.

Theo stood next to them smoking a cigar, while Gabriel chomped on a cookie. When one of them spat in my direction, Gabriel tossed the cookie at his head and shoved him with a well-placed boot.

Gabe and I exchanged a nod of respect.

Next to the twins sat Mr. Clean and Opie. They were handcuffed together but not secured to anything. When Mr. Clean stood up, wobbled, and fell back down, I understood why. Meanwhile, Gin talked to them about how to avoid ending up as bloody as the twins.

"It's like I tell my students, your choices determine your outcome. So, what have you learned from your choices tonight?"

I elbowed Jackson. "Gin thinks those guys are redeemable. Do you?"

He leaned toward me. "That's up to them. Choices determine your outcome," he smiled.

A few feet down the bridge, Jude What's-His-Name stood on the outside of the bridge railing looking ready to jump. His tossed cigarette would be cooled off by now. And swept away downstream. Jude blinked into the blackness with a sheen of sweat glistening in the moonlight. He looked like a guy who could use another smoke.

"What's going on here?" I asked Hal, who leaned on the railing to watch Jude, while snacking on potato chips.

"What? Him?" He nodded toward Jude.

"Yeah, him. Smart-mouth."

"We gave him the best seat in the house. Look at the view this guy's got."

I shivered at the thought. "I've seen it."

Hal chomped on another chip. "And now he can, too."

I took a cautious step closer to get a good look at Jude. His left eye had already swollen shut, his lower lip kicked a chorus line of blood, a cut sputtered red from a cheek, and fingers on his right hand bulged beyond the norm.

That had to hurt.

"Terrifying, isn't it?"

Jude jerked his head in my direction. His mouth fell open, and his one functioning eye bulged. "How are you alive?"

I whispered, "What makes you so sure I am? Maybe I'm dead. Maybe you're dead, too, and I've come to drag your soul to heaven or hades or wherever men like you go."

For a cold-blooded killer, he sure scared easily. Jude stumbled sideways, losing his grip. As his body tilted outward, I grabbed the back of his collar with my workable hand. The force of it jerked me against the railing, which caused an instant scurrying behind me. Hal stepped up to the rail to watch. Jackson wrapped one arm around my waist and took a handful of Jude's shirt to lighten my load.

What he didn't do, bless him, was pull Jude back, yet.

"Pull me back! Please! Pull me back!" Jude's arms failed and flapped to balance in the nothingness. "I'm afraid of heights."

"Yeah? Me, too…now. And, let me tell you, you were right. It's quite a fall. Plenty of time on the way down to think about what's coming." I leaned in. "But it'll be a quick end."

"Come on! Pull me back! You're no killer."

"I wasn't this morning. But it's been a long day, and a girl has the right to change her mind. So, if you want to live, change my mind. Tell me, Jude. Who's 'they?'"

Hal looked at Jackson. "They?"

Jackson, who I'd told earlier, replied, "I'll tell you later."

"'They,' Jude. Who's 'they'? I know 'they' exist. You're not a good enough actor to play this off. Who are you working for? What do 'they' want?"

Jude reverted to his denial. "What 'they'?! I don't know what you're talking about. Please!"

Hal leaned his back against the rail. "Let him fall. It'll be good for him. He likes it when others fall. He should get the experience himself."

Was Hal serious? Then my eyes dropped to his feet. Kermantle rope, the pasty-colored kind from Theo's truck, had been wrapped around Jude's ankles and the bridge railing.

Well played, Hal.

Jackson raised his eyebrows at me for direction, his way of letting me decide.

I considered it. "I mean, Hal does know what he's doing."

We both let go.

Jude yelled for a second. Then, the rope yanked and stopped him. He swung upside down a foot below the bridge. "Please! Don't leave me down here!"

I yelled down at him, "Be right back! Gonna grab a soda. Dying is so dehydrating."

When I turned away, Hal patted me on the shoulder. "We'll let him hang there for another minute to rethink his life choices. Then, I'll get Theo and Gabe to pull him back up."

"Does someone like that ever rethink their life choices?"

Hal checked his watch. "For the next 54-seconds, yes."

"Addison." Det. Casey eyed me with his skeptical gaze, while his hair puffed in the moist evening air. "I'm never surprised to see you at a crime scene anymore. You account for thirty percent of all my calls."

I snorted, treating it as a joke. I don't think it was.

Authorities arrived by the time Jackson and I made it to the snack tables. Officer Reilly was first on scene and, luckily, had a key to remove the handcuffs still cinched around my wrist. After talking with Hal and Jackson, he called in other emergency personnel, including Detective Casey. The Dive and Rescue Team arrived in the next half hour to search for Marilyn's body. Other officers from the city, county, and highway patrol arrived about once every ten minutes. The word had gone out about Trudy's food and, suddenly, we were awash in civil servants. They needed a pat on the back every once in a while, and Trudy loved feeding people. So, it was a win-win.

The thugs were hauled off without snacks and sent to face their iffy futures. Thanks to Gin's "tough love" talk, however, Mr. Clean appeared to be having second thoughts about his life choices. Or, he was still concussed.

Meanwhile, Jackson and I gave Casey the rundown of everything we'd learned tonight, along with Trevor pitching in his part while holding an ice pack to his head. Things were about to get messy for Robert Maessen, but I knew the Maessen Publishing Group would survive. They still had Trevor, and Trevor was being given the chance to make up for past mistakes.

Casey allowed the sidekick girls to steal me away for a few minutes, which meant Angel and Trudy went into make-up mode again.

"Girls. Seriously." I motioned for Angel to put the mascara away. "The beauty pageant was cancelled."

They offered wet wipes, lip balm, and sandwiches for Jackson and I, along with strawberry slushies. Theo's tailgate became our table and, while Casey continued his grilling, we ate, nodded, and offered what explanations we could. The superhero stuff we left out, of course. He couldn't know that. He wouldn't even want to once he did. But the rest was his to scribble into his tiny little notebook.

When he was finished, Trudy magically appeared with a sandwich and slushie for him, too.

"Try it. Officer Reilly said you frequently consume his strawberry soda. So, you'll like this." She passed it over with a napkin. "Also, you need to stop eating his food. Come find me when you're hungry. I'll feed you."

With that, Trudy spun on a heel and headed back to food central. Reilly, stationed on this side of the bridge as traffic control, was a hit with the girls. With no vehicles likely to appear for weeks, he regaled them with stories of our adventures together last month.

"And then she forced me to join this dating service," Reilly told an attentive audience.

"They don't work, by the way." Lauren bit into a cookie. "I've done the math. It's statistically impossible to find love through the process of strangers matching other strangers."

Greta, perched on the end of a table, shrugged. "I think there's more to it than that."

"Nope." Lauren grabbed another cookie. "That's the gist of it."

Jerry nodded. "They don't work." When everyone turned to her in surprise, she gave a, "What? I'm not dead."

Beside me, Jackson returned from rummaging in Theo's pickup cab and draped his suit jacket over my shoulders. "You're shivering."

It was either my plummeting adrenaline, aftershock tremors, or the second strawberry slushie dropping my temperature. I shoved my left hand in the arm and pulled it around me.

Jackson helped. "Better?"

I nodded gratefully. "Better."

"Okay. Sit tight. I want to check on how much longer we need to be here. I'll be right back." Jackson rubbed my shoulder and walked over to Casey, who was discussing with Gin and Angel the strength of materials used in vehicle production and how they compared when slammed into each other.

Behind them, located on the opposite side of the bridge, the Dive and Rescue Team was regrouping. So far, no luck, no Marilyn. From what I could tell by their actions, it looked like they were moving further down the river. She was in there somewhere. Waiting…

The thought sent icy fingers walking along my bones. I tightened Jackson's jacket around me and felt a lump in his inside pocket.

Whatever it was, was not my business. But I was bored. Sitting on a tailgate. In the middle of nowhere. Done eating. Waiting to go home. I had time to kill and curiosity to satisfy. I fished the lump out and found a ring box.

~

"Hey, Casey says we can go. He'll—"

"Have more questions later," I finished for Jackson, after he walked back up.

"Exactly. Do you want me to take you home? Or back to the cabin?"

All I cared about at that moment was a shower, a bed, and greasing my finger to get the ring off.

Yes, I opened the box. Yes, I slipped on the engagement ring. Yes, it was stuck.

That ring wasn't coming off without ice, oil, and possibly amputation. And I couldn't let Jackson know. What if he hadn't planned proposing tonight? What if he carries around purple diamond heirloom rings like I carry around lip balm? What if he hadn't made up his mind about marrying me, yet?

He'd earned the right to decide when and if he wanted to propose. So, my hand stayed in his jacket pocket.

If he had asked, would I have accepted?

I did love him, but we'd only been dating a week. Getting engaged after a week seemed unreasonable. Unless you looked at it in dog years, which equaled six months. Getting engaged after six months of dog years was reasonable.

So, yes. I was a yes. I was a hell yes. I couldn't live without the man. I didn't even like it when we weren't in the same room. Or when we were in the same room but he was on the other side of the room. Or, when we were in the same room, on the same side, but something or someone blocked my view of him.

I had it bad.

I wanted to be his bride more than I wanted anything ever. And that's why I put on the ring.

Besides, the ring wasn't an innocent bystander here. Nestled in the black felt, polished and elegant, a purple diamond encircled with white diamonds, it dared me to put it on. It practically bullied me into it.

"How about the cabin?" I needed to get it unstuck and back in his jacket before he checked.

"Climb in the truck. Theo and Gabe can grab a ride with Trudy."

I hesitated. "There aren't any seats in the back of her van. And the refrigeration kicks on periodically."

Jackson paused at the cab. "Gabe shoved you back there, didn't he?"

Oh, yeah. "Point made."

He opened the passenger door as Reilly walked up with a strawberry slushie. "Here you go, Sam."

I hesitated before climbing in. "What's this for, Reills? I already had two."

He motioned behind him. "Jerry said you wanted another and asked me to bring it to you."

I leaned around Reilly to get a look at the woman. She sat at a table, slurping on a slushie, and cocked an eyebrow.

Oh, crap. She knew.

I straightened up. "Nope. Jerry's wrong. She often is. Don't want it."

Reilly handed it over. "Well, take it anyway. You might change your mind. You often do."

"I won't."

Jackson watched the exchange suspiciously.

"Give it to someone else, then. Or take it back, if you like." Reilly held it out again. "Casey needs me on the other side. I'm headed in the opposite direction."

I sucked in heavily through my nose. The issue was, as Jerry well knew, the only hand capable of grasping that drink had an engagement ring stuck on it. If I removed it from Jackson's jacket pocket, he'd see it. If I didn't, he'd wonder why.

I hated that woman. "Jerry, you're a menace!"

She raised her slushie in salute.

"Thanks Reilly. I'll take it." I exposed my hand and gripped the frozen drink. The coldness soothed the throbbing.

"Enjoy Sam. Oh! And congrats on the engagement you two. Nice ring." With that, Reilly ambled away with his utility belt playing its favorite squeaky tune.

Beside me, Jackson cleared his throat.

"Right." I exhaled loudly. "I know this line. We need to talk."

Epilogue

Earth, Wind, And Fire asked me if I remembered September as the city streets passed in a blur. I turned right, merged with traffic, and considered what I remembered about September.

It had only been three months ago, but it felt like a lifetime. Maybe because it was.

September had been the closing of my previous life. September was before Jerome Deluca dragged me into an alley. September had been before Black-Hood Guy crunched a tailgater around a tree. September was when I still saw Jackson Christy as a cold, distant, unfriendly enigma. September was when I was still hiding at Promotions Magazine and watching the world go by.

In September, I saw myself as a woman permanently damaged by her past. In September, I didn't believe in restoration or miracles. In September, I'm pretty sure I didn't believe in love anymore, either.

Then, October came. And, with it, danger and fear and bruises and life and joy. They came as a package, per usual. In October, I faced danger. And death. A few times. And I found hope.

It's true there are things in life worth dying for, toothpaste not being one of them. But love is. And, in November, I found it. Sandwiched between heartbreaks and growing pains and one too many near death experiences. But love never asks more from you than everything you've got. It's a fair price, I think.

Now, finally, we'd reached December and I was two weeks away from gaining a husband and losing my last name.

So, yes. I remembered September, but every day with Jackson I forgot it more and more. If the memory ever left completely, I wouldn't miss it.

The song, however, was really good.

∼

Our first official date did become our engagement. My man never does anything halfway. He'd originally planned an elaborate romantic evening with Chef John and the Durant Hotel all to ourselves. A night of fine dining and dancing and, finally, a proposal.

That didn't happen.

Instead, we got the initial start of a romantic evening, while the rest consisted of bombs and kidnappings, a near drowning and a hard landing. I was broken and bruised. He was bleeding. We were both dirty and tired and jittery from a slushie sugar high, but Jackson proposed anyway.

"So, you found it." His face unreadable, his tone flat.

I rubbed the ring against my leg hoping to dislodge it. "I'm sorry, Jackson. I wasn't snooping. I mean, I was snooping. But I wasn't thinking. Then, I saw it. And I stopped thinking more than what I was already not thinking. Now, it won't come off."

He took my hand gently, wiggling the ring, straightening it, inspecting my finger. "It fits."

"I'll get it off. And we can pretend I never saw it, okay? No pressure here. Not that I'm making assumptions it was for me or anything. Because, you know, maybe you carry engagement rings around for other reasons."

Jackson pressed his thumb reassuringly on the back of my hand. "So, no pressure?"

"Nope. None."

"You'll forget you saw it?"

"Already forgotten."

Jackson nodded. "Or, how about this?" He dropped to one knee.

Holy crap.

"How about you agree to marry me, and we leave it on?"

I looked up to find the sidekicks all huddled around the snack tables and watching the exchange from a safe distance.

"Jackson," he looked so tired and alive and handsome all at once, "you don't have to do this."

"Yes, I do."

"No. No you don't. This was a mistake on my part. Whatever you had planned, or didn't have planned, I know it didn't include proposing at a crime scene. So, let's forget it." I called to the ten pairs of curious eyes. "Trudy? Have you got any mayo or anything? Something greasy."

She looked too frightened to answer. "Yeah. Okay." She didn't move.

"Trudy?" Jackson called out.

The redness in her hair increased another shade. "Yeah?"

"Hold on the mayo."

She swallowed. "Okay."

I shook my head. "Jackson, don't be stubborn."

He shifted on his knee, got into a more comfortable position, and gave me a look that shut me up. "Samantha Eloise Addison, I love you. I've been waiting seven years for you. Why, woman, would you want to make me wait more?"

I took in the chaos around us. The cops swarming in and out of the snack area. The red and blue flashing lights bouncing off the aging bridge. The beeping from the wreckers. The general chatter and laughter and shouts from rescue personnel. The generators powering lights on the scene above and below the bridge.

"This isn't what you wanted."

Jackson shook his head. "You're wrong. You are what I want. And this," he motioned to the chaos, "is my life, Sam. Not every day, maybe. But this is going to happen. Broken dates. Ruined evenings. Bruises and exhaustion and amazing meals missed, replaced by sandwiches and slushes. This, my love, is what life is going to be like with me. So, this is the perfect place to ask. Take a hard look around. Do you want this?" He took a beat. "Do you want this with me?"

In the background, another generator kicked on. One wrecker whined under the tension of pulling that metal monstrosity onto its bed. Officers were shouting over the noise at other officers to organize the ongoing search for Marilyn's body. An ambulance arrived but forgot to shut off its sirens.

It was enough to unsettle the steeliest of nerves.

I turned back to Jackson, his face grimy and unguarded, and felt my heart beat down in my toes.

"Trudy?" I called out.

She still hadn't moved. "Yeah?"

"Cancel the mayo."

~

Tonight was date night. Nothing extravagant. Just Tex-Mex and a movie with my baby. Simple evenings worked best for us. No major plans to ruin should ruining happen. Besides, we didn't need anything that required too much energy. We were two weeks away from our wedding and wishing we'd eloped already.

Getting here hadn't been easy. I still had nightmares about Marilyn. They never did find her body. And, I had anxiety about Jackson's father, Lucian. I learned the night of our engagement that THE Lucian, the urban legend, just happened to be my future father-in-law. A man's name that had haunted me for years turned out to be the father of the love of my life. Go figure.

I haven't met him, yet, but we've talked on the phone several times. He's the sweetest thing with a voice that could speak worlds into existence. I now know where Jackson gets his charm and his heart. I still have no idea how Lucian became the symbol he did.

I asked Jackson not long ago if he could explain it, and he said it was his reputation for being just, fair, but brutal.

"He's a good man, but not a safe one, Honey. Not for people like Jude or Marilyn or Robert Maessen. They would prefer to believe he isn't real than that he is and their comeuppance will eventually be due."

"So, he's like you, then."

"I'm like him," he corrected.

I'd smiled, caressing his face. "No wonder I like him."

I'd finally meet him face-to-face at the wedding. If we could grab a moment alone, I wanted to ask him about the 'they' Jude still refused to acknowledge. When Jackson and I talked about it, he only repeated that same line as before. "There is always another villain." But my curiosity would never let me leave it there. Who was this 'they'? And what was this 'they' planning next? Maybe Lucian knew. And maybe he'd share some of that insight with his new daughter-in-law.

Until then, I relished life without assassins hiding in every shadow. I'd been able to return to a more normal existence, if you didn't count my sidekick training exercises nearly every weekend. With my hand finally healed, Gabe took that as a sign for me to hit him in various body parts until it broke again. And Hal agreed, usually with his feet propped up on an exercise bench and a cigar stuck between his teeth.

~

When I pulled onto my street, I spotted Jackson's SUV parked in front of my house. He knew I needed an hour after work to shower and change, but he often came early so he could rearrange the books in my living room while I got ready.

As I pulled closer and passed, my eyes adjusted to the window tint. That wasn't Jackson inside. It was two men. One bulkier and behind the wheel. The other squatier and in the passenger seat. His gold-rimmed glasses caught my vehicle lights and twirled them around his circular frames.

I parked in my driveway, reached into my purse, and gripped my Triple Defense Pepper Spray gun. If these guys were Mormons, I'd apologize. But I'm not the house where strangers should come knocking.

I climbed out of my new Jeep, identical to the one I'd lost in the flooding, and stood my ground. The gun remained behind me out of sight.

The passenger door opened, and Gold-Rims climbed out. And I do mean climbed. He had the girth of a man with an inactive lifestyle and the height of an eight-year-old boy. There wasn't room enough for all that he was to spread out. His trunk held everything on top of itself. One organ stacked upon another. When he walked, the organs shifted and twisted his body to the left then right. His legs didn't step forward, they pivoted side to side, like a plastic soldier forced to advance.

I didn't know whether to be leery or entertained.

"Miss Addison?"

The voice I recognized. Slushy voices are distinctive. "Virgil Fairchild?"

That caught him off guard. "Why, yes." He stopped and the rounded organ part of his body shimmied and stilled. "I'm surprised you remember."

I remembered because the guy's number was disconnected when I tried to schedule our interview for his article. It'd been my fault we never connected. He called multiple times last month, but I was always busy being kidnapped or hit from behind by a car. The guy had lousy timing. When I finally got around to ringing him back, the number was no longer in service. Delaney got so annoyed at missing the sale, she threatened to take it out of my paycheck. So, I threatened to quit, and she revoked her threat.

"What are you doing at my house, Mr. Fairchild?"

He smiled, showing teeth with gaps all on the bottom. "I came by to deliver a wedding present." He motioned to the vehicle and the human bulk behind the wheel exited with a blue box wrapped in white ribbon and an elaborate white bow the size of a shih tzu. The big guy resembled the unrelated thug twins' older brother, if they had one and if they were related. When he approached me, he held out the box waiting for me to take it.

"It won't bite, Miss Addison." Fairchild teased. "It's only an olive branch. Intended to create good will."

I wasn't ready to take it, yet. "Why do you need to build good will with me, Mr. Fairchild?"

Fairchild laughed. "Oh, Miss Addison. You are delightful. It's not from me."

With that, he motioned to the human refrigerator to set it at my feet, and they both stomped and wiggled their way back to the SUV.

Jackson, arriving early per usual, pulled into my driveway as the SUV departed. He found me still on my front lawn, still staring at the box.

"Who was that?" He nodded to the departing SUV.

I nudged the box. "I honestly don't know."

"What's in the box?"

I squatted down to take a closer look. "I don't know that, either."

"Is there a card?"

Hey, now that's a thought. I cautiously slipped my fingers under the white shih tzu and found a card.

"Got it." I stood up, flipped it open, and laughed. "It says, 'Congratulations on your upcoming nuptials. I wish you and the stud muffin the best. Hope to catch up soon.' And it's signed, you won't believe this, 'Marilyn.'"

Jackson took the card and reread it. Checked the back of the card.

Then nudged the package with his shoe, too. "Huh."

Marilyn McBride was alive. Doesn't that woman beat all.

"You're smiling," Jackson observed. "You're glad she's alive?"

Was I? Yes. I really was. "I am, actually. I'm thrilled."

"As much pain as that woman caused you, not discounting her enthusiastic attempts at killing you, I'm surprised. Impressed, actually."

I took the card from him and reread it. "I know. She's psychotic. And a tad evil."

"Tad?"

"But death is so final, Jackson. That's the end of it all. At least now I know she may still be redeemable. Choices determine your outcome, remember?"

He smiled, leaning over and kissing me softly. "I remember. And I'm proud of you."

I was kind of proud of me, too, actually. "I'm turning into a real optimist. If you can love me, what other miracles are possible?"

"'If' I can?" He raised an eyebrow.

I leaned into him, happier than I ever remember being. "Let me rephrase. 'Because you love me…' How's that?"

"Better." He pulled me close, his lips lingering on mine. "Much better."

As soon as we started making out on my front lawn, the box at our feet started humming.

"That's odd." I didn't nudge it with my toe this time.

Jackson stepped in front of me, automatically placing himself between me and the box. So I stepped around him.

"Sam…"

"Let's not immediately jump to conclusions." I held up my hand to quiet him. "Give it a minute. Maybe it's some kind of clock. Or battery-powered toaster or something."

Marilyn McBride wasn't to be trusted. I knew that. She'd more than proved her wickedness. But I'd grieved her death for more than a month. Well, grieved my inability to stop her death, anyway. Now that she was alive, I could release that guilt. All I wanted now was a clean slate with her. Surely, she wasn't still determined to take me out. What would be the point?

"You're giving her the benefit of the doubt?"

"I am."

"You shouldn't." Jackson noted a new development. "It's vibrating."

"So," I scrambled for a reasonable answer, "maybe it's one of those back massagers. You know. The kind you put on your car seat, and it heats, vibrates, and works the kinks out while you drive."

Jackson wrapped his arm around my waist and walked me back a step. "The humming is getting louder."

"It could be one of those heat lamps. They hum."

"Sam…"

"What? They do."

The humming changed.

"Now it's beeping," Jackson pointed out.

"So, maybe I was right about the clock."

Jackson gave me a 'you don't believe that' look.

"Do toasters beep?"

He shook his head.

The beeping increased in speed until it shifted into a blaring alarm.

I looked wide-eyed at Jackson. "Ok! I admit it! That woman's insane!"

He grabbed my hand, "Run, Sam!"

And, together, we ran like lightning.

Note To The Reader

Dear Friend,

Some readers have asked where my story came from, which is often the question authors can never answer. Usually, ideas are amalgamations. They are stews of known and unknown ingredients. A dash of experience. A sprinkle of research. A fistful of overheard conversations.

Few authors write down their recipe. It's better when made fresh. But, in this instance, I happened to have a pen handy.

The Another Story came to me one afternoon while reading the book of Isaiah, and I fell into the rabbit hole of a single verse. "But they that wait upon the Lord shall renew their strength; they shall mount up with wings as eagles; they shall run, and not be weary; and they shall walk, and not faint." Isaiah 40:31

Now, that's interesting. What would it look like to run and not be weary?

And the lightning speed was born.

What would it look like if the spiritual gifts in scripture, like prophecy, knowledge, encouragement, and tongues, were used more like superpowers?

And Jerry, Lauren, Trudy, and Greta were born.

What about other biblical promises being superpowers, too, like living without fear and living with unexplainable peace?

And Theo and Gin were born.

This created a fun group of characters, but it wasn't the heart of the story. To find strength that soars, like Isaiah describes, you need a love that can work miracles. That came to all of us through the sacrifice of

God's only son, Jesus. For my story, it would come through a Christ-like figure.

And Jackson Christy was born.

This superhero needed a damsel to save, as all great love stories in capes and tights do. But this girl wouldn't be typical. She would be a victim and a hero, too. She would be, in many ways, like most of us: strong but also a little broken.

And Samantha Addison was born.

She struggled. She doubted. She tried. She failed. She tried again. Her story was never going to be neat and tidy. She was far too interesting for that. Aren't we all? But she would have the adventure of a lifetime, find the love of a lifetime, and take us all on a hilarious journey on her way there.

Samantha taught me that doubting wasn't the problem but giving in to those doubts was. Failing wasn't shameful, but quitting was. Experiencing fear wasn't unnatural, but letting it rule you was. Being human wasn't the worst thing ever, but wasting that human life was.

So, my friends. Here's my hope for you. That when you doubt, you don't give in. When you fear, you don't quit. When you are fearful, you're still courageous. Whatever good and bad life brings, you make it an adventure. And, at the end of the day, I hope you take off running just for the heck of it. And maybe, just maybe, you won't feel weary at all.

Your friend,

Tara Lynn

ABOUT THE AUTHOR

Tara Lynn Thompson is an Emmy and Addy-award winning writer and author of The Another Series.

Made in the USA
Columbia, SC
26 January 2021